A SPECIAL PLACE

Jill got out of the pool and walked toward the lounge chair that she had left her towel on. Suddenly she stopped, as she noticed a pair of dusty cowboy boots in front of her. Slowly she lifted her head, until her eyes rested on the soft brown gaze of the man who stood before her.

"Are you looking for this?" he asked in a soft, sensuous voice.

Jill went to take a step back and tottered at the edge of the pool. In one quick motion, his arm was around her waist and he gently pulled her toward him.

"You must be Jill. I'm Kyle Roberts," he said as he tried to hand her the towel again. He took his arm from around her waist, but still stood in close proximity.

Jill said nothing, though she recognized him from the brochure. She stared at him as if it were her first time seeing a man.

"I'm sorry if I startled you."

"That's okay, I just wasn't expecting to see anyone standing there," she said, telling only half the truth.

"So how are you enjoying Durango?"

"It's beautiful. "I've never been to Colarado before."

"If you'd like, I would love to take you around," Kyle said keeping his eyes focused on hers.

"I have lots of work to do, but when I get a good start on it I'd like to take you up on your offer," Jill said with a nervous smile.

I'm always here, just let me know when you're ready."

Kim Carrington

A Special Place

BET Publications, LLC
http://www.bet.com
http://www.arabesquebooks.com

ARABESQUE BOOKS are published by

BET Publications, LLC
c/o BET BOOKS
One BET Plaza
1900 W Place NE
Washington, D.C. 20018-1211

All Kensington Titles, Imprints, and Distributed Lines are
available at special quantity discounts for bulk purchases for
sales promotion, premiums, fund-raising, and educational or
institutional use. Special book excerpts or customized print-
ings can also be created to fit specific needs. For details,
write or phone the office of the Kensington special sales
manager: Kensington Publishing Corp., 850 Third Avenue,
New York, NY 10022, attn: Special Sales Department,
Phone: 1-800-221-2647.

BET Books is a trademark of Black Entertainment Television,
Inc. ARABESQUE, the ARABESQUE logo and the BET
BOOKS logo are trademarks and registered trademarks.

First Printing: September 2004
10 9 8 7 6 5 4 3 2 1

Printed in the United States of America

This book is dedicated to my sister,
Toni, who made me believe in dreams.

ACKNOWLEDGMENTS

There are so many wonderful people who have helped to bring this work to print. It truly has been a labor of love, one which would have never seen the light of day without my God. Thank you my Lord, for making way out of no way, each and every day.

Thank you Linda Gill and Demetria Lucas for giving me the opportunity to write for BET/Arabesque.

I would especially like to thank Christy Stechman, Lynn Barrett, Jamel Dunn, Krystal Sahli, and my dear friends Zola and Diane, for all their support and assistance in helping me make this dream a reality. I truly couldn't have accomplished this goal without all of your help. I would also like to thank Ray Farah and Kim Smith at Farah Printing for giving me quality printing that is worthy of any publisher's desk.

To my husband, James, I would like to say thank you for all the tender love, concern and support you have given me, not only during the writing of this book, but throughout our marriage. I love you, baby.

To my beautiful daughter, Antonia, thank you for celebrating all the wonderful high points with Mommy during the development of this book. Most of all, thank you for entertaining your little brother while Mommy worked. You are my inspiration and I love you.

Marc, Mommy can never thank you enough for being the sweetest little boy a mother could wish for. Thank you for supplying me with my favorite candy (Red Hots) while I wrote. You are the light of my life and I love you very much.

If it wasn't for the love of my sisters, I don't know where I would be. To my sisters—Toni Mebane, Terri Rucker, and Karen Adams—thank you so much for all your love you have given me over the years, and the support you showed during the creation of this book.

Chapter 1

Jill Alexander had been in the office since six o'clock that morning. It was now almost seven-thirty at night. She had become used to the long workdays that being a public relations executive warranted. Unmarried with no children, she didn't mind sixty-hour workweeks much, as her time was all her own.

Over the years, she had stopped counting the times her friends and coworkers had tried to matchmake or set her up on blind dates. She never clicked with any of the men they chose for her anyway. Besides, she thought, she was attractive enough to find her own man. If only she slowed down long enough to find the time.

She pulled up in front of Clayton's in Lower Manhattan at eight o'clock. She and her friends ate there almost every Friday night as their way of celebrating the weekend's arrival. Jill happily parked in front of the restaurant, checking her makeup in the mirror and applying a little lipstick before she stepped out of her silver-gray Mercedes.

As she pressed a button on her key ring to lock and arm the vehicle, the car made an unusually loud beeping sound, causing a couple to look over. The woman was sitting in the car waiting for her date to close the door, but the man stood watching the five-foot-eight bronze beauty walking toward the entrance of the restaurant. "Why don't you go after her if you want her so bad?" the girlfriend yelled at him.

He jumped at the sound of her loud voice and tried to make an excuse for his inattentiveness. Jill, as usual, was unaware of the commotion she caused.

She entered Clayton's, which was always dimly lit, the music always light and mellow. People were laughing, talking, and eating and the usual guys were there trying to make that big score with someone for the weekend, or longer. Jill smirked at the leisurely social scene. In between her hours at the office and the work she took home, she wouldn't have time for a weekend fling even if she'd wanted one.

She had been working for Iguana since she graduated from college, and since then she'd made a name for herself in the world of public relations. The company paid her very well and she had a nice office to match. Several firms had tried to lure her away over the years, but they couldn't compete; she loved the people she worked with and the developmental freedom she had. Her wonderful expense account, company credit cards, and her frequent cross-country trips were nothing to complain about either.

She walked through the restaurant slowly. To the right of the room, in the back, she saw a hand waving at her. It was Lois, and sitting next to her was Diane.

"Hey, girl, you finally made it!" Lois said, when Jill reached the table.

"If you spent any more time at work I'd think you had a man there," Diane said, laughing.

Jill smiled sarcastically. "As many problems as I see you having with men, Di, I am not in a big hurry to be in your shoes. Were you guys waiting long?" she asked.

"No, girl, we've only been here twenty minutes or so," Lois replied.

"Hello," a waiter said, interrupting the threesome's banter. "Can I get you something from the bar?"

"Yes, I'll have Chambord and soda with lime please," Jill answered.

"Will do," he said, leaving to fill the order.

"Now, that one was kind of cute," Diane said when the waiter departed.

"Yes, he's cute, but he's not Jill's type," Lois added. "Jill needs someone who can handle being with a strong woman, someone who can afford her too, not some waiter, Di."

"What's wrong with a waiter, as long as he's good to her?" she shot back.

"Thanks, ladies, but I don't need any man right now. I am happily married to my job, so you can both stop trying to matchmake," Jill said contently. "Let's just enjoy ourselves and enjoy the night. Can't we talk about something besides who I'm dating?"

"It's more like who you're not dating, Jill. We're just worried about you," Diane told her. "I know none of my relationships have been lasting, but they were good while they did last. You're not getting any younger and—"

"And I don't need you to remind me. Look, I am perfectly happy with my life. And let's not forget that it is my life. Now I need you two to back off," she said abruptly and more harshly than she intended.

Realizing that Jill had enough talk about her love life, Lois quickly changed the subject. "Guess where Curtis is taking me on vacation?"

"Where?" Diane asked her.

"You'll never guess, so I might as well tell you. We're going to Hawaii for two weeks!" she said excitedly.

"Curtis is taking you to Hawaii? How can you two afford it? Just last week you wondered how you were going to take care of all your bills. Now you can go to Hawaii?" Diane inquired nosily.

"I think it's wonderful. When are you going?" Jill asked.

"We're going to go as soon as I can get Mrs. Williams to approve my vacation time."

"All right, let me ask my question again, what funds are you getting to Hawaii on?" Diane said, determined to get an answer.

"Well, we kind of lucked into the trip," Lois said coyly.

"Lois, how did you and Curtis just luck into a trip to Hawaii?" Diane demanded.

Just then, the waiter returned with Jill's drink. "Thank you," she said as he put the glass down.

"Are you ladies ready to order?" he asked politely, realizing that he was interrupting an intense conversation. He stood, taking in every aspect of Jill's beauty, but she paid him no attention. She ordered what she always ate when she went to Clayton's: grilled chicken salad with garlic bread.

"I'll have ribs, coleslaw, and fries," Lois said when Jill was finished ordering.

With her eyes never leaving Lois's face, Diane gave the waiter her order. "I'll have the grilled chicken, baked potato, and whatever else comes with it," she answered offhandedly. "Now tell me, how is it that you two can't pay your bills, but you can go to Hawaii, Lois?"

"Can't you just be happy that they are going?" Jill said to her, trying not to giggle at Diane's irritation.

"No, I can't! Now are you going to tell me, you little witch, or do I have to slap it out of you?" Diane and Jill both fell out laughing. "What's so funny? Are we all going, and no one told me?"

"All right, Di, I'll tell you," Lois said. "It's a gift from

Jill. She wanted to do something special for us for our
fifteenth wedding anniversary because we've been having such a rough time."

"Jill, why didn't you just give them a nice night on the
town? Isn't Hawaii a little much?"

"Hey, don't talk her out of giving me a trip to
Hawaii," Lois said, laughing. "Di, I just love to get you
going. Everything seems to bother you."

"Everything doesn't bother me. I just couldn't figure
out how Curtis could take you to Hawaii for two weeks.
I should have known he wasn't behind it."

"Yeah, well, we might have our money problems, but
I know that he loves me. Besides, this is just a moment
in time. We won't always have financial problems."

"Well, all I got you was a new toaster oven," Diane
said flatly.

"Thanks, girl, I need that too." Lois leaned over and
gave Diane a big hug.

The waiter returned with their orders. He served them
quietly and left. This time he didn't try to catch Jill's
eye.

"I know you don't want to hear it, but that waiter was
trying to get your attention, and you never looked at him
once, Jill," Diane said. "You have needs like everyone
else. What's wrong with satisfying them every once in
a while?"

"I will satisfy them, just not right now. Right now I
am just busy with work. I don't have time for a relationship," Jill said, defending herself.

"Well, what about just getting out and enjoying yourself now and then? It wouldn't hurt you to enjoy a man's
company," Lois said as they ate.

"Or even go on a wonderful vacation with a nice gentleman," Diane added.

"I really don't need to take a vacation. Most people

take a vacation to get away from their jobs or coworkers. I love what I do and I love the people I work with," she replied matter-of-factly. Besides, I get to travel all over the country working for Iguana. So you see, there really isn't any reason for me to take a vacation," she said, smiling, having made a good point.

Laughing and talking, they leisurely finished their dinner, paid their bill, and left the restaurant.

"What I want to know is, how can we all work for the same company and only one of us drive a brand-new Mercedes convertible?" Diane asked in mock jealousy, as the threesome stood outside the restaurant admiring Jill's car.

"That would be because we aren't one of the top executives. We also have husbands and kids," Lois replied teasingly.

"And you both know that you wouldn't trade the husband or the kids for a car. You've got great lives, and you wouldn't change a thing, would you?" Jill replied.

"I don't have a husband, but you should have asked me that question last week when Tiffany decided to skip school," Diane said. She gave Lois and Jill a kiss on the cheek. "I'll see you ladies on Monday. Lo, you stay out of trouble, and, Jill, you try to find some," she said as she waved good-bye and made her way to the subway entrance.

Lois paused once again to thank Jill for the wonderful anniversary present before she quickly caught up with Diane. Jill looked at her watch and saw that it was only nine-thirty. She didn't want to go home, but there really wasn't any place else to go. Reluctantly, she started her engine and headed there. As she drove, she admired the New York bustle. Having lived in Manhattan since she'd graduated from college, she missed her hometown of Pittsburgh very little. When Jill did visit her parents, she was always anxious to get back home. She loved New York's excitement and its energy. It was definitely the place to be as far as she was concerned.

Jill continued her drive home to Park Avenue. She parked her car in the underground garage and took the elevator to her eleventh-floor apartment. After unlocking the door and turning on the lights, she picked up the mail from the table in the foyer and saw that Marie, her maid, had left her a note.

Good evening, Ms. Alexander,
Your dinner is in the refrigerator and only needs to be heated. I picked up your dry cleaning and made arrangements for your carpets to be cleaned. Your mother called. She asked that you call her tomorrow.

Have a nice weekend
Marie

Jill kicked off her shoes and went to get the meal Marie had left. Though she'd just eaten, she picked at the delicious food before she put it into the garbage disposal. Marie was a fabulous cook, and Jill didn't want her to ask how dinner was and know she had not even tasted it.

Walking into the living room, she noticed the housekeeper had left fresh white roses in a vase. As she deeply inhaled their scent, she again realized how fortunate she was to have Marie.

She opened the doors to a huge oak armoire that revealed a television, then sat down on the bone-colored leather sofa and grabbed the remote. As she turned on the television, Jill remembered she still hadn't watched the episode of *Survivor* she'd taped the night before. Though she didn't like the lying and trickery, she was amazed at what people would do to win a million bucks. She was even more astonished at the people who managed to make a love connection. Jill always wondered if she would last a week in the overheated shelters, searching to find drinking water. She thought it would be almost impossible for her to put up with people she really couldn't stand and sleep in such close quarters with them at night. Then in the morning they would try to work well together, but whisper secretly to the camera how they couldn't wait to vote someone off.

There was a very handsome man on the show. The sun glistened on his bare shoulders as he carried heavy branches to help make the shelter. His name was Tyrek, and he was a physical education teacher from Houston, Texas. Though she loved the idea behind *Survivor,* Tyrek was the real reason she watched with such interest.

Were Diane and Lois right? Did she need a man in her life? She was happy with the success she found in her career, but she didn't kid herself. Of course, marriage was in her plans, it just wasn't on her list of things she needed to do right now. But why was it such an issue for her friends and why was it always an underlying thought for her?

The show ended, but Jill left the television on, disliking the silence of the apartment. She went to the bathroom and prepared a bath in her sunken tub, pouring jasmine-scented salts into the water. Back in her bedroom, she turned on the lights as she stood in the doorway. Jill looked at her huge king-sized bed. Hugging herself, she closed her eyes. Yes, it would be nice to share that with someone, she admitted as she opened her eyes and shook her head. Crossing the room to her walk-in closet, she chose a beautiful silk teddy with a matching robe to wear after her bath.

Stepping into the tub, she let the hot water relax her

tired body. She felt tense, but she couldn't understand why. Her mind wouldn't let go of all the people who had tried to match her up with their brother, their cousin, their coworker, or their friend. Even when she went back to Pittsburgh, her mother always tried to match her up with her friends' sons or someone from church. What was wrong with them? she wondered. Why did everyone always feel the need to fix her life?

Or is it me? Maybe something was wrong with her thinking, and everyone else could see it. No, it was *her* life. She, more than anyone else, knew what she wanted. Jill tried to brush the thoughts out of her mind, but what Lois and Diane said at dinner kept running through her head. "It wouldn't hurt you to enjoy a man's company," Lois had said.

Sinking deeper into the tub, she convinced herself a man wasn't what she wanted right now. A husband and children would only hold her back. Her sister, Barb, had been in law school when she got married and after the kids, she never finished. Her husband, Rick, made a good living and Barb said she was happy with her life, but in Jill's eyes, her sister had settled, she hadn't finished what was important to her. "I don't want that," Jill said out loud.

She relaxed in the tub with her eyes closed for a while longer before she got out. As she was drying off, the phone rang. It was Phil Harmon from work.

"Hey, Jill, how are you?" he asked.

"I'm fine, Phil, is everything all right?"

"Yes," he answered quickly. "I just wanted to make sure that you were going to be in the office early on Monday. We have a new client out West, and I think we will need you out there next weekend."

"I don't have any special plans for that weekend.

About how long will I be there?" she asked, pinning the towel around her chest.

"At this point, I really don't know. I guess for about a week, but I'll have more details on Monday. Just keep that time open. Matt doesn't want anyone to handle this new account but you."

"Why is it so special, and why only me?"

"Well, Matt just feels like you'd be just the perfect person for this one. It's a new spa that is opening in Durango."

"All right, but I still don't understand. The firm has handled many new spa openings," she said, placing her foot on the edge of the tub as she applied lotion to her leg.

"This one is not just a spa, it's a spa located on a ranch."

"Well, that is a little different."

"That's not all. The ranch is owned and operated by a wealthy group of African-American investors. In all actuality, Jill, they asked Matt to make sure you had their account. He promised them you would. It seems that once again your reputation precedes you," he told her with a smile in his voice.

"My reputation, huh? Nice touch! See you Monday, Phil."

"Good night."

A couple of weeks at a spa would be just what she needed. As much as she loved New York, it would be good to get away for a while. No one knew her in Durango. There would be no one trying to get her a man. Obviously it had to be a five-star place. Matt Singletary, the president of Iguana, only represented top-notch clients. Iguana charged a hefty sum, but their customers were always satisfied. After the firm had finished with a client, people knew their company's name and what they stood for.

Jill slipped into her silk teddy and put on a nighttime facial moisturizer. She grabbed *A Love So Special,* a book that she had been trying to read for the last couple of nights, from her nightstand and climbed into bed. She wasn't past the first chapter when she fell asleep.

Jill awoke to the sound of the telephone ringing. She hesitated to answer it when she glanced at the clock and saw it was only seven A.M. Who would call her this early in the morning? she wondered. Jill tried to ignore it, but whoever it was would not leave her alone. Fearing it could be important, she finally picked up the phone.

"Hello," she said, a mixture of irritation and sleepiness in her voice.

"Good morning, Jill!" the man on the other end of the phone said. It was Lois's husband, Curtis. "I just wanted to thank you personally for the trip you gave Lois and me. Jill, you know you're like a sister to me, right?"

"No, I didn't know that, but thanks anyway. I just want you to take care of my friend. You both deserve a nice vacation, Curtis. I know it's been a rough year for both of you. I hope you have a great time."

"In Hawaii, I'm sure we will. I know I woke you up, but I have to leave for work early, and I wanted to make sure that I got a chance to talk to you today. Anyway, thanks again, Jill."

"Bye, Curtis," she said, clicking off her phone and nestling back into her blankets. She closed her eyes and tried to go back to sleep. Finally, she threw back the covers and let out an exasperated sigh when she realized getting more sleep was not going to happen.

After turning on the coffeemaker, she ate her breakfast, a bowl of cereal with a banana, and planned out her day. Of course she had to call her mom back, but later this afternoon she would have to go visit Darlene Alceveda, her next-door neighbor. She and her husband, Mike, just had a baby girl and Jill had been meaning to go over to congratulate the couple on the birth of their first child. Today she would make it a priority. She knew she had to go shopping for her upcoming business trip and she would get something for the baby then. As she sipped her coffee, Jill picked up the phone and dialed her mom's number.

"Hi, Mom," Jill said, in her most cheery morning voice.

"Good morning, sweetheart, you sound very happy today," her mom said.

"Well, I was awakened by Curtis this morning."

"Lois's husband, what's he doing there?" her mom asked with concern.

"No, Mom, he's not here. He called to thank me for the trip to Hawaii."

"Oh, that was nice of him. I'm sure they will enjoy their vacation. You told me they have had a pretty rough year. I hope things get better for them."

"I hope so too, Mom. I have to go on another out-of-town job this week."

"Where to?"

"Durango, Colorado, to a ranch."

"A ranch, with real cowboys on it?"

"I guess so. I mean that's where you would find a cowboy, Mom."

"Don't be sassy, Jill."

"Yes, Mom," Jill answered, giggling. "There is supposed to be a spa on the ranch too. I don't have all the information. Phil called me last night and told me that he would give me more details on Monday. He said that

Matt wanted me on this project because the investors requested me specifically."

"That's because you're good at your job, baby girl. I've never been to a ranch. I wish I could go with you."

"Mom, what would you do on a ranch? I really can't imagine you on a horse."

"I can't imagine myself on a horse either, but since I never have, I would like to try. You did say that there is a spa on the ranch too, didn't you?"

"Yes."

"Well, that's something I would enjoy. Maybe one day I'll take a nice vacation myself. What are you going to do today?"

Jill ignored her mother's obvious ploy to get invited to the ranch. "I have to go out and do a little shopping, and I am going to visit my neighbors. They had a baby a couple of days ago."

"I'll talk to you later then, Jill."

"Love you, Mom," Jill said. She hung up the phone and drank the last of her coffee.

Driving in the direction of her favorite department store, Jill turned on the radio and rolled down the windows. She was singing along with the radio and thinking of what to buy for Darlene and Mike's new baby. She wondered if the baby looked like Dar, or more like Mike. What would her own baby look like? Would she even ever have a baby, and why did she care about things like that now? She was driving aimlessly when she realized she missed a parking space.

"Damn! That's probably the only one in the city," she said aloud.

Thirty minutes later, Jill found another parking space and quickly went inside Bloomingdale's. She knew she wanted to pick up a few pairs of jeans, and found three pairs of boot-cut Seven jeans and two trendy denim jackets to match, before she headed to the baby department. She was amazed at how much stuff a little one would need. She marveled at how tiny the dresses were and fell in love with two of them, a yellow one and a beautiful pink one with lavender teddy bears. She bought the baby a blanket, a bottle warmer, a set of bottles, and a sterling silver piggy bank, in which she put a hundred-dollar bill. To top it off, she bought a huge teddy bear that came up to her hip. She felt that she'd gone overboard with her gifts, but she did like Dar and Mike and she was very happy for them. She imagined that there would be many sleepless nights in their future.

Pulling into the garage of her building, she asked the attendant, Bob, to help her with her gifts.

"Sure, Ms. Alexander, I'll be happy to help you. Just give me a second; I have to let Tommy know that he will be down here by himself."

Jill parked her car in its usual spot, and a few minutes later Bob arrived to assist her. "It looks like you tried to buy out the store, Ms. Alexander," he said, laughing.

"It sure looks like it, doesn't it?" she replied. "I think I bought just as much for myself as I did for the Alcevedas' baby girl."

"You got all this for their baby?" he asked as he lifted several bags from the backseat.

"Yes. I know I went a little crazy, but I couldn't help myself," she told him as they took the elevator to the eleventh floor. "There were so many things to buy for babies and I couldn't choose just one or two things, so I got only my favorites. I hope they like everything," Jill said.

"I'm sure they will," Bob answered.

"Do you know if they're in?"

"Mr. Alceveda only goes out for baby supplies and groceries. Mrs. Alceveda hasn't gone out at all," he told Jill matter-of-factly.

"Good. I want to catch them before I have to leave town."

Jill opened the door to her apartment. She and Bob set all the packages on the sofa, and she gave him a large tip. "Thanks for helping me, Bob," she said politely.

"No problem, Ms. Alexander. Thank you," he responded as Jill walked him over to the door.

Jill quickly wrapped her gifts and placed huge pink bows on all the boxes. Amazingly, she gathered everything in her arms and went next door to the Alcevedas'. Jill knocked on the door and was greeted by Mike.

"Jill, we were wondering when we were going to see you," Mike said as he opened the door.

"Hi, Mike. I am so sorry I didn't get to see you guys in the hospital, but I just couldn't get out of work early enough to make it over there," she explained.

"It looks like you really did some major shopping. This all can't possibly be for Helena?" he asked, taking some of the packages out of Jill's hands.

"Actually, it is all for her. What a beautiful name, and I can't wait to see her. Where is Dar?"

"She's in the bedroom with the baby. Let me see if she's ready for company before I take you in," he said, smiling, as he left the room.

As Mike went to notify Dar, Jill sat down on the sofa. She looked around the room at all the baby stuff. Mike and Darlene's place looked cheery, happy, and homey, she thought. There were pictures all around their apartment of the two of them on their wedding day and on vacations. They made a beautiful couple. Darlene owned a clothing boutique and Mike was a real estate developer, and in fact, he owned the building they all lived in. With two very busy careers, they always made time for each other. Jill remembered Darlene telling her that they made a date at least once a month for dinner and a movie or sometimes a play or dancing. The point was to always make time for romance and Jill hoped she would remember that advice if she ever got married.

She was lost in her own thoughts when she finally realized that Mike had been calling her. "Jill? Jill, are you with me?" he said, realizing that she was deep in thought.

"Oh, I'm sorry. I guess I was just daydreaming."

"Dar is ready for you. I'm sorry that it took so long, but she had to pull herself together. You know how you women are," he joked.

"Dar always looks great."

"She'll be happy to hear that."

"I can't wait to see Helena," Jill said sincerely. She hadn't realized the heightened excitement she was experiencing until Mike was leading her back into the bedroom.

He opened the door slowly. The room glowed in gentle sunlight and Darlene was sitting in the bed with Helena resting in her arms. The baby looked like a little angel. She was dressed in a pink nightgown with pink bows in her hair.

"Oh, Dar, she's beautiful! Congratulations," Jill said in an excited whisper as she bent to kiss her friend.

"Thank you, Jill," Dar whispered back to her. "Would you like to hold her?"

"I would love to, but I don't want to wake her up. I imagine it's hard for you to get rest with a new baby. I won't stay long," she said nervously.

"No, please stay. It's almost time for her to wake up

anyway, and I haven't had much company since I've been home."

"Are you sure?"

"Definitely. Pull over that rocking chair and sit next to me." Jill did. "Here, hold her," Darlene said.

Jill stood and took the baby from Darlene. "Oh, Dar, she is beautiful," Jill said again, her voice filled with awe. "I can't imagine ever having something so wonderful happening to me." The words were out before Jill had realized it.

"It will, Jill. One day it will just happen and you'll wonder how your life became so complete without you even working on it."

"My life is so full right now, it doesn't seem like there's time for anything else. I don't know how you and Mike do it."

"I don't know. I guess we just try to make each other a priority in one another's life. I have so many married friends whose relationships are like two ships passing in the night. It's like I'll see you when I see you. Marriage takes work like anything else."

"I guess you're right." Jill looked down at the little baby sleeping in her arms. It seemed like she had been staring at her forever, instead of a few moments. She looked up to see Dar looking at her with a slight smile on her face.

"You look so natural in that rocking chair. I wouldn't doubt you're having a little one of your own soon."

"I think you see something I can't."

Mike returned with an armful of the gifts Jill had bought for Helena. "Are you ladies ready for the gifts?" he asked them.

"Auntie Jill, I think you went a little overboard," Dar said with a big smile on her face.

"I'll be right back," Mike said. "There's more still on the sofa."

"Jill, you really shouldn't have," Dar said as she opened the first gift.

Mike returned with the huge teddy bear and set it in the corner where the baby's crib was. "This is from Auntie Jill, too," he said as he handed Dar the sterling silver piggy bank.

"Jill, everything is beautiful. You really went all out for this kid." As Dar admired the piggy bank, she noticed that there was money already in it. She undid the bottom of the bank, and out fell the hundred-dollar bill. Dar smiled. "I need a hug."

"And you'll get a big one too." Jill looked down, and to her surprise Helena was awake. She lay quietly in Jill's arms looking up at the person who held her. Inside Jill, something was stirring, but she wasn't sure what. She couldn't remember ever feeling this completely serene. "Dar, she's awake," she whispered as if she were afraid she would startle the baby.

"See? I told you it wouldn't be long. It's time for a feeding and she could probably use a clean diaper. If you lay her next to me I'll change her."

"I'll do it, Dar. If you tell me where everything is, I'll give diaper changing a try."

"Are you sure you want to do it?" Darlene asked skeptically

"Sure. She's so cute and little, how bad can it be?" Jill said, laughing lightly.

"Behind you in the corner is a changing table, everything you need is there."

"Okay, here we go, Helena," Jill said, cuddling the bundle.

Jill went to the changing table carrying the baby. She undressed and changed her as if she had been doing it forever. After she finished, she threw the dirty diaper in the pail and went back to Dar. As she held Helena, the baby turned in the direction of Jill's breast.

"I think she's hungry, Dar, and I can't do anything for her in that department," Jill joked as she handed Helena back to her mother.

"You changed that diaper like a pro," Dar said, undoing the front of her nightgown preparing to feed her baby.

At first, Jill didn't know whether to watch as Dar breast-fed or to look away. She felt awkward looking around the room, but she didn't want to make Dar feel uneasy either.

"Jill, do you feel uncomfortable with my breast-feeding Helena in front of you?" Darlene asked, surprised by Jill's reaction.

"A little, but I was more concerned with making you feel uncomfortable with my being here while you fed her," Jill replied.

"I'm fine, but if you want me to cover up I will."

"No, Dar, that's not necessary," Jill said, relieved. "She certainly is hungry."

"She has three main functions, eat, sleep, and leave a little something in her diaper for me," Dar told her, laughing.

Jill sat quietly for a moment. She watched as Dar nursed her daughter. Did she want what Dar had? Maybe one day. Right now, her time was all her own and she could do with it what she pleased. She blinked her eyes several times and slightly shook her head. Jill convinced herself that she was just confused by all the things Diane and Lois kept telling her; now she sat in a room where her friend was breast-feeding her beautiful baby girl. Of course she was in a quandary, but she was happy with her life, and she wasn't about to let anyone make her think that she wasn't.

"Well, Dar, I better get going," she said as she stood to leave abruptly.

"Auntie Jill, thanks for coming by to see us," Dar told her, gazing at her daughter.

"Thank you for having me," Jill said as she leaned over to give her friend a kiss on the cheek and a gentle hug, then she kissed Helena, too.

"See you later, Auntie Jill. Do you have to leave town again soon?" Dar asked her.

"As a matter of fact, I do. I have to go away next weekend."

"I have a feeling you will have a wonderful time," Dar said as she winked at her.

"No, Dar, this is all business," Jill answered, pushing the rocking chair back to where it belonged. "At best, I'll get some rest and relaxation. Take care of your little family, and I'll see you when I get back."

Jill walked down the hall toward the living room. Mike was folding laundry and watching the football game on television when Jill entered. "I'll see you later, Mike."

"Hey, Jill, thanks for coming by. I'm sure Dar appreciated the visit. She has been kind of lonesome. The doctor won't let her go out shopping, and she hasn't had much company. Everyone is so busy, I guess," he said as he walked Jill to the door.

"She has you, Mike. You two make such a wonderful couple. I think people realize you two need time alone with that precious baby girl, and they are trying to give Dar time to bond. After she's back on her feet, this place will be jumping with visitors, I promise," Jill told him confidently.

"Thanks for everything, Jill."

Jill walked slowly back to her own apartment. They were a lucky couple, she thought. They had all they needed in each other. She flopped on her sofa and thought of Mike folding clothes as his wife tended to their baby and rested. Though Lois's husband was good to her, she really couldn't see him tending to her needs like Mike did for Dar. As she thought about it, she didn't see the kind of passion and commitment that Dar and Mike had in anyone else she knew. Not even her parents had that kind of fire in their relationship. Though they loved each other and got along well, it wasn't like that.

She turned on the television and absentmindedly watched a show. She was thinking she might go to Pittsburgh to see her own family before heading out to Durango. Picking up the phone, she called her mother again.

"Hi, Jill," her mom said.

"Cursed caller ID," Jill retorted.

Her mom laughed. "Two calls in one day, what's going on?"

"Hey, Mom, I was thinking of coming to Pittsburgh on my way to Durango."

"Oh, that would be wonderful. What day of the week were you planning to come?" her mother asked anxiously.

"Is Thursday good for you?"

"Yes, I have to call Barbie and let her know that you're coming. She will be so excited to see you."

"Now, Mom, don't go planning anything elaborate. I just want to spend some time with you and the family. Please don't invite any strangers over."

"Strangers, never. Everyone will be someone we know."

"Fine, but will they be someone I know, or someone that you'd like for me to know?"

"We'll see," her mother said in a voice that confirmed Jill's suspicions. "I can't wait to see you, baby girl. Bye for now."

"Bye, Mom," Jill said, with lighthearted affirmation.

Chapter 2

When Jill awoke Sunday morning, she decided to just relax. She had tossed and turned in bed all night long, and didn't feel well rested. She made herself breakfast and read the newspaper.

She went into the living room and turned on the television. As usual she wanted it on more for the noise than for entertainment. She sat quietly thinking about Dar's baby girl. Little Helena was certainly blessed to have such loving parents; they were as devoted to her as they were to each other. Jill resisted the urge to go back and visit. She didn't want to become a pest, though Dar certainly seemed to enjoy her company. But the real reason she didn't go was that she didn't want to appear emotionally needy. Jill felt so lonely that she thought her heart would break. She wouldn't dare admit that to anyone, fearing countless available bachelors being thrown at her door. A man would only get in the way of her goal of opening her own public relations firm, she reasoned.

She spent the remainder of the day tidying an already clean apartment and ignoring the phone. Jill couldn't help the tears that rolled down her cheek; she felt so confused and emotional, but she didn't know why. She went to bed early, eager for the workweek to begin and anxious to speak with Phil Harmon.

* * *

Morning found Jill in the kitchen making coffee before her alarm clock went off. She went to the fitness center in her building and did her usual forty-five-minute workout, then returned to her apartment for a quick shower and cup of coffee before heading to work. She was excited about the job in Durango, as she had never been to Colorado before. The idea of visiting a ranch and spa interested her, and she was curious as to what the client would need.

It was seven-thirty A.M. when she arrived at Iguana's offices on the twenty-third floor, and Lois was already there. She was the secretary for several of the executives, including Jill, and usually came to work before anyone else. Diane worked in payroll and didn't come in until closer to eight o'clock.

"Good morning, Jill," Lois said, greeting her friend cheerily.

Jill turned around just in time to see Lois sit down at her desk. "Good morning, Lois. How was your weekend?"

"Wonderful. All weekend long Curtis and I made plans for our trip. My mom is going to keep the kids while we're gone."

"That's great. Did Mrs. Williams sign off on your vacation request?"

"Yep, it was in my mailbox when I got in this morning," Lois answered her happily.

"Well, girl, you're all set then. Have you seen Phil Harmon yet?"

"No, I haven't. Why?"

"It looks like I'm going to be heading West next week. He said we would go over all the details with me today. I think I'll really like this assignment. It's supposed to be a ranch with a spa on it and I really could use a wonderful spa vacation right now."

"I thought you said this trip would be for work."

"It will be. I'm just thinking that I might stay out there a few extra days after the job is over and get a little Jill time in."

"I hear you," Lois said, smiling and shaking her head.

"Will you buzz me when Phil gets in?"

"You got it," Lois said, then answered her ringing phone. "Good Morning, Iguana Public Relations Group."

Jill started down the corridor where her corner office was located. After turning on the lights and hanging up her coat, she looked briefly at the mail and messages left on her desk by Lois and quickly decided which ones needed her immediate attention. Jill turned on her computer and sent off a couple of urgent e-mails to her last two clients. She ended each e-mail with *If there is anything else I can help you with, please contact my office.* Jill always made herself available to her clients and liked being able to service their needs as quickly as possible.

Suddenly, Lois buzzed her phone. "Jill, Phil is in. He said to come down to his office whenever you get a chance."

"Thanks, I'll be right down," Jill told her.

With Phil's being the company's vice president, his office was much nicer than Jill's. Though she had a corner office too, she couldn't have fit his desk, a huge mahogany piece with a matching chair, or the several pieces of fine art hanging on his walls, in her space. Phil had a taste for the good life, and everything he surrounded himself with showed that aspect.

"Good morning, Jill," he greeted her.

"Hello, Phil," Jill said, as she looked around the room.

She noticed that Matt Singletary was with them. "Matt, I didn't know that you were going to join us," she said as she eyed Phil suspiciously. "This must be a big one for you to come in this early."

Matt gave her a polite kiss on the cheek as he pulled a chair out for her. "Jill, this is big. That's why I want to make sure you're on board for this project."

The two men sat, and Matt explained the details of the project. "Jill, we have on our hands a group of very wealthy African-Americans who are friends of my wife. I'm sure Phil has told you that this group is opening a ranch and spa in Durango, Colorado. The grand opening is in one month. They just don't feel like they are getting the kind of exposure they need for the kind of clientele they want to attract."

He handed Jill a brochure of the resort and she looked at the cover. She saw the beautiful building that obviously was the resort. In the forefront of the picture stood three very tall, incredibly handsome African-American cowboys. Jill opened the brochure and began to read its contents, hoping to disguise her interest in the men on the front. Secretly, she hoped that they weren't just models, but actually worked on the ranch. She wouldn't mind a little romance while she was in Durango.

Jill brought her attention back to the meeting. "I understand all that, Matt. What I don't understand is why it is so important that I take this client. Phil said that you, as well as the client, wanted only me. Why?" she asked, already knowing that she would accept the assignment, if only for the chance to meet the tallest cowboy on the cover of the brochure.

Phil and Matt smiled at each other before Matt said, "Jill, that would be your personal cheerleader's fault."

"Joan," Jill said, knowing just whom he was talking

about. Joan was Matt's wife, and everyone in the office teased Jill about how the wife of the company's owner was her number-one fan. Even Matt teased her about it. Joan had been immensely impressed with Jill ever since she pulled her butt out of the fire two years ago on the Morgan account.

Paulina and Alex Morgan of Morgan Fiber Optics had needed a public relations representative. Joan had offered to find them someone at Iguana and picked Bill Winslow at random, but he had bombed on the account, and Joan was desperate to save face with the Morgans. Jill was new, and the only executive available, so Matt asked her to take on the mess. Jill handled the account like a seasoned veteran, and Joan had been singing her praises ever since.

"I should have known it had something to do with Joan." Jill smiled as she shook her head.

"Jill, this account is huge. Even if Joan hadn't insisted on you handling the account, I would have. You're smooth, smart, and efficient. You're just the person for the job. Are you on board?" Matt asked her directly.

"You already know I'm on board, Matt. I'd do anything for my favorite cheerleader," Jill said with a wink.

Matt winked back. "Thanks, Jill," he said as he stood to leave. Phil will fill you in on all the particulars."

"Tell Joan I said hello and give her my love," Jill told him as he began to leave.

"I sure will," he replied. "Now, if you'll excuse me, I have to get into my own office. There are a few things I have to do before I meet Jones and Kendall for golf at the Windsor Country Club."

"Windsor Country Club? Isn't that in Miami?" she asked him, a confused look on her face.

"That would be true, Jill. Thank goodness Kendall

has a company jet at his disposal, huh?" He laughed as he left the room.

"What a character," Jill said to Phil.

"Yeah, I wish my friends had a company jet they could use any time they wanted," Phil said with a smirk on his face.

"I have friends who would be quite happy with that Hummer and thirty-five-foot boat you have. You shouldn't complain."

"Who's complaining?" he joked. Turning serious, he said, "Well, Jill, you'll be leaving Sunday night. Davis, Sterling, and Roberts, the primary investors who have hired us, won't be at the ranch until the grand opening."

"Who is my contact person there?" Jill asked.

"Bebe Simmons is the manager. She has already faxed us everything we need. Frank, from Personal Limousine Service, will be picking you up to take you to the airport. You get into Durango at two P.M., and Bebe says that she will be waiting for you."

"What's my expense account looking like?"

"The sky's the limit. The investors want you to have every thing you need to make this opening magnificent," he said, handing Jill an envelope and Bebe's business card.

Jill opened the envelope and took out its contents. It was an American Express business card, with a note that read *If you need anything else, let Bebe know, she will be sure to get it for you. Thanks, Samuel Roberts*. Jill looked up with a slight smile on her face; she bounced her eyebrows. Phil bounced his back.

"I'll have Lois arrange your flight and then I'll get back with you."

"Phil, I think I want to start out earlier than Sunday. I'm going home for a few days."

"Pittsburgh?"

"Yes. I'm going to go visit my family. I want to leave early Thursday. Will that be a problem?"

"Absolutely not, I'll have Lois take care of that for you."

"Thanks, Phil," she said as she stood to leave. "You know, I'm kind of excited about this trip. I think I need to get away for a while. How long do you think I'll be out there?"

"Hmm, I'm thinking you'll only need to be there for a week or two. But you'll have to go back out for the opening. Then again, you can stay the whole month if you want, just play it by ear."

"Sounds good to me, Phil, thanks," she said as she left his office.

Jill quickly walked back to her office, pleased with her assignment. Though she wanted to meet Lois and Diane for lunch, she had mountains of work to finish, and tons of things to do before Thursday. She could count on Lois to help her with the office work, but she had to go shopping again. She couldn't possibly go home without taking her family something from New York.

"Lois, can I see you for a minute?" she asked as she walked by her friend's desk.

"Sure thing, Jill, just give me a second, Phil wants to see me too."

"Take your time," Jill said, knowing what Phil had to speak to her about.

In her office, Jill began to wrap things up. She still had several calls to make on behalf of her clients, she reminded herself as she went to her file cabinet and pulled some accounts. She had planned on working on them throughout the week, but since she'd be leaving soon she decided to get done as much as she could that day. She hated to leave any of her clients to someone else in the firm, because her own work ethic was high. That was the reason people asked for her, she never left them hanging.

"So you're going to Durango!" Lois said as she entered Jill's office. "Why didn't you tell me?"

"Lo, I didn't know myself until Saturday night. Phil called and told me a little bit about it, but said he couldn't give me particulars until this morning. I'm kind of excited about this assignment though. I think I need a little getaway."

"You're married to your job," Lois said, shaking her head at Jill. "But it seems like this time you can mix a little business with pleasure."

"I just prefer working vacations," she said as she smiled at her friend.

"You are a workaholic Jill," Lois cautioned. "What did you need me to do?"

"Oh, I really need your help. There is no way I can get all the work done and be ready to leave Thursday morning. Can I give you half of my files to fax? If you can do that for me, I can do the rest. Can you also make my return phone calls? And then I still have four letters I have to send out. I was going to start on another assignment, but it will have to be given to someone else," Jill explained in a hurry.

"Jill, just give me all the files. You just concentrate on your letters and your phone calls."

"Lois, are you sure?"

"Sure I'm sure. I'll fax them all off as soon as we get back from lunch. We are still on, aren't we?"

"I can make it now."

"Great. I have several airline arrangements to make for Phil, not including yours. I'll get all that done before lunch so I can concentrate on your stuff afterward. Just let me know who needs what and where it's to be sent."

"Oh, and, Lois, could you—"

"I know, I know. Make the necessary follow-up calls on your behalf to make sure they received everything, and ask if there's anything else we can do for them," Lois said as she stood to leave.

"You're a lifesaver," Jill told her.

"You know I'm here for you, girl. Let me know if there is anything else I can do."

"Thanks, Lois."

"Don't mention it. See you at lunch," Lois said as she left Jill's office.

Jill was busy with all the work she needed to do. She had an hour and a half to make a dent in her workload before she had to meet Lois and Diane in their usual lunch spot, the eatery on the lower level of the building. It wasn't a fancy place, but the food was good, and since they didn't have to travel far they could use the whole hour gabbing.

Nearly two hours later, she headed down to the cafeteria to meet Diane and Lois. When she arrived, they had already found seats close to a window and had saved one for Jill.

"So I hear you're going to Durango," Diane said sullenly. "Why does everyone in our office get to travel but me? Even Lois gets to travel."

"And did you hear the ranch has a spa on it?" Lois said teasingly with a childish smile on her face.

"Di, it's all work related," Jill explained. "Though I do plan on getting a little relaxation and some sightseeing in, but that will be after I'm finished with work."

"Jill, you're so committed to your job, I hope you really get some rest in," Lois told her.

"I'll give you that, you are a hard worker," Diane

added softly. "Everyone knows it. I hope you meet a really nice man who can take your mind off work at least for a little while."

"Di, that's not my goal."

"I know, but I'm just hoping for you. I can see that you could use a good man, even if you won't admit it."

"You sound like my mother, Di."

"Well, maybe it's time you listened to us."

Jill rolled her eyes. "What do they have good to eat today?" she asked her friends.

"You know I always get my usual, a grilled tuna sandwich, and as usual it's great. Want a bite?" Diane offered.

"No, I just can't make up my mind. I'll be right back," she told her friends.

She left the table, and Diane and Lois continued on with their lunch.

"Di, why do you ride her back so about finding a man? She will in her own time," Lois said.

"It's obvious she's lonely. The only thing she has in her life is this job and you and me."

"Well, she says all that's enough for her."

"Lois, you have Curtis and your kids. I have Tiffany and an occasional boyfriend or two. Jill has two girlfriends that she meets up with every Friday night and for lunch at work. How much of a life is that for her?" Diane asked.

"It's not a life. Maybe she's afraid, and you know she wants to get ahead in her career. It doesn't matter. Whatever she does, it's got to be her choice. She's smart, she's beautiful, and—"

"And she's not getting any younger. Lois, she's thirty years old. Her looks aren't going to hold up forever, you know."

"Well, maybe never having married or having kids

would be all right for Jill. We can't push her into a relationship."

"No, we can't," Diane replied. "But we can try."

"We'll argue about this later. Here she comes."

"Did you find something good?" Diane asked Jill.

Jill sat down in her seat. "I got the chicken noodle soup. Nothing else appealed to me. Hey, Lois, did Phil tell you that I want to leave on Thursday for Pittsburgh?"

"He sure did. I just need to know what time of day you want to catch your flight."

"I want to leave as early as possible. I'll only have three days to visit my family. I have to leave Sunday for Durango."

"Your mom is a sweetheart. Tell her I said hello," Diane said.

"I will."

"You need to bring her to New York again on your way back home," Lois added.

"I can see your evil plot brewing right now, Lois. You would love to get together with my mother and matchmake."

"Who, me?" Lois said coyly.

"Well, I don't think I'll be able to bring her back anyway."

"Why?" Diane asked.

"Because Phil says that I will definitely be out there for a week or two. After that, it's up to me, but I have to be back there for the grand opening."

"Why don't you take her out there for the grand opening?" Lois asked.

"At first I was thinking about it. She was even hinting around that she would like to come. I just know that she would start husband hunting, and since I really have to work I didn't think it would be a good idea."

"Jill, she only has your best interests at heart. We all do," Diane told her.

"I know. I just want things to happen when they feel right to me."

"Ladies, it looks like we're running low on time," Lois said as she glanced at her watch. "If I am going to get my work and your work done, I'd better get back."

"Thanks again for your help, Lois."

"Don't mention it."

Jill went straight to her office. She made all her phone calls and finished up the files she couldn't pass on to Lois.

She became momentarily lost in thought. She sat quietly thinking about Barb and Rick. Her sister met Rick Hamilton during her second year of law school. Rick was in his last year of law school and had a promising career as an attorney. With several law firms already interested in him, Rick would go on to pass the bar on his first try. Right after he started working with Cafaro, Jones, and Freidman, he and Barb were married and she never finished law school. Barb would reason that two high-powered careers such as theirs would be devastating to the marriage she wanted to create. But Jill felt as though Barb's getting pregnant right after the wedding was the real reason.

They did have a happy marriage, Jill thought. Her sister was always e-mailing her pictures of her kids. The little family had two boys and one girl. Rick Jr. was the oldest at eight; Lacy was five and had just started kindergarten; James was the baby at only three. Barb certainly seemed content, but Jill couldn't understand how her sister could have so easily given up her dream of being an attorney. Jill knew she certainly couldn't give up her job for a man. She could only think of all the times she and Barb would sit and talk about all the wonderful vacations they would take together when they both finished school. Then Rick came along, and all the plans and dreams seemed to be forgotten by her sister.

Jill came back from daydreaming and said aloud, "That won't happen to me." She grabbed her purse and her coat and headed out the door.

She hailed a taxi and just as she got into the car she realized she forgot her laptop. "I don't know what's wrong with me. I need to get away more than I think." She sighed. She made a mental note to remember to get it when she went into the office in the morning. Right now, she wanted to get home and make a phone call.

At home, she quickly took a shower. She would figure out what to have for dinner later as it was still early. After she dried off, she picked up the phone and called her mother. It rang several times and Jill was just about to hang up when she heard a man's voice answer.

"Hi, Daddy," she said in an excited voice. "It's Jill."

"Hey, baby girl, how are you?" he said, glad to hear from his daughter.

"I'm fine," she answered, happy to hear his familiar "baby girl" again. He had sweet pet names for her and Barb. When they were growing up, he had even called all their girlfriends sweet pea, or precious, but baby girl belonged solely to her.

"I was calling to let you know that I am coming home for a long weekend."

"When will you be here?"

"Thursday morning, but I can only stay for three days," she explained.

"I can pick you up at the airport. Do you know what time your flight will be in?"

"Not yet. All the plans for this trip are coming together this morning. I have to leave for Durango, Colorado, Sunday morning."

"Business trip?"

"Yeah, but I'm trying to get in a little family time before I go out there. I have an assignment to do some public relations work for a new ranch. I have to stay for two weeks, but after that I'm not due back in Durango until the grand opening."

"So that's what your mother was talking about. It sounds like she would like to join you, but instead of just enjoying herself she would be busy husband hunting," her dad said knowingly.

"Bingo! And that's why I really don't want her to come. This job is really important to the firm. I need to concentrate on my job, not finding a man."

"I can understand you don't want to be pressured into a relationship right now, but you know that you're not getting any younger," he said sympathetically.

"I know that, Dad. There is always that chance that I will never get married. I'm not going to marry just anyone to satisfy everyone else, and I certainly am not going to marry before I'm finished doing what I want to do with my life. I don't want to end up like Barb."

"Jill, don't get upset. I guess we all just worry about you. We want to make sure that someone will take care of you."

"Daddy, I think I've proven time and time again that I am quite capable of taking care of myself," she said flatly.

"I've got to give you credit, you have proven that. Just make sure that I see more grandkids, okay, baby girl?"

"We'll see, Daddy. I have to call you back tomorrow with my flight information. Do you remember Lois, the secretary at Iguana?"

"I sure do. I remember the fabulous meal she cooked

at your place when we came up to visit," he said, making Jill laugh.

"Well, she'll probably give you a call with my flight information if you don't hear from me. Hey, where's Mom? I better say hello to her before I hang up."

"She's not home right now. She went over to Barbie's to see the kids. Do you want me to have her call you back when she gets home?"

"No, that's okay. I'll just talk to her later," Jill said quietly. "I have to go, Daddy. I love you and I'll see you soon."

"Bye, baby girl. I love you."

Jill hung up the phone and sat on the sofa lost in thought. Once again she doubted herself. According to everyone she knew she was going to be some pitiful old maid, with an empty life. Didn't anyone understand that right now she was content with her life? How could she be happy? Everyone she knew was convinced that she was missing out on something special.

She wasn't completely unaware of how holding Darlene's baby affected her, or how every time her mom and dad mentioned how happy Barb was being a wife and mother, she felt so forgotten and empty inside.

Jill tried to push the thought from her mind. She busied herself writing a note to Marie. She wouldn't see the housekeeper for two weeks, so she left the address and phone number where she could be reached in the case of an emergency. Jill put the information on the table in the foyer, along with Marie's paycheck. Next, she called her building's management office to notify them of her extended business trip and explained that Marie Watson would be the only person authorized to be in her apartment while she was away.

Feeling a little hungry, Jill made herself a sandwich. She bit into it and suddenly wished she had a plate of

Marie's cooking instead. She sat at her kitchen table in silence, noticing her apartment felt lonely and cold. Thoughts of Dar floated into her head again, followed by thoughts of Barb playing with her kids. For the life of her, she couldn't figure out what was going on in her head.

Chapter 3

Jill woke up a little before five A.M. and shut the alarm clock off. She quickly dressed and went down to the fitness center. When she arrived, Dar's husband, Mike, was working out with another man who looked very much like him. She walked over to get on the stationary bike and said hello to the pair.

"Hey, Jill, how's everything?" Mike said. He had finished lifting weights and was getting up from the bench.

"Just fine, how's that sweet little baby girl of yours?" she asked him, smiling.

"She's growing more beautiful every day," he said, turning to the man beside him. "Jill, I want you to meet my big brother. Jill, this is Andre. Dre, this is my baby girl's adopted aunt Jill Alexander."

"It's very nice to meet you, Jill," Dre said as he extended his hand to shake hers. Jill noticed immediately that his hands were huge and strong. Dre stood a few inches taller than Mike, and had broad shoulders and full lips that curled into a sensuous smile. She smiled back effortlessly.

"Hi, Dre, it's nice to meet you, too," Jill said, still holding his hand. "I didn't know Mike had a brother," she continued, as she slowly released it, taking notice that there wasn't a wedding band.

"My brother didn't tell me that he had such a beautiful neighbor either," Dre said, as he gave his brother a quick side glance.

"My apologies to both of you, but, Dre, we can't keep Jill. She's a public relations executive and is usually up and out the door early."

Jill quickly glanced at the clock on the wall. "Your brother is right. I usually get in a quick workout before I head off to work. I better get a move on."

"We better get going too, Dre. I have to get to work also," Mike said as he nudged his brother. He walked toward the door and a smile formed on his lips.

"Jill, would you like to go out with me one evening?" he asked almost shyly.

"Yes, I would. Oh no, I can't!"

"What's wrong?" Dre asked, confused.

"I'm sorry, Dre, I leave on Thursday for possibly a month," Jill told him.

"I tell you what, why don't we just plan a date a month from today? I'll still be interested, I can only hope you'll be," he told her.

Jill smiled as Dre walked away to join his brother. She only had twenty minuets left to work out, and it flew by like five.

Back in her apartment, Jill took a quick shower and dressed for work. She hated being late, but meeting Dre made it almost worth it. She couldn't believe that he had made her blush like a schoolgirl.

While the elevator rose to the twenty-third floor, Jill pulled out a mirror and checked her makeup, combing her hair with her fingers and letting it fall on her shoulders. The elevator stopped and she got out.

"Good morning, Jill," Lois said, from behind her desk.

"Good morning, Lois. How are all the arrangements coming along?" Jill asked her.

"You're just about ready. Your plane tickets are being picked up by the courier, and do you see the little stack of files right there?"

"Yes."

"That's all that is left of the pile you gave me to take care of," Lois said, proudly.

"Oh, Lois, as always, I owe you big."

"No, you don't. That trip to Hawaii has your account paid in full for a long time. Just remember to tell your family I said hello, especially your dad."

"I called him last night. He was talking about your cooking. Oh, just in case I forget, could you call him and let him know all my flight information?"

"I sure will."

"I'll be in my office if you need me," Jill said as she headed down the hall.

"Are we on for lunch, or are you leaving early?"

"I'm leaving right after lunch. I'll see you and Di downstairs."

Jill finished the last of the files in her office and made a few phone calls to her clients. She put her laptop next to her purse, which reminded her to check her e-mail. She replied to all of her messages and then went back to Lois's desk.

"Lois, if you're finished, I can file those before we head down to lunch."

"Do you need any help?" Lois said as she handed Jill the stack of files.

"No. I'll be quick, and I'll meet you and Di downstairs," Jill said.

"Sounds good to me. Oh, the file on top is for you to take with you to Durango. I compiled some information from the Web about the area, as well as any information we had about the resort. I thought it might be useful."

"I'll put it with my laptop. Thanks, Lois, for every-thing," Jill said.

She went back to her office and filed the last of her clients' information. Then she grabbed her purse and her laptop and went to meet Lois and Diane.

When she got to the cafeteria, they had just bought their food and were looking for a seat. Finally, they found a table and sat down.

"Jill, are you all ready for your trip?" Diane asked her.

"Yes, I am. You know, I think one day we all need to take a vacation together," Jill told them.

Diane's face lit up until Lois's voice of reason dimmed it. "You know that the firm couldn't run with all three of us gone."

"We could go for a long weekend or something," Jill told them.

"That would be great. I sure could use a vacation," Diane said anxiously.

"I have some other news," Jill said with a sly smile on her face.

Lois and Diane looked curiously at each other, and then in unison said, "What is it?"

"Well, I have a date," she said.

Diane stopped chewing, and Lois almost choked. Both women looked at their friend in amazement. When Lois cleared her throat she asked, "A real date, with a real man?"

"Yes," Jill said, still smiling.

"Who is he? Do we know him?" Lois asked, curi-ously.

"No," Jill answered, laughing.

"Give us details, Jill. When is this date going to hap-pen?" Diane demanded.

Jill laughed harder. "The date isn't for another month.

I won't be back in town for at least two weeks, and the job won't be completed until two weeks after that," she explained.

"Do we know him?" Lois asked again. She was sure it was one of the other executives.

"No, you don't know him," Jill said as she stood and picked up her purse and laptop. "He's my next-door neighbor's brother. That's all I can tell you ladies until next month."

"Lois, we better be happy for that," Diane said contently. "Are you coming in tomorrow?"

"No. I'm going to pack tonight and shop tomorrow. I'll give you both a call before I leave town," Jill said and leaned over and gave her friends a good-bye kiss on the cheek. Lois and Diane were like sisters to her. She would miss them terribly, especially their standing Friday night date.

Jill was headed home in a cab when she asked the driver to stop so she could pick up a bottle of wine. She just wanted to relax, listen to music, pack, and if she was lucky see Dre, who she hoped would still be at Mike and Darlene's. She hated to admit it, but she was a little excited to have the attention of the tall Latino man.

After she picked up the wine, she stopped by the Candle Emporium and bought several scented candles. Feeling like she had what she needed to ensure a wonderful evening, she walked the rest of the way home.

Unlocking her door, she entered her apartment and set her laptop and purse on the sofa. Jill put the bottle in the fridge to chill before she looked around her apartment, trying to decide where she wanted to place the candles. She placed the large, three-wick vanilla-scented one on the coffee table in the living room and the two smaller matching candles on the mantel. She put the others in her bedroom, though she knew she wouldn't let things with Dre get that far.

Jill opened the solid mahogany armoire and turned on her favorite jazz CD on the stereo. Then she went into her bedroom and put on a comfy pantsuit that she loved to lounge in. She went into her bathroom and brushed her teeth, fixed her makeup, and combed her hair. "No sense in waiting for him to knock on my door," she said aloud.

Jill went to Mike and Darlene's, stopping to listen at the door. She could hear Mike's voice clearly and she thought she heard Dre talking too. They were obviously up to having company. She quickly knocked and waited eagerly for an answer.

Darlene answered the door. "Hey, Jill, how are you?"

"I'm great, Dar," she said as her eyes fell on Dre. He sat on the sofa with a woman sitting comfortably on his lap.

"Come in and meet everyone. Do you have time?"

Jill stared in Dre's eyes. The smile disappeared from his face. From where she stood, she could see Mike drop his face in his hands. Dre looked to his brother for help, but Mike had none.

"Jill, do you want to come in? Are you okay?"

"Oh yeah, Dar, I'm fine. I . . . I just wanted to let you know that I have to leave town Thursday morning," she stammered. "I'll be gone for a while, and I wanted to say good-bye," she added, trying to cover her original intention.

"Well, if you're leaving town, surely you can come in for a little bit," Dar said.

"No, I really have to be going. I have a lot to do before I leave. Kiss Helena for me," Jill said as she backed away from their door.

Darlene, sensing that something was wrong, stepped

into the hallway and partially closed the door behind her. "Jill, what's wrong? Please tell me," she pleaded.

"Nothing, Dar, really, I have to go. I'll be in touch as soon as I get back in town." Jill hurried back into her own apartment, not wanting Dar to see the tears in her eyes.

She wasn't hurt because she had seen Dre with a woman in his lap; she was hurt because she had let herself get sucked into the idea of romance again, only to be let down. The look on his face when he saw her at the door told her that the woman meant something to him.

She grabbed a tissue and flopped on the sofa. She allowed herself to have a brief cry. "Why do men act the way they do?" she wondered out loud. Jill turned off the CD and allowed the radio to play. She pulled herself together and went into her bedroom.

Opening her suitcases, she packed, making a conscious effort not to forget her makeup or any of her other essentials. When she was done, she had four large suitcases. Jill wanted desperately to call Lois and Di, but she didn't, she would talk to them tomorrow. Right now she wasn't up to all the questions they would have as to what went wrong. How could she answer them? She wasn't sure herself. All she knew for sure was that she allowed other people's opinions of what her life should be like influence her.

There was a light knock on the door. Jill instinctively knew who it was and wasn't interested in any apologies. She ignored it and turned the music up louder. She waited a few minutes before she turned it off altogether. Shortly after, the phone rang. She ignored it too and turned on the television. Jill lay across the sofa and watched the movie *The Best Man,* holding the brochure with the handsome cowboys on it that Matt had given her. She looked at the tall, dark cowboy in the center and wondered if he was at the resort right now, and if so, would she get to meet him? She stared at his face until she fell asleep.

When Jill woke up, it was morning. She turned off the television and went into the kitchen to make breakfast. She didn't work out because she wanted to avoid running into Dre in the fitness center. She sat at her table and ate, sipping her coffee slowly and thinking about the previous night's events. Having slept on it, she felt she had let the situation get the best of her. Though she had hoped to spend time with Dre, she certainly didn't owe him anything, nor did he owe her. She felt good and remembering that she had an interesting and exciting assignment ahead of her changed her frame of mind.

Jill took a shower and dressed. She grabbed her purse and keys and left. As she closed the door to her apartment, she noticed a note taped to it. She balled it up and tossed it in the trash can as she got into the elevator.

Playing the radio, Jill sang along with Whitney Houston's "One of Those Days" as she drove. She promised herself that she wouldn't think anymore of the high hopes she secretly had for Dre. She had let her mind play the love game too fast and she knew to keep that in check from now on.

First, she went to FAO Schwartz to buy her nephews and niece some toys. Rick Jr. was deeply interested in science, so she bought him a telescope and a book called *Earth, Space, and Science.* She bought Lacy books and a doll to add to the collection Jill had given her. The baby, James, was still very easy to impress. She bought him a battery-operated fire truck that would light up and the little fireman inside yelled commands.

Jill went to Saks for her mother and bought her a coral-colored silk pantsuit. Her dad was the easiest to shop for and would hope for his usual, cigars from the Pipe and Cigar Factory, the only place that sold the brand that he wanted.

It was almost time for dinner when she was finished shopping, and Jill was getting hungry. Knowing that there wasn't anything great at home to eat, she decided to stop by the Olive Garden.

"How many are in your party?" the maitre d' asked, shortly after she walked in.

"Just me," she answered and was quickly ushered to a table. Jill sat down and looked around the room. She was the only one sitting by herself. There was a family across from her, two couples to her right, and another behind her. She wasn't sure if the two men to her left were a couple or not. Nonetheless, she felt awkward sitting alone. When the waitress came to take her order, she asked for a take-out menu instead. She ordered stuffed chicken marsala with mashed potatoes and headed home.

Outside her door were the plane tickets Lois had sent to her apartment by courier. Next to the tickets was another note. Assuming it was from Dre, she threw it away. Jill ate quietly in her apartment, then finished her packing before she called Lois.

"Hello," her friend answered.

"Hey, Lois, it's just me. How was work today?"

"It was fine, but not the same without you. Are you all ready for your trip?"

"I think so. I got all of my shopping done, and I got the plane tickets, thank you."

"You don't sound as excited about your assignment as you did yesterday. Are you sure you're all right?" Lois asked again in a voice that revealed her worry.

"I'm fine; I won't be going on that date though."

"Oh, Jill, I'm so sorry. What happened?" Lois asked.

"Let's just say that it wasn't meant to be."

"Jill, how can you say that? The date wasn't for another month."

"I don't want to date somebody who already has a woman," Jill said softly. She had promised herself she wouldn't tell Lois about Dre, but she had to talk to someone about it.

"Is there anything I can do, baby?" Lois asked, sympathetically.

"Actually, there is. Please don't ask me any more questions, at least not tonight."

"I won't."

"I better go. I have to be up early tomorrow to catch that flight." Jill was choking back tears and didn't want Lois to know how upset she was.

"I'll talk to you later, Jill. Have a safe trip."

"See you later."

Chapter 4

In the morning, Jill put all her suitcases and laptop next to the door so she wouldn't forget them. Her laptop and purse were the only things she would carry on the plane. Thank goodness her father would be there to pick her up, she thought. She didn't know how else she would manage all of her bags.

Jill made a pot of coffee and slowly drank a cup as she got dressed. She curled her hair in hot rollers and did her makeup, then she put on an above-the-knee, cream-colored skirt, with a matching silk top. She finished the rest of her coffee with a bagel, and then took out the rollers. Brushing the soft curls, she let her hair frame her face. She decided to wear her cream and brown stilettos with a matching handbag.

The driver who would take her to the airport rang the buzzer just as she put her dishes in the sink. She asked him to come upstairs and help her with her luggage. Jill quickly checked herself one last time in the mirror and slid on her suit jacket. She was putting her necessities into her purse when there was a knock at the door.

"Good Morning, Ms. Alexander," said Frank, a stout man with silver-gray hair. "You're in luck, they sent me today."

Jill smiled back and offered her hand to shake. "Good

morning, Frank. Thank you for coming for me," she said, stepping aside so he could enter the apartment.

"Is this everything?" Frank asked, pointing at the suitcases and laptop case.

"Yes, this is it."

"I can carry these three, if you can manage that piece," he told her.

"I can do that," Jill answered and picked up her purse and laptop with her free hand.

The two made their way down to the front of Jill's building where Frank had parked his limo. They placed all Jill's suitcases into the trunk of the car; then he opened the door for her to get in.

A half hour later, he pulled up in front of United Airlines.

"How did you know what airline I was taking?" Jill asked him curiously.

"Lois from Iguana told me." He winked at her.

"I should have known," Jill said. "Lois is on top of everything."

"She also told me to give you this," Frank said as he handed her a newspaper and an umbrella. Jill laughed; it was a joke between the two women. It seemed whenever the two got caught in the rain, only one of them had an umbrella and the other had to use a newspaper.

At the gate, Jill had a twenty-minute wait before her plane started boarding. She was happy to be on her way to Pittsburgh and was anxious to see her family. Hopefully, she would have some time alone with Barb. Even though her sister had a pretty full life, Jill wondered if she would be able to steal her away from her family for one night. It had been a year since they had spent any time together, and she missed Barb more than she wanted to admit.

When her flight was called to board, Jill was not only

happy to be on her way, but also thankful that no one was sitting beside her in first class. After the plane took off, she stored her purse and laptop holder in the vacant chair as she clicked away on her computer, writing letters she would need to send out after she landed. Next, she looked at the information Lois had given her on A Special Place. Jill read the information thoroughly since she had never been to Colorado; she figured it would be useful to know a little about the town she would be visiting.

As she read, Jill grew even more excited about Durango. The area was rich in Native American history, which interested her, since her great-great-grandfather was from the Ute tribe. She read on, making mental notes to rent a car and visit the Mesa Verde National Park.

"Would you like something to drink?" the flight attendant asked her.

Jill looked up from her reading and asked for a Sprite. Thanking the flight attendant for the drink, she turned and stared out the window. She still hadn't overcome the excitement she felt about this assignment. Though Dre had dampened her spirits briefly, she was back on track again.

She returned to her reading and saw that Durango had lots of activities to keep her busy. She wouldn't mind rock climbing since she had done that before, but hot-air ballooning was out of the question. There were many luxurious bed-and-breakfasts around the area. Jill quickly remembered how she had felt at the Olive Garden, surrounded by all the couples, and knew to steer clear of the little romantic inns.

When the captain announced that they were approaching Greater Pittsburgh International Airport, Jill put her laptop and file back in their bag, tucked them under the seat in front of her, and fastened her seat belt.

After Jill exited the plane, she grabbed a luggage cart and walked toward the baggage claim area. She waited patiently for her luggage to arrive. When it did, she collected all her bags and placed them on a cart, then headed for the main entrance. Once outside, she looked around trying to spot her parents' car. She could see her father waving to her and she started walking in his direction.

"How was your flight, baby girl?" he asked, obviously happy to see her, as he kissed her cheek.

"It was fine, Daddy. Were you here long?"

"Not at all, Lois called to let me know what time to be here, and said she would call if there were any changes in your arrival time. I told her she didn't have to do that, but she insisted. Since I didn't hear from her, I assumed your flight was on time."

"She has been really great. She pulled this trip together for me fast, and even handled some of my office work. I don't know what I would do without her."

"I can believe that. I still think you should have brought her with you. I sure could use some of her cooking. Not that your mother is bad, I just like that good old Louisiana cooking she does."

"Where's Mom?" Jill asked.

"She didn't want to park so she's circling around," he answered as he looked around to see if he could see his wife. "Here she comes now," he said as he signaled to her.

Jill's mom pulled up to the curb and got out. She ran over and gave her youngest daughter a hug. "Oh, Jill, you're finally here. I'm so happy to see you!"

"I'm happy to see you too, Mom," Jill said, smiling.

Her father put the suitcases into the trunk while the two women greeted each other.

"Step back; let me take a look at you," her mother said

Jill did as she was told, realizing that her mother was sizing her up for another round of matchmaking.

"You're stunning!" her mother announced. Jill had hoped that her mother wouldn't start right away on finding a mate for her. She was wrong.

"Thanks, Mom. I try to keep my looks up. It's hard when you hit thirty," Jill said, with sarcasm in her voice.

"Jill, that was a compliment."

Before Jill could reply, her father beeped the horn for them to get into the car. Her mother sat in front and she sat in the backseat, thankful that her mother couldn't see the look she shot her.

"You know, Jill, Barbie wanted to pick you up from the airport, but your father insisted that he come. She's at our house waiting for you."

"Good. I can't wait to see her," Jill said, and her mood lifted. She was excited that she wouldn't have to hunt Barb down.

"She's making a wonderful lunch for you. I hope you're hungry, or did you fill up on airplane food?" her mother asked.

"No, the flight wasn't very long. I had a little Sprite and read. I'm really excited about this assignment. I've never been to Colorado," Jill said excitedly.

"Neither have I. Take lots of pictures," her dad said, glancing back at her with a smile.

"You know, Barbie and Rick are going on a trip real soon too. Rick is taking her to Barbados for their anniversary," her mother said proudly.

"That's nice," Jill replied flatly.

Her father glanced at his wife, obviously annoyed

with her. "Tell us more about your assignment, Jill. It sounds like it'll be great," he said.

"Maybe we can talk about it later. Mom wants to tell us about the wonderful trip Rick is taking Barbie on," she said slowly.

Her mother continued. "Barbie says that they are going in August. They plan on staying for a week. I told her I would watch the kids for them," her mother said, oblivious that Jill had stopped listening.

Jill sat quietly in the backseat staring out the window. Her father noticed, but decided that it was best to leave the situation alone. Jill had tuned her mother out, and for the moment, so would he.

As her father pulled into the driveway, Jill saw Barb's kids playing in the yard. She smiled at them when they ran toward the car. As soon as Jill got out, she was surrounded by two children calling her name who were extremely happy to see her. She bent to give each of them a kiss.

"Hi, sis!" Barb said as she came out of the house to greet her sister. Though she had James in her arms, she managed to give Jill a hug. "It's good to see you."

"It's good to see you, too. I missed you. E-mail has nothing on seeing you in person," Jill said as her sister led her into the house. Ricky helped his granddad bring his aunt's luggage in.

Inside, the family gathered in the dining room. Barb had made a wonderful lunch of fried chicken, potato salad, baked beans, and lemonade. The family ate and asked Jill numerous questions about New York and her assignment in Colorado.

"Jill, how long are you going to be in Durango?" Barb asked.

"I'll be there for about two weeks. After that, I have to play it by ear until the grand opening."

"You have such an exciting career."

"You know, Jill, Barbie—" Her mother didn't finish her sentence before her husband interrupted her.

"Ah, honey, can I see you in the kitchen for a minute," he said as he stood up.

"Rob, what is it?"

"It will only take a minute, Maddie, please," he said, and she reluctantly got up and followed him into the kitchen.

Not wanting to overhear anything, Jill took the opportunity to give the kids the presents she had bought.

"Ricky, do you think you're strong enough to pull that big suitcase over to me?" Jill asked her oldest nephew.

"Aunt Jill, please," he said as he stood and rolled up his sleeve. "Look at this," he said, showing her his imaginary muscle.

"Wow!" she said in mock astonishment. "Have you been working out?"

"Yep," he said, with a wide smile on his face, happy his aunt had noticed. He pulled the suitcase toward Jill and then sat back down.

"This is for you, Ricky," she said, and handed him the telescope. "Are you still into stars?" she asked him

"Yes! Thanks, Aunt Jill!" He gave her a big kiss.

"What did you bring for me, Aunt Jill?" Lacy asked anxiously.

"Oh, Lacy, you know I didn't forget my sweetheart," Jill said. Reaching into her suitcase, she brought out a big doll. Lacy grabbed it and squeezed it tight.

"I love her!" Lacy said. "I love you too, Aunt Jill," the little girl said, hugging her aunt, before she ran to her mother to show her the doll.

Jill watched her sister as she looked at the doll she had given her daughter. She paid close attention to everything her little girl was saying. Sensing Jill's eyes on her, Barbara looked up.

"Jill, you're a wonderful auntie," Barb said, making her sister smile.

"This is for James," she said as she handed the fire engine and the books she had bought for the kids to her sister. "I couldn't decide what to get you and Rick, so I thought I would watch the kids one night and send you two out for the evening."

"Jill, that's a wonderful idea. Are you sure you want to take on these three?"

"Sure. It'll be fun. Besides, I'll have Big Rick here to help me out. I'm sure he can help me with the little ones," she said, smiling at her nephew. He smiled back, happy to be considered so mature.

Her parents came back into the room and Jill pulled their gifts out of the suitcase.

Her mom sat on the sofa nearest Jill, and her dad sat in his recliner.

"Mom, this is for you," Jill said as she handed her a package. "I hope you like it," she added.

"Jill, it feels like Christmas when you come home," her mom said with a smile. She opened the package and saw the beautiful silk pantsuit her daughter had bought her. "Oh, Jill, this is lovely. The color is beautiful. Thank you, sweetheart," she told her as she leaned over and kissed Jill's cheek.

"Daddy, there's no surprise in your gift; I got you the usual," Jill said walking over to him.

"Thank you, baby girl. I knew you wouldn't let me down." She handed him two boxes of his favorite hand-rolled cigars. He took one out and smelled it. "Ah, I'll save this for after dinner," he announced as he stuffed it into his shirt pocket.

"Jill, your room is ready if you want to get settled in," her mom said.

"I guess I would like to freshen up a little. I'll help clean up first though."

"No, don't worry about it. I'll clean up. Barbie, you help your sister with her suitcases. Rob, can you keep an eye on the kids?"

"What kids?" he replied. "There aren't any kids here, these are all grown folks," he said, laughing, as he reached out to grab Ricky. Ricky playfully dodged his grandfather's grasp and sat down to help keep an eye on his younger brother and sister.

The two sisters made their way upstairs, each one with a suitcase in her hand. Jill carefully balanced her purse and laptop in her other hand.

"I'll go get your other suitcase," Barbara said.

"Thanks, Barb. I'll start unpacking," Jill said.

Barb left the room and returned momentarily with Jill's last suitcase. She put it in the corner with the others and sat down on the bed.

"You still have an amazing figure," Barb told her sister as she slid into a pair of jeans. "What are you, a size four?"

"No, I'm a six. You don't look bad yourself, Barb."

"Thanks. Flattery will get you everywhere."

"You've got to remember, you've had three kids and you're in great shape. What are you, a size eight?" Jill asked, giving her sister the once-over.

"I'll take that as a compliment, but I'm a size ten."

"Let's do something together while I'm here."

"Just the two of us?" Barb asked.

"Yes, just the two of us. I know Mom will be happy to watch the kids. Let's go shopping or to the movies, or both."

"What makes you think Mom would be so happy to watch the kids?" Barb asked.

"I guess because she's always telling me that she is watching the kids so you and Rick can go out. Doesn't she watch them for you?"

Barb stared at her sister sympathetically and said, "Jill, Mom watches the kids now and then, mostly when Rick is working late and I have something important to do. I had to beg her to watch the kids while we go on vacation."

"Why does she do that to me?" Jill said.

"Probably because she wants you to see us as the couple that is so much in love, and spends countless hours gazing into each other's eyes," Barb said as she pretended to look lovingly and longingly at a man. Jill laughed at her sister.

"She still has no right to make me feel guilty for choosing the path I feel is right for me."

"Don't let her get to you, Jill," Barb said, reaching out to hold her sister's hand.

"I won't, I'll just get even."

"Jill, be warned; don't play with fire," Barb told her younger sister. "When Mom's on a mission, nothing can stop her."

"Oh, I'll be careful, but I think Mom would benefit from a little burning this time," Jill said. "Hey, let's go out tonight. I know where I can find you a babysitter, and she's right downstairs."

"Jill, I don't think Mom will babysit, so we can just hang out. Rick won't be home till late tonight."

"You don't know your little sister very well," Jill said as she slipped on a different blouse. She put on another pair of shoes and went downstairs with Barb.

Their mom was sitting on the living room floor playing with Lacy, and their dad was still in his chair.

"Hey, Mom, would you like to spend time with the

kids? Barb and I want to have a little time together before I have to leave."

"Tonight, Jill?" her mother asked, trying to hide her
shock.

"Tonight would be perfect, thanks, Mom," Jill said excitedly as she bent down to give her mother a kiss. She
grabbed her sister's hand and said, "We won't be late.
Bye."

"Thanks, Mom," Barb said, picking up her purse and
her car keys.

The two sisters said nothing to each other until Barb
had pulled off, then they burst into laughter.

"Jill, you make it look so easy," Barb told her after
she caught her breath.

"Oh, that's just the beginning."

"I'm afraid to see what's next. Well, where are we
going?"

"Why don't we skip the movies and go down to the
Sheraton at Station Square? We could listen to some
live jazz and get a drink," Jill suggested.

"That sounds good. I haven't been to Station Square
in months. Jill, tell me more about your assignment in
Durango."

"Do you mean what my job entails there or about the
city itself?"

"Both. I sit at home all day with James, take Lacy and
Ricky to school, cook dinner, and run errands. Rick is always so busy with work. By the time he gets home, we
both are usually worn out. I need to hear something exciting, and you're it," Barb explained.

"But you two are happy, right?" Jill asked, concerned.

"Yes, we're happy. I guess I'm just missing some of the
fire we used to have. Maybe we'll rekindle some of that
romance when we go to Barbados."

"I'm sure you will, sis," Jill consoled her.

* * *

She pulled into Station Square and quickly found a parking space in the garage. It was early evening, and the weather was warm. There was a slight breeze coming off the river. Walking with her sister, Jill looked up at the star-filled sky. She had a sense of inner peace and attributed it to being with Barb.

They entered the dimly lit lobby and heard the music softly filtering through the air. Two seats were empty near the corner of the room, and they made their way toward them. A waitress came over and took their order. "Can I get you something from the bar?" she asked.

"I'll have Chambord with soda and lime," Jill ordered.

"And I'll have Khalua and cream please," Barb said.

"I'll be right back with your orders."

"You still haven't told me anything about your assignment or your job," Barb said when the waitress departed. "I know you are a public relations executive, but what do you do?"

Jill could tell that her sister was truly interested in her job. Though she had been at Iguana for a few years, Jill realized that she and Barb had never talked about her job. Jill always knew that Barb accepted her just the way she was. She didn't push her to find a man, or play any games. Barb was Barb, accepting, loving, and nurturing. Even when she was dreaming of a career in public relations, and moving to New York, it was Barb who had supported her.

"Well, Barb, what I do isn't really hard, but I love my job. When someone has a new company or business, or even if they want to drum up some business or recognition for an existing company, I help them with that. I work on their publicity and actually anything else they need."

"And that pretty much takes you all over the country?"

"Yes, only because of the company I work for. Iguana is widely known, and much of their business is through word of mouth. It's still a great place to work. We're like a little family there."

"What will you do in Colorado?"

"I have to prepare a press release for the newspaper and contact the media about the ranch's grand opening. I'm also responsible for organizing their coming-out party," Jill told her.

The waitress returned with their drinks and set them down. "Let me know if you need anything else," she offered.

"Thank you," Barb said as the waitress walked away. "I remember Lois and Diane, they're very nice. Lois made quite an impression on Dad with her cooking."

"I know. No matter where she is, she feels right at home in the kitchen," Jill added.

"Do you know anything about Durango?"

"I know a little bit. Lois printed some information from the Internet. It sounds like a very exciting and interesting place. Of course, there is ranching and river rafting, but I'm anxious to see the national forest," Jill said as she took a sip of her drink.

"That all sounds so fabulous. Will you have time to get all that in?"

"Maybe not all of it, but I hope to get some of it done."

"I wish I could go with you," Barb said with a sigh and took a sip of her drink.

"Now, that would be great. There are hot springs there; I can see us lounging in one right now. I wish you could,

Barb. Mom hinted around that she would like to come with me, but I know that she would only be on a quest to find a man for me," Jill said as she rolled her eyes.

"You'll settle down when it's your time," Barb told her simply.

"Thanks, Barb," Jill said as she looked sincerely into her sister's face.

"Thanks for what?"

"For your love and acceptance. Sometimes people treat me like there's something wrong with me because I'm not married. I'm happy with my life, but even if I wasn't I wouldn't get married just to please everybody else."

"If you did that, you would miss out on all the wonderfulness of being single," Barb told her sister lovingly.

Jill loved her big sister. Just like when they were little, Barb had a way of making everything all right, or at least seem right. It was her mother that made her feel like a failure, for not being married with children like Barb.

"Let's go look in some of the shops before they close," Barb suggested. "It's been so long since I've been out of the house without the kids; I just want to get in as much as possible."

Jill insisted on paying their tab, and then the two sisters walked across the street into the shops at Station Square. They weren't really shopping as much as enjoying each other's company. Jill bought her sister some candles, and Barb purchased a glass bluebird for Jill.

"This is your bluebird of happiness," she told Jill as she gave it to her. "Never let anyone tell you what your dreams are; always be happy knowing you're making the right decision for Jill."

"I will, Barb," Jill told her sister, once again finding confidence in her life choices.

"We better go home. Mom is probably all played out

by now," Barb said with a laugh, remembering the trick Jill had played on their mother.

The two sisters headed back outside to the garage where Barb's car was parked. They got in and headed home.

"I wish you could come home more often. I know we couldn't have nights like this all the time, but it would be more often than once a year," Barb said.

"Maybe one day I'll come back home to stay. I wish we lived closer to each other too, but right now my job keeps me in New York."

"Well, I won't hold my breath. I know just how much you love your job. To be honest, I would love your job too."

"Really? Why do you say that?" Jill asked her sister, obviously puzzled.

"Jill, come on! You have to know how fascinating your career is. You make a great living, and you fly all over the country meeting all kinds of people. I didn't even finish law school," Barb said sadly.

"Barb, you have a great husband and three beautiful children. You have a wonderful life," Jill told her sister as she caressed her arm.

"I know, and I am very thankful for my life. It's just that I feel unfulfilled personally. Sometimes I think I would like to go back to law school."

"If that's what you want, I think it's a great idea. Have you talked it over with Rick?"

"Not yet, but I'm going to. I don't see any reason why he wouldn't support me on this. Ricky and Lacy are in school now, and I could find a day care for James. By the time I finished with school and started to work, James would be in school too."

"Go for it," Jill told her.

Chapter 5

When they reached their parents' home, it was nine-thirty in the evening. They went inside to find everyone in the house still awake except their dad. Their mom sat on the sofa and looked like she was exhausted. She lifted her head slowly from the sofa to see who was coming through the door. Trying to appear not as tired as she was, she greeted her daughters with as much enthusiasm as she could manage.

"Did you two have a nice time?" she asked.

"We sure did, Mom. Did the kids give you any trouble?" Barb asked.

"Not my angels, Barbie. Where did you go?"

"We went to the Sheraton in Station Square, and then we went over to the shops," Jill told her mom. Barb kissed Lacy on the cheek, then was made to kiss the baby doll the little girl hadn't put down all evening.

"Barb, Rick called. I told him you and Jill went out for a little while."

"Why didn't he call me on my cell phone?"

"I don't know. I guess he just wanted to give you some time alone with your sister."

"Well, I guess I'd better get going," Barb said.

"Saturday I'm planning to have a little party for Jill. I'm just inviting a few family friends over, but would you two like to go do pottery with me Friday afternoon?"

"Sure, Mom, I'm free," Jill said.

"Let me see if I can get a babysitter, and I'll let you know," Barb said. Noticing the pleading look on her sister's face, she winked at Jill to assure her that she would do her best to find a sitter.

Jill and her mother helped Barb out to her car with the kids. The family kissed each other good-bye, and Barb left for home.

Back inside the house, Jill helped her mother straighten up the living room. When her mom took a couple of glasses into the kitchen, Jill used that time to make a quick phone call. Her mother came out of the kitchen just as Jill had finished talking.

"I'm going to bed, Jill," she said as she gave Jill a good night kiss.

"Good night, Mom," Jill said, smiling as she and her mother hugged.

"Do you need anything?"

"Not right now, but if I do I know where everything is."

Maddie smiled at her youngest daughter and went to bed.

Jill walked over to the coffee table and picked up the family photo album. She sat on the sofa and flipped through it. She had seen the album many times before, and it always took her mind to a place that was familiar and warm; it embraced her and told her that she belonged. Jill looked at each picture, as if to burn it into her mind's eye again. She lovingly touched the pictures of her and Barb sitting on her father's lap Christmas Day, her fifth birthday party, and her mom standing with her outside the classroom on the first day of kindergarten. There were pictures of Barb's sweet-sixteen birthday party, and her own high school graduation and prom. She stood there beaming in her prom dress, with Calvin Haskins's arms around her waist.

Then came the pictures Jill loved the most, of her mother and father dancing at their twenty-fifth wedding anniversary party. Jill closed the photo album as she wondered if she would ever have a twenty-fifth wedding anniversary of her own.

No, she thought. She wouldn't let her mind go in that direction tonight. Barb had done such a wonderful job of lifting her spirits; she wouldn't let her thoughts get carried away into sadness.

She put the photo album back in its place and went upstairs to her room. Jill changed into her nightgown and lay down in bed. In her room, which was illuminated by moonlight, she couldn't stop thinking about Barbie. *Barbie.* She had stopped calling her sister that a long time ago. She couldn't remember exactly what had happened to make her stop calling her Barbie, except that she was jealous of how her mother had always made it seem that Barb was so wonderful for getting married and having children. Her mother would go on and on to anyone who would listen about the wonderful life "Barbie" had.

Jill thought long and hard, and couldn't remember a time when her mother had carried on so about her. Even so, she didn't think it was fair to harbor resentment toward her sister for how her mother made her feel. Just like tonight, Barbie was there for her, letting her know that she was perfect just the way she was. Her sister had never failed to let her know that she was in her corner. Jill realized that she adored her sister, and having made peace with this insecurity, she fell asleep with a smile on her face.

* * *

Just as Jill came downstairs the doorbell rang. "I'll get it," she yelled out to her parents. She opened the door to find a deliveryman from Swissvale Florist.

"I have a delivery for Jill Alexander," he said.

"That's me," Jill said excitedly.

"Can I get you to sign here?" he said, pointing to a place on his clipboard.

"Thank you," Jill said as she took the box into the house.

"Who was that?" her mother asked.

"It was a deliveryman from Swissvale Florist," Jill told her as she walked toward the sofa and sat down.

"Is that for you?" her mom asked, noticing the white package with a large red bow.

"Yes," Jill said, opening the card that was attached to the box. She smiled warmly and returned the card to its envelope.

"Well, who is it from?" her mother asked, not able to hold her curiosity in any longer. Jill handed her the envelope and began opening the box. Inside was a beautiful arrangement of long-stem red roses surrounded by baby's breath.

"These are just gorgeous!" She gasped in amazement. "I have to put them in water right away. Mom, do you have a vase I could use for them?"

"Jill, this young man seems to be quite in love with you," her mother said excitedly.

"Oh, Mom, it's really nothing."

"How can you say it's nothing? He says to have a great time in Durango, that he'll miss you, and then he signs it 'with love, L.' I think it's more than what you're letting on. Honestly, Jill, you should know that I would be happy for you."

"Mom, you're reading way too much into this."

"Does your father or Barbie know about this person?"

"No, they don't. I didn't tell them anything, because there is nothing to tell," Jill said honestly.

"Well, your secret is safe with me; I won't say a thing until you're ready."

"Mom, can I please have a vase to put them in?" Jill asked again.

"Sure, I'll get you one right now," her mother said happily as she left the room. She returned with a beautiful large glass vase that was just perfect for Jill's arrangement.

"Here we go, sweetheart," her mother said, handing Jill the vase and still happy to be of service.

"Thanks, Mom."

"No problem. I was just wondering, though, what should we say to your father and sister when they ask who sent the flowers?" her mother asked, hoping to get a bit more information.

"Well, we don't want to lie, so just tell them that they are from a friend," Jill said as her mother beamed, overjoyed to have been taken into her daughter's confidence.

"I'll go get a pitcher of water," her mother said, squeezing Jill's arm softly as she started to leave the room.

"I called Barbie, she said to tell you that she did find a babysitter. Her next-door neighbor will be keeping James."

"Oh, that's fine," her mother said casually.

"She also said that she'd be here early so that we can beat the crowd."

"I hope she doesn't come too early. I have several phone calls I have to make before we go anywhere," her mother said as she hurried into the kitchen. She returned with the pitcher of water, and her husband in tow.

"Rob, look at the beautiful roses Jill's friend sent her," her mother announced as she gave Jill a wink.

"They're beautiful. Who are they from?"

"They're from a friend," Jill said nonchalantly.

With nothing else to say about the flowers or whom they came from, he left the room.

"I'd better take a shower and get ready for our day. I have so much to do. I hope Barbie isn't too early."

"Don't worry, Mom; if she is, I'll keep her busy until you're ready."

"Thanks, sweetheart," her mother said and quickly went to get ready.

Jill leaned back into the sofa and smiled at herself. Her mother was so transparent. From the moment she laid eyes on the flowers, her little wheels were turning. Things that mattered to her, all of a sudden didn't anymore. Her game plan for the day had changed now, and probably, Jill imagined, for tomorrow too.

Her parents were two totally different people, with two totally different outlooks on life. Though she knew they both wanted to see her married, her mother would stop at nothing to see her dream realized, while her father took a more relaxed approach. His only effort made in that area was to make occasional comments about her getting married one day soon. He didn't participate in any of his wife's tricky matchmaking schemes.

Jill sat up and took a different photo album from under the coffee table. This one contained pictures of Barbie and Rick's wedding. She opened the book and saw a picture of her sister on her wedding day. *She really did look like a Barbie doll,* Jill thought. Her sister was tall, slender, and beautiful. She stood there in a sleeveless wedding gown that was tight in the waist with a plunging back. The dress had beautiful crystal beads sewn on the bodice, and at the hem were tiny white roses all the way around the ten-foot train.

Jill turned the page and there were pictures of Barbie and Rick. They faced the camera, his arms around her waist. Barbie looked so happy and serene, as if she knew what she wanted and went for it. Her smile radiated from the photograph, knowing she had found her Prince Charming.

Jill put the album back where she had found it. She sat back and again wondered if her parents truly saw her as a failure. If they thought a career wasn't as important as being married. Did her finishing college and having a successful career mean nothing to them?

She shook her head in confusion and silently hoped that Durango would help clear her mind. She was still anxious to get there. Jill couldn't think straight here with constant reminders of her not being married.

The door opened and Barbie came into the house. She looked as beautiful and as shapely as she did the day she was married.

"Hi, sis," she said, happy to see Jill again.

"Hey, how did everything go with your next-door neighbor?"

"Fine, Brenda has watched him lots of times. She and I take turns watching each other's kids. She has three kids too," Barbie explained as she walked over and sat next to Jill.

"I'm just glad you made it. I didn't want to go alone."

"Wow, those are gorgeous! Who are they for?" Barbie asked as she stood and walked over to the vase of roses.

"They're for me," Jill said, smiling.

"Who sent them?" she asked as she smelled the fragrant flowers.

"Oh, a friend sent them to me."

"A friend? What did Mom say?" Barbie asked, giving her sister a suspicious look.

"She was terribly excited for me and wanted to know

who the admirer was," Jill told her, unable to keep a straight face.

"Who is L?" Barbie asked as she looked at the attached card.

"I'll tell you like I told Mom, a friend sent them to me."

"Your sister is being very secretive about her love life, Barbie," their mother said as she entered the room. Jill and Barbie turned around surprised to see her standing there.

"I see, Mom. I'm not able to get anything out of her either."

"I guess we'll have to respect her privacy until she's ready to reveal her secret," Maddie told her oldest daughter as she sat next to Jill.

"And you're not going to keep digging until you have all the information now?" Barbie asked her mother surprisingly.

"No, I'm not. I think it's time I stopped pushing your sister and let her make her own decisions," she told them.

Jill put her hand on her mother's forehead. "She's not warm, Barbie," she said as she and her sister snickered.

"Oh, stop," Maddie said as she stood to leave the room. "I have to make a few phone calls, then we can leave. I won't be long."

"Jill, I don't know what you've done; I just don't want to be here when the fireworks go off," Barbie told her as she sat down.

"Hopefully, I'll be gone by that time and only have to experience her rage long distance."

"What time is your flight on Sunday?"

"Two in the afternoon. I was hoping to spend some time alone with Ricky."

"Well, he'll see you at the party Mom planned for

tomorrow evening, but why don't you spend the morning with Ricky? Is that all right with you?"

"That's great; I just want to take him someplace special. You'll have to be with me when I spend time with Lacy and James; they don't like to go anywhere without you," Jill said. "Do you think Ricky will like going to Chuck E. Cheese?"

"I think he would love it, Jill. You're such a wonderful sister. I'm going to miss you so much when you leave," Barbie said, leaning forward and hugging Jill.

"Don't start crying, Barbie, or I'll never be able to leave," Jill told her as she returned the hug.

"If that's all I have to do to keep you here, then I can produce some tears," she said, but didn't cry.

Their mother came back into the room with her purse in hand. "I'm ready to go, girls. Who's driving?"

The two sisters exchanged glances quickly and in unison said, "You are." They stood up and followed their mother out the door, who didn't protest. Maddie was walking on a cloud, happy to have both her girls with her, and hopeful of another wedding on the way.

When they arrived at the Ceramic Depot, they each chose a piece of art to paint. They sat together at a table and began working. The three women were relaxing and enjoying the pleasure they derived from being creative. No one spoke. They worked in silence and quietly enjoyed each other's company.

Jill was surprised when she glanced at her watch and saw that they had been in the shop for several hours. Though the hours flew by, her body was stiff from sitting in the same position for so long. She looked over and saw that her mother and sister were both putting the finishing touches on their work.

After spending the day at the Ceramic Depot, the three walked outside, feeling as though they had just spent a day at the spa. They got in Maddie's car and she started the engine and pulled off. Jill hadn't felt this relaxed since she left New York. She felt as if her brain had taken a mini, but much needed, vacation.

"That was fun," Barbie said.

"Yes, it was," Jill agreed.

"Do you two want to go have dinner somewhere?"

"I can't, Mom. I have to go pick up James," Barbie told her. "Brenda picked up Lacy and Ricky from school, so she has had six kids for a few hours. I have to go bail her out before she goes crazy."

"Jill, do you think you want to go get something to eat?"

"Not really, Mom, I think I want to go over Barbie's house for a little while. I'm going to visit the kids tonight, and I haven't spent time with Rick since I've been here."

"I guess I'll just go home and have a quiet dinner with your father then," Maddie told them with a slight disappointment in her voice.

"Do you want to come with us?" Jill asked.

"No, actually, I have a few things to do to get ready for tomorrow. You two have fun, and I'll see you later tonight."

They pulled up in front of the house just as day was turning to dusk. Soon the soft glow of streetlights would illuminate the yard, adding a final touch of serenity to Jill's day. This day wasn't filled with questions of marriage, or surprise meetings with her mother's friends' sons. Her mom had been totally relaxed, and Jill had enjoyed her company for the first time in years.

"Thanks, Mom, for a wonderful day, I really enjoyed it," Barbie said as she kissed her mom.

"Thanks, Mom," Jill said, kissing her mother's cheek too. "You made today really special and memorable."

Maddie smiled at her girls and replied, "You're welcome." Then she headed into the house.

"Are you ready, sis?" Barbie asked Jill.

"I'm all ready, let's go."

They got into Barbie's car and started down the street. As Barbie came to a stop sign, something hit Jill in the back of her foot. She bent down to pick up a Sippy cup. She set it on the seat next to her, realizing that Barbie's car was filled with children's things. She turned and noticed that there was a car seat in the back, along with Lacy's doll. Ricky had several of his comic books in the backseat too. She turned back around and noticed a pack of bubblegum on the dashboard.

Jill didn't expect Barbie's car to be filled with toys. She was so used to her own neat and tidy car. But Barbie was a mother who zipped around town delivering her kids to school, T-ball, the library, and who knows where else? Why wouldn't her car be filled with her children's belongings? Would her own car look like her sister's one day? Jill shuddered at the thought.

"I know you're not cold, Jill?"

"Oh no, I'm fine, Barbie," Jill answered as they pulled up into Barbie's driveway. She hit the button for the garage door to open and drove inside.

Jill was again surprised to see so many bikes, baseball bats, dollhouses, and toys inside the garage. Barbie pulled in expertly, leaving lots of room for them to get out on either side.

"Go on inside, Jill, I have to go next door and get the kids. I'll be right back."

Jill walked through the garage and into the kitchen. She turned on the lights and found her way to the living room. She had a seat on the sofa and admired Barbie's clean house. She expected to see the kitchen sink filled with breakfast dishes, and the living room to be filled with toys. She was pleasantly surprised at how her sister juggled her busy family with such coordination. She seemed to get everyone everywhere they needed to go, and still get everything done that she needed to do.

Ricky and Lacy came running in, calling her name excitedly. They found her on the sofa and covered her with hugs and kisses. Barbie came into the room last, carrying James, who was sleeping.

"Jill, I'm going to leave you with your fan club, while I go put James to bed," Barbie said as quietly as she could."

The evening was just as magical as when they were kids. First, Jill and Barb watched a murder mystery, then a scary movie. Rick had come home and was allowed to join them only if he promised not to talk. With the exception of kissing Jill and welcoming her home, he kept his promise. All three of them fell asleep in the living room and woke up to the sounds of Lacy turning on her favorite cartoons.

Jill took a shower and changed into an outfit she borrowed from Barb. Her sister was a little larger than she was, so Jill was happy she found something to fit. Under the urging of her nephew, she quickly ate her breakfast and the two were out the door. Jill felt odd driving her sister's minivan, and silently wished for her own car. She glanced over at Ricky, who had a big grin on his face.

"What are you grinning for?" Jill asked him.

"I'm just happy to be with you."

Jill and Ricky spent a fun-filled day at Chuck E.

Cheese, and afterward Jill was exhausted but thankful for the time they'd spent together.

Leaving the restaurant, they headed for Jill's parents' house. When they got there, Maddie was busy making sure the house was neat and clean and setting her dining room table. Her father was busy cooking for the party. Keeping out of the way, Ricky went down into the game room to play pool.

"Jill, you need to hurry. People will be arriving in a little over an hour, and I want you to be ready," her mother said with a sense of urgency.

"I can be ready in no time at all, Mom. You never told me who you invited to this shindig."

"Well, of course I invited our neighbors: the Joneses and the McPhersons. Uncle Ray and Aunt Jean are coming, as well as Uncle Tommy and one of his ex-wives. He has been divorced so many times, I don't know which ex-wife he'll bring tonight," Maddie finished with a chuckle.

"I know that isn't the end of your guest list, is it?" Jill eyed her mother suspiciously.

"Of course not, I also invited a few members from our church. Reverend Gregory and his wife are coming, and a few other church members and their families. I think that is pretty much the entire guest list. Now hurry, Jill, I want you to be ready when they arrive."

Jill walked upstairs wondering what surprises her mother had in store for her. Though her mother was a little vague about who would be coming with whom from the church, she didn't put it past her to make sure at least one eligible bachelor would attend the party. Jill had hoped tonight would be just a nice little party with friends and family, not another of her mother's quests to marry her off.

* * *

She quickly showered and put hot rollers in her hair. She chose a burgundy sundress that flowed with her every move. Over beautifully manicured feet, she put on a pair of matching burgundy sandals with high heels that had little gold suns decorating them.

Jill had the same beautiful mocha skin tone as her mother. She did her makeup in colors that complemented her complexion and put on black eyeliner to accentuate her almond-shaped eyes. Then she applied a beautiful brown lipstick with matching blush before she undid her hot curlers and brushed her hair gently, letting it fall freely in soft curls. She opened her jewelry box and took out a pair of medium-sized Italian gold hoops and put them in her ears. She held up their matching bracelet for a moment, trying to decide if she wanted to wear it or not. She decided to wear it, then dotted herself with her favorite fragrance, Chloe Narrcisse, and went downstairs.

Maddie, who had been sitting on the sofa talking to Barbie and her husband, stopped in midsentence when Jill entered the room. She stared at her daughter in awe, having forgotten what a true beauty she was. Maddie stood up and walked over to her.

"Jill, you look amazing," she said as she held her daughter's hand.

"You look awesome, sis," Rick chimed in, and Jill playfully stuck her tongue out at him.

"I know this isn't high on your list of priorities, but I promise you one day soon, someone is going to sweep you off your feet," Maddie told Jill, in all sincerity. The doorbell rang, and she went to answer it.

"Jill, look who's here, it's the McPherson family," Maddie announced as she let in Elaine and Henry McPherson and their thirty-two-year-old unmarried son, Daryl.

Barbie stood up and walked over to her sister and whispered in her ear, "Mom never put out a spread like this for me." She smiled.

Jill gave her sister a slight grin and walked over to meet her guests.

"Hi, Mr. McPherson. Mrs. McPherson, how are you?" she said as she gave each of them a kiss on the cheek.

"Jill, we haven't seen you in ages, how are you doing, baby?" Mrs. McPherson asked as she made her way into the room.

"I'm fine. Do you remember my sister, Barb, and her husband, Rick?"

"I sure do." She walked off to talk with them.

"Jill, every time I see you, you get prettier and prettier," Mr. McPherson said. "Have you gotten married yet?"

"No, I haven't," she answered as politely as she could.

"Well, that's music to my ears, because Daryl hasn't either," he said as he turned to his son. "Daryl, do you remember Jill? You two used to be inseparable." He pushed his son toward Jill.

"Hi, Jill. Long time, no see," Daryl said.

"Hello, Daryl, how have you been doing?"

"I been doin' all right. I been lookin' for a job though. They ain't been hirin' round here. What's it like in New York?"

"It's pretty slow there too, Daryl," Jill said, and was thankful that her mother was calling her to come and greet more guests.

"Hi, I'm so glad you could come over," her mother said as she greeted her neighbors Eleanor and Mike Jones. They had no sons, which Jill was thankful for. Instead they had two daughters, Cheryl and Danielle. Cheryl was the oldest, and from what Jill could tell, never refused a meal. She gave Jill a dry hello and was on her way to see what was for dinner.

Danielle, whom Jill always called Dani, was very excited to see her. She threw her arms around Jill and gave her a big hug. "Oh, Jill, it's so good to see you!" Dani said.

"It's good to see you too, Dani," Jill said as she returned the hug.

"We have so much catching up to do."

"We'll squeeze some time in later to chat," Jill said.

Dani leaned toward Jill and whispered in her ear, "That Daryl McPherson is staring this way. He's kind of cute. Are you going for him?"

"No, girl, that one is all for you," Jill whispered back, with a sly smile and a wink. Dani returned the wink and went to pursue Daryl.

Jill smiled and walked toward Mr. and Mrs. Jones. Jill liked Dani's parents. They were some of her parents' oldest and dearest friends, and the two families had seen each other through many changes. Eleanor Jones was a beautiful woman who smiled easily. Her husband, Mike, was more reserved and liked going fishing with her father. Dani and Cheryl were both still unmarried. Their parents, like Jill's, were anxious to get both of their daughters married off.

Jill felt as though she were standing at a revolving door as guest after guest came through her parents' door. Reverend Gregory and his wife were the last guests to arrive. They came through the door with not only one, but with all three of their sons in tow. Jill didn't know their sons, so her mother introduced them. Reverend Gregory had gotten his sons' names straight out of the Bible, Matthew, Mark, and Luke. As her mother introduced them to Jill, Luke gave Jill an appreciating once-over and then a slick grin.

As if he knew that Jill needed to be rescued, Jill's father came into the living room and announced, "Dinner is ready, everyone; but first, I would like to thank you all for coming over to see my Jill. We don't get to see her much. Jill, this is just our way of letting you know that you are love and missed." He then gave his daughter a kiss on the cheek. "Now, if Reverend Gregory will bless the food, we can all get to eating."

Reverend Gregory stood up and said a blessing that included food, friendship, and love. Jill sensed someone staring at her, so she looked up. It was Luke. He licked his lips and blew her a kiss. Jill lowered her head and closed her eyes and listened to the rest of his father's prayer. "Help me through this long evening, Father," she whispered quietly to herself.

"Maddie, these roses are beautiful. Did Rob buy them for you?" Jill overheard Mrs. Gregory asking her mother after the prayer was finished.

"No, they're not even mine. They belong to Jill. An admirer of hers sent them here," her mother said proudly and loud enough for everyone to hear.

Jill smiled to herself, realizing why her mother wasn't pushing every available male in her direction. Her plan had worked.

Her father had set up a buffet in the kitchen. He had cooked a ham, fried chicken, greens, macaroni and cheese, potato salad, and his own homemade dinner rolls. For dessert, he had made Jill's favorite: peach cobbler. Jill got in line with Barbie and Rick to make a plate. She saw her nephew and signaled him to her. Ricky walked over toward his aunt and Jill let him in front of her in line.

"Ricky, will you be Aunt Jill's escort tonight?" she whispered in his ear.

The young man puffed out his chest and answered, "I sure will, Aunt Jill."

Her father put on his favorite jazz CD, and the atmosphere became mellow. Some of the guests had gone out to sit on the lighted patio, while others went down to the game room and played pool while they ate. Still others remained in the living room, which was full of conversation, and in the dining room, to be close to the food.

It amazed Jill to see who was attracted to whom. Her mother had hoped Cupid's arrow would soon find Jill, but it wasn't to happen tonight. Tonight, Dani had found Daryl, and her sister Cheryl had found another plate of food.

Chapter 6

It was Sunday morning, and much to Jill's surprise, she wasn't ready to leave. She had enjoyed her brief visit with her family. She sat on the bed and looked out the window of what used to be her room. She remembered the many times she and Barbie had exchanged secrets and sat up late at night talking about everything, and sometimes about nothing at all.

Jill picked up her purse, laptop, and a suitcase and headed downstairs. Her father was already waiting in the living room.

"Good morning, sweetheart," he said sadly.

"Daddy, please don't look like that," she said as she gave him a long hug.

"How else am I supposed to look? My baby girl is getting ready to leave again, and I'm not happy about that. I'm going to miss you, Jill."

"I'll be back before you know it," she said, still wishing she didn't have to go.

"I made you breakfast. Go ahead in the kitchen; your mother is in there. Are your bags ready?"

"Yes, Daddy, they are."

"I'll go and put them in the car," he said.

Jill walked into the kitchen. Her mother was sitting at the table having breakfast. She looked sad too, and Jill hadn't realized till now how much this visit meant to them.

"Good morning, Mom," she said as cheerfully as she could, and bent down to kiss her mother on the cheek.

"Good morning, Jill. Did you sleep well?"

"Not really, I'm not ready to leave."

Maddie smiled and reached over to squeeze Jill's hand. "Your visit was a wonderful thing for all of us, Jill. I think your leaving is going to be really hard on your father. He tossed and turned all night. I know it was because his mind was on you. Please keep your promise and come back home soon. I don't think my own heart can stand not seeing you for a long time again," she told her daughter as she fought back tears.

"Mommy, I promise," Jill said as if she were a little girl again. "I will be back sooner than you think. I won't give you a chance to miss me like this," she added as a tear slid down her cheek.

"Now, we can't do this. If your father sees us crying, he won't be able to take it. Sit down and have some breakfast. You know how he feels about breakfast; it's the most important meal of the day, he says," Maddie told her, smiling.

"I better eat, I don't know what they'll be serving on the plane, or if it will be edible," Jill said with a light laugh. Her mother smiled as her husband entered the kitchen.

"Jill, these letters are for you; one is from Barb, and the other is from Ricky. They asked me to tell you not to open them until you were on the plane," he said, handing her the envelopes.

Jill took them and put them into her purse. She knew she would probably cry if she read them right now and Jill definitely didn't want to cry in front of her dad.

"Thanks, Dad. I really have to think of something fun

to do with Ricky while he's out of school for summer vacation," she said.

Her parents exchanged glances, realizing that they would see their daughter again as soon as summer. Their moods lifted a little, and Jill noticed.

Jill sat down with a plate of pancakes and sausage. Her father poured her a glass of orange juice. She ate quickly, keeping an eye on the clock.

"Did you enjoy the party last night, Jill?"

"I really enjoyed myself. It was good to see everyone again."

"What did you think of Reverend Gregory's sons?"

"That youngest one is a pervert, and I don't think Daryl McPherson ever got out of the fifth grade."

Jill's father started laughing and said, "I think you're a pretty good judge of character. I always thought something was wrong with both of those boys." He smiled at his wife. Noticing that she wasn't smiling, he turned and left the room.

"We better get going. I don't want you to miss your flight," her mother said as she stood up and put her dishes in the sink.

Jill finished the last of her food and put her dishes beside her mother's in the sink, then she followed her mother outside to the car.

The ride in the car was quiet. Jill's father made an occasional comment about the traffic, but other than that, nothing much was said. When they arrived at the airport, Rob pulled up to the curb and parked. Maddie got out of the car and stood solemn-faced in front of her daughter, as Rob unloaded her suitcases and placed them at the curb. Afterward, he stood near Jill and his wife. He, too, had a sad expression on his face.

"Now, baby girl, I want you to have a safe flight," he

said, concerned. "I'll miss you," he added as he kissed her, his voice filled with sorrow.

Jill could feel her heart breaking as she prepared to leave her parents. "Daddy, I'll see you in a few weeks. I'm going to come back to Pittsburgh on my way back to New York," she said, noticing that her mother was fighting back tears.

"I didn't know that you were planning to come back through. You just give me a call and I'll be right here to pick you up," he said. Some of the sadness left his heart knowing he would see Jill again soon.

"Maddie smiled as her tears dried. She said, "I can't wait to see you again, Jill." She leaned forward and kissed her daughter on the cheek. "You be safe and remember that I love you," she finished, and rubbed her daughter's shoulder.

Jill waved good-bye and walked inside the airport. An hour and a half after her parents dropped her off, she was ushered to her seat in first class. She put her laptop in the overhead compartment, then she took her seat, placing her purse on the floor next to her feet. She took out the letters from Barbie and Ricky. Jill was ready for two sad good-bye letters, but instead, each one had written a note telling her how much fun they had had with her, and wished her a safe trip and a quick return home.

Jill returned the letters to her handbag and fastened her seat belt. She listened to the roar of the plane's engines, and the voice of the flight attendant, but her mind was a million miles away. She sat staring out the window as the plane taxied down the runway.

Finally, she was on her way to Durango. She had been feeling anxious for the past week, and could only figure she just needed a break from the New York rat race. She hoped to get a chance to use the spa's facilities. She knew she was long overdue for relaxation. Her job had kept her so busy that she never took time out for herself. She silently promised that she would make time for herself in Durango, even if she had to take some vacation time from work to get it in.

The flight attendant came by and offered Jill something to drink. She slowly sipped a cola, and was happy that once again no one was assigned to sit next to her. She put her purse in the empty seat and took out her book. "I am going to finish you if it's the last thing I do," she said, determined to get through several chapters before she landed.

Jill looked out the plane's window again. She watched as big puffy clouds majestically glided by, enveloping the craft in their billowy softness. She rested her head against the headrest. Jill hadn't felt more at peace with herself since she had left New York. She closed her eyes, allowing the clouds to dance in her mind, and fell fast asleep.

When she awoke, the sun was no longer as bright in the sky. She quickly glanced at her watch and realized that she had been sleeping for almost three hours. The flight attendants were taking dinner requests. Though she wasn't really hungry, she ordered the chicken. She didn't want to refuse the meal and later regret it.

Jill got the brochure from A Special Place out of her purse and was once again enchanted with the picture of the tall, handsome man on the cover. She stared at the face of the cowboy as if to commit it to her memory. Then she opened her book and started reading again. She was at the part where the guy in the story finally let the woman know that he loved her. Jill closed the book and put it back into her purse.

She didn't feel like reading about love right now. Why did everything have to revolve around love? She thought of Barbie and Rick, her mother and father, Lois and

Curtis; all of them were so happy. Was she just not ready for love or afraid of getting hurt?

Jill had been hurt before, but not so badly that she wanted to ward off men. She did feel as though she had narrowly dodged disaster with Dre. Was she really so in love with her job that she didn't have time for a relationship, or was it all something she made herself believe so that she wouldn't get hurt or lose sight of her goals? Jill shook her head, trying to clear her thoughts. She didn't want to go crazy trying to figure it all out right now.

The flight attendant brought her meal. Jill sat eating quietly, chewing on chicken that tasted like the cardboard it came in. She took another bite and decided that she could wait until she landed at three P.M. to get something decent to eat.

Jill got up and walked to the restroom. She hated using the tiny bathroom and always feared she would get stuck in the toilet. When she returned to her seat, she looked disapprovingly at the empty chair next to her. At first, she was happy to have it vacant, now she felt lonely. Maybe she should have brought Diane with her, or at least her mother. She closed her eyes in exasperation, not noticing the flight attendant. Jill let out a long sigh as she opened her eyes.

"Oh, I'm sorry. I didn't realize you were there," Jill said, surprised someone was watching her.

"That's okay, you looked like you needed to exhale. I thought I would just give you a little time," she said, smiling. "Would you like something to drink?"

"I would love a Chambord with soda and lime please."

The flight attendant bent over her cart and prepared Jill's drink. "I hope you enjoy this," she said as she handed it to her.

"Thank you so much, this is just what I need."

"Enjoy," she replied, and moved on to the next passenger.

With the first sip of the raspberry liqueur, Jill felt her mounting tension ebb. In a while, she would be in Durango. She thought of the beautiful pictures Lois had given her of the ranch, and Jill felt her excitement mount. She loved horses and couldn't wait to get a chance to ride. That and a relaxing Jacuzzi would be a wonderful release for her. She hoped to get in a lot of sightseeing too, since she had never been there.

She finished her drink and set the glass aside. She felt mellow, warm, and relaxed. Like a genie, the flight attendant reappeared.

"Would you like another one?" she asked Jill.

"Sure, I'm not driving," Jill joked as she smiled, and the flight attendant laughed. She made Jill another drink and handed it to her.

"Let me know if there is anything else I can get you."

"I think this will be it, thank you," Jill said, and the flight attendant smiled again and left.

Jill closed her eyes again and allowed herself to daydream. She felt warm, moist lips softly kiss her neck and a masculine hand gently caress her hair. He held her tightly to him, as if he were afraid she'd slip away. She allowed herself to enjoy his touch, his scent. Her fantasy had take on the face of the cowboy from the cover of the brochure.

She opened her eyes abruptly. No one was standing there, but she felt as though what she was thinking were written on her face. She took another sip of her drink and glanced at her watch. She stared out the window as if she could will the plane to fly faster.

Why am I doing this? she thought. She couldn't understand what on earth was going on. Maybe it was her

biological clock ticking so loud that it was yelling at her.
Though she tried to ignore it, the sound was coming
through loud and clear. Jill thought of Dar and Helena.
She couldn't help wanting a little one of her own as she
held the baby. She thought back to when Barbie had her
kids. Jill was there for each of their births, and she
didn't feel like this then. Was that what her body was
telling her, that it was time to either have a baby or forget it? No, she wouldn't allow herself to go into this
crazy thinking now. She had just gotten her mind
straight. She took a last sip of her drink. It helped to
clear her head. She decided to read for the fourth time
the information Lois had printed out for her.

Colorado looked so vast and different from what she
was used to, she thought, looking at the pictures. In
New York, everything was so fast-paced and everyone
moved as if they should have been at their destination
yesterday. Every building was connected; apartments
were stacked high on top of each other. From food to
transportation, everything was at a super speed. Jill
wondered if she would be able to slow down and enjoy
the atmosphere, or would she do like she usually did
and jump into her work and stay there? She would have
to make a conscious effort not to do that.

The captain's voice came over the speaker and announced that they would be arriving in Durango/La
Plata County Airport in about twenty minuets. He also
said that the weather was sunny and about ninety-two
degrees, and Jill hoped that she had brought along
enough cooler clothing. Except for a couple of sun-
dresses and a pair of shorts, she had only brought along
business clothes and the jeans and jackets she had just
bought. If she had to go shopping again, she would be
more than happy to.

She put the papers back into her purse and stood to

retrieve her laptop from the overhead compartment. She didn't want to wait till the last minute to get it, for fear she might get off the plane and forget it in all her excitement. She returned to her seat and fastened her seat belt as instructed.

The plane landed, and the captain's voice once again came over the speaker. He gave the local time and then thanked everyone for flying America West Airlines. The flight attendants, still smiling, told the passengers good-bye as they left the plane. Jill walked down the long ramp to the gate.

New passengers waited anxiously to board the plane. Mothers, weary of travel and holding babies, tried to muster energy to finish their trip. Jill wondered if she would look so disheveled if she were traveling with children. She imagined she would and suddenly felt sorry for the busy moms.

Jill was pulling her suitcases on a cart and was on her way outside when a woman approached her.

"Jill Alexander?" The woman stepped close to her and extended her hand to shake.

"Yes," she answered, curious to know how the stranger, who was walking toward her, knew her name.

"I'm Bebe Simmons," she said.

"Oh, hi, how did you know who I was?" Jill asked as she juggled her things in order to shake Bebe's hand.

"Lois faxed me a picture of you."

"She's amazing. I don't know what I'd do without her."

"I have to admit, she's pretty efficient when it comes to making everything run as smoothly as it can. I've even picked up a couple of tricks from her, and I've never even met her," Bebe said as they continued to walk. "I can carry your laptop if you want."

"Thanks," Jill said and handed it to her. She noticed

that Bebe was dressed in business attire too. The woman was about her height, and looked to be the same size and age.

As they began to walk, Jill noticed a tall, broad-shouldered man wearing a cowboy hat coming toward them. He smiled easily, revealing perfect white teeth, and Bebe introduced her to the muscular, brown-skinned man.

"Jill Alexander, I'd like you to meet Eric Roberts. Eric, this is the woman we've all been waiting for, Jill Alexander."

Jill extended her hand, and it was enclosed in a large, rugged, bronze grasp. "It's nice to meet you," Jill said confidentially as they shook hands and she realized that he had a wedding band on.

"It's nice to meet you too, Jill. We've all been waiting for you. Rumor has it that you're the best at what you do."

"Well, I'm good, but I don't know if I can live up to the rumor," she said as she laughed lightly. "Those four are mine," she said, pointing to the conveyer belt.

Eric reached out and grabbed all four bags, and seemingly had no trouble carrying all of them at once.

"We'll take you to the ranch right now, so that you and I both can get into something more comfortable," Bebe said.

"I can't wait to see it. I'm sure the pictures I received don't do it justice," Jill said as they got into Bebe's car. "What do you do on the ranch, Eric?"

"I work with my brothers; we run the stables."

"Do you have very many?" Jill asked.

"Brothers?"

"No, do you have many horses?" she said, laughing, but quickly felt as though she should have let him answer that question too.

"Actually, we have quite a few horses. Aside from the ones that are owned by A Special Place, we board horses too," he said as he put Jill's luggage into the trunk.

The three got into the car and Jill sat up front with Bebe. After a little driving, they got on U.S. 160 and headed for Durango.

"Is the resort pretty big?" Jill asked Bebe.

"It's moderate in size. We're not a ski resort like Durango Buena Vista, but we have more land, five thousand acres. The resort itself only occupies a few of those acres, including the pools and hot springs. The rest of the land is basically for the horses."

Jill turned around so that she could see Eric's face. "Do you let your guests ride off alone, or do they have to be escorted by a guide?"

"It's up to them. If they are experienced riders, and feel comfortable enough to ride alone, that's fine. Some are experienced enough but are unsure of the area and the terrain. In that case, we can have someone ride with them."

"What do you do if someone gets lost?"

"We break up into teams and go looking for them. The teams stay in touch via two-way radio. We can usually find someone in no more than a couple of hours. Are you an experienced rider, Jill?"

"I thought I was. I think the terrain would make me feel a little intimidated too. I would probably want someone to come with me at first; then I would probably feel comfortable going off by myself after that."

"Well, here we are," Bebe said as she drove through the high wrought-iron gates.

Jill turned around in her seat to seen the beautiful A Special Place Resort and Spa. As Bebe pulled up into the rotunda, Jill saw a huge statue of a man on a horse. "Who is the statue of?" she asked.

"That's Decatur Roberts, he passed away about twenty years ago, and owned much of the land that A Special Place sits on," Bebe told her.

"This place is beautiful," Jill said as she stepped out of the car. Standing in the foreground of mountains, the resort looked elegant, yet rugged enough to be called a ranch. The sun shined bright as the clouds danced majestically across the unyielding blue sky and cast their shadows on the ground before her. Jill felt as if they were giving her their personal welcome, and she didn't try to hide the approving smile that graced her face. As the clouds moved on, another burst of sunshine came through. The building seemed to glisten in the sun's rays. She was happy to be here.

"Jill, I'll take your things to your room," Eric said, smiling, amused at her enthusiasm for the place.

"Thanks, Eric, I'll see you later."

Bebe left the car running and a valet came and took it to park for her. Jill followed Bebe into the lobby, which had floors that were done in a beautiful brown ceramic tile. The registration desk was in a marble that had several shades of brown and cream in it. Several large pictures of cowboys and horses were hung on the walls, and there were Native American artifacts decorating the lobby.

"This is the main lobby," Bebe said. "It's called the main lobby because there are two smaller buildings that have lobbies too."

"What is the function of each building?" Jill asked her.

"This is naturally the building that houses the guests. All guest rooms are on two levels. There is a spa house, which is near the hot springs, and the ranch house,

where the stables are. There is a restaurant in this building, which is for more formal dining. The restaurant in
the ranch house is called just that, 'The Ranch House.'
It's very informal and will be used basically for the
guests who just come off the trails, and the staff. The
more formal dining room hasn't been named yet."

Jill paid close attention to everything that Bebe was
saying, nodding occasionally. They walked through the
resort as Bebe continued to fill Jill in.

"Exactly when is the grand opening?" Jill asked.

"One month from today. We weren't supposed to
open for another two months, but the owners want to
push up the opening. They're in competition with another resort opening in Silverton, and they want our
resort to open first. Do you think you can do the job in
a month?" Bebe asked hopefully.

"I'm quite sure I can," Jill told her.

Bebe's tense posture relaxed. "I have been instructed
to get you anything you need to make this opening
come together," Bebe told her, happy to extend herself.

"Thanks, Bebe. I'll keep that in mind."

"Come on, I'll take you to your room. I think you'll
love it. I put you on the first floor. All the rooms on the
first floor have private patios, and the ones on the second floor have balconies. I think the patios are more
beautiful and personal. They have privacy partitions on
each side, and you don't have to take the stairs several
times a day. That gets pretty tiring by the end of a workday."

"I'm sure I'll love it."

"If you don't, just let me know and I'll have it
changed for you," Bebe offered.

"Bebe, how much staff is here now? I didn't notice
any help behind the registration counter."

"That staff won't be in until the end of the month. The

Ranch House Restaurant staff is all here, and that restaurant is fully operational. The main dining room is still waiting not only on its name, but also on the rest of its staff, which will be here by the end of the month too. Pretty much everyone else is already here. The ranch hands have been here for a while, and the spa personnel have too. They have been unpacking supplies and equipment getting the spa ready for the grand opening."

"When will the spa be operational?"

"In time for the grand opening. All but one person has submitted their license," Bebe said as she stopped at room 110. "This is your room," she said, unlocking the door.

Jill stepped into the room and her eyes widened. She had never seen a room as inviting as the one before her. It was done in dusty peach and mauve. The same Native American décor from the lobby was used in her room. Hanging over the bed was a beautiful painting of a naked Ute woman, bathing in a river. Jill walked out onto the patio and knew just what Bebe had meant. The patio was covered in beautiful greenery, which helped aid in giving a sense of privacy. A chaise longue faced the beautiful mountains that the sun was getting ready to disappear behind.

"Is this room acceptable?" Bebe said, with a knowing grin on her face.

"It's perfect, Bebe. Thank you so much for all your help," Jill said, noticing that Eric had put her luggage in the room already.

"You're welcome, Jill. I'm going to go to my room and shower and change too. Why don't we meet in the lobby in about an hour, and we'll have dinner together?"

"That sounds great. The food on the plane wasn't what I was looking for."

"I can understand that. I'll see you in a bit," Bebe said as she left Jill's room.

Chapter 7

Jill sat down on the chaise longue and looked off into the beautiful mountains. All of her assignments had always taken her to busy cities, with only cars and tall buildings as testaments to their greatness. Here it was different. She looked at the slowly setting sun, the mountains, and the ever-changing sky; it was as if God Himself had put His stamp of approval on this place. She had never known such beauty as she saw right now. She felt a sense of completeness within herself, as if she was in the right place at the right time.

She walked back into her room and picked up the phone to call Lois. The phone rang several times before Lois answered.

"Hello," Lois finally answered. Jill could hear the television playing in the background.

"Hi, Lois, it's me," Jill said cheerfully.

"I've been waiting for your call. Are you in Durango now?" Lois asked anxiously.

"Yes, I am. Lois, I love it here. The pictures you gave me don't do the place justice."

"I had a feeling you'd love it. How is Bebe?"

"She is a real sweetheart. She reminds me of you; she's very thoughtful and likes everything to run as efficiently as possible. Bebe's real down-to-earth, not pretentious at all."

"Good. Did you like the roses?"

"Yes, but not nearly as much as my mom did. I hated doing that to her, but if I didn't she would have pushed every bachelor she could get her hands on into my lap."

"Jill, you know that she only wants to see you happy."

"I know, I just want to do it on my own terms and in my own time."

"Oh, before I forget, Darlene Alceveda called you. She left a message with me to tell you she's sorry about everything. Does that have to do with your mystery date?"

"Yes, but Darlene had nothing to do with it. She was stuck in the middle of the situation. I don't blame her and I hope she doesn't think that I do. I'll make sure I go see her as soon as I get back."

"She said that she had left you a note, but you didn't reply. If I were her, I'd think you were upset with me."

"I didn't know that she left me a note, I thought they were all from her brother-in-law."

"Diane told me to tell you hello, too."

"Tell her I said hi. Don't you two go having all kinds of fun without me. I'll be back before you know it."

"We miss you, girl," Lois said sincerely.

"I miss you, too. Take care."

"Bye."

Jill looked at her watch and saw that she only had twenty minutes to shower and dress before she was supposed to meet Bebe for dinner. Jill opened her suitcases and unpacked as quickly as she could. She was thankful just about everything she had brought needed little or no ironing. Jill chose a denim sundress with a halter back.

She ironed out the wrinkles in it and then went to take a shower. Afterward, she dressed quickly and pulled her hair in a sleek ponytail. She pulled a cute pair of match-

ing blue Prada sandals with small heels from her suitcase. She then put on her diamond stud earrings and her
tennis bracelet. She sprayed on her favorite scent and
headed out the door to meet Bebe.

When Jill arrived in the main lobby, Bebe was already
there. She had on a beautiful yellow sundress that gave
her brown skin a radiant glow.

"Don't you look beautiful?" Bebe was the first to say.

"I have to say the same for you. You look lovely, too,"
Jill said sincerely.

"Since we have no male escorts, I guess we have to
compliment ourselves," Bebe said, laughing. "Come on,
let's get something to eat, then I'll show you some more
of the property."

"That sounds great to me," Jill agreed.

The two women headed for the Ranch House Restaurant. They walked through the back of the main lobby
and went outside. They passed a beautiful lighted swimming pool and then the spa building. Just before the
stables was the restaurant. The sign on the front of the
building had a picture of a cowboy on a horse, along
with its name.

True to Bebe's word, the restaurant was very informal. There were booths that would seat four, and a bar
where you could sit and just have a drink. The décor was
also very midwestern, and Jill loved it.

"We will always have music playing in here. Joe is the
manager, and can you guess what kind of music he is
partial to?" Bebe said.

"Oh, let me guess: western?" Jill said teasingly.

"Bingo!" Bebe said as they walked over to a booth.

There were quite a few people in the Ranch House.
Jill noticed that Eric was there sitting in a booth with a
woman that Jill guessed was his wife. He nodded a
greeting to Jill and she politely nodded back.

"Is that his wife?" Jill asked, feeling as though she would burst from curiosity.

"Yes, that's Sharon. They've been married for about a year now," Bebe said as they looked over the menu.

"They make a beautiful couple," Jill added.

A waitress came over to take their orders.

"Hey, Bebe, how's it going?"

"Just fine, Grace, how are you?"

"I can't complain."

"Grace, this is Jill Alexander; she'll be part of our family for a while."

"Hi, Jill, it's nice to meet you," Grace said. She wiped her hand on her apron before extending it to shake Jill's.

"It's nice to meet you too, Grace," Jill replied.

"Jill's the woman we've been waiting for from New York, but I think she'll fit right in around here," Bebe said, smiling.

"What can I get you ladies?" Grace asked.

"I'll have my usual: steak medium well, fries, and coleslaw. Oh, and don't forget my beer."

"Gotcha. What about you, Jill?"

Jill looked at Bebe and closed her menu. "I'll have what she's having," she told Grace.

"I'll be right back with your orders, ladies," Grace said.

"She seems like a nice person," Jill said.

"Yes, she is. Just don't tell her anything that you wouldn't mind being general knowledge. A few weeks ago she almost broke up Eric's marriage."

"How did she do that?"

"Eric was in here having lunch with a few of the ranch hands. One of them was interested in one of the waitresses. Eric mentioned that he thought the girl was pretty and that the ranch hand should ask her out. Grace only heard part of the story and went and told Sharon what she had heard. Sharon was so upset that she packed her bags and was ready to leave Eric."

"Why would she do such a thing? She could have ruined their marriage."

"I don't know if she's learned her lesson or not. I just tell her very little concerning private matters. Eric, as you can see, was able to explain everything to Sharon. He has always only had eyes for that girl, and she's crazy about him too."

Jill looked back over at he couple. He was holding her hand and listening intently to whatever she was saying. "You can see that they are very much in love," Jill said.

Grace returned with their beers and said, "I'll be right back with your food."

"Thanks, Grace," Bebe said. After Grace left their table, Bebe continued, "Don't get me wrong, Grace is really a nice person, and that unfortunate incident probably would never have happened if she and Sharon weren't so close. Grace was just trying to look out for a friend. I just operate by the motto 'once bitten, twice shy.' But I bet she'll think twice before running her mouth again." She took a drink of her beer.

"You know, the more I talk to you the more I like you. Bebe, you seem to operate in the same mode I do. I get the feeling that you've been burned a time or two with love."

"Yes, I have, but it hasn't turned me away from the idea of marriage; I've just become more cautious in approaching it is all."

"I'm not against the idea either. I just want to do it in my own time. My mother can't wait for that day to arrive though." Jill rolled her eyes, and Bebe laughed.

Grace returned with their food and the two newfound friends ate heartily. Jill saw a lot of herself in Bebe, and this made it easy to talk to her. Lois and Diane would really like this woman too, she thought.

A tall and masculine man who was dressed like one of the ranch hands came over to their table. "Hey, Bebe, what's going on?" he said as he bent down to kiss her cheek and stole one of her fries.

She brushed his hand away. "Get your own food, Tony!" she snapped at him with a faint smile on her face.

"Why would I do that when I can just sit here and eat yours?" he said teasingly as he quickly snatched another fry.

"Jill, this is the ranch pest, Tony Roberts," Bebe said in lighthearted irritation.

"It's nice to meet you, Jill."

"It's nice to meet you too," Jill replied.

"Be careful what you say, Jill, you might regret it later," Bebe said as Tony pulled up a chair. "As you can see he's kind of annoying."

"He seems nice enough, as long as he keeps his hands out of my food," Jill said, laughing.

"Tony is Eric's baby brother."

"I see the family resemblance," Jill told him.

"Yep, but I'm the one that got all the looks," he said, smiling. "Ladies, I'm going to have to excuse myself. I see my brother over there. Jill, welcome to A Special Place, let me know if there is anything I can do for you." He stood and took Jill's hand and kissed it. Snatching another of Bebe's fries, he left to see his brother.

"I told you he was a pest," Bebe repeated herself.

"But he is a handsome pest," Jill replied. "He certainly is more outgoing than Eric."

"Yes, Eric is shy," Bebe said as they finished the last of their meal. "Are you ready for your tour?"

"I'm ready; I have to use the ladies' room first," Jill said, and she stood up.

"Just go to the end of the bar and to the left; you'll see it. I'll wait right here for you," Bebe told her as she walked off.

"Hey, Bebe. How are you?" said a ruggedly hand-some man as he bent down to kiss her cheek.

"Hi, Kyle, what have you been up to?" Bebe asked.

"You name it, I've been doing it," he said in a deep exhausted voice. "Right now I have to get my brothers. We have to round up the horses for the night."

"Have fun," Bebe told him.

"Yeah, right; the fun won't begin until I hit the bed. I'll see you later."

"See you later, Kyle," Bebe said as he walked over to where Tony and Eric were. He spoke to them for a minute, then the three left. They were a handsome lot, Bebe admitted to herself.

"Jill, you just missed Kyle. I wanted you to meet the last brother," Bebe told her when she returned to the table.

"Did he just leave?" Jill asked as her eyes quickly sur-veyed the restaurant, and she wondered if Kyle was the guy from the brochure.

"Yeah, they all went to round up the horses. You'll probably see them out in the stables," Bebe said.

"Don't we have to pay?" Jill asked as Bebe started to leave.

"No, as part of the staff we don't. It's one of the perks of working here," she said. "Let's start from the stables and work our way to the front of the property. I don't want to rush you, Jill, so if you're not up to this right now, just let me know."

"No, I'm fine, Bebe. I want to know as much about the resort as I possibly can. I only have a month to pull this opening together. I would rather you give me as much information as you can, and as quickly as you can."

"Well then, let's go," Bebe said.

They walked outside and could see the ranch hands corralling the horses. Jill couldn't make out any of their faces, but assumed Eric and Tony were out there.

As they briefly walked through the stables, watching where they stepped, Bebe gave Jill all the fine details about the ranch that she would need to make her press release. Jill was surprised that inside the restaurant you couldn't smell the stables. They walked around toward the back of the stables and then down a narrow path. At the end of the path was the hot spring. It looked so inviting; however, no one was enjoying it. Jill knew that once the place opened, the hot spring would not lack for guests.

On the side of the hot spring was an entrance to the spa building. They went inside and Jill saw about a half dozen private massage rooms. There was a steam room and a sauna, too. There were separate locker rooms for the men and women, complete with showers and blow-dryers. They left out through the other end of the spa, which opened at the Olympic-sized swimming pool.

Following the tour, Jill went into her room and opened the sliding glass door that led out to her patio. A gentle breeze blew through the door, as the twinkling lights from the pool illuminated the area. She looked up at the night sky and once again was happy she was there. She walked back into the room and started to change into her nightclothes. Feeling safer than she had ever felt in New York, she didn't bother to close the blinds. She dimmed the lights in her room, then she went out on the patio.

She sat down on the chaise longue and looked up at

the stars. She felt so blessed to be there. She sat there for a long time just letting the warm gentle breeze caress her, and thinking of all the people she'd love to share this place with. Though it was a very romantic place, she couldn't think of any man she would like to share it with.

Jill got up and went inside. She picked up a pencil and paper from the desk in the room and began to write a list of things she would need to do the following day. She wanted to contact all the local television and radio stations, to make sure they would broadcast the news of the opening. She also made note that the local newspapers should print the event. She decided to hire a party planner for the grand opening. A month would hardly give her enough time to take care of all the necessary details herself. She had done it before; she would simply have to oversee the person, to make sure that everything was done to her specifications. They would work jointly on finding a caterer. Jill hoped she could find a print shop that could deliver quality invitations fast. She wanted to make sure that all the town's VIPs were personally invited sooner rather than later.

Feeling as though she had a good idea of what she needed to do to get this project started, she put the pen and paper on the nightstand and lay down on the bed. For a second, she thought about getting her book out and trying to read. She decided against it. Right then, she didn't want to read about anyone, pretend or not, falling in love. Instead, she closed her eyes and went to sleep.

Chapter 8

When Jill awoke, the sun had been up long before she had. Sunlight glistened through her room as if it were late in the day. She glanced at the clock; it was eight. She had never slept in that late. She got up and washed her face and brushed her teeth. Then she changed into a pair of jeans and a white button-down cotton shirt. She pulled her hair back in a ponytail and put on a pair of boots. Grabbing a leather purse, she put her wallet, hairbrush, and a lipstick inside.

Jill walked to the main lobby and found it empty. Looking behind the counter for a phone book, she was searching through it when Bebe walked in.

"Good morning, sleepyhead," she said playfully to Jill.

"Good morning," Jill said, smiling as she closed the phone book. "I was just trying to call a car rental agency. I want to find a place where I can rent a Jeep."

"No need, there's a Jeep here that you can use. I told you if you needed anything to just ask me, Jill. You're going to make things harder on yourself than they have to be," she said playfully.

"Well, I didn't think you would have a Jeep at my disposal," Jill answered as she put the phone book back where she had found it and came from behind the registration desk. "So tell me, all-knowing one, where can I get some breakfast around here?"

"I know a fabulous little place not far from here. In fact, it's in walking distance," Bebe teased.

"Would this fabulous little place be called the Ranch House?" Jill asked as they walked in the direction of the restaurant.

"As a matter of fact, that is the name of the place," Bebe said, smiling.

As they entered, Jill saw that the place had more patrons in it than last night. She could see Grace in the back of the room.

"Come on, Jill, I see a booth in the back," Bebe said as the two women made their way to the seats.

"Are all these people employees?"

"Yes, there are about seventy-five full-time employees. Only the ranch hands actually live on the property. There are about twenty-five of them," she said as they sat down.

"I'll be right with you, Bebe and Jill," Grace yelled to them over the noise, and Bebe nodded in acknowledgment.

"Do the twenty-five that live here stay in the hotel?" Jill asked.

"Oh no, just past the mountain behind the ranch are a few houses. That's where most of the ranch hands live. They all take turns sleeping over in the stables. They do that just in case something goes on with the horses," Bebe explained. "The rest live in town."

"What can I get you for breakfast, Jill?" Grace asked.

"I'll have pancakes, sausage, and orange juice," Jill said.

"All right, I'll be right back with your food," Grace said and left to fill Jill's order.

"Aren't you going to have anything to eat?" Jill asked Bebe.

"I had breakfast almost two hours ago. You're the one who's just waking up, remember?"

"You know, I can't believe I slept that late. In New York, I'm usually up at five A.M. and out the door a little over an hour later."

"Why do you leave for work so early?" Bebe asked in astonishment.

"I like to get a jump on the traffic. You haven't lived until you have fought New York traffic, complete with ten thousand taxis. I really don't have to be at work until eight, but I like to get in early and get started."

"I've never been to New York. Actually, I have never been out of Colorado."

"You'll just have to come and visit then. New York is very busy and fast-paced. It's a beautiful city, but it's nothing like Durango. New York has a lot of man-made beauty; here it's all natural, just the way God made it," Jill told her.

Bebe smiled at the way Jill contrasted the two cities in simple yet eloquent words. Bebe had expected a hoity-toity princess from New York; instead, she got a really sweet, funny, down-to-earth woman. She promised herself that she would go and visit Jill in New York when she had a chance.

Grace returned and set Jill's breakfast in front of her. "Let me know if you need anything else," she said as she left.

"Thanks, Grace," Jill said, and began to eat.

"Good morning, ladies."

Jill looked up to see Eric and Tony standing in front of her. She recognized them as two of the men on the brochure. She wondered where the handsome third one was. The two brothers were fine, she admitted to herself.

"Hello," Jill said, with her mouth full.

"What are you two up to?" Bebe asked them.

"Kyle wants to get an early start with the horses. Randy and a couple of the other guys are going to work on some of the fencing. Some of the horses are getting out at night," Tony told them.

Jill was thankful that Bebe was carrying the conversation. She wasn't sure she could trust her mouth. She took a good look and realized that she had never seen black cowboys before. The two men stood there, each over six feet tall and both incredibly broad-shouldered. Thick leather belts accentuated their narrow waists, and Jill tried not to blush as she imagined ripped muscles underneath their tight shirts. Each man had a strong jawline, full sensuous lips, and amazing dimples when they smiled; and each had high cheekbones and deepset, soft brown eyes. She quickly stuffed her mouth with pancakes again.

"You're pretty hungry, Jill," Tony said jokingly.

"Maybe she's trying to keep her food from you," Bebe said in Jill's defense.

"It's going to be a long day for me, but I have noticed that my appetite has been a lot healthier since I left New York," Jill replied.

"Well, we better get going," Eric, said. "If you see Kyle, tell him we'll be waiting in the stables."

"I sure will," Bebe said.

"Thanks, Bebe," Tony said as they put on their hats and turned to leave. "See you later, Jill."

"Bye, Jill," Eric said and then left.

"Bye, guys," Jill replied, watching intently as they walked away. She turned to see Bebe smiling at her.

"What?" Jill smiled back at Bebe, though she was confused as to why amusement played upon her face.

"Wonderful eye candy, aren't they?"

"I don't know what you're talking about," Jill said as she continued to eat.

"Come on, Jill, thank goodness you're not a magnifying glass, you would have burned those two to death," Bebe said, laughing.

"I wasn't staring!" Jill said, laughing in mock defense.

"Whatever you say," Bebe relented. "Hey, do you want me to go into town with you, or would you rather go alone?"

"Oh no, I'd love company. Besides, I really could use a guide. It would cut my time in half, not having to figure out where everything is," Jill said.

"Great, are you ready to go?"

"Yes, I am. I just have to make a pit stop in the little girls' room, and then we can go," Jill said as she wiped her mouth on the napkin and stood to leave.

Bebe turned around to see Kyle coming through the door. She looked back toward the direction Jill had just walked in, only to see the ladies' room door close behind her. Kyle made his way over to where Bebe sat.

"Hey, Bebe, have you seen Tony and Eric?"

"Well, good morning to you too, Kyle."

"I'm sorry, Bebe, good morning. I'm just anxious to get a ton of work done," he said, bending down and kissing her cheek.

"You just missed them. They told me to tell you that they would meet you in the stables."

"Thanks, Bebe," he said as he started to leave.

"Hey, wait a minute; I want you to meet someone."

"I don't have time, Bebe. I've got lots of work to get done; maybe later," he said, heading out the door.

As the door swung closed behind him, Jill came out of the ladies' room. Bebe let out an exasperating sigh and dropped her chin in her palms.

"I'm all ready," Jill announced. Bebe stood and the two women left the Ranch House.

Bebe led Jill to the end of the parking lot where several Jeeps were parked. She opened the door to a white one and pulled down the sun visor. A set of keys fell out, and Bebe tossed them to Jill.

"You're driving," she said as she put on her sunglasses and got in on the passenger side.

Jill smiled and got in the driver's seat and started the engine.

"I want to find some decorations that would enhance the beauty of the main lobby, and I need to find a party planner," Jill said.

"Then why don't we go over to Mesa Verde Company in Mancos? It's about an hour and a half away; they have wonderful stuff," Bebe suggested.

"Sounds good to me, just show me the way."

Bebe gave Jill directions to get onto Route 160; it was a straight shot west to Mancos and Mesa Verde. Jill turned on the radio and the two headed out of Durango.

"What kind of things are you looking for in particular?" Bebe asked her.

"I want to keep the same motif going in the lobby; I just thought I'd add some more interesting objects. I mean, the lobby is decorated beautifully, but for a party it needs a little more pizzazz." Bebe nodded, and Jill continued. "I guess I'm looking for anything that would give the place a festive Native American and cowboy flare."

"I think you'll like where we're going then. Mesa Verde and Mancos both have wonderful shops that carry all kinds of the things you're looking for."

"Bebe, have you ever been married?" Jill blurted out the straightforward question, which had been on her mind. Bebe was certainly pretty enough, and smart enough. But at almost thirty, like herself, Jill wondered why marriage had eluded her too.

"I guess I just never found that special someone that I would consider spending the rest of my life with," she said honestly.

"You haven't mentioned anyone. Are you even dating right now?"

"Nope, right now I am sort of involved with my job. I really love working at the ranch, and I love the people. I've been on board with this project since before they broke ground on the main building."

"I'm surprised one of the cowboys hasn't caught your eye," Jill said.

Bebe sensed that Jill was fishing for information; she looked at her friend and said, "I grew up with Eric, Tony, and Kyle. We've known each other since elementary school, so they're like brothers to me. While Grace isn't like a sister, we've known each other for a long while too. Now it's my turn. Why aren't you married yet?" she asked, turning the tables on Jill.

"Marriage is a huge step. You're promising to be with someone for the rest of your life. I don't know about you, but marital longevity is a strong suit in my family. I don't want to promise to love, honor, and cherish someone who I almost wished were dead," Jill said, making Bebe laugh.

"I know what you mean," Bebe said. "So tell me truthfully, Jill, has any cowboy caught your eye?"

A playful smirk crossed Jill's lips as she twisted the end of her ponytail. "It's like you said, Bebe, eye candy."

"Oh, come on, Jill, that's not an honest answer," Bebe

said, laughing at Jill's playful attempt to avoid the question.

Jill looked off into the never-ending Colorado sky and saw huge clouds rolling by as if dancing just for her. She looked at the mountains peeking and ducking behind each other. Once again, Jill felt a oneness with this place, and felt safe opening up to Bebe. "To be honest, Bebe, they have caught my eye. I mean Eric did at first, then I found out he was married. Then Tony caught my eye, but he is a tad too playful for my taste."

"I think you mean immature."

"Yes, but I was trying to be polite. Besides, I think he has eyes for someone else." Jill smiled. "I haven't had a date in months," she said, before telling Bebe about the disaster with Dre.

"And that really bothered you?" Bebe asked sympathetically when Jill finished.

"No. It just reminded me of another guy I used to date a long time ago. My mother had fixed me up with one of her friends' sons. She went on and on about what a great catch Roger was, so I gave in and went out with him. We dated for several months, and I thought I was falling in love with him. One day I went over to his house and caught him with another woman. I didn't say anything, but he saw me. I turned and left, and he didn't even come after me."

"Later that day, he came over to my parents' house. I was home alone. I told him that we were through and that I didn't want to see him again. He told me don't get so upset, that she meant nothing to him. I told him to get out, and as I turned to walk away I tripped and fell," Jill said, her voice shaky as she pulled off the highway. A tear rolled down her cheek as she got out of the Jeep. She leaned against the vehicle, sobbing heavily.

Bebe got out and went over to console her. "Oh, Jill,

I'm sorry. I didn't mean to conjure up bad memories," she said as she held her friend. "At least you were smart enough to dump the clown."

Jill pushed Bebe back a little and undid her jeans. She lifted her shirt to reveal an ugly scar on the left side of her abdomen. "Isn't that the most hideous thing you've ever seen?" The jagged scar was only a couple of inches long, but hadn't healed properly.

Bebe grimaced unintentionally and said, "It really doesn't look that bad, but how did it happen?"

"I tripped over a glass coffee table, it broke and cut me. I didn't see a doctor. I stopped the bleeding myself and kept bandages on it."

"Jill, weren't you afraid it would get infected?"

"It did, I just took an unfinished bottle of penicillin my mom had in the medicine cabinet."

"You hid this from your family?"

"I had to. My mother would never have forgiven herself. She doesn't deserve that," Jill said. "She only wanted good to come of the relationship. If she knew the trouble Roger had caused, she would have been devastated, and my father probably would have killed him. It was just better all the way around to keep it to myself. No one knows about this except you, Bebe," Jill said, realizing that she had never even told Barbie, Lois, or Diane.

"Your secret is safe with me," she told Jill and gave her another hug. "Come on, let's get going," she said as Jill tucked in her shirt and fastened her pants before wiping her face with her sleeve.

"How's my face?" Jill asked.

"You look beautiful," Bebe told her with a smile, and the two women got back into the Jeep and continued on their way.

They rode in silence the rest of the way, each digesting what had just transpired between them. Jill wondered what had made her open up so to the woman she had just met. She felt comfortable talking to Bebe. It was as if she had known her forever and didn't have to hide her true feelings.

Though Bebe had never gone through anything like Jill had, she certainly had known women who had. She liked Jill a lot and saw in her a woman of deep feelings, especially for her mother. It was obvious that Jill was smart and capable; otherwise she wouldn't have come so highly recommended for this job. She saw another side of Jill that was funny, compassionate, and sincere. Bebe could only hope they would continue their friendship long after her job in Durango was done.

"Do you see those buildings up ahead?" Bebe asked.

"Yes, it looks like a little town."

"That's Mancos. We'll stop there first, and if you don't find anything that you like, we'll keep going to Mesa Verde."

"Oh, I'm so excited. I can't wait to get out and shop," Jill said. She noticed as she got closer that Mancos wasn't as small as it had first appeared. They drove past beautifully colored houses on the outskirts of town, and larger, but just as colorful, shops as they got to the center of the city.

"Jill, let me remind you, this isn't New York. You're not going to find all kinds of fancy little quaint boutiques here," Bebe warned.

"I know, and I'm glad. One thing about me, Bebe, is that I love any kind of shopping," Jill said as they entered the little town.

"Let's try the Mesa Verde Company first," Bebe suggested.

Jill found a parking spot close to the entrance of the

shop. She parked the car and they went inside. Jill was thrilled with everything she saw.

"Oh, Bebe, look at this!" Jill held up a beautiful Navajo rug. The colors were exquisite, and she thought a few of them spread around the floor of the main lobby would look wonderful against the ceramic tile. Then she found a fascinating collection of woven baskets and decided that they would look marvelous on the registration desk alongside the beautiful ceramics she had found. Jill wanted to bring out more of the Native American culture in the décor, since the western cowboy culture was already heavily represented. She wanted to create a sense of balance in the room.

"Jill, did you see these?" Bebe said as she held up two big beautiful dream catchers.

"Those are lovely. Where do you think we should hang them?"

"How about one in each of the lobby windows, and one on each of the pillars behind the front desk?" Bebe suggested, happy to be included in the decorating.

"That sounds great."

"Can I help you ladies?" a salesperson asked.

"Yes, we're going to need a ton of help. We need ten of the Navajo rugs and two sets of the woven baskets. Bebe, how many dream catchers do you think we'll need?"

"I think six will do it," she told the woman. "We need the large ones," she added.

Obviously happy for the huge sale she was about to make, the shopkeeper said, "I'll start collecting those things for you. Feel free to keep shopping, and call me if you need anything." Then she dashed off to fill their order.

"That pretty much wraps up the lobby for now. I think I'll get some souvenirs for my family," Jill said.

"Do you have any nieces?" Bebe asked her.

"Only one; Lacy is five years old."

"Then she'd probably like this," Bebe said, holding up a doll. "This is a kachina, a Native American doll."

"She's beautiful. Lacy would love her. She has such a huge collection of dolls, but that's all she really wants as a gift. I have two nephews. Ricky is eight years old and a little more difficult to buy for than his three-year-old brother, James."

"Does he like musical instruments?" Bebe asked, holding up a handmade flute.

"Not in particular. Though he loves science, Ricky is more of an adventurer," Jill said, holding up a reproduction of a classic bow and arrow and smiling as she thought of what Barbie would think of her gift. "I'll get this," she said, pleased with her choice. She decided to get James a little drum set. Jill knew Barbie wouldn't appreciate the noisemaker, but she couldn't resist.

Next, they walked over to a jewelry display case, which held a large variety of beautiful southwestern jewelry. The case held an exquisite collection of silver and turquoise items. Jill chose five beautiful silver rings: each had a turquoise figure on it, a sun, a moon, a cactus, an eagle, and mountains.

"Do you see something else you like?" the saleswoman asked when she returned.

"I'd like to see your rings please," Jill told her. The woman quickly walked behind the case and unlocked it. Jill pointed to the ones she wanted, and the woman handed them to her.

"These are perfect. Do you have shipping?"

"Yes, we do."

"Good, I need to have four of these rings shipped," Jill said as they all walked to the counter for her to pay for the items.

Jill opened her purse, pulled out the American Express business card, and paid for all the decorations for the main lobby. Then she pulled out her personal credit card to pay for her own purchases.

"I can start loading this stuff into the Jeep," Bebe said.

"Thanks, Bebe," Jill said.

Jill wrote quick notes for each ring and made address labels for each. She sent one to Lois and one to Diane. Then she addressed two more labels for her mother and sister, making sure the saleswoman knew to ship the doll and the bow and arrow with her sister's ring. She wrote little notes for Ricky, Lacy, and James, too. Bebe returned and Jill handed her a little box.

"Jill, you should put this in your purse, I'm afraid it will get lost in the back of the Jeep."

"No, silly, this is for you. It's just a little thank-you for all your help, and for being a new friend."

"Jill, you didn't have to do that," Bebe said as she took the box. She opened it and saw that Jill had given her the ring with the sun on it. "It's beautiful, thank you," Bebe said and hugged Jill. She put the ring on, and it fit perfectly.

As Bebe finished loading the Jeep, Jill signed for her charges and then joined her.

"I'm starving, aren't you?" Jill asked her.

"Yes, I am. I don't know anywhere good to eat around here. Let's head back to Durango. I know a place there, and it's not on the property this time," Bebe said, smiling.

Jill started up the engine and headed back toward the ranch. Before they went too far, Jill stopped to fill the Jeep with gas.

"Don't you ever have to go to the bathroom?" Jill asked Bebe.

"I have to go now, but I don't think I go as much as you do," she answered teasingly.

They got their gas, used the restroom, and bought something to drink for the long drive. Jill started driving east on 160, back toward Durango. She hoped they would get there quickly, because she was hungry and didn't know how much longer she could wait. She glanced over and saw Bebe admiring her newest piece of jewelry.

"You know, outside of the people at the ranch, I really don't have any family," she said in a low sad voice. "And no one has ever given me a ring before."

"Where are you parents?" Jill asked cautiously.

"They died in a car accident when I was little. I was raised by an aunt, and she passed away a few years ago."

"Oh, Bebe, I'm so sorry. I go on and on about my family; I didn't mean to be insensitive," Jill told her.

"No, Jill, it's all right. I am just so touched by your gift today. I'm always around the guys, and men aren't always in tune with your emotions. They're great and all; I guess I need to be around the gentler of the sexes more often."

"I can understand that."

"I love the ring, thank you," Bebe said again.

"You're welcome, Bebe. This was a wonderful little trip. I think we both learned a lot about each other."

"I'd say we did. I wasn't even planning on a deep soul-searching journey. I thought we would get some shopping done."

"Yes, and grab a bite to eat and get in some girl talk; that's all I was banking on," Jill agreed.

"We got so much more out of our trip."

They chatted and reminisced about the success of the day, and it did make the trip to the restaurant fly by. Jill was thankful, because now she was really starving by the time they arrived.

Pulling in front of the ranch after lunch, Jill and Bebe
unloaded all their purchases. It took them several trips,
but they eventually got it done. Then the valet took the
keys and parked the car.

"Want to have a couple of drinks out by the pool?"
Bebe asked Jill.

"Sure, there are a few things I still need to go over
with you if you don't mind."

"Not at all, I'll get our drinks and meet you poolside."

"Sounds great," Jill said as she tossed the keys to
Bebe. "I'll see you in a few minutes."

Jill went to her room to put her purse away. She
washed her face and hands and then walked out onto the
patio. The sun was setting, giving the mountains a
golden hue. In the distance, she could see the ranch
hands rounding up the horses for the night. Jill walked
out a little farther. She could make out the figures of
Eric and Tony, the only two men she knew. She noticed
one cowboy seemed to be in charge and giving all the
orders, and wondered who he was.

She reached in her purse and pulled out the brochure.
She knew Eric and Tony were two of the cowboys on the
cover. Her heart pounded excitedly as she came to the
conclusion that the third man wasn't a model either and
was somewhere on the ranch. Smiling, she returned the
brochure to her purse.

Her mind quickly drifted back to breakfast, when she
had become overly titillated while looking at Eric and
Tony Roberts. She had never seen such magnificent-look-
ing men, not to mention fine, bronze cowboys.

Less than ten minutes later, she walked out to the pool
where Bebe was already waiting with a beer for each of
them. Jill sat down in a lounge chair next to her.

"Here you go, Jill," Bebe said, handing her a mug. "What did you want to talk to me about?"

"I want to hire a party planner. I don't have much time to get ready for the grand opening. I need someone who can put up the decorations, order invitations, and get us a caterer. I have a ton of things I have to do myself, and I think I'm going to need a little help. Do you know someone competent enough to take on this project?"

"I know someone who can do the job and feels as passionate about this project as you do," Bebe said confidently.

"Who? Are they available?"

"Jill, I'm talking about me."

"Oh, Bebe, I hate to put all this on you. You already have so much to do around here."

"That's true, but I think it will be fun. Besides, I can do everything you just named," Bebe said with assurance.

"I know you feel as passionately about the opening as I do, probably even more so, but are you sure you want to do it? This is going to be a hectic four weeks."

"Yes, Jill, I'm sure. Just give me a list and let me at it," Bebe said with a smile on her face.

"Okay then, the job is yours, and it pays the standard fee party planners receive," Jill told her.

"That's fine by me. It will be great to work together."

"Then it's a deal," Jill said.

"It's a deal," Bebe repeated in assurance. They toasted their business relationship with their mugs of beer and drank them down.

After chatting with Jill for several hours, Bebe stood to leave. "I'm exhausted. I think I'm going to go to bed. Are you coming?"

"Not yet, I think I'm going to take a swim."

"Have fun, I'll see you in the morning."

"Thanks for everything, Bebe."

"Don't mention it," she said as she walked down the path to the main building.

Jill finished the rest of her beer and walked down the same path. She went to her room and found her swimsuit. She desperately needed to exercise. Since she had been in Colorado she had been eating like a pig, and she'd burned off none of the calories. She didn't want to get back to New York and find herself weighing ten pounds more than when she had left.

She slipped into a tangerine and gold one-piece bathing suit that was cut high in the thigh and low in the back. She never wore a bikini, because she was so ashamed of her scar. Still, she looked beautiful.

Jill grabbed a towel and headed back up the path toward the pool. When she arrived, she threw her towel over the back of a chair near the deep end. She walked over to the diving board and climbed up. Balancing at the end of the board, she bounced twice before she took flight in the air. Her long body made a nice clean cut into the water. With her hair flowing gently behind her, her body glided sleekly through the tranquil water. Jill flipped and kicked off the other end of the pool. She did twelve laps before she took a break.

Jill got out of the pool and walked toward the lounge chair that she had left her towel on. She bent her head down as she squeezed the excess water from her hair. Suddenly she stopped as she noticed a pair of dusty cowboy boots in front of her. Slowly she lifted her head, until her eyes rested on the soft brown gaze of the man who stood before her.

"Are you looking for this?" he asked in a soft, sensuous voice.

Jill went to take a step back and tottered at the edge of the pool. In one quick motion, his arm was around her waist and he gently pulled her toward him.

"You must be Jill. I'm Kyle Roberts," he said as he tried to hand her the towel again. He took his arm from around her waist, but still stood in close proximity.

Jill said nothing, though she recognized him from the brochure. She stared at him as if it were her first time seeing a man. Kyle Roberts was taller than both of his brothers, and had definitely taken all the best of their good features. He looked to stand at least six feet three and was just as broad-shouldered as they were. His waist was small, and judging from the embrace Jill had just received, his chest was well chiseled. He had full lips and irresistible dimples, and every time he spoke, his words, like the water she was just in, wrapped themselves around her.

"You are Jill, aren't you?" he asked again.

"Yes-yes, I'm Jill. It's nice to meet you."

"It's nice to meet you too. I'm sorry if I startled you."

"That's okay, I just wasn't expecting to see anyone standing there," she said, telling only half the truth.

"So how are you enjoying Durango?"

"It's beautiful. I've never been to Colorado before. I want to try to get in some sightseeing while I'm here," Jill said as she gently dried her dripping hair and wrapped the towel around her.

"If you'd like, I would love to take you around," Kyle said, keeping his eyes focused on hers.

"I have lots of work to do, but when I get a good start on it I'd like to take you up on your offer," Jill said with a slight but nervous smile.

"I'm always here, just let me know when you're ready."

"I sure will, Kyle, thank you. I have to be going. I'll

see you around," she said, praying that there wasn't too much hope in her voice.

"See you later, Jill."

She turned and walked around the pool toward the path that led to the main building. She didn't want to but she looked back to see if he was still watching. He was.

Chapter 9

Jill walked back to her room with a smile on her face. She thought of her chance meeting with Kyle Roberts. He was incredibly handsome, Jill thought, and smiled to herself. He was tall, strong, and a gentleman. Kyle wasn't as reserved as Eric, or as playful as Tony. Jill realized that he must have been the one in charge of the men and the stables. His brothers were always waiting for his instructions.

Jill walked into her room and closed the door slowly behind her. She went into the bathroom and prepared to take a shower. While she waited for the shower water to warm, she turned on some music. She hadn't found a good jazz station since she had arrived, but she liked the station that was playing now. Luther Vandross was singing his rendition of "Always and Forever." Jill turned the volume up. The music filled the air, and she sang along as she walked back into the bathroom.

Jill slipped out of her swimsuit and into the shower. She continued singing as she worked up a soapy lather. She didn't rush through her shower like she always did in New York when getting ready for work. She took her time, enjoying the warm, pulsating water, the music filtering into the bathroom, and the peace she had found since she had been in Colorado. Jill stopped singing abruptly as she realized that it was a love song that she was singing. She hadn't listened to love songs in a long time, always preferring jazz. She didn't want to let her mind slip into thoughts of romance.

From the moment she had stepped off the plane and met Bebe, she had liked the woman, and from the moment she arrived in Durango, she had fallen in love with the place. Since arriving, she had felt free to be herself. She began to sing again and allowed herself to enjoy the love song.

She finished her shower and dried herself off before she slipped into a powder-blue nightgown. Catching a glimpse of herself in the mirror, she saw how much she looked like her mother and smiled.

Jill left the music playing and went outside on the patio. She looked out toward the mountains, which had faded into the night sky; only the twinkling stars gave evidence of the divide. She sat down on the lounge chair and thought about her day. She and Bebe had a wonderful time in Mancos. Jill was so happy that they would be working together. They got along so well and Jill was sure they would make a good team.

Lying back and enjoying the stars, Jill found her thoughts drifting back to Kyle. He was cute. Then she shook her head no, a smile forming on her lips. "He's magnificent," she said out loud. Kyle wanted to take her to see some of the sights of Durango if she had time from work. She would make time, she thought. Still, she fought that something deep inside that was whispering to her heart, *Take a chance.*

Jill went back into her room and turned off the music and the lights. She lay down in bed and fell asleep, wondering what tomorrow would bring.

Jill awoke at five o'clock pretty much like she always did on a workday morning in New York. Though it was still dark outside, she got up and dressed. Pulling her hair back into a quick ponytail, her favorite hairstyle, she left the room.

Jill walked out to the Ranch House, where she found Grace getting ready for her workday.

"Good morning, Grace."

Grace jumped at hearing someone's voice so early in the morning. "Oh, Jill, you scared me," she said, trying to balance the tray full of glasses.

"I'm sorry. I didn't mean to startle you."

"Don't worry about it. It's just that I wasn't expecting anyone for almost an hour. Can I get you anything?"

"I don't want to stop you from what you're doing. Just tell me where the coffeepot is and I'll make some."

"That's the first thing I get started as soon as I get here. It will only take me a second to get you a cup. I'll be right back," Grace said as she left.

Jill sat down at the bar and decided that after she had her coffee she would go back to her room and get a little work done. She wanted to be ready when Bebe got up.

Grace returned with her coffee and Jill took a sip. "Grace, this is wonderful, and just the way I like it. Thank you."

"You're welcome. You're the only new face I've had to remember, so it was easy to remember how you take your coffee," Grace said, smiling. "So tell me, how do you like Durango so far?"

"Grace, I'm falling more in love with this place each day. I've never seen such beauty in one place."

"It is pretty amazing, isn't it?"

"I think it will be hard for me to leave when my job is done," Jill said sadly.

"I'd like to think you'd come to visit us once in a while; you're like family here now."

Jill smiled at the thought of being considered one of them. "Thanks, Grace. I'll see you later," she said.

"Where are you headed?"

"I was going to go back to my room and get some work done, but I think I'll go and see the horses first. I haven't seen them yet. Bebe and I have a lot of work to do, but I'm afraid I'm up a little too early for her. If you see her before I do, would you tell her where I am?" Jill asked.

"I sure will. Will I see you later for breakfast?"

"You can count on it."

Jill walked out of the Ranch House and headed down the path toward the stables. As she walked through she noticed that only a handful of horses were there. Skye, Six Foot, and Chocolate Dancer were some of the names she read on their doors. The one that quickly got her attention was a horse at the end named Patches. Looking over his stable door, he threw his head back and neighed, as if he wanted Jill to come visit him.

"Well, hello, Patches, how are you?" Jill said, patting the horse's head. Patches immediately calmed down and enjoyed the woman who was gently stroking his mane. "You're beautiful, no wonder your name is Patches," Jill said, noticing the chestnut-brown horse had a white streak running not only the length of his nose, but also on his back and his left hind leg. Jill lay against the stable door as she rubbed his soft coat. He was a magnificent animal, and she could tell that the owner took excellent care of him. She stood in the quiet of the morning, enjoying the horse, when a man's voice startled her.

"Would you like to ride him?"

Jill jumped and turned around in the direction in which the voice had come. Tony was leaning against the stable's entryway. He had a mischievous smile on his face, having found pleasure in scaring Jill. "I didn't mean to frighten you," he said as he walked toward her.

"Yes, you did, and judging from the smile on your face, you enjoyed it," Jill said in playful anger with her hands on her hips.

"I'm sorry, Jill, but would you like to ride Patches? He seems to have taken a liking to you," Tony said as he patted the horse's head, too.

"Aren't the horses in here all boarders?"

"Yep."

"Well, don't you think the owner would mind?"

"I know the owner of this horse and he's a pretty nice guy. I'm sure he wouldn't mind at all if you rode Patches."

"All right then, I'd love to ride him," Jill answered.

"Good, I'll get him saddled up for you," Tony said as he went to get the horse ready.

Jill stood and watched as Tony worked quickly putting on the horse's saddle, bridle, and reins. "Have you worked on the ranch long?" she asked, noticing how fast and expertly his hands worked.

Tony looked up and smiled at her, and then answered, "All my life." He pulled the Arabian horse by the reins out of his stable and outside. "Have you ridden before?"

"Yes, I'm a pretty good rider, I should be fine."

"We have three trails that are marked red, yellow, and green, just like the traffic signal. The green is the easiest trail and the red is the hardest. Being that you're not familiar with the terrain, I suggest you take the yellow trail."

"Thanks, Tony," Jill said as she stuck her left foot into the stirrup and with a big hop, threw her right leg over Patches's back and sat down in the saddle. Tony handed her the reins and she headed out past the corral.

The sun had begun to rise, and Jill felt exhilarated as

she deeply inhaled the fresh Colorado air. Patches trotted across to the edge of the ranch as if he knew exactly what he was doing. Jill let him lead since the horse obviously knew where he was going. *He should,* Jill reasoned, he *lives here.*

Patches headed down a dirt path, which led toward the mountains. Jill relaxed in the saddle as the horse led her through the pine trees. He walked with assured steps as he climbed the side of a small mountain. Jill noticed the yellow arrows Tony had talked about, and she knew Patches was on the right trail. Patches walked until he got to the other side of the mountain. Once there, he paused as if to give Jill a chance to take in all the beauty beyond the ranch.

Jill looked down the mountain and into the tiny valley. There was a lake tucked between the surrounding mountains, with even taller pine trees surrounding it. She could see huge rocks closer to the bottom of the mountain she and Patches were on, and worried whether the horse could navigate the terrain.

As if he could read her thoughts, Patches gracefully started down the side of the mountain. Jill clutched his reins tightly and leaned back in the saddle.

Patches trotted around the side of a lake before cutting up the side of another mountain. He broke into a full gallop. Jill smiled and leaned into the wind. "Okay, Patches, show me what you've got," she whispered to the horse.

Patches ran even faster. Jill smiled, enjoying the horse's speed and agility. She pulled on the reins, and Patches slowed his speed. "Whoa, whoa," Jill said as the horse came to a clearing. "I think someone lives up here."

Through the trees, she could see a beautiful log cabin. The horse tried to get closer to the cabin, but Jill wouldn't let him. "We don't want the owner to see us," she whispered to the horse, trying to keep him at a safe distance. She made Patches circle the edifice while she admired the architecture. It was a two-story building with a beautiful porch that ran the entire length of the front of the cabin. Jill could tell that whoever lived here had a love of horses, because in the back of the house were several other horses grazing. They raised their heads and neighed as Jill and Patches circled, and she guided Patches away before the owner could come out.

"I better get back to the ranch, Patches, I have to get to work," she said to the horse as he took her on another wonderful ride. Patches ran for a long while, and didn't slow his gait until he reached the lake. He took a drink there, and Jill decided that she needed a break too. She dismounted and rubbed the cool water on herself. She sat on a huge rock and admired the mesmerizing view. She could hardly wait to tell her family and friends of the amazing place she was visiting.

Off in the distance she saw someone fast approaching her on horseback. Jill stood to get a better look at who was coming. She squinted in the sunlight, trying to make out who it was. It was Kyle Roberts.

Jill moved closer to Patches and grabbed his reins, wondering why the man rode his horse so fast toward her. As Kyle got closer, she noticed that he was smiling.

"Good morning, Jill," he said.

"Good morning, Kyle, is everything all right?" she asked slightly nervous.

"Everything is just fine. Tony thought it would be funny to give you my horse."

"Oh, I'm so sorry. I didn't know Patches was yours. Tony said he knew the owner, and that he wouldn't mind," Jill said as it slowly dawned on her that Tony had tricked her. "I think that jokester brother of yours set me up."

Kyle smiled. Dropping his head, he shook it and laughed. "No, Jill, it's really all right. If he had given my horse to anyone else, I would have been upset," he said, making Jill blush slightly. "Besides, Tony is making me late for work, so I gave him my job to do."

"That sounds fair," Jill said, smiling. An awkward silence fell, and Jill noticed that Kyle was staring at her. She looked away for a moment, then managed to say, "I guess I should get your horse back to the stables."

"There's no need to hurry now. I have someone filling in for me. Would you like to go for a ride with me?" Kyle asked.

"I'd love to, Kyle, but Bebe should be waiting for me. We're supposed to start working together today, and we have a lot to get started on," she explained.

"Well then, we'll just make it a quick ride," he said with persistence.

"All right, a quick ride then," she said, smiling up at him, making his grin broaden.

Jill mounted Patches and asked, "Which way are we going?"

"Follow me," Kyle told her and had his own horse head up the mountain behind them.

Jill followed closely behind him. She watched his strong back, as every muscle worked with the horse as they climbed up the slope. She wondered why he was so persistent on going for a ride with her right now, and where he was taking her. She wondered if Bebe was at the Ranch House waiting for her, and hoped she wouldn't keep her waiting long. Right now, Jill allowed herself to enjoy the ride, and enjoy watching Kyle Roberts.

When they came to the top of the mountain, Kyle stopped and dismounted his horse. He walked over and helped Jill down off Patches. He placed one hand on either side of her tiny waist and gently guided her toward the ground.

When her feet finally touched the ground, Jill felt as though she had been holding her breath forever, and hoped Kyle hadn't noticed her finding pleasure in his touch. He took her hand and walked over to the mountain's edge.

"It's beautiful up here," she exclaimed as she surveyed the surrounding view.

"Look over there," he said, pointing out the ranch in the distance.

"I didn't realize the resort sat on so much land."

"The property is quite extensive, but we are still one of the smallest ones around."

"The more I see of this place, the more I love it," Jill said, turning to see Kyle looking at her intensely.

"Come over here," he said as he again took her by the hand and led her to the other side of the mountaintop. "That's the lake we just left."

"It's so relaxing up here, I could just stand here forever," Jill said, closing her eyes and enjoying the sun's warmth on her face.

"Me too," Kyle said and watched the sun glisten on her brown skin.

Sensing that he was staring at her again, Jill opened her eyes. "I better get back. I don't want to keep Bebe waiting," she said, heading toward her horse. Reluctantly, Kyle followed her and did the same.

Kyle led the way back to the ranch. Jill didn't know how long they had been riding. Though she had enjoyed herself, she wrestled with letting herself admit it.

They reached the bottom of the mountain and cut across to the corral and into the stables. Kyle dismounted and walked over to Jill. He helped her off her horse, in the same manner he had before.

"Thank you for the ride, Kyle, I really did enjoy myself," she said, smiling.

"You're welcome, and thank you for coming along with me. It was a quick ride; maybe we can do something else later. You know, once you and Bebe get a good start on your work," he teased.

Jill laughed. "I'd like that very much. I'll see you later," she said and walked in the direction of the Ranch House.

"See you later, Jill."

As she was walking, she turned to see if he was watching her, and just like last night, he was. She waved to him before she entered the restaurant, and he waved back.

Kyle grabbed the two horses by their reins and led them to the corral. Tony and Eric rode up next to their brother, and Tony said, "Eric, I think I won the bet, he wasn't gone nearly as long as you thought he'd be."

"I had money on you for at least three hours," Eric said as he handed his brother a five-dollar bill. Kyle looked up at his brothers in irritation and a playful smile came across his face as he threw his hat at Tony.

"You're almost thirty-one, man, when are you going to settle down?" Tony asked, snatching the five-dollar bill from Eric as he made his horse take off into a full run. Kyle jumped on Patches and chased after his playful brother, and Eric followed them.

Chapter 10

Jill entered the Ranch House and saw Bebe sitting alone. She was busy writing when Jill sat down at the table with her.

"Hey, Jill, Grace told me you were probably the first one up on the ranch," Bebe said to her.

"Yes, I was up kind of early, so I decided to go for a ride."

"Did you enjoy your ride?"

"I loved it, this place is amazing. I find something new and wonderful everywhere I look," Jill told her as a bright smile appeared on her face. "Did you eat yet?"

"No, I thought I might as well wait for you. I haven't been waiting long," Bebe said as Grace approached them.

"Jill, I see you're back in one piece," Grace said, smiling.

"I stayed on the yellow trail. The horse seemed to know what to do," Jill said.

"Are you to ready to order?"

"Yes, I am. I'm starving, Grace. I'll have a western omelet, grits, toast, and orange juice," Jill said.

"You really worked up an appetite. How do you stay so small eating like that?" Bebe asked.

"At home, I don't eat like this at all. Well, I do when I visit my parents. My dad makes everyone eat a hearty breakfast. In New York, I usually have a bowl of cereal, a banana, and coffee," Jill said.

"I'll have a ham and cheese omelet, toast, and orange juice, Grace," Bebe said, and Grace wrote down their orders.

"I'll be right back," she told them.

"Jill, I made a list of all the things we need to do in order to be ready for the grand opening. I pretty much concentrated on my responsibilities in looking for a caterer and getting invitations, and I'll take care of putting up the decorations. Is that all right with you?"

"That's fine, Bebe. I think you were right, you are the perfect person for the job."

"I also got you a list of addresses and phone numbers for the local radio and television stations, as well as the newspapers and the mayor's office," Bebe said as she looked up and handed Jill the paper with the information on it. Jill's attention was focused on the door.

Kyle, Eric, and Tony had just entered the restaurant. Eric went immediately over to see his wife, and Kyle and Tony walked over to see Bebe and Jill.

"Hey, Bebe, girl, what do you know good?" Tony asked her playfully, walking toward the table. He gave her a kiss on the cheek as he sat down beside her.

"I know that Grace hasn't brought me my food yet, so you can't steal anything, Tony," Bebe said to him as Kyle sat down next to Jill. "Kyle, you're probably the last one to meet Jill."

"Actually, Bebe, we met last night when I went for a swim," Jill told her. Bebe's eyes widened as a faint happy smile played upon her lips.

"We also had a brief encounter this morning on the mountain. Tony thought it would be funny to give Jill my horse. So I went looking for her," Kyle added, his eyes never leaving Jill's.

"Now, Kyle, I haven't been able to figure that one out, why did you go after her? You could have used any horse we have to get your work done until she returned," Tony said.

"I wanted to use the opportunity to meet Jill during the day," Kyle said, smiling at Jill, making her blush.

Grace arrived with Jill's and Bebe's orders and said, "I'll be right back with your juice. Kyle, Tony, can I get you anything?"

"I'll have the usual, Grace," Kyle told her.

"I will too," Tony added.

"All right," Grace said, leaving to fill their orders.

"Bebe, I offered to show Jill around Durango while she is in town, but she says that you have a lot of work to get started on. Do you think by the end of the week you'll have gotten enough done so that I could steal her away for a day?" Kyle asked.

"Kyle, that's so nice of you to offer to do that. We'll get as much done as we can, but that won't hinder your taking Jill out," Bebe said, ignoring the kick under the table that Jill had given her.

Grace returned again with platters filled with pancakes, bacon, grits, toast, and coffee for Kyle and Tony. "Here you go, fellas, and don't forget my tip," Grace teased.

"I won't, Grace," Tony said. "Just leave me the bill," he said jokingly. Grace waved her hand at his silliness. "So, Jill, did you enjoy your ride today?" he asked her.

"Yes, I did, but I see that I have to watch out for you. You set me up today."

"I did, and I've already been punished for being a bad boy. Kyle had me do his work, too," he said, trying to sound like a sullen child.

Jill tried, but couldn't hold back her laughter.

The group of friends ate together and discussed what

would be going on in the weeks to come on the resort. As he listened to what Jill and Bebe discussed, Kyle realized just why the two women were going to be so busy. Still, he wanted to go out with Jill. Though he didn't know why, he got the feeling that Jill was afraid to be alone with him. She had seemed a little tense and uncomfortable on the mountain when they were alone. But now, with a group, she was relaxed and spoke freely.

"Excuse me, I have to make a trip to the little girls' room," Jill said, having finished her meal. "I'll be right back."

"I'll see you guys later, I'm going to go say hello to the fellas over there. Bebe, girl, don't get into any trouble," Tony said. He put his hat back on and left the table.

"I'm not you, Tony, trouble doesn't find me, nor I it," she teased. Her eyes fell on Kyle, and she smiled at him. "So what do you think of Jill?"

"Bebe, I think she's amazing. I would really like to get to know her better, but I get the feeling she isn't interested," Kyle said.

"Kyle, give her some time. She's got issues she's trying to work through too."

"Do you mean she's married or is she going through something with an ex-boyfriend?"

"No, nothing like that, she just wants to take slow and cautious steps. It's up to you, Kyle, but I think you shouldn't make your first time out with her so much of a date."

"What do you mean? How else am I supposed to get to know her, Bebe?" Kyle asked in confusion.

"Well, maybe you should consider making it a group thing. You know, invite more than just Jill. It's up to you, but I just think she wouldn't be so uptight if more people were around. After that, try the one-on-one thing."

"I get it. Bebe, girl, you're worth your weight in gold," he said, just before Jill came back to the table.

"All right, Bebe, I'm ready to get started," Jill said.

"Let's do it then. I thought we could work in my office; it's in the back of the main building," Bebe told her.

"Kyle, thanks again for this morning, I hope we get to go riding again, it was fun."

"The pleasure was all mine, Jill. I'd love to go riding with you again. Next time we'll take a different trail and see more of the property," he said, smiling. He stood and put on his hat. "I'll see you ladies later," he said.

Jill watched intensely as the cowboy walked over to his brothers and the other ranch hands. They all were laughing and talking, and Kyle gave the men their assignments for the day.

Jill slowly looked around the entire room. Never in all her life had she seen so many well-built men in one place. There were a couple of Native American and Hispanic ranch hands, but the room was mostly populated with tall, dark African-American men.

"Jill, I get the feeling that this one is more than eye candy," Bebe said as she got Jill's attention once again.

"No, it's eye candy, nothing more. Come on, let's go to your office," Jill said. She stood and walked toward the door, and Bebe followed.

The two walked in silence all the way to the main building. Bebe took her keys from her pocket and unlocked the door to her office. Sitting behind her desk, she looked at her friend.

"Bebe, I'm sorry. I should have brought my laptop with me. That way we both can get on the Web and take care of business. I'll go get it now."

"No, wait, Jill. I want to talk to you for a minute."

"What's wrong, Bebe?" Jill asked, sitting down in a chair.

"I know that I am probably way off base here, but I have to ask. I know that you and Kyle have only just met, but you do realize that he wants to get to know you."

Jill sighed deeply and then said, "Bebe, a blind man could see that, and I really enjoy hanging out with him too. I mean, what's not to like? He's tall, dark, and handsome, not to mention, sweet, kind, and considerate. But every time I've thought I had love by the tail, it dragged me through the dirt. Besides, I just want to stay focused on my dreams. One day, I want to open my own public relations firm in New York. I'm so close, I don't want things to turn out for me like they did for my sister, Barbie."

"What happened to her?"

"She is happily married, with three beautiful kids."

"Okay, Jill, I'm missing something here, isn't that what you want to happen to you some day?"

"Yes, but Barbie let go of her own dream. She wanted to be an attorney, but instead she got married and never finished school. Now she wants to finish school and has to balance the kids, a husband, and a house in order to go back."

"I see."

"Kyle is the kind of man I could lose myself in. Last night, when we met at the pool, I almost fell back in the water. He caught me and pulled me close to him. He wrapped his arms around me, and I could have just melted in them. Bebe, you know what scared me? Though I don't believe in love at first sight, for an instant I did."

"You know, Jill, sometimes we don't get to decide

who we'll fall in love with, or when we'll fall in love. It just happens."

"I know, but for as long as I can I'll try to dodge it. I better go get my laptop. I'll be right back," Jill said.

Jill walked back to her room, thinking about what Bebe had asked her. Obviously she and Kyle had been talking. It seemed, no matter where she went, the dating game followed her. Jill toyed with the idea of telling Kyle she wouldn't have time to go out with him. That would be the safest way for her to avoid his advances, she reasoned. How she wished she had someone to talk to about this. She just wanted to validate her feelings. Right now, she felt as though she were the one in the wrong. But how could that be? she wondered. It was her life. She was free to do with it what she wanted. Jill reached her room and grabbed her laptop. She headed back to Bebe's office, determined to get some work done.

After an hour had passed with Bebe and Jill working on their promotional materials, Bebe broke the silence. "I was thinking, maybe we should hire two bands, so we could have a band in the main lobby and outside near the pool. Wouldn't that be nice?"

"Bebe, you have a natural talent for the party-planning thing," Jill said, making Bebe's smile broaden. Jill glanced at her watch and realized that it was past lunchtime. "Bebe, what do you say to lunch? I'm a little hungry."

"I was just thinking the same thing. I just want to put this call into the band's agent."

"I am going to my room to make a few phone calls. Why don't I meet you in the Ranch House in about a half hour? Is that enough time for you?"

"It should be, but if I'm not there just wait for me."

"Where else could I go?" Jill teased as she left the office. She walked back to her room, feeling that she and Bebe had gotten a lot accomplished. Jill entered her room and lay across the bed. She reached for the phone and decided to call Barbie first.

"Hello?" said the familiar voice of her sister.

"Hi, Barbie, It's me."

"Jill, I've been waiting to hear from you. How is everything going?"

"Fine, everything is going really well as far as work is concerned."

"Is there something else going on?" Barbie asked, sensing something was on her sister's mind.

"No, why do you ask?"

"You just sound like something is bothering you."

"No, I'm fine."

"Well, just know that I'm here for you if you need me. I guess I should tell you my exciting news."

"What is it, Barbie?" Jill said with a little excitement in her voice.

"I talked to Rick, and he thinks my going back to school is a great idea!"

"Oh, Barbie, I'm so excited for you," Jill said sincerely.

"I'll start this fall, and Rick says he'll help out as much as he can with the kids and the housework."

"Barbie, you have to be so excited. I am so proud of you."

"Thanks, sis, that means a lot to me."

"Do Mom and Dad know?" Jill asked.

"Yes, Dad's excited, but Mom has mixed feelings. I guess she thinks she'll get stuck watching the kids," Barb said, and they both laughed.

"Barbie, I have to go. I have to make a few more calls. I'll be in touch soon."

"All right, sis, I'll talk to you later, I love you."

"I love you too," Jill said and hung up the phone.

She still lay across the bed, and her mind drifted back to Kyle. She knew just why she hadn't told Barbie about him. She didn't want her to feel as though there was more to the friendship than what was there. Her sister would only have showed her love and support. Jill thought back to the night they were at Station Square, and everything Barbie had said to her, making her feel as if she was making the right decisions in her life.

Jill closed her eyes. Why was all of this so hard for her? she thought. What was there to hide or explain? Why couldn't she just be friends with the man, and no one, including herself, expect more than friendship? "Because I want more," Jill admitted aloud to herself. She opened her eyes and a tear rolled down her cheek. She picked up the phone and called Barbie back.

"Hello."

"It's me again," Jill said, trying to conceal the fact that she was crying. But it was of no use. Barbie knew her sister, and knew something was bothering her.

"Jill, what is it? I know something is not right. Why won't you tell me? Whatever it is, Jill, I'm here for you," Barbie said, in a unique mother-sister-friend voice.

Jill burst into tears.

"Oh, Barbie, what's wrong with me? Why can't I just let happiness have its way with me? Why do I always fight it?"

"I get the feeling that you have met someone, sis."

"I have," Jill said, continuing to cry. "Barbie, I've only know him for a day, but he wants to take me out. I'm finding all kinds of reasons why I shouldn't go."

"Why, Jill, is he ugly?"

"No," Jill said, laughing. "As a mater of fact, he's very

handsome. His name is Kyle, and I want to go out with him, but I'm afraid."

"Jill, what is it that you're afraid of?"

"I'm afraid that I won't get to realize my own dreams. Barbie, you know that I want to open my own firm someday. I don't want to have to choose between work and family life. I don't want my dreams to be put on hold."

"You mean like I did?"

"Barbie, you have a wonderful life, and you are happily married. I just want to take a different road to the same happiness you've found."

"I can understand that, but why do you think you can't have both? I chose the path that was right for me. My path might not have worked well for you. Jill, already your path is quite different from mine."

"Are you upset with me," Jill asked her.

"Don't be silly, how could I be upset over something like that? I told you I'm here for you, and I meant it. Jill, do you see my life as a failure?" Barbie asked directly.

"No, Barbie, I see it as a success. I just don't see myself being able to manage it all like you. I don't think I could do the job of wife, mother, daughter, and sister, like you do, and still have a career."

"Jill, you have to make the right choices for yourself. One last piece of sisterly advice, please allow yourself to enjoy life, and to enjoy love."

"Thanks, Barbie, I'll try," Jill said as her tears started to dry.

"I have to run some errands before I have to pick up the kids. Call me anytime for anything, promise?"

"I promise, sis. Talk to you later," Jill said and hung up the phone. Barbie had succeeded in making her feel better again.

Jill knew she was putting the cart way in front of the

horse. It was possible that Kyle only wanted to be friends and that the ideas of anything more were all in her head. Bebe had said Kyle wanted to get to know her, but maybe he just wanted to get to know her as a friend. At any rate, she would place herself in control of the situation. She would take Barbie's advice and enjoy herself, and she would know when to pull up on the reins.

Jill got off the bed and walked into the bathroom to freshen up. She threw cool water on her face, and reapplied her makeup before she brushed her hair and decided not to pull it back into a ponytail.

She left her room and walked to the Ranch House to meet Bebe. Entering, Jill saw that her friend hadn't arrived yet. Though the place was packed, she found a table in the back and claimed it for them. Jill looked around and saw that most of the ranch hands were at the bar throwing back a cold beer. The scent of barbecue filled the air, along with mood-relaxing conversation and laughter. Jill could see that the people were happy to work here. Tony and Eric were making their way toward her. Eric was holding his wife's hand as he walked.

"Hey, Jill, sorry I didn't get a chance to say hello earlier. I wanted you to meet my wife. Sharon, this is Jill Alexander," Tony said.

Sharon extended her hand to shake Jill's. "So you're the pretty New Yorker we've been waiting for. Bebe said that you were a powerhouse in your field."

"I think we should wait until I'm done with the job before I accept any accolades. Bebe is very generous with her compliments. I hope I live up to all of your expectations," Jill said, a little embarrassed by the flattery. "Bebe should be here any minute, do you want to have lunch with us?" she offered.

"We'd love to but we can't. I just came to steal my

husband away, we're going home for lunch," Sharon said as she gently caressed Eric's arm, blinding Jill with the huge diamond in her engagement ring. "We'll see you all later," she said.

"Tony, tell Kyle that I went home for lunch. Jill, I'll see you around," Eric said as he was led away by his wife.

"Bye, Sharon, bye, Tony," Jill said, smiling at the couple.

"I'll do just that, big brother," Tony told Eric. "Jill, would you mind if I had lunch with you, or is this going to be a working lunch for you and Bebe?"

"We might do a little shop talk, but you're welcome to join us."

"Hey, guys, I'm sorry I'm late. I was put on hold so many times I forgot who I was holding for," Bebe said, rushing over to the table.

"Hey, Bebe, girl," Tony said. His face lit up as she sat down, and for a brief moment, Jill wondered if more wasn't going on between the two than Bebe let on.

"Did you order already?" Bebe asked them.

"No, I was waiting for you. I hope you don't mind. I told the pest that he could join us," Jill said teasingly.

"I think you've been hanging around this one too much," Tony said, taking his hat off and putting it on Bebe's head. Bebe smiled, took the hat off, and placed it on a hook on the wall.

"Don't look now, but here comes another pest," Bebe said.

"Hey, big man, are you going to join us?" Tony asked Kyle.

"You should eat now, Kyle, you've got more work to do too," Jill said. She smiled up at him and scooted over to make room for Kyle to sit down.

"Since you put it like that, I guess I'd better," Kyle

said. He hung his hat on a hook next to Tony's and then sat next to Jill.

"Well, well, the gang's all here," Grace said as she approached the table. "Can I interest you in today's special?"

"What would that be, Gracie?" Tony asked.

"Barbecued ribs, fries, and coleslaw," she announced.

"That sounds good to me," Kyle said.

"Yeah, I'll have what my brother is having," Tony told her.

"What about you ladies?" Grace asked.

"Grace, I think I'll have a taco salad," Bebe said.

"I'll have a grilled chicken salad," Jill said.

"Let me see, beers for the men and lemonade for the ladies, right?"

"Grace, you're good," Bebe told her.

"How hard can it be? I've known you all forever. Jill is the only new member of the gang. I'll be right back with your drinks," she said, then left.

"Bebe, did you book the band?" Jill asked.

"I got one band booked. Tomahawk is a local Native American band. I've heard their music before, and they're great. Their agent says they can definitely do the opening. They'll be out near the pool, but I haven't found anyone for the main building yet."

"You'll find another group," Jill said.

"We have another problem, Jill. The main dining room doesn't have a name yet."

"Who's responsible for that?"

"The investors should name it. I'll get in touch with them and see what they want to do," Bebe offered.

Grace returned and set their drinks in front of them. "Your food will be ready in a minute," she said and dashed off.

"Thanks, Gracie," Tony said.

"I know you ladies have a ton of work to do, but I have an idea for Saturday," Kyle said, his gaze fixed on Jill. She shifted nervously in her seat, afraid of the romantic date he was about to announce he wanted to take her on. "I thought it would be nice if we all went white-water rafting," he said, cocking his head to the side, hoping he would receive an enthusiastic answer from Jill. Her eyes widened and a smile came across her face.

"Kyle, that sounds great. I haven't been rafting in a long time," Jill said.

"We've all been rafting recently, so you won't be at a loss for help," he assured her.

"I haven't been rafting in a while either," Bebe told him.

"We should see if Sharon and Eric want to come," Tony added.

"Let's make sure we tell them today. Not that they have such a busy social calendar, but they would rather stay home and make love all day than go out," Bebe said, laughing.

Grace returned with the food. The group ate heartily and talked endlessly about work and rafting. Jill relaxed and found herself caught up in a private conversation with Kyle. She struggled to hear over the music, and found herself leaning toward him. Someone had started the jukebox and Bon Jovi's "Dead or Alive" was playing. Jill couldn't help feeling that she was in the right place at the right time. She was doing what she loved, in a place that she loved, and in the process had made new friends.

Bebe glanced over to see her friend laughing. She didn't know what Kyle had said to Jill, but he had definitely tickled her funny bone. Bebe was glad that he had taken her advice. Jill wasn't ready for anything heavy. If he really wanted to get to know her, he would have to do it on Jill's terms.

Chapter 11

The group finished their meal and left the Ranch House. Kyle and Tony were hoping to find that Eric had returned from home and would be ready to start work. Bebe and Jill still had much to finish before the day ended.

"Where are you two off to?" Tony asked.

"We're going into town. We have to see a printer about the invitations for the grand opening and we also have to visit a caterer," Bebe told him.

"I'll see you later then, Bebe, girl," Tony said as he gently touched her cheek. "See you later, Jillian."

"How did you know that was my name?" Jill said, looking at Tony quizzically.

"I didn't," he said as he put his hat back on. "I just like to play with people's names. I guess I hit right on with yours."

"I think it's beautiful, Jillian," Kyle said, smiling.

Jill blushed slightly and gently rolled her eyes. "See you guys later."

She and Bebe began walking back to the main building. She quickly glanced over her shoulder and saw Kyle still watching as she walked away.

"Jill, I have to get my purse out of the office. I'll meet you at the Jeep in a few minutes," Bebe said.

"I'll have to go to my room to get mine, and then I'll be right there."

The two women parted and went their separate ways. Bebe returned first and got into the Jeep. She was sitting in the driver's seat when Jill returned.

"You aren't going to make me drive?" Jill teased.

"No, I think you deserve a break. Besides, we aren't going that far."

Jill walked around the Jeep and got in on the passenger's side. Bebe started the engine and drove off. It was already three-thirty P.M. Jill worried whether they had enough time to get everything done.

"Bebe, do you know what time the printer and the caterer close? We only have two hours before it's five-thirty, and I'm afraid everything will be closing," Jill said.

"Don't worry, Jill, we're going to the printer first, because they do close at five. Then we'll go to Paulina's, because she stays open late. I already called and told her we wouldn't be there until after five, and she said that would be fine."

"Good, I feel like we're getting a lot done today," Jill said.

"Yes, I feel really productive too. I just hope we get everything done in time."

"We will if we stay focused and do as much as we can each day."

"Jill, you are so dedicated. I can't imagine any client ever being dissatisfied with their project after you've finished with it," Bebe said in admiration. She hoped she was doing a good job for Jill, and not being more of a hindrance.

"Bebe, every project comes together smoothly when everyone involved with it works together and gives one hundred percent. Back in New York, Lois is my right

hand. She's one of my best friends, but she's also dedicated to Iguana like I am. You're like us. You are
dedicated to the successful opening of A Special Place.
You're doing twice the work just to ensure it. Like I said
before, you're great at this," Jill said sincerely.

"Thank you, Jill. Sometimes my ego needs to be
stoked too," Bebe said, smiling.

They arrived at Diamond Mine Printing Company,
and Bebe parked in the rear of the building. They exited
the car and walked around to the front entrance. Inside
were several tables with all kinds of huge books with invitation samples on them. Along the walls were
different patterns of stationery, and everything one
would need to fill one's writing and printing needs.

Jill walked up to one of the tables and opened a book.
She and Bebe had been looking for a few minutes when
a saleswoman came and asked if she could be of any assistance. Jill explained what type of invitations she had
in mind, when she would need them, and about how
many she would need. The woman showed Jill another
book that contained more formal invitation samples,
and Jill found just what she was looking for. She
showed Bebe a beautiful cream-colored invitation with
matching envelopes that had a rich burgundy lining inside. The salesperson assured Jill that if she placed an
order now, she would put a rush on the project and have
them ready in a week or two.

"That would be perfect," Jill told her thankfully. She
reached into her purse and pulled out the paper con-
taining the grand opening's information. She handed it
to the woman and explained the font and style she
wished to be printed on the invitations.

"This is for the grand opening of A Special Place?" the saleswomen asked Jill excitedly.

"Yes, it is," she said, smiling. "Have you heard of it?"

"I think everyone in town has heard of it. We even have visitors that were hoping to still be here for the opening. Do you work at the resort?"

"No, I don't work there, but she does," Jill said as she nodded her head toward Bebe.

"Is must be great to work there," the woman told Bebe excitedly.

"I have to admit, it is a nice place to work," Bebe said as she glanced at Jill and rubbed her hands nervously together.

"Is the place as beautiful as I've heard? Do you have the best-looking cowboys in town working there?" the woman continued, firing questions directly at Bebe.

"I-I guess we have good-looking cowboys," Bebe continued nervously, unsure if she was handling the situation the way Jill would. "The resort is beautiful though, you'll have to come out and see it."

"Is there any way I could come to the grand opening?" the woman asked with a wishful twinkle in her eyes.

Unsure of how she should answer the question, Bebe quickly looked to Jill for help. But this was Bebe's moment, and Jill let her have the spotlight. "Ms. Simmons, I went over our numbers earlier. I think you could extend an invitation to her."

"I guess we'll see you at the grand opening. I'll make sure we get an invitation out to you, Ms. . . ."

"Sanchez, Delores Sanchez," she said, extending her hand and shaking Bebe's in appreciation. Delores turned and said, "I'm sorry, I didn't get your assistant's name."

"Oh, she's no—"

"I'm Jill Alexander," Jill said, interrupting Bebe. She too shook Delores's hand and told her, "We have to be going, please call us at the number on the bottom of the instructions when the invitations are ready." She and Bebe walked to the door.

"I sure will. It was nice meeting you both. Have a wonderful day," Delores said, holding the door open for the two women.

Jill and Bebe walked toward the back of the building, where the Jeep was parked. They got in, and Jill noticed a faint smile on Bebe's face. Bebe leaned back in her seat and looked at Jill. She wondered how this woman who sat next to her had become such a gracious person. Jill never seemed to need to be the person in the spotlight. She was happy making others shine. No wonder she was so good at her job, Bebe reasoned. But on a personal level, even in the little things, Jill had a giving and gracious spirit.

"All right, Bebe, why are you staring at me?" Jill finally asked, laughing.

"I have never met anyone quite like you, Jill. At every turn I learn something new about you. You are so gracious with your time, yourself, and your kindness. You never grandstand, or act as if it all has to be about you," Bebe said in admiration. "I'm not a bad person, but you are certainly teaching me how to be a better one."

"You are exactly the same way, especially when it comes to your friends."

"I'm so very happy to have met you, Jill Alexander. I only wish you never had to leave," Bebe said sadly.

"Bebe, just because I have to go back to New York doesn't mean it will be the end of our friendship. It just means I have another home to visit. You are now an extension of my family, and I hope I'm an extension of yours," Jill said.

"Of course you are," Bebe told her as she wiped her eyes. "We better get going. We still have to visit Paulina's." Bebe started the engine and drove toward the restaurant, which was only a few streets away. When they arrived, Bebe was able to park right in the front of the building. They got out of the Jeep and went inside. Instantly, they smelled the wonderful dishes that were being prepared in Paulina's kitchen, and their bellies reminded them that they hadn't had dinner yet.

"Well, hello, ladies," said a heavyset, golden-skinned woman who was walking up to greet them. "You must be the people I'm expecting from the resort," she said assuredly, as she shook both their hands.

"That's us," Bebe said. "How did you know who we are?"

"You're my last appointment," the woman said, winking her eye, revealing her mystic powers.

Jill and Bebe laughed, trying to lighten up from the serious conversation they had just had in the Jeep.

"I am the owner, Paulina Cortez," she said with a thick Spanish accent. "And you must be Bebe Simmons," Paulina added, looking at Bebe.

"You're right, how did you know that I was Bebe?"

Paulina threw her hands in the air and said, "Lucky guess. I don't know your name though."

"I'm Jill Alexander. I'm working with Ms. Simmons," Jill told her.

"Well, now that we all know each other, let's get down to business," Paulina said, leading them to the back of the building where her kitchen was. There were a few employees there, but they paid no attention to Jill and Bebe and kept working. Paulina led them to a table with about twenty plates of food on it.

"I have prepared authentic Mexican and Mexican-American dishes, as well as Spanish, Italian, and

American. Please try them and tell me if you like them," Paulina said, handing them silverware.

Jill and Bebe sampled dish after wonderful dish. Paulina explained her favorite Southwest specialties as they ate. She had prepared venison quesadillas, grilled lamb, and a roast chicken breast with green-chili stuffing. Paulina had Mexican, Spanish, and jasmine rice, all of which went well with each dish. She also had them sample paella she thought they would enjoy, and they did. There was also lasagna, stuffed shells, and manicotti, but Jill and Bebe had already decided to go with Paulina's Southwest specialties, and asked that she include salad with the meal. For dessert, she offered them flan, key lime pie, strawberry cheesecake, and fried ice cream. Though neither of them tried any of the tempting desserts, they decided to have all of them offered at the grand opening. Paulina saw the look in the women's eyes, and had one of her employees box some of the goodies for Jill and Bebe to take with them.

Paulina wrote down everything they had ordered, and Bebe gave her the address and confirmed the date and time on June 5. Having their menu in place, Jill and Bebe prepared to leave Paulina's and thanked her for everything.

"Don't worry, darlings, the food at this grand opening will be the talk of the town, I guarantee it," Paulina promised as she walked her clients to the door. They told the woman good-bye and to call if she had any problems or questions. Though she could foresee none, she promised them she would.

"Bebe, I can't believe this is coming together so smoothly. I hope my part comes together this nicely," Jill said as they got into the Jeep.

"Hey, you're the pro at this, Jill. Your part is going to come together as smooth as butter."

"I doubt it, Bebe. In this business you either have a rough start or a smooth finish, or vice versa, you don't get both," Jill said, laughing, and Bebe started the engine and headed toward the resort.

When they returned to the resort, the sun was beginning to dip behind the mountains. Bebe parked the Jeep in the rear of the resort and got out. She stretched and said, "The muscles in my back are so tight. Jill, want to join me in the hot spring, or are you going for a swim?"

"No, the hot spring sounds like a wonderful idea. I think I'll join you. Give me a few minutes and I'll meet you there," Jill said.

They both walked to the main building and went to their rooms. Jill entered hers and turned on the lights. Her patio door was still open, and the evening breeze blew in, welcoming her. Jill set her purse down and walked outside. She could see the horses in the corral and wondered if Patches was in there too. She loved the horse, and wasn't surprised at all to discover it belonged to Kyle.

Her thoughts lingered on Kyle. Jill hugged herself as she thought about the embrace he had given her before. Bebe said he wanted to get to know her better, and Jill would have a hard time resisting him. She knew that she wanted to get to know him, too. She wanted to know how he took his coffee, did he like to sleep in late? what kind of movies did he like? and could he cook? Jill let her mind drift even further and wondered what his lips would feel like against hers, and did he get as much pleasure from holding her as she received from being held? She made her mind stop there, and stood up and went back inside.

Back in her room, she slipped out of her clothes and back into another bathing suit. Jill grabbed a towel and went to the hot spring to join Bebe. When she arrived, her friend was already in the water.

"Come in, Jill. It's perfect," Bebe said, cupping a handful of water and pouring it over her shoulder.

Nearby, patio lights glistened off the water, making it shimmer, and music filtered out from the Ranch House. The atmosphere made Jill realize that this was the rest and relaxation she had been dreaming of when she was back in New York. She stepped into the water and slowly lowered her body. She gave each inch of her tired form a chance to thoroughly enjoy the mystifying waters.

"Oh, Bebe, this is what we need to do every night," Jill said, leaning back in the comfortable water. "A few minutes of this and my body will be as good as new."

"We had a hard day, we should reward ourselves. Let's try to make this a ritual."

"Yes, every time we get a lot accomplished or just have a rough day, we'll come here to rejuvenate our tired souls," Jill said, laughing.

"What do we have to do tomorrow?"

"I have to go talk to the radio and television stations about running a spot. I also have to contact the newspapers to place an ad. These are excellent mediums for reaching people and we need to reach as many as we can. We have to reach as many visitors as we can, too."

"Why do we need to reach the visitors? They're only on vacation, and will be leaving soon," Bebe asked.

"Because if they enjoy their trip to Durango, they will more than likely return; and when they return, we want them to remember our name," Jill explained. Bebe nodded in understanding.

"The stations and papers that I use will also be invited to cover the event. We want to let people know about the resort and its amenities, as well as letting them know about the grand opening," Jill said.

"Let's try to start out a little earlier tomorrow."

"Good, I'll meet you in the Ranch House and after breakfast we'll leave," Jill suggested.

"That's fine by me. I don't know about you, but I'm ready to get out. I'm getting all wrinkled," Bebe said, examining her skin.

"Me too, I'm going to change and get something to drink," Jill said, getting out of the water and grabbing her towel.

"Are you going to the Ranch House now?"

"I really want to go back into town for a drink. I love the Ranch House, but I want to see more of town too."

"Great, we can go back into town. I could use a different atmosphere too," Bebe said. The two women went back to their rooms and agreed that whoever finished first would knock on the other's door.

Jill took a quick shower and dressed in a lavender-colored sleeveless dress that fell to five inches above her knees. She put on a beautiful pair of lavender and black Prada dress sandals and was ready to go. She grabbed the matching purse and put a few essentials in it. She dabbed on her perfume and left the room.

Jill was just about to knock on Bebe's door when she opened it. "Wow! Don't you look great?" Jill said. Bebe had on a burnt-orange skirt set. The top had spaghetti straps, and the skirt had a slit running up the side and showing off her beautiful long chocolate legs. "We're not trying to pick up any men, are we? Because you certainly are going to attract attention," Jill said, smiling.

"No, I just felt like looking tantalizing," Bebe said. Her makeup was done in soft natural tones, and her own shoulder-length hair was left flowing in a gentle flip. "I'm ready if you are."

They walked through the main building to the lobby and ran into Kyle, Tony, and Eric.

"You two look like you're going to get your party on," Tony said, looking at Bebe with an appreciative smile on his face.

"Actually, we're celebrating getting so much accomplished today," Jill told them. Though she tried to avoid Kyle's eyes she looked up, and as she suspected, they were fixed on her.

"Where are you going?" Tony asked.

"I thought I'd take Jill to Roland's. We're just going for drinks really," Bebe said.

Tony looked at her in disbelief and raised his eyebrows.

"Bebe, that place is known for its nightlife. They have great food and music, but the guys there are looking for one thing," Tony said.

"Tony, that may be true, but Jill and I are just looking to enjoy some music and have a drink."

"Would you mind if I tagged along? I'd love a change of scenery," Kyle said.

"Not at all Kyle; we'll wait for you," Bebe said. "Tony, you can come along too, if you promise not to be a pest."

"I'm not going to promise anything I can't deliver," he replied.

"Eric, you and Sharon should come too," Jill said.

"I want to go, but I'll have to run it by Sharon first," he said.

"I'll be ready in a minute," Kyle said. He hurried off to get ready, and his brothers followed close behind.

"Well, Jill, so much for it being just us," Bebe said as she leaned against the Jeep.

"That's all right, the more the merrier. Bebe, I think Tony really likes you," Jill said, smiling.

"I really like him too," Bebe said, hoping Jill would let the subject go.

"No, Bebe, I mean I think he's in love with you. I see the way he looks at you, and he is very protective of you too."

"What do you mean, Jill?"

"He's always kissing your hand, and just now he was worried that some other man would pick you up. Something is there between you two; either you're trying to hide it or you really don't see it."

Bebe blushed and turned her head from Jill. "You're right, I have been trying to hide it. I've been in love with him for years, and I know that he's in love with me too."

"So tell me where the problem is," Jill said, confused.

"The problem is that they are all like brothers to me. Like I told you, Jill, I don't have any family, and I don't want to ruin my relationship with them. Right now, what Tony and I have is safe. I don't expect anything more from him than I already have."

"But you could have so much more," Jill said.

Bebe smiled. "But I can't afford to lose what I do have. We'll talk about this later, here comes Kyle and Tony."

"Where?" Jill asked, looking around.

Realizing that Jill had no idea what Kyle drove, Bebe smiled and pointed, saying, "He's headed right toward us."

Jill looked at the midnight-blue Lincoln Navigator that pulled up in front of them. Kyle was driving, and Tony, Sharon, and Eric were in the back. Though she said nothing, she wondered how the ranch hand could afford such a vehicle.

"Ladies, your chariot awaits," Tony called out to them as he got out of the backseat and opened the doors for

Jill and Bebe to get in. Bebe got in the back and Jill sat up front with Kyle.

"This is a beautiful vehicle," Jill said to Kyle as she started to fasten her seat belt.

"Thank you, but I'm afraid that it's not as beautiful as you look tonight, Jill."

She blushed slightly, hoping Kyle wouldn't notice. She continued to fasten her seat belt. "So this Roland's is a fun place to go?" Jill asked.

"Yeah, it's a fun place all right, Jill. It's like I said, they have great food and great music. The atmosphere definitely puts you into a happy thank-God-it's-Friday mood, but the guys are always on the prowl," Tony said.

Jill gave Bebe an I-told-you-so glance and then turned back around in her seat.

Jill glanced over at Kyle, who sat quietly as he drove. The music was low, and he had a faint smile on his face. Sensing Jill's eye's on him, he turned and looked at her. Though he said nothing, his smile broadened and he returned his attention to the road.

Jill crossed her legs and pressed herself firmly against the back of her seat. Eric, Sharon, Tony, and Bebe were all engaged in conversation, but Jill was lost in her own thoughts. What was it about Kyle that made her want to run away as fast as she could, but not so fast that he couldn't catch her? He could mesmerize her with just his smile. Every time he looked at her, it was as if he were staring at the center of her very soul, knowing just what she needed and how to give it to her.

She looked out the window, realizing that outside of the obvious physical attraction she felt, she knew little about the man sitting next to her. Would she get to know him better, and would she dare let him get to know her? Though he could make her laugh and was well spoken, was Kyle Roberts even able to hold her attention intellectually? Jill never considered herself to be a shallow person, but knew that a couple should be intellectually equal for a relationship to have longevity.

"Bebe, did you ask Eric and Sharon about Saturday?" Kyle asked, bringing Jill's attention back to the group.

"No, Kyle, I hadn't had a chance to. We're all going white-water rafting on Saturday, would you two like to come along?"

"Do we have anything going on Saturday, babe?" Eric asked his wife.

"No, I don't think so. I'd love to go rafting. We haven't been in a long time," Sharon said.

"Great, I'll make the reservations for all of us," Kyle told them. He pulled up into the parking lot of Roland's. It was full and they could hear the music coming from inside. After driving around for a few minutes, Kyle finally found a parking place.

The group exited the Navigator and went inside. The atmosphere inside Roland's was just as Tony had described. The music was loud and everyone was on the dance floor. Jill could smell wonderful food, and noticed guys eyeing Bebe and herself as they entered. She was immediately thankful that Kyle and his brothers had decided to come with them. Though the idea was to get a drink and enjoy each other's company, Jill had a feeling that she and Bebe would have spent most of their time fighting off unwanted advances if they didn't have escorts.

There weren't any tables available, so the group made their way to the bar. The guys all ordered a beer, and Bebe and Sharon both had rum and Coke. Jill had her usual, Chambord and soda with lime.

The beat of the music had found its way to Tony, who started dancing by himself. Unable to suppress the urge to hit the dance floor any longer, he grabbed Bebe's hand and said, "Come on, Bebe, girl, let's show them how we do it."

Bebe smiled reluctantly, but followed Tony to the dance floor. Jill watched as the two moved to the music. She had no idea that Bebe was such a good dancer. She and Tony moved in such a way that Jill realized that they had shared many dances together.

"We're not going to let them show us up. Come on, Eric," Sharon said as she grabbed her husband's hand. Jill saw that Sharon liked to be in control, and Eric obviously didn't mind.

With another swallow of his beer, he said, "I'm right behind you, honey." The dancing between Eric and Sharon was more sensual. Sharon raised her arms above her head, and Eric rubbed his hands slowly down her body until they rested on her hips. He pulled her close to him, and then she turned and pressed her back into his chest. He kissed her neck softly, and Sharon smiled. Reaching back, she gently played in her husband's hair. It was all too erotic for Jill to watch, feeling as if she were peeking into their bedroom. She turned her head and took a sip of her drink. As she looked up, she found Kyle staring at her in amusement.

"And what's so funny, Mr. Roberts?" she asked. Jill hoped that he didn't notice her discomfort at watching his brother and his wife.

"No, nothing is funny. I was just thinking that as beautiful as you look right now, you should be on that dance floor, too. May I have the pleasure of this dance, Ms. Alexander?"

Her first instinct was to say no, but her mouth and heart worked in unison and she said, "I'd love to." Jill set her drink down, and Kyle took her hand and led her to the floor. A fast song was playing and the floor was packed. They made their way through the crowd and began to dance. Jill quickly noticed that Kyle was an excellent dancer. He didn't try to rub and grind on her, which would have sent her running. Instead, he made a few moves up of his own, which made her laugh. She let herself go, letting herself enjoy the music, the atmosphere, and the man.

The music ended, and a slow song began. The dance floor began to empty except for a few couples. Jill turned to walk away, but Kyle caught her hand. His eyes were soft and pleading, and she felt herself being pulled into his masculine embrace. Her mind flashed back to the night at the pool, when he pulled her close to him. She remembered how she enjoyed his touch, and right now her body ached to be held by him again. Kyle said nothing, but gently continued to embrace her. Jill let herself delight in his touch. She closed her eyes and let the warmth of his body pleasure hers. They danced slowly, but not erotically. Jill had no idea how long the song lasted, but at that moment it was as if they were the only two people in the room.

The song ended, and Kyle released her from his arms. Reluctantly, Jill stepped away, and the two became aware that Bebe, Tony, Sharon, and Eric were watching them. Jill waited for her old familiar feeling of embarrassment or being uncomfortable to return, but it didn't. She felt good, and she hoped that Kyle felt the same way. Barbie's advice was working. She was allowing herself to enjoy life.

As they returned to the bar, no one said anything to them. The music returned to its quick tempo, and the dance floor was flooded again. The three couples finished their drinks and talked about everything imaginable. Knowing that they all had a big day ahead of them tomorrow, they left Roland's early and headed back to the resort.

The drive back was still filled with lots of conversation. Jill could hear Bebe laughing as Tony told one funny anecdote after another, making everyone in the vehicle burst into laughter. Tony had a natural gift for imitating people and was telling the story about one of the ranch hands. He had an uninhibited personality, and Jill thought that he and Bebe would make a wonderful couple. She wished that Bebe would consider letting their relationship go further.

When they arrived at the resort, Kyle pulled to the curb in front of the building. He left the Navigator running and put it in park. He got out and went around to open the door first for Jill and then for Bebe. The women got out and he closed the doors behind them.

Bebe took a few steps away, but Jill stood there, expecting Kyle would want to tell her how much he enjoyed her company, or maybe he wanted to tell her he couldn't wait to see her again. Instead, he turned and started back to the driver's side of the vehicle and said, "Good night, ladies, see you tomorrow at breakfast." Kyle jumped back into the driver's seat and drove off.

Jill turned around and saw Bebe trying to suppress a giggle. "What are you laughing at?" she said.

"Come on, Jill, admit it, you were expecting more just now, weren't you?"

"I don't know what you're talking about."

"It's written all over your face. I don't know if it was a kiss, a hug, or just an I enjoyed your company, Jill, but you thought there would be more."

"You know what? I was. And for the first time since I can remember, I really let myself enjoy a man's company," Jill said, smiling.

Bebe slipped her arm through Jill's, and the two women started walking toward their rooms. "I'm happy for you, girlfriend. You deserve all the happiness a man has to give."

"Well, so do you. I saw you and Tony out there on the floor. You two move together as if one was just made for the other."

"I don't know about all that, but I did enjoy myself," Bebe said.

"I enjoyed myself too. I'll see you bright and early in the morning, Bebe."

"The Ranch House?"

"The Ranch House. Good night."

"Good night, Jill," Bebe said, and they went into their rooms.

Chapter 12

In her room, Jill quickly took a shower and slipped into a beautiful white silk nightgown. She wanted desperately to call someone and tell them of the wonderful night she had had, but it was way too late. She walked over to the patio doors and opened them. She stepped out and gazed up at the stars. A gentle breeze greeted her, catching her silk nightgown in its wind and making her mind think instantly of Kyle.

Tonight she had seen a funnier side of him, when he decided to create some of his own dance moves. He was definitely a gentlemen, and obviously well spoken for a ranch hand. She sensed he was more educated than his profession let on. Jill had many unanswered questions about the handsome cowboy. She decided that she did want to get to know him better. A smile played across her face as she came to that conclusion.

Jill walked back inside and left the sliding glass door open. She pulled back the bedding and climbed in. She reached over and turned out the light on the nightstand. As she closed her eyes, her mind was filled with thought of things that could be. She fell asleep with dreams of love and passion, of things that could be included in her life, only if she let love have its way with her.

* * *

Sunlight glistened into Jill's window, and the rays played across the floor, inviting her to get up and go outside. Jill stretched and smiled to herself. She was falling more in love with this place.

She looked at the clock and quickly picked up the phone. Though it was early, she imagined that Barbie was up and tending to the kids. Jill dialed her sister's number and hoped Barbie was already awake.

"Hello," Barbie said on the other end.

"Hey, sis, it's me."

"I had a feeling it was you calling."

"Did I wake you up?"

"Are you kidding? Lacy beat you to the punch about an hour ago; of course she woke James up before she woke me. Jill, thanks for all the wonderful gifts, the kids just love them."

"I can't believe that you got them already."

"I want to give you a special thank-you for the ring; it's beautiful, Jill!"

"You're welcome, sis."

"Before I forget, thank you for Ricky's gift too."

Jill smiled to herself, knowing exactly what Barbie meant. "I couldn't resist, Barbie," she said as she let out a chuckle.

"You sound mighty happy, what's up?"

"Well, I guess I am. I took your advice."

"You did? Tell me more, what's going on out there?" Barbie asked excitedly.

"I met someone, Barbie, and he seems really nice. His name is Kyle, and he is a cowboy."

"A cowboy, huh? I didn't take you as one to fall for the cowboy type. He must be quite handsome."

"He's tall, dark, and handsome, not to mention smart, funny, and a gentleman. Barbie, I am so attracted to this guy. He's like no one else I've ever met. In a way, I guess that's what's scaring me."

"Don't let it, Jill. Just relax and enjoy yourself. He hasn't proposed marriage yet, has he?"

"No, of course not."

"Well then, keep enjoying the ride. By the time you get back to New York, you'll be happy you did. Who knows? Maybe more will come of it, but for right now enjoy it. I know I would," Barbie said, making Jill laugh and appreciate the wisdom of her older sister.

"Thanks, Barbie, you always know just what to say. You're so smart."

"That's because I'm older."

"Then I'll never catch up with you. I'll always be a few years behind in the brains department," Jill said, making Barb laugh.

"I have to go; Lacy is trying to make her own oatmeal. I love you, Jill."

"I'll see you later, sis, love you too," Jill replied and hung up the phone.

She glanced at the clock and saw that she was running late. Jill jumped out of bed and dressed quickly. She knew that Bebe was probably at the Ranch House waiting for her, so she hurried to meet her.

As she walked through the doors of the restaurant, she wasn't surprised to see Bebe waiting. Jill walked over to her friend and sat down.

"Bebe, I'm so sorry. Have you been waiting long?"

"Not at all, I just got here a few minutes ago. I guess I was pretty worn out from last night. The guys haven't been in yet either, but I think they have a lot to do today."

"Well, we have a lot to cover today, too, Bebe. I want to make a call to the radio and television stations, but hopefully I can just fax the information to the newspaper."

"I agree, it's going to be a very busy day. I want you to listen to Tomahawk's CD, so that you will have an idea of what will be playing at the grand opening."

"Fine by me; we can do that as soon as we get to your office, then I'll make my calls."

"Once I figure out who the inside band will be, then all we have to do is the little stuff like check the wine and champagne to see if it's what you want, and if we have enough on hand."

"Right, Bebe, I also want to see the china we'll be using. Do you think we'll have enough?" Jill asked.

"I'm sure of it; I was hoping we could use Styrofoam plates and cups for the guests outside. If we do that, we have more than enough."

"That's appropriate since they'll be by the pool," Jill agreed.

Grace returned with their orders and set them down. "I'll be right back with your orange juice and coffee," she told them.

"This looks wonderful. Thanks, Gracie," Jill said.

Grace stopped in her tracks and turned to look at Jill; a wide smile formed on her face. "Only family calls me Gracie." She winked at Jill and continued on her way to get their beverages.

Jill smiled at Bebe. "Since I'm family now, would you mind telling what Bebe is short for?"

"Bebe is short for Rebecca. Tony gave me the nickname a long time ago, and it just stuck."

"Well, I like it, and it fits you," Jill said as she quickly blessed her food and began to eat.

Grace returned with their beverages and told them to let her know if they needed anything else. Jill and Bebe ate and discussed what they needed to accomplish.

When they were finished with their meal, they headed straight for Bebe's office, anxious to get started.

Bebe walked over to her stereo and put in the CD. "This is Tomahawk's latest, *Broken Arrow.* I think you'll like it, Jill. It's keeping our theme for the grand opening intact."

The music filled the room with the soft beat of a drum, combined with the gentle sound of a flute. "This track is called 'Pounding Heart,'" Bebe said. This time she offered no summary of what Jill was about to hear. She listened as the sound of a sultry flute filled the air. It was joined by a viola and the low beat of a drum. A man's voice sang softly, and Jill's gaze drifted outside. The man's alto voice sang of his love for a woman, and that he would follow her to the ends of the earth until she agreed to be his. He professed his love for her and called her his pounding heart. He said that like any man, without his pounding heart he would fall dead. The song ended with the faint beating of a drum.

"So, Jill, what do you think?"

Jill flinched, startled at the sound of Bebe's voice. She had taken her own sojourn into her soul and only returned when she heard Bebe speak. "I love it, Bebe. I think I want this CD, too."

"I'll get you an autographed copy," Bebe said, smiling.

"Won't they be great outside near the pool?" Jill asked.

"They'll be perfect out there. Their music will create a natural, Native American ambiance."

"Can I use your phone? I have to make those calls to the stations."

"Sure," Bebe said, handing Jill the telephone and the list of numbers she needed to call. "Do you think they will be able to fit you in today?"

"I don't know, but at least I can make an appointment," Jill said as she dialed the number to Channel 4. The phone rang several times before the operator answered. Jill held a brief conversation, before she hung up the phone with a satisfied smile on her face.

"Bebe, this just keeps getting better and better," Jill said.

Bebe looked up from her work and smiled, but said nothing. Jill was already dialing the radio station. When they answered the phone, Jill asked to speak to the advertising department. After a short conversation, Jill said, "All right, Charmaine, I'll be there within the hour." She smiled smugly as she hung up the phone.

"Bebe, this is coming together so smoothly. I should start worrying now," Jill said.

"Why would you start worrying? I thought you said that everything was coming together smoothly."

"Yes, but I also said that you either get a smooth start or a bumpy finish, you don't get both at either end," Jill said, smiling. "Right now I guess I just have to enjoy the smooth ride."

"Do you mind if I tag along?"

"What do you mean tag along? We're partners, *mi amiga*. This project is a joint effort," Jill said. "Besides, although I wrote down the directions, I would probably still get lost."

"Let me get my purse and we'll be on our way," Bebe said, thankful to be reminded of her importance in this project. Once again, she noticed how gently and unwittingly Jill made people feel like their thoughts and opinions counted to her. Bebe had never met anyone as generous as her new friend.

Jill and Bebe grabbed their purses and headed out to the parking lot. The morning sun was high in the sky. Though the weather was hot, there was a gentle breeze greeting them. Jill looked up to see huge beautiful clouds drifting by. It was the same type of day that had greeted her when she arrived at the ranch. She got into the Jeep realizing that she no longer just admired this place for its beauty, but she had actually fallen in love with it.

As Bebe started the engine, Jill looked off toward the corral in hopes of seeing Kyle. The men were rounding up the horses. Through the thick clouds of dust, she could not determine if he was out there or not. Bebe tapped her on the shoulder and pointed toward the south end of the corral. Jill looked and could see Kyle working hard.

Bebe backed out of the parking spot and Jill continued to look at Kyle. Was she falling in love with A Special Place, or was she falling in love with Kyle? One was safe to love, and the other she perceived as hazardous.

"You're falling for him, Jill, aren't you?" Bebe asked softly.

"I think I am, Bebe, but right now isn't a good time for me to fall in love," Jill said. She fixed her eyes on the road. Jill tried desperately to stay focused on her own dreams, but knew each time she was close to Kyle, they seemed to fade in importance. She didn't want her dreams and aspirations to disappear like her sister's.

"Jill, you can have it all."

"Maybe, but I don't want to risk it," was all she offered before she changed the subject. "Bebe, do you want to record the spot for the commercial?" Jill said, smiling and handing Bebe the directions.

Bebe laughed and said, "Jill, you have to be kidding. I could never do something like that. I don't have the voice for it," she answered, quickly looking over the directions before getting on the main road.

"You have a beautiful voice, and I think your love for the ranch will be apparent to the listeners when they hear you."

"You're not kidding, are you?"

"No, I'm not kidding. You're knowledgeable about the subject and you have a passion for it. I think you should do it," Jill said honestly.

"Well, let me think on it a bit. I've never done anything like this before, and I don't want to mess up for the ranch by sounding like a fool."

"If I thought you would sound like a fool, I never would have suggested you do it. Bebe, you will sound great and you'll do a great job for the ranch. Can you imagine the guys' faces when they hear your voice?"

"Yeah, they'll probably all start laughing," Bebe said as she rubbed her forehead.

"I can think of one cowboy who won't laugh."

"Tony will be the one laughing the loudest."

"I think he would support you in this, especially if he knew you felt strongly about it too."

"I do feel strongly about it, and I would love to do it. I just want this opening to be perfect. If you think I won't come across sounding like an idiot, then I'll do it," Bebe said. She was still unsure if she was making the right choice, but she trusted Jill's instincts.

"Great, we won't tell them about this. We'll wait until it airs to get their reaction. Don't worry, Bebe, I'm sure it will all be positive."

"You're the professional, Jill. I'm going to trust you on this one," Bebe said as calmly as she could. She refused to reveal how nervous she was.

"Did you make any progress getting another band lined up for the opening?"

"Yes, I did. While you were on the phone I e-mailed two agents from local bands. I'm hoping that we'll hear something from them by the time we return. I gave them all the pertinent information."

"When we get back, let's try to check the bar to see if we have enough champagne, wine, and liquor."

"That sounds good. I want to show you the table linens that we have, as well as the china. Let me know if we need to change anything or if you think we don't have enough of something. If I put a rush on it, I can probably have it by the opening," Bebe told her.

"I guess we only have a few things to check on and we'll be ready. Or I should say as ready as we can be."

"Jill, stop being so negative. You're doing a great job, and everything is going to turn out beautifully," Bebe re-assured her. "You're great at what you do. I know this because Davis, Sterling, and Roberts wouldn't have gone to such great lengths to get you if you weren't. What I don't understand is why you are so nervous about this opening. I know that you've done this type of work before, and you always make the company shine. I just don't . . . Hey, wait a minute. I think I'm finally seeing the big picture here," Bebe said as she came to her own revelation.

Jill looked over at Bebe, not knowing where she was going with the conversation. "What on earth are you talking about?" she said.

"There is a lot more riding on this opening than just your reputation; there's Kyle Roberts to consider," Bebe said knowingly.

"Bebe, how does Kyle fit into my work?"

"You would do your best work no matter if there was a man involved or not. But you want to leave a lasting impression on Kyle too. He works here, and you want him to see you at your very best."

Jill said nothing, but continued to stare out her window smiling.

"Judging from your silence, I would have to say that I hit the nail right on the head," Bebe added.

Jill finally turned around to face her friend. With the smile still on her face, she said, "Bebe, what am I going to do? I love Durango and I could easily fall for Kyle."

"I think you have already fallen for Kyle. You mean you don't want to let your heart take control of your head, because if it does, Cupid will have his way with both of you. I see the way he looks at you, Jill. He's already yours. All you have to do is reel him in."

"I know he's interested, but—"

"Don't think that you don't play an intricate part in this love game," Bebe said, cutting Jill off. "I see how you look at him too. Even as we were leaving the resort, you couldn't wait to lay eyes on him. Your brain keeps telling you no, but your heart might have something else in mind."

Chapter 13

They entered the radio station and were greeted by the receptionist. Jill asked for Charmaine Perry, then she and Bebe had a seat in the reception area. After a few minutes of waiting, Charmaine arrived.

She introduced herself and shook their hands, then led them to her office. Charmaine was a very attractive woman, who Jill guessed was a Pueblo Native American, with thick black hair hitting her backside as she walked. She was a friendly woman, yet was all about business and was anxious to get started on the commercial. She offered them something to drink, and as they discussed the ad, Charmaine handed Jill a contract, which Jill read thoroughly and saw what the station planned to deliver and what they charged.

"Do you have any questions?" Charmaine asked.

"No, it's all clear to me," Jill replied. She took a pen from Charmaine's desk and signed the contract. "I'll mail a check to you within a couple of days."

Bebe looked at Charmaine nervously and said, "I'm ready when you are," as she took a long drink of her water.

"Fine, let's get started then," Charmaine said as she led Bebe out of her office.

Jill gave Bebe the thumbs-up sign as she left the room, but Bebe still looked a little hesitant. After they were gone, Jill sat and thought of Kyle. Bebe was right, her heart did have other plans for her. She could feel herself giving in every time she was near him. Each time she saw him or smelled him she wanted to make love to him.

She forced the thoughts of Kyle reluctantly from her mind, making herself concentrate on the job she was hired to do. Glancing at her watch, she wondered how the radio commercial was coming along.

Just then, Bebe entered the lobby smiling. Charmaine was close behind her and it was obvious that the recording was a big success.

"I can tell by the look on your face that you achieved perfection," Jill said as she stood.

"We'll have to call it perfection, for lack of a better word," Bebe said, beaming. She picked up her purse and thanked Charmaine for her assistance.

Jill shook Charmaine's hand good-bye and the two women left the building. They walked to the station's parking lot and climbed into the Jeep. Jill had exactly fifteen minutes to get back to the resort before her one o'clock appointment. They had missed lunch, and decided not to eat until after the appointment with Don Ashton of Channel 4.

Bebe drove back to the resort as fast as she could. Though they were five minutes late, Don had not arrived yet. Bebe quickly parked, and the two women decided to go to their rooms to freshen up. As they reached the front of the resort, Don pulled up in a van with the Channel 4 logo on it.

"Well, I guess Don will just have to take us as we are," Jill said.

"We don't look too bad. Come on, let's go introduce ourselves," Bebe said.

The van parked and three men exited and walked to

the entrance of the resort. "Excuse me, do you know where I might find Jill Alexander?" Don asked.

"You've found her," Jill said, extending her hand to Don.

"Hello, Ms. Alexander. It's nice to meet you. I'm Don Ashton," he said, firmly shaking Jill's hand.

"This is my coworker, Bebe Simmons," Jill said.

Bebe held out her hand and greeted Don also. "It's nice to meet you, Don. Thanks for coming."

"It's my pleasure. Actually, any station would have jumped at the chance to do this assignment. This place is exquisite. When it opens, you'll be booked for months in advance. I'm sure we can capture all the beauty and charm that this resort has to offer." With a slight wave of his hand, Don introduced the man to his right. "Ms. Alexander, Ms. Simmons, this is Fred. He's the best cameraman around." Fred held a television camera, so he couldn't offer a hand to shake. Instead, he nodded his head in greeting. "And this is Bobby, Fred's assistant," Don added.

Though he was holding cords for Fred, Bobby still managed a hand free to shake hands. "It's nice to meet you both," he said.

"It's nice to meet you too, Bobby," Jill replied.

"Well, let's get down to business," Don said. "If it's possible, I would like to get a tour of the property. As we go, please let me know of any areas of the property that you would want highlighted. Does that sound all right?"

"That sounds perfect," Jill agreed.

The group walked around to the front of the property. Jill wanted to be sure that the opening shot was of the front of the resort. It was a breathtaking view, with the sun-kissed mountains glistening in the background. From there they went into the main lobby. Both Jill and

Bebe wanted to include it in the commercial, as well as the main dining room. Aside from showing off the ranch's rugged beauty, they wanted to include its elegance as well.

Don and his coworkers were amply impressed with the tour they were receiving. Though they hadn't started filming yet, their eyes gave away just how in awe they were of A Special Place. Bebe smiled constantly as she and Jill led the three men toward the spa. She made sure they noted the indoor pool, steam rooms, hot tubs, and massage and sauna areas. They went through the rear exit of the building and headed toward the outdoor pool.

They came to Jill's favorite part of the resort, the ranch. Though she loved every aspect of the place, she had come to love the Ranch House Restaurant the most. It was where she would meet her friends and unwind. And of course, it was where she always ran into Kyle. She smiled and followed the group inside the Ranch House. Kyle wasn't there, and Jill was disappointed at not seeing him. "The Ranch House is a more relaxed dining experience for our guests. It is currently used only by employees, but when the resort opens, guests will be welcome to patronize it as well," she said, putting her disappointment aside and continuing on with her work.

Finally, the small group came to the corral and stables. The ranch hands were busy working, but Jill still didn't see Kyle. "We have quite a few horses for the guests to choose from," Bebe explained, noticing that they had momentarily lost Jill's attention.

"Yes, and the trails are wonderful and range from the very experienced horseman, to the novice," she added. Realizing that she was paying more attention to Kyle's whereabouts than to her job, Jill tried to stay focused on what she was being paid to do.

Feeling as though he had an idea of what the two women wanted included in the piece, Don told them that they would start filming. "Have you decided who will be doing the commercial?" he asked.

Jill only smiled as Bebe said, "That will be me."

"Great, after we're finished filming, I'll need you to come down to the station and view the tape first. If you like what we've done, then you can do the voice-over," Don told her.

"That sounds good, Don. Will I be doing it today?"

"Oh no, after we're done filming we have to take the tape back to the station and edit it. After we're finished editing, then we'll have you take a look at it and do your voice-over."

"About how long do you anticipate this will take?" Jill asked, worried about her time line. "Unfortunately, I need to have the commercial running soon."

"We'll have it running in the next couple of days, that is, if Ms. Simmons can come down to the station tomorrow afternoon."

"I can be there, Don, but will you be ready for me so quickly?"

"Ordinarily, I couldn't be, but for A Special Place, I'll personally put a rush on everything," he said, still thrilled to be the only television station covering the grand opening of the hot, new resort.

"Thanks, Don, I really appreciate it," Jill said as she extended her hand once again to shake Don's. Bebe did the same. "If you need anything, just let us know," Jill told them.

"And if you want to get something to eat or drink, just come on over to the Ranch House," Bebe added. Then she and Jill headed over to the restaurant themselves.

Jill looked at her watch and saw that it was already three-thirty. She was starving and couldn't wait to sit down and eat. As she entered the restaurant, the air-conditioned room took the heat out of her skin. She welcomed the cool air and the fact that the restaurant was practically empty. When she had brought the camera crew in earlier, there had been more people, but she was happy that was not the case now. No music was playing, and she and Bebe were almost the only ones there. They sat in the first booth they came to. Looking into each other's tired eyes, they started to laugh.

"I am exhausted." Jill sighed.

"Me too. I think it's because we've been on the go since early this morning, we've been out in the sun for several hours with nothing to drink, and we missed lunch. I think we have a right to be exhausted," Bebe said, leaning back in her seat. "But it does feel good getting so much accomplished."

Jill smiled back and said, "Yes, it does. Are you sad that the project is so demanding?"

"Not at all. I haven't had this much fun in a long time. I can't image you doing all this by yourself, though."

"I do it all the time, Bebe, but I'm used to it. Working with you has made this assignment my most memorable yet," she said sincerely.

"I still wish you never had to go back to New York. When you leave, it'll feel like I'm losing a sister," Bebe said. Her eyes brimmed with tears.

"Bebe, please don't think of my going back to New York as the end of our friendship. I feel as close to you as you do me. We'll stay in touch, you'll see," Jill said. She went to Bebe and gave her a hug. Jill was genuinely touched by the fact that Bebe considered her as close as a sister. She handed Bebe a napkin and grabbed one for herself before she sat back down. She didn't know how they would control their emotions when Bebe had to take her back to the airport.

"What are you two blubbering about?" Grace said tersely.

Jill and Bebe looked up to see Grace standing next to their table. Though her manner was harsh, they knew that that was just Grace's nature. They also knew that the woman couldn't possibly realize just how close they had become.

"Oh, Grace, I just think we both know that we're going to miss each other a lot when Jill goes back to New York," Bebe said. She continued to dry her eyes, trying not to rub them red.

"You two are as close as peas in a pod. I don't see how geography can destroy your bond," Grace said. "Now, what can I get you?" she said, her eyes never leaving her pad. Jill and Bebe hadn't ordered, but Grace continued to write. She held the pad a little closer to her face, fearful that they would see the tears in her eyes, too. She too had grown fond of the friendly New Yorker and had hoped she would stay with them.

"What's the special today, Grace?" Bebe asked, finally drying her eyes.

"Barbecued pork sandwich, fries, and coleslaw," she answered quickly.

"I'll have that," Bebe said.

"I'll have the same," Jill told her.

"I'll be right back," Grace said and quickly disappeared.

"She didn't ask what we wanted to drink," Jill said.

"She was crying too, Jill. I guess she doesn't want to see you go either."

"Oh, Bebe, I didn't know she was crying. I don't understand why she would be."

"Everyone is happy you've come out here, Jill. Aside from Grace being sad to see you go, she's probably sad to see us so unhappy too."

"I didn't think she would feel so deeply about my leaving though."

"You have that affect on people, Jill. You've made me feel like there's nothing I can't do. You've taught me how to be a more kind and gracious person, and that it's all right to share the spotlight with others. You've taught me that the gifts I should cherish most are the ones that don't diminish when shared with others. I have grown as a person because of you. You've taught me all of this in just a few short weeks and you've affected Grace and others in the same way. How can we not be sad to see you go?"

Jill turned and looked at Grace, who sat waiting for Jill's order to be prepared by the cook. Treating others as you would want others to treat you was one of the commandments her father had instilled in her. Only now had she any idea how profound a meaning the words had. Silently, Grace had let her know just how much she cared for her.

Grace turned and looked in Jill's direction. The woman stood and walked back over to their table. "I'm such a bubble brain; I forgot to ask what you'd like to drink," she said, trying to speak in her usual, offhanded way, but Jill could see right through her now.

"I'd like iced tea, a really big one, Gracie," Jill said, smiling at the woman.

"And I'll have a lemonade, the same size please," Bebe added.

"I'll be right back with your orders," Grace said. She rested her hand on Jill's shoulder briefly, then walked back toward the kitchen.

Jill fought the urge to hug Grace. She didn't want to make her cry again. Jill knew that leaving would be hard on her too. She had never become close with any of her clients, and once again was caught in not understanding something. Why was this place so special to her? And why was she so special to the people here? It had all happened so fast that she didn't have time to figure any of it out. Her heart was taking her on a fast, furious, and amazing journey that left her mind in a whirlwind.

"Grace is right about one thing," Bebe said, breaking the silence. "Geography won't break our bond."

"No, it won't, Bebe."

"Here we go, ladies," Grace said. She placed two of the biggest mugs they had ever seen on the table. "You asked for really big ones, and here they are. Let me know if you need a refill," she said, laughing as she walked away. "I'll be right back with your food," she yelled over her shoulder.

"Wow!" Jill said, laughing.

"I guess we should have asked for a medium," Bebe said, looking at the drinks in amazement. "I didn't think we had mugs this size."

"I guess we won't be asking for refills any time soon," she joked.

They were thankful that Grace managed to lighten the mood, and shortly she returned with their order. As they ate, they laughed and talked about their day and made plans for the following morning. The Ranch House started to fill up just as they finished their meal. Jill wondered if the television crew was still at the resort. They hadn't come in for anything to eat or drink, so she decided to see how the filming was coming along.

The two women left the restaurant and went in search of Don and his crew. They walked to the front of the resort and saw that the station van was gone.

"That was quick. I hope they didn't forget to film anything," Bebe said.

"I'm sure they didn't. Don seems just as excited about the opening as we are. He'll make sure everything goes off without a hitch," Jill said confidently. "We should go back to your office and finish up for the day."

"Fine by me," Bebe said.

They walked back to Bebe's office and got right to work. It was approaching early evening and both were anxious to end the long workday. Bebe checked her messages and was excited to hear from both bands.

"Jill, I got a reply back from both bands. City Slickers' agent says that they are already booked. I got a yes from Gentlemen of the Four Corners."

"Good, do you know anything about them?"

"Yes, they're a local band. I've seen them perform a couple of times. I know of about a dozen local bands, but I categorized them from my most to least favorite. Thankfully, two of my top three can do the opening," Bebe said, satisfied with how she was handling her end of the job.

"Do you have one of their CDs?" Jill said.

"As a matter of fact I just got it. It's in my room. I'll run and get it."

"No, Bebe, you don't have to do that now. I can listen to it later."

"It's no trouble. It will only take me a minute. I'll be right back." Bebe quickly left the office.

Jill stretched in her chair and turned and looked out the window. She rubbed her temples and tried desperately to make sense of everything that was going on around her. It wasn't the assignment, everything was going along smoothly. She loved working with Bebe, but hadn't planned on getting so attached to her. She hadn't gotten this close to anyone outside her family since Lois and Diane. Jill knew it would kill her to leave A Special Place. She loved the free and easy style of the ranch and all the people on it.

She continued to stare out the window, and once

again her gigantic clouds put on a show for her. They created such beautiful shapes in the sky that she found it hard to keep her eyes off of them. Jill knew in her heart that one of the people she would miss the most would be Kyle. Perhaps if she were further along in her own career goals she would have found it a little easier to let herself be swept off her feet. But for now, she would do exactly as Barbie had instructed her to do: enjoy the ride.

Smiling, Bebe returned with the CD. "Jill, I think you're going to love this group too." She quickly put the disc into the CD player and adjusted the volume. Gentlemen of the Four Corners' music was a mixture of western, country, and R&B, and they played all genres very well.

"Bebe, they're wonderful. I would be up dancing to their music too, if I weren't so tired."

"I'm glad you like them. Do you want me to e-mail them and seal the deal?"

"Yes, and we'll have to have both groups sign a contact."

"I was wondering about that. I'm not sure what to do on that end."

"I'll e-mail Lois and have her overnight express both groups a standard contact, with instructions to send the signed contact to us at the resort," Jill said. She turned around to her laptop and started typing out an e-mail. "Do you have an address where both groups can be reached?"

"I have it right here," Bebe said and handed the address to Jill.

Jill finished typing and included a personal hello to her buddy. "There," she said, clicking the send button. "I think that takes care of that. Now how do you feel about going to check on the wine and champagne lists?"

"All right," Bebe replied tiredly.

"Come on, girl. That's the last thing we have to do today, and then the rest of the evening is ours," Jill promised.

"Good, then I have a date with the hot spring. My back is killing me, and I sure could use a nice soak," Bebe said. She raised her tired body out of her chair and followed Jill to the main dining room.

Jill quickly went over the wine list and saw that the restaurant had quite an extensive and impressive list. She hoped, as she followed Bebe into the cellar, that everything that was named on the list was actually in the cellar. As she walked through the cellar Jill counted the cases and found that every bottle of wine, champagne, and top-shelf liquor was accounted for.

"I think there is more than enough here to take care of the grand opening," Jill said thankfully.

"And for those who are dining outside, the Ranch House will be providing beer. I already checked with Grace and she said she would let her manager know that their service would be needed."

"My, my, Ms. Simmons, aren't you the efficient one?"

"Ah yes, that would be me," Bebe said, laughing.

Bebe showed Jill the table linens and china she hoped they would be using for the grand opening. Everything met with Jill's approval, and she felt as though they had more than enough china for the guests being served in the main dining room.

"Bebe, let's get some much-deserved rest," Jill announced when they'd finished. She entwined her arm in Bebe's as they headed toward their rooms.

"Jill, I'm really wiped out. I think I'm going to go to my room and take a nap," Bebe said.

"I'm tired too. I think I'll do the same, but I have to make a few phone calls first."

"Do you need to go back to my office?"

"No, I can make them from my room. I'll see you later, Bebe. Thanks for everything," Jill said. She and Bebe separated, each happy to have accomplished so much.

Jill entered her room and opened the sliding glass doors. She walked into the bathroom and undressed, leaving on only her underclothes. She washed her hands and face and then went back into the bedroom. She looked outside and saw the horses grazing peacefully. The sun was beginning to set, and the mountains would soon lose their golden hue. Jill would miss this view. Every time she looked at the mountains or trees, the horses, and the clouds, she instantly felt at peace with herself. The Colorado sky stretched on endlessly, and at nightfall it always put on a spectacular show of twinkling stars.

She couldn't remember ever seeing stars in New York. She tried hard to recall, but the only thing that came to mind was the dazzling Broadway and Times Square lights. Though they were beautiful in their own right, nothing could compare to the show Mother Nature could put on.

She lay across the bed and grabbed the phone, deciding to call her parents first.

"Hello?"

"Barbie?" Jill said, surprised.

"Yeah, Jill, it's me. How is everything going?"

"Great. How are Mom and Dad?"

"They're fine. Dad is right here. Hold and I'll let you speak to him," Barbie said.

A moment later, her dad was on the phone. "Hi, baby girl," he said, instantly making Jill wish she could see his face and hope that next week could come sooner then it would. "I just wanted to let you know that I'll be back in Pittsburgh next Thursday."

"That's fine, I'll be sure to pick you up from the airport. Your mother is in the shower, but I'll tell her you said hello."

"Thanks, Dad. I'll see you soon. I love you."

"I love you, too, baby girl. Good-bye," he said and hung up the phone.

Jill hung up too and laid her head back on the pillow and fell asleep. She hoped for a peaceful sleep, a restful sleep; instead her mind was flooded with dreams. She tossed and turned as one vision after another filled her mind.

She dreamed of raging rapids tossing the little craft that carried her out into a rough sea. She held on tightly, even though an evil sea witch tried to pry her fingers open. It seemed as if she put up the tiring fight to save herself for days, but the evil sea witch was unrelenting. Finally, the rough waves tossed her close enough to shore and a huge tree bowed its branches and pulled her from the tiny sea-ravaged vessel.

Then Jill's mind took her on another confusing dream. She was falling down a deep black hole. She waited and waited, wondering when she would stop, and was afraid of the terrible landing she would receive. She clawed out at the wall, but it was just an illusion.

Jill's body jerked and then stiffened in bed, and then her eyes flew open. Her mouth was dry, and she felt as if she had been running for hours. She glanced at the clock and was surprised to see that she had slept for three and a half hours.

She sat on the edge of the bed and rubbed her head.

"Wow, that was some dream!" she said aloud. Jill walked into the bathroom and threw cold water on her face, swallowing several handfuls. She redressed, putting her swimsuit on underneath her clothes, and then headed to the Ranch House.

Chapter 14

The sun had set, and the temperature had dropped slightly. As Jill walked to the Ranch House, she looked up into the star-filled sky. The slight breeze tossed her long hair gently, and she brushed it out of her face. She had combed it but hadn't pulled it back into a ponytail. She ran her fingers through it and hoped it didn't look too messy.

Jill entered the Ranch House. The music was playing loudly, and people were enjoying themselves on the dance floor, eating and throwing back a cold beer or two. Jill quickly glanced around the room and was happy to see Bebe and Tony were there. They were standing at the bar, and Jill walked over and joined them.

"Well, good evening, sleepyhead. Bebe was just saying that she wanted to go and check on you," Tony told her.

"I guess I was really worn out. I didn't mean to sleep that long. I wish you had wakened me, Bebe. I don't know how I'm going to get to sleep tonight."

"I slept for about two hours myself, but I know I will fall right off to sleep as soon as my head hits the pillow tonight," Bebe said. "Are you hungry?"

"No, just thirsty."

"What can I get you, Jill?" Tony asked.

"An iced tea, please. Thanks, Tony."

"Don't mention it, you can treat me later."

Jill laughed and glanced around the room. At first she didn't see him, but then she spotted him toward the back of the room. Though she could only see his back, she knew it was Kyle. She wanted desperately to walk over and start up a conversation, but felt awkward doing so. Bebe only looked at her friend and smiled. Jill quickly looked at Tony and was thankful that his head was turned. He was still trying to get the bartender's attention.

Bebe leaned over and whispered in her friend's ear, "Jill, he doesn't bite. Go on over and say hello to the man."

Jill said nothing and only shook her head no. Bebe was well aware of the electricity that was transmitting between Kyle and Jill. Kyle was ready to love Jill with all of his heart and then some. Jill, on the other hand, would need some coaxing. Bebe knew they were perfect for each other, but she had to be careful not to betray either of her friend's trust.

With a smile on her face, Jill continued to stare at Kyle. *God's own masterpiece,* she thought. Jill let her eyes take in their fill of him. From the tip of his toes, to the top of his head, she could only see perfection. She stared at his strong muscular back, which led to his tapered waist. Thick strong thighs supported his tall frame. With his skin the color of smooth, rich chocolate, Jill found herself hungering for a taste.

"Here you go, Jill," Tony said. Breaking Jill's concentration, he handed her a glass of iced tea.

"Oh, thanks, Tony," She took a long sip on the cold drink and then focused her attention on Kyle again.

Tony's eyes followed Jill's, and he saw that she was closely observing his big brother. Pulling his hat down over his brows, he looked at Bebe and smiled, then leaned his back against the bar.

Jill was toying with the idea of going over and talking to him. Bebe knew what was on Jill's mind, and once again whispered in her ear, "I could be wrong, but wouldn't you rather be gazing into his sexy dark brown eyes than staring at the back of his head? And wouldn't you rather be up close and personal to that well-chiseled chest than just staring at his muscular back?" Jill coughed, choking on her iced tea, but Bebe continued telling her titillating tale. "Sooner or later a slow song is going to come on. I know that you want to find yourself in his strong embrace, and feeling every inch of him."

Jill turned around, looking into her friend's smiling eyes, and said, "Bebe, can you hold my tea for a minute? I see someone I'd like to say hello to."

She handed her drink to Bebe and quickly made her way through the crowd over to where Kyle was standing. Tony, who had been pretending not to pay the women any attention, turned around from the bar and gave Bebe a high five.

Kyle had a beer in his hand and was laughing and talking with some of his friends. His face lit up as soon as he laid eyes on Jill. It was as if no one else in the room existed when he saw her face. Though he tried hard not to show too much excitement, he couldn't resist the temptation to kiss her.

"Hey, Jill, I was wondering if I would get the chance to see you this evening," he said, quickly kissing her on the cheek.

His heart pounded hard in his chest. Nervously, he looked into her eyes for any sign of discomfort from his kiss. Jill only smiled and explained how the workday had worn her out.

Kyle's own smile broadened as he told her he thought she truly was working too hard. He made no excuses to his friends, but happily walked away with Jill. The two found a booth and sat down.

"Do you have much more to do on your assignment before the grand opening?" he asked.

"No, everything is pretty much wrapped up. I only have a few small things to do, and then I'll be finished. Bebe has been a tremendous help, too."

"She's a sweetheart. I noticed that you two have gotten quite close. I never see one without the other. Well, except for right now," he said, laughing.

Jill blushed as she thought of what Bebe had said to make her get Kyle's attention. "Yes, Bebe and I are very close. I really will hate to leave next week."

Kyle's smile faded. "You're leaving next week?"

"I'm leaving for Pittsburgh next Thursday. I want to see my family for a few days before I go home to New York," Jill explained.

"I thought you would be out here until after the grand opening."

"That was the plan if I didn't get everything finished in time. With Bebe's help, I'm ahead of schedule," Jill said. She saw that Kyle wasn't happy about her leaving Durango either. She knew he wanted to get to know her, but she didn't think he would be this disappointed. "I really miss my family, and they are all so anxious to see me again too."

"I was hoping to spend some time with you. I mean I want to get to know you, Jill. I have been trying to give you time to get your work done, and I tried to play it cool and not scare you off. Now it's time for you to go, and there's just so much I wanted to do with you."

Jill cocked her head to one side and gave Kyle a crooked smile.

"No." He laughed. Shaking his head and bending down, he said, "I don't mean sex. I mean I honestly wanted to take time to get to know you. No, that's not true either. What I meant to say is, I already know everything I need to know about you, and I like what I see. I wanted to give you time to get to know me. I know that's what you want."

"What I want right now is for you to take a walk with me," Jill told him.

Kyle tipped his hat as he stood up. He walked over and pulled Jill's chair out and took her hand, and then guided her out into the cool Colorado air.

Hand in hand they walked in silence. Neither one of them knew what to say next. Jill hadn't expected Kyle to lay his cards on the table tonight, but he had said everything she secretly wanted to hear.

They kept walking quietly until they found themselves at the hot spring. Kyle turned and took Jill in his arms. They could still hear the music from the Ranch House. It was a slow song, and Kyle was happy to have a chance to dance with Jill the way he had really wanted to the other night at Roland's.

He held her gently like a delicate flower as his hands caressed her back. He rubbed his cheek against her soft hair. Jill relaxed in his arms and let her body enjoy every part of him that touched her. Her arms lay softly over his shoulders, and she lovingly caressed the nape of his neck. She could feel his hands sliding down her body, until they rested on her hips. Then he pressed her firmly to him. Both of their eyes were closed, as they dreamed that they would never have to part.

The music ended and slowly their bodies untwined. Jill stepped back from Kyle and started to undress. She took off one shoe and then the other. She started to unbutton her blouse, and Kyle found himself only able to stand there and stare. He started laughing when he realized that she had a swimsuit on underneath.

"Let's get in the hot tub," she said, laughing too.

"You had me scared there for a minute."

"A big guy like you scared? I don't think so," Jill said, smiling.

Kyle still stood there. He looked at Jill in utter amazement. She was the most beautiful woman he had ever seen. She was smart and funny, and apparently didn't mind being with a ranch hand. He wanted to tell her one important thing about himself, but had to find the perfect time to do it.

"Kyle, what's wrong? Aren't your getting in?"

"I-I don't have my swim trunks on," he stammered. "I didn't think the evening would find us here."

"Then swim in your underwear. You do have some on, don't you?" she said playfully.

"Yes, I do," he replied, laughing again at her remark. His smile faded as he looked at the gorgeous woman before him. "You are so beautiful, Jill," he said in a deep, sincere voice.

Kyle stared at her amazing body and wanted to hold it again, but if he did, he knew he would desperately want to make love to her. He wouldn't risk even holding her, not wanting to chase her away.

"Please, you're making me feel self-conscious," she replied.

He watched as she lowered her body into the water. Kyle knew that he couldn't trust himself, so he declined the offer to join her. Instead, he knelt by the side of the spring and gave her a massage. He kneaded and rubbed her shoulders and neck. Jill lay back and enjoyed the masculine hands that worked tirelessly on her.

"Kyle, that feels wonderful. Where did you learn to do that?"

"Oh, just a little something I picked up."

"So you're a man of many talents."

"As a matter of fact, I am. Before you leave, you have to taste my cooking," he said proudly.

"You cook?" Jill said, surprised. She stood and turned to get out of the hot spring.

"Yes, señorita, I do. Be prepared because I will dazzle you with my culinary skills," he said. He took her delicate hand and gently assisted her out of the spring.

"I can't wait," Jill said.

"Neither can I." He quickly grabbed Jill in his arms and held her wet body close to him. He kissed her long and passionately, letting his mouth explore hers. He tasted the sweetest lips he had ever encountered. Kyle had known from the moment he laid eyes on Jill that she was the one for him.

Jill allowed herself to enjoy his passionate kiss, and felt her knees tremble as he pulled away. "I could get lost in loving you," she said. She was shocked she had said the words aloud. Jill pulled away from Kyle and started to dress. "Kyle, I'm sorry. I never should have said that. It slipped out."

"Did you mean it?"

"What does it matter if I meant it or not? I never should have said it."

"It matters to me, Jill."

"Kyle, I don't want to lead you on. You're wonderful, and if I had my life together, you would be perfect for me, but—"

Kyle grabbed Jill by the wrist and looked deep into her eyes. He asked again, "Jill, please tell me, did you mean what you just said?"

A tear rolled down her cheek as she answered him truthfully, "Yes. Kyle, I meant every word I said. That night by the pool when you tried to hand me my towel you said, 'Are you looking for this?' Do you remember?"

"I remember every detail."

"You're what I've been looking for all my life."

"Doesn't that make everything perfect for us?"

"No, it doesn't. I have dreams I want to make a reality first, and I won't give up on myself. I just can't do this right now, Kyle. You want more, and I can't give you more," Jill said. She started walking back to her room and prayed Kyle wouldn't follow her.

On her way to her room, Jill ran into Bebe, who smiled excitedly at her friend, until she saw that Jill was crying.

"Jill, what's wrong?" she asked.

"Nothing, Bebe, I just want to be alone right now," Jill said. Tears were streaming down her face and Bebe couldn't imagine what had happened. The only thing she did know was that she wasn't going to leave her friend alone.

Jill reached her room and went inside. Bebe followed her and shut the door behind them.

Jill went into the bathroom and locked the door. Bebe was scared, not knowing what had made Jill so upset. She listened at the door and realized Jill was only taking a shower. She sat in a chair and waited for her to finish.

Twenty minutes later, Jill emerged. She was wrapped in a white terry cloth robe and drying her hair when she looked up and saw Bebe was still there. "Bebe, I said I don't want to talk about it."

"Jill, it's going to take more than that to get rid of me. I just can't leave you crying."

"I'm not crying anymore."

"Good, then I won't have any trouble understanding you when you explain what's wrong, will I?"

Jill sat on the edge of the bed and fumbled with her fingers. "Bebe, I love him," she said simply.

"And that has you crying?"

"No, but I told him I love him."

"I still don't get it, are you upset because he didn't say it back?"

"He didn't say it back, but not because he didn't want to, but because I didn't give him a chance to."

"Girlfriend, you've got it bad, don't you?"

"Bebe, I'm leaving for Pittsburgh next week. I have a life and dreams of my own that I have to get back to. I knew going into this that I had to return to the real world eventually. Kyle told me he how he felt about me, and he said everything I ever wanted to hear. Then I realized that it's everything I've ever wanted to hear, but just not right now. He's perfect for me, Bebe, and I'm going to lose him."

"You don't have to, Jill."

"If I don't go after my own dreams, I will lose myself. Bebe, I'm really tired. Would you please leave now?" Jill said. She smiled, knowing she had asked as politely as she could.

Bebe smiled back and said, "Sweet dreams, Jill." She kissed her friend on the forehead and left the room.

After Bebe left, Jill lay across the bed and fell fast asleep.

Chapter 15

The sunlight glowed in Jill's room as she awakened and stretched in her bed. She rubbed her eyes and walked to the bathroom. Looking into the mirror, she saw that her eyes were very puffy. Jill threw cold water on her face and patted it dry. She slowly walked back to her bed and sat on the edge thinking of the night before.

She had enjoyed every minute of her time with Kyle. She tried to smile, but remembered what she had said. "How could I have been so stupid?" she said aloud and fell back onto the bed. She wondered how she could have let the words slip out of her mouth. Jill had admitted to Kyle that she could fall in love with him right now. All her actions had shown it too. She wanted someone to love.

She reached for the phone and called Barbie at home.

"Hello," said a young voice on the end.

"Hi, Ricky, it's Aunt Jill," she said. Her sadness melted away slightly when she heard her nephew's voice.

"Aunt Jill, Mom told me that you would be home next week. I can't wait to see you!" he said excitedly.

"I can't wait to see you either, Ricky. How are Lacy and James?"

"They're fine. Lacy really liked the doll you sent her. Mom wasn't too happy with the gift you sent me though," he said. Jill could hear the amusement in his voice as he gave a little snicker.

"I couldn't find anything that James would like, so I'll just have to do something special for him later."

"Mom said that he was happy just playing with the boxes. I have to go, Aunt Jill; Mom is ready for the phone. I love you."

"I love you too, Ricky. Bye."

"Hey, sis, how is everything going?" Barbie asked.

"Hi, Barbie. I am so glad you're home. I really need to talk to you."

"What's wrong? You don't sound too happy," Barbie said, concerned.

Jill took a deep breath, and said, "No, Barbie, I am not happy. I took your advice and everything was going well."

"Do you mean with the guy you wanted to go out with, Kyle?"

"Yes, I told him that I could love him."

"Jill, you just met the man. Why would you say that?"

"I didn't mean to say it; it just slipped out. Besides, it's true. I love him, Barbie. I don't know how it happened or when it happened, but it did. You know how I feel about my career; I want to finish on top. Getting seriously involved with someone right now would only jeopardize my own goals, and I don't want to do that."

"He feels the same way about you, doesn't he?" Barbie asked knowingly.

"How did you know? How is it that you always know?"

Barbie gave a slight laugh and said, "Jill, everything you've ever done has been deliberate. You might not have meant to say the words at that exact moment, but you did want to let Kyle know how you felt. So there's some truth to that love at first sight thing, huh?"

"I guess so, but I don't know what to do from here," Jill said sadly.

"Jill, you let it play out. Let the chips fall where they may. This situation could blossom into the relationship you want and deserve, or it could dissipate right before your eyes. In either case, you have to prepare for the worst and hope for the best."

"How do I do that, Barbie?"

"I stand by my original advice, allow yourself to enjoy life, Jill. If love comes along in the process, well, that's just an added bonus."

"I'll try, Barbie. Have I thanked you today for being my sister?"

"No, I don't recall you mentioning that."

"Barbie, I don't know what I would do without you. Thanks for helping me manage my life. Thanks for being my sister."

"Thanks for being my sister too, Jill. I am always here for you, babe."

"I know that, and I love you for it. I have to get to work, I'll talk to you later, sis."

"Call me anytime, Jill," Barbie said and hung up the phone.

Barbie had succeeded in giving Jill some peace of mind. Jill stood up and walked back to the bathroom. She looked in the mirror and saw that her eyes were still puffy. "I must have had a real good cry last night," she said to herself. She reached into her cosmetics bag and pulled out her eye-moisturizing cream. If she were home she could put cool tea bags or cucumbers over her eyelids, but she couldn't manage getting that from the Ranch House now.

Jill dressed in a pair of tight-fitting jeans and a white, tailored, button-down blouse. She left the top three buttons unfastened, and slid a tooled leather belt around her waist. There was nothing else she could do about her puffy eyes, so she slipped on a pair of Gucci sunglasses. They were a little to fancy for the ranch, but they were the only pair she had brought with her. She would rather no one see that she had spent the night crying. She hoped the puffiness would disappear soon as she applied a little lip gloss and then some blush to her cheeks.

After speaking to Barbie, Jill had a fresh perspective on how she should handle things with Kyle. Maybe she was getting way ahead of herself with this whole relationship thing. Regardless of what happened now, she was going back home in less than a week. Barbie was right, she had to let the chips fall where they might. She had a job to do now, and dreams of her own to satisfy. If Kyle Roberts fit into her plans, then it would be; but she couldn't worry about that right now.

Jill left her room and headed toward the Ranch House. She now felt lighthearted and wondered why she had taken everything so seriously in the first place. She knew Barbie was right. She did calculate her every move, but she did feel as though she had acted impulsively in telling Kyle how she felt.

She walked into the Ranch House and was happy to see Bebe was there. She walked over to her friend and sat down.

"Good morning, Bebe," Jill said sheepishly.

"Hey, Jill, how are you doing this morning?" Bebe replied, staring at Jill's sunglasses.

"I'm doing fine, but I'll be doing much better after I apologize to you. I am so sorry for pushing you away last night."

"No, Jill, it's fine really. I just wanted to make sure that you were all right."

"No, it's not fine. You are my friend, and I should have let you in. It's just that I was hurting and ashamed of myself. My emotions were just everywhere, and I didn't know what to do next. Bebe, I'm sorry."

"Jill, you don't have to apologize. I know exactly what you're going through. I just wish there was something I could do for you and Kyle."

"There's nothing you can do, Bebe; we just have to see where things lead us. I have my own goals and aspirations, and I won't let anything get in the way of them. Kyle is wonderful, but I'm afraid that I can't give him what he wants right now."

"Are we still on for tomorrow?" Bebe asked.

"Do you mean the rafting trip?"

"Yes."

"Of course we are. Why wouldn't we be?"

"I just thought that because of last night you might feel uncomfortable around Kyle."

"I can handle being around Kyle, I just can't handle a heavy relationship right now. You know, it sounds funny to hear myself say that. When I was in New York, I still tried to have tunnel vision where my goals were concerned, but I didn't have a problem wanting to date someone. It's so different with Kyle. It's like I can sometimes see my life played out before me with him in it."

"Is it a happy life?"

"Yes, it is, but it's just a dream. I don't know if it could be my reality."

"You can lose the glasses, I already know you were crying," Bebe said.

Jill slipped the sunglasses off and laid them on the table. "Do my eyes look real bad?"

"No, you can hardly see it. I bet in a little while, it won't be noticeable at all. Are you hungry?"

"I'm starving. I guess I really worked up an appetite with that late night cry."

"Grace should be coming back in a moment. She was going to bring me another cup of coffee."

"That's fine. Did we get a call from Don yet?"

"Yes, he left a message saying that the commercial was ready and he would like for us to come to the station today."

"What time?"

"He said to come over this morning, but I called him and told him I had to clear it with you first."

"This morning is good for me."

"Good morning, Jill. What can I get you for breakfast?" Grace said. She set Bebe's coffee down and looked at Jill. She noticed that Jill's eyes were puffy, but said nothing about it.

"Good morning, Grace. How are you today?"

"I'm fine, honey."

"I'll have a western omelet, toast, grits, and coffee please."

"Coming right up," Grace said and left.

"Jill, the invitations arrived today. They're in my office," Bebe said.

"Great, after we come from the station I want to get busy and send them out. We have to listen to the radio. Your spot should be airing soon."

"It's already airing," Tony said. He walked over and sat down next to Bebe. Kyle was behind him with Eric. Kyle sat down next to Jill, and Eric pulled up a chair. "Bebe, girl, you sounded great on the radio. Now A Special Place has its own celebrity."

Bebe looked at Jill and threw her hands over her face. "Did I sound like a fool?" she asked, laughing.

"No, Bebe, you did a great job. If I didn't already live here, I'd want to come and visit the place. Whose idea was it for you to do the commercial?" Tony asked.

"Jill's," she told them.

"Jill, you didn't mind sharing the spotlight?" Tony asked her.

"The spotlight shouldn't be on me. It should be on the resort. Bebe did a wonderful job. She was the perfect person to do it because she loves this place," Jill said sincerely as she smiled at her friend.

Jill looked over and saw Kyle staring at her. Her own smile faded as she saw the look of concern in his eyes. She could tell that he knew she had been crying, and she regretted taking off her sunglasses.

Grace arrived with Jill's food. Kyle, Tony, and Eric ordered a cup of coffee. Grace gave Kyle a quick side glance of disapproval, and left saying nothing. Jill immediately felt bad, but was afraid to say or do anything.

The group began to talk about their upcoming rafting trip. Though they were all excited, everyone noticed how quiet Kyle and Jill were. Unable to take the strain any longer, Kyle stood and said, "Well, I better get going. I have a few things I need to take care of."

"Wait up, Kyle, I'll go with you," Eric said and started to stand.

"No, you stay and finish your coffee, I can handle everything," he said. Having made his excuse, he quickly left the table.

Eric sat back down in his seat. He looked at Tony, whose eyebrows had furrowed. They didn't know what was going on with their brother, but had a good idea it had something to do with Jill.

Jill stared at Kyle's back as he left the Ranch House. She knew exactly why Kyle had left the table so abruptly, and she felt like it was all her fault. She was acting like a silly schoolgirl, and that wasn't the image she wanted to portray. This was Kyle's home, and somehow she had managed to make him feel uncomfortable in it. Right now, she hated how she felt inside.

"Excuse me," Jill said and left the table. She walked quickly after Kyle, but her own fast pace was no match for the giant strides he took. She called out to him, but he kept walking toward the barn. Jill started running and she caught up to him as he entered the stables.

"Kyle, please wait," she said as she grabbed his sleeve. Inside the barn, she stood in front of him and stared into his smoldering brown eyes. He stood rigid in front of her and waited to hear what she had to say. "I'm sorry," Jill said softly. She dropped her arms at her side. "I didn't mean to hurt you." Kyle turned and continued to walk away. "Kyle, we can't just stop talking to each other. What do you want from me?"

He stopped walking and turned around and said, "I want you to be honest with yourself. I want you to be honest with me."

"I am being honest with you, what are you talking about?"

"Jill, something is already happening between us, but you won't even give it a chance. I understand that you have dreams, and I'm man enough to let you pursue them, and patient enough to wait for you. But you can't be honest with yourself enough to say, 'This is what I want.' I don't know if you're afraid of love or what, but I can't meet you halfway if you won't even be honest with me."

"Kyle, you're asking me to step out on a limb and open up to you. We've known each other for less than two weeks. You're right, I'm not being honest with you. I don't know if I can trust you that way. But I want to try," Jill said. She fought hard to keep her tears at bay.

Kyle walked over to her and put his arms around her. "Jill, you don't have to be afraid of me. I love you, too. Yes, we just met each other, but something inside me said, 'This is the girl for you,' the moment I laid eyes on you."

He kissed her cheek softly and just stood there holding her. Jill rested her head on his chest and let her body relax as she listened to his heartbeat. The lyrics of Tomahawk's song "Pounding Heart" filtered through her mind. Jill began to hold Kyle's body as tightly as she could. It was almost as if she were afraid he would slip away. She wanted the moment to last forever. She knew she was fighting a losing battle. But right now, she didn't want to think about that.

It seemed they had stood that way for eternity, and neither wanted to let go of the other. No more games were being played, and they allowed themselves to be completely honest. It felt good to let go, and Jill wanted to keep the momentum.

Kyle began to kiss Jill's neck across her collarbone, and she wanted nothing more than to be his at that very moment. She felt his hands slide from her waist to the top button of her shirt. He continued to kiss down the center of her body as he undid each button. When he reached the last one he began to unfasten her pants.

Realizing that Kyle was only inches from her scar, she instinctively pulled her shirt closed so that he couldn't see it.

Kyle's brow furrowed as he wondered what was wrong. Jill clearly wasn't signaling him to stop, but she was hiding something. Gently, he moved her shirt aside and looked at the scar she was hoping he wouldn't notice. Kyle rubbed his thumb over what seemed to him like a small imperfection, then pressed his lips firmly on it in a moist kiss.

Jill felt his passion and acceptance for her body, and didn't know if she was going to cry or faint. All she knew for sure was that she wanted to give herself to him right now. She stepped out of her jeans and as Kyle stood, she began to undress him in the same manner.

She was glad that Kyle was a responsible lover and had protection. Without destroying the heat of the moment he slid it on, and Jill found herself in awe of his considerable sexuality.

Kyle began to say something, but Jill stopped him. "Shhh, don't say a thing. Just make love to me, Kyle." She took his hands and wrapped them around her waist. She could feel the warmth of his body searing through hers. Feeling his need for her mounting, she parted her lips to welcome his tongue.

Without letting go of each other, their bodies melted to the floor. It had been a long time since Jill had been with a man, and Kyle was pleasing her in ways she had been dreaming of. The two lovers gave no care to time and place. All they cared about was the perfection of the moment, and they would let nothing come between fulfilling their desires.

Jill lay on the floor with Kyle on top of her. He kissed her body from head to toe, then he held her as if she were a precious gem as his tongue gently sucked each of her breasts as if they were a delicious dessert. His titillating action bought about a low moan from deep inside her, and it let Kyle know that she was ready for him.

Still, he wasn't ready to pleasure her yet. Kyle slowly rolled Jill over onto her stomach and began taking long, deliberate strokes with his tongue up and down her back, as he continuously massaged her backside with his strong, firm hands. When he placed his hand between her legs, he saw that she was more than ready for him.

Rolling Jill onto her back, Kyle positioned himself close to her until she could feel the full thickness of him entering her body. She arched her back to accommodate his massiveness. Another deep, hungry moan escaped her lips, letting him know that he was just what she needed.

Jill's legs instinctively wrapped around Kyle's body as she felt her passion mount. She held his body close to hers and didn't try to hide her need for him, as her body moved in order to receive its pleasure. Letting out what had been captive in her body for months, she could hardly catch her breath as she experienced all the intensity Kyle was thrusting inside her. Her lips found his and she began kissing and stroking his back and body. He held her tightly as his thrusts became more powerful and deliberate. Any second he would erupt inside her, she thought, and though her own body was spent, she summoned what strength she had left to bring him to his peak.

In unison with his movements, Jill began moving her body back and forth until she had achieved her goal.

"Oh, Jill, I love you, baby," was all Kyle managed to say, before lying on top of her in exhaustion.

When they were finished, Jill lay in Kyle's arms completely satisfied. She was thankful to have found such a compassionate and loving man, and was happy he was such a skillful and patient lover. Kyle had not left her hanging and didn't finish until she had.

Kyle lovingly stroked and kissed Jill's hair. "Let's go for a ride," Kyle whispered softly in her ear.

Jill knew that Bebe was waiting for her to go to the station to see the commercial, and she had the invitations to mail out today. Somehow it all paled in importance to being with Kyle. "All right," she whispered back.

They quickly redressed, and Kyle saddled up Patches. He mounted the horse and then leaned down and offered a hand to Jill. He hoisted her on the horse behind him, and Jill wrapped her arms around Kyle's waist.

At first Kyle let the Arabian stallion walk slowly, enjoying the movement and the warmth of Jill's body so close to his. Then he said, "Hold on tight," as he urged his horse into a full run.

They cut through the wind like lightning, and Jill's long dark brown hair flowed wildly behind her. She didn't know where Kyle was taking her and it didn't matter, she was enjoying herself and loving the feel of the man to whom she held tightly.

Though they started out in the direction Patches had taken her before, the path Kyle took was a little different. He cut up the mountainside and past the same lake she had seen the time she rode alone. Before she knew it, she was at the same log cabin she and Patches had visited.

Kyle slowed the horse's gait as he got closer to the cabin. The horse walked to the back of the cabin and Kyle dismounted. With a hand on either side of Jill's waist, he helped her off of Patches's back. Once Jill was off, Patches walked into the stable, which housed the other beautiful horses.

"The day that I took Patches for a ride, he brought me here. Now I see why. He lives here," Jill said, smiling.

"So do I," Kyle said. He took her hand and led Jill to the front of the cabin and opened the door. He hung his hat on a hook and then followed her inside.

Jill walked inside and looked around. "Wow, this place is beautiful!" she said in amazement.

"Do you mean beautiful for a bachelor?"

"No, I mean beautiful for anybody. I know you didn't decorate this place yourself, did you?"

"I would like to take credit for it, but no, I didn't do the decorating. I had an interior designer do that for me.

I did, however, design and build the cabin myself," Kyle said proudly.

"You did?"

"Yes, well, with a little help from Eric and Tony. Have a seat. I'll get us something to drink," he said.

Kyle disappeared into the kitchen, and Jill continued to marvel at the exquisite interior. Kyle had done his cabin in a Spanish theme, with beautiful, rich earth tones. He had all the toys one would expect of a thirty-year-old bachelor. Next to the huge flat-screen television, he had every game system known to man hooked up to it. Toward the back of the room was a pool table and a dartboard. Two large, comfortable sofas filled the living room, and a matching recliner was off to the side. There was a giant cactus in the corner. Upon closer examination, Jill saw that it was real. He had beautiful Spanish-inspired paintings hung around the room with a few Native American artifacts too. All in all, Kyle's place had a very comfortable, relaxing appeal.

He returned with two tall glasses of iced tea and placed a slice of lemon on the rim of each. He handed Jill a glass and sat down.

"So, what do you think of my humble bachelor pad?"

"This place is anything but humble. I see where you spend all your money."

Kyle bowed his head. When he looked up, Jill was smiling at him, and he melted all over again. "Come on," he said as he stood. "I'll show you the rest of the cabin."

Kyle took Jill's hand again and led her past the powder room to the kitchen. Jill looked around in surprise. Kyle had a kitchen that would rival Martha Stewart's. A set of copper pots hung over the kitchen's island, which housed a double-sided sink. Jill noticed not a single

dirty dish anywhere in the kitchen. A beautiful silver
Sub Zero refrigerator hummed quietly next to the stove,
which had six burners. Kyle's kitchen had all the bells
and whistles, and he enjoyed seeing the shocked look on
Jill's face.

"Kyle, this kitchen is absolutely fantastic!" she said.
Jill turned around to look at Kyle's face and saw the
amusement that filled it. She smiled. "I guess you
weren't playing about your cooking expertise?"

"No, señorita, I wasn't, and if you ever give me a
chance I'll make you a dish that you'll be talking about
for years to come." He looked at Jill and realized that he
was fighting the urge to kiss her. Kyle looked away, in
hopes of breaking the spell Jill had unknowingly cast
upon him. "Follow me," he said. Kyle turned and
walked through a doorway that led to a massive home
office.

The room was bright and sunny, and Jill could see
Patches and the other horses through a giant window
that ran the entire length of the room from ceiling to
floor. Two other walls were covered by bookshelves.
There was a brick fireplace in the corner and an oversized recliner. It was obvious to Jill that Kyle loved to
read.

She stood for a second and visualized the masculine,
six-foot-three cowboy, drinking his coffee as he read a
good book by the fire. She smiled again and looked at
the rest of the room. There was a huge mahogany desk
toward the back with his computer and printer on it. Jill
wanted to get a better look at the beautiful piece of fur-
niture, but didn't go any closer. There were some papers
on the desk and she didn't want to seem intrusive.

"Kyle, everywhere I look, I find out something new
about you," Jill said. With her head tilted to the side and

her arms folded, she added, "And I'm completely fascinated."

"That's good. I was afraid that you would find me a bore," Kyle said. He was smiling and Jill saw his gorgeous, deep dimples. Kyle had perfect white teeth and sensuously full lips. Jill wanted to kiss him again and again. Kyle walked closer to her and Jill held her breath in hope. But instead, he took her hand and led her up a flight of stairs.

At the top of the stairs Jill was greeted by plush, pale blue carpet. They walked to the end of the hall and Kyle briefly showed Jill the only two guest rooms in the cabin. They were of medium size, but tastefully decorated. There was a hallway bathroom and a linen closet that separated the two rooms. They walked back down the hallway and went into the last room, Kyle's master suite. The same beautiful sunlight greeted Jill as she walked in. She was immediately impressed by the sheer style and sophistication of the room. Kyle had decorated it in beautiful soft tones and it wasn't overdone. Jill felt the gentle breeze of the ceiling fan and could hear jazz playing softly. There was a massive king-sized bed, which was neatly made. Jill walked over and ran her hand along the edge of the hand-carved oak headboard. Her thoughts quickly went back to the love she had made to the man who slept here, and the thoughts caused her to smile.

There were matching nightstands on either side of the bed. An oak armoire that housed a television was against the wall, and a beautiful, tall yucca plant stood next to it. Jill went farther into the room and saw that Kyle had a gigantic walk-in closet, and she silently wished her closets at home were that big. She looked but didn't go inside, not wanting to be intrusive. Instead, Jill walked to his bathroom. Every room she had seen so far was immaculate. She began to wonder just how much time Kyle actually spent here. She saw that he had an oversized whirlpool tub and guessed that it was probably just what he needed after a long day's work on the ranch.

Jill came back out and joined Kyle. He still had a smile on his face and Jill smiled shyly too. "Kyle, you have a beautiful home. It must have taken you some time to complete it," she said.

"It took about six months. We probably could have completed it sooner, but working on the ranch took precedence."

"Kyle, would you mind if I took a quick shower before we head back to the resort?"

"Not at all. Would you mind if I took one with you?"

Jill took Kyle by the hand and walked back into his bedroom. "I wouldn't mind at all, as long as you keep your hands to yourself," she said, smiling.

"I won't make any promises I can't keep."

They walked into the bathroom and began to undress. Kyle turned on the shower and adjusted the water to a temperature that matched his mood. Jill stepped into the tub and he followed her. She lathered a washcloth and began bathing herself. Kyle watched as Jill cleansed her perfect body. In his eyes she was the epitome of beautiful. He wanted to make love to her again and again, hoping to reaffirm that she wasn't a mythical creature here to bring him to his knees and then disappear.

He took the washcloth from her and finished cleaning her body. Jill smiled as Kyle kissed her neck while he scrubbed her back.

When he was finished, she took the cloth and began to bathe him as well. She began washing his shoulders and admired their broadness and strength, but quickly found herself running her tongue longingly across his muscular chest. Her hand found his manhood, and she saw that he was in need of her again.

They found themselves once again kissing and locked in a passionate embrace. Kyle pressed Jill's body against the shower wall as his hands firmly grasped her buttocks. Jill looked down and saw that he had applied protection so that he could pleasure her once again the way he had not even an hour earlier. Lifting her slightly, he lowered her body onto his hardened member.

Jill caught her breath and hoped she wouldn't pass out. She couldn't decide if it was the steam from the warm water that made her feel light-headed, or if it was the sheer pleasure she was receiving from Kyle, and the force with which he delivered it, that caused her dizziness. It didn't matter. She knew that the strong arms that held her wouldn't let her go.

Though she was tender from their earlier lovemaking session, she could not deny her need for him again either. Their bodies were as one and Jill felt her passion mount and release several times from Kyle's own. She could feel his hands all over her body and especially enjoyed how he used his tongue along her neck with such mastery. Every time he pleasured her body with his tongue he licked her as if she were a sumptuous treat, and she felt as if her body belonged to him.

She had not received all the pleasure she could when Kyle pulled out of her. She opened her eyes and he could see her confusion. Kyle smiled and kissed her lips and every other inch from her neck down to her lower abdomen, until he reached the soft place between her legs.

Gently, he again used his tongue to bring out all the sensual cries Jill had inside her. This time her moans of passion were full and breathless. Her hands massaged his head, yet they couldn't resist pressing him deeper into her flesh.

Kyle continued to do what Jill wanted until she begged him to stop. When he did, he stood to see that he had done what he had set out to do, to make her feel as beautiful as she was, and to make her see that he was truly in love with her.

Kyle stood holding Jill's exhausted body in his arms as the water continued to spray over them. Jill realized then that Kyle had every part of her: mind, body, and soul. He was capable of handling her, she thought, but was she ready for all that he wanted to offer?

Kissing her a final time, Kyle released Jill and they stepped out of the shower and quickly dried off and re-dressed.

Kyle took Jill in his arms again and said, "Jill, I just want you to know that what happened today was real."

Jill felt her old emotions trying to regain control of her heart, and struggled with a reply. "Kyle, I enjoyed being with you very much, but remember, we're going to wait and see where this thing takes us." She didn't want to say anything that would come back to haunt her later, so she added nothing else to explain their relationship. "I really hate to leave, but I have to get back to the ranch. Bebe and I have a few things to wrap up before the weekend."

"I hope you rest up for tomorrow though, we're going to start out right after breakfast and won't be home until evening. Rafting is a lot of fun, and a lot of work," he told her with a serious face.

"I'm not too worried about that," she said coyly, looking up through her thick lashes. "I'll have you with me," she added.

Blushing, Kyle playfully rolled his eyes before letting them again rest on Jill. "I don't want to either, but I think you're right, we better get going." He turned and headed out of the room and Jill followed him back down the stairs. "Would you like something to drink before we head back?" he asked.

"No, thank you."

"Jill, can I ask you something before we leave?" Kyle asked hesitantly.

"Sure."

"What is it exactly that you are afraid of? Is it me?" he said, trying to maintain eye contact. Jill looked away.

"No, Kyle, it's not you, really. It's me," she said. Jill slowly raised her eyes to meet his. She wanted to turn and run away. *Why did he have to ask me that now?* They were having such a wonderful time. Why did he have to get heavy on her? She wanted to avoid the conversation, but without looking childish, there simply was no way. She walked over to the sofa and sat down. Kyle followed her.

"Kyle, right now I am terribly afraid of being honest with you."

"Why? Are you married or something?"

Jill smiled slightly as she played nervously with her fingers. "No, I'm not married, and I never have been. I fear that I won't complete my career goals," she said.

"We've already been over that. You know that I want you to obtain your dreams. I would never hinder you from your aspirations. If you weren't happy, I wouldn't be happy."

"That's just it, Kyle, you make me laugh, you're smart and completely devoted to your family. You're the most handsome man I've ever laid eyes on, not to mention an incredible lover. Finally my dreams have taken shape, and they come in the form of you. I know in my heart that I could stay here forever," she finished softly.

Kyle lifted her chin with his finger and said, "I want you to stay forever."

"I would be happy in your world, but then what would happen to mine? Would I end up regretting my choices? Would I resent you? We both know I have to go back to New York next week, but that doesn't mean it's the end of us. Can't we just wait and see where this thing between us goes? If what we feel is real, we'll eventually find ourselves together, and not ruin our lives by making rash decisions."

Kyle smiled at how reasonable Jill had made everything seem. Still, he didn't want to risk losing her, and decided to let her know it. He began to stand, and as he did he took Jill's hand and made her rise too. Kyle pulled her close to him and gave her a hug. Then he looked at her and said, "Jill, I don't want to lose you. Everything in me tells me you're already mine. I want to be patient, but please don't hold it against me if I keep trying to show you what I already know," he said huskily, and then planted another kiss on her beckoning lips.

It was a moist, passionate kiss, and when their lips parted, Jill said, "I would seriously be disappointed if you didn't." She kissed him again. "I think I had better get you back to the ranch."

Kyle walked over to the door and opened it for Jill. She squinted in the bright sunlight and regretted having left her sunglasses back at the Ranch House.

Kyle closed the cabin door behind them and grabbed his hat off the hook. He stepped out to the edge of the porch and gave a loud whistle. A moment later Patches appeared before them. Jill was amazed at how smart the animal was and stepped down to pat the horse. Patches rubbed his nose against her face in acknowledgment of his beautiful rider's attention.

Kyle saw the effect Jill had on his horse. Patches really didn't like to be ridden by anyone other than himself, so he was surprised at the bond the two had formed. "Easy, boy, she's already taken," he said playfully to his horse.

Patches threw back his head and snorted, making Jill laugh. She mounted the horse and then Kyle got on behind her. They both held on to the horse's reins, and Patches started on his trek back to the ranch.

Jill felt Kyle's masculine chest against her back, his long strong legs cradling hers. She felt secure with his arms around her, and was glad Patches was walking, giving her time to enjoy his master. She felt the warmth of the sun on her face and closed her eyes briefly, enjoying its rays.

Kyle wrapped one arm a little tighter around Jill's waist and then he urged Patches on faster. The stallion broke into a full run, giving Jill the thrill of her life. With his mane flowing freely through the wind, Patches ran expertly through the trees, and only slowed down once they arrived at the lake. His two riders dismounted and let the horse rest a moment.

Jill and Kyle stood nearby and listened to the natural sounds of their surroundings. They listened to the trees make music with the wind, and the birds sing sweetly to each other. They said nothing, but enjoyed the immense pleasure they received from holding each other. When Patches was finished he walked over to the couple and waited for them to mount him again.

Kyle and Jill mounted the horse in the same manner they had before, and Patches walked the rest of the way to the ranch.

Patches walked up to the corral and came to a stop. Kyle jumped off of his horse and turned around to help Jill down. He placed a hand on either side of her waist and guided her down gently, until her feet touched the ground. He kissed her again and whispered, "Will I see you tonight?"

"You can count on it, cowboy," she answered, touching the rim of his hat. Jill turned and walked in the direction of the Ranch House. Kyle watched her walk away. He seemed to never grow tired of watching her. From the first night he saw her hips in motion, it was a pastime he had grown to love.

Chapter 16

After Jill entered the Ranch House, Kyle started toward the barn with Patches. He looked up and saw Eric and Tony sitting on the fence of the corral. Eric looked at his brother and tried to decipher just what kind of mood he was in before he approached him.

Tony wasted no time and started right in on Kyle. "Hey, big brother, did that little philly calm you down?" he asked. A huge grin formed on Tony's face. Kyle walked over to his brothers with his head bowed.

When he reached them, he lifted his head and said helplessly, "I love her."

"Well, we already knew that," Tony replied. "But does she love you?"

"She does, but she's not ready to admit it yet. Jill doesn't want to make any rash decisions."

"I don't blame her there," Eric said.

"Neither do I," Kyle agreed. "Come on, let's go get some work done."

Tony and Eric jumped down from the fence and followed their brother. It was good to see him happy. They thought that, of the three of them, Kyle would be the first to marry. But it seemed that no woman he had ever dated was quite what he wanted, until now.

Inside the restaurant, Jill could not find Bebe anywhere. She quickly left and headed toward her office. When she arrived, Bebe had just finished a phone call.

"Oh, Bebe, I am so sorry that I was gone so long."

"Hey, Jill, don't worry about it. I knew something heavy was going on between you two."

"I still shouldn't have done that. I know we have some odds and ends to tie up."

"Yeah, and they were only odds and ends. We can catch up in no time. You seem to forget, we're the dynamic team of Alexander and Simmons," Bebe said, smiling. "There's virtually nothing we can't accomplish."

Jill walked over and gave Bebe a big hug. "Thanks for being my friend," she whispered.

Bebe stood and hugged Jill back. "Don't be silly, girl, it's easy being your friend." Bebe sat back down in her chair, and Jill sat across from her. "Is it all right to ask how things went between you and Kyle?"

"Yes, it's fine. Bebe, I'm sorry I've been acting like such a nutcase."

"Jill, stop apologizing. I think I already know what you're struggling to figure out."

"Oh yeah? What's that, Miss Know-it-all?" Jill asked, laughing.

"That you love Kyle something terrible, but don't want to lose yourself in him," Bebe said honestly. The smile on Jill's face faded, and Bebe sat back in her chair and gave Jill a moment to ponder her answer before she asked, "Am I right?"

"You've hit the nail right on the head. Kyle and I talked about what we wanted out of the relationship, and agreed to just take it one step at a time."

"I think that's wise, but I still get the feeling that neither of you want to take too much time trying to figure out what you both know in your hearts."

"Yes, but it's better to take time than to do something you'll both regret."

"Jill, I try to stay clear of playing Cupid, but I want you to know that there is more to Kyle Roberts than what meets the eye."

"He has a past?" Jill asked, fearing the worst.

"Yes, and it's all good. Now, I'm not anxious to find myself in the same predicament Grace found herself in, but just suffice it to say that Kyle is everything you think he is and then some."

A bashful smiled formed on Jill's lips as she thought back to her morning with Kyle. Slowly, she raised her eyes to see Bebe looking at her. "Bebe, Kyle is so perfect for me," she said. Her face was radiant as she spoke.

"Oh, Jill," Bebe said as she finally composed herself from shock. "You and Kyle did more than just talk, didn't you?"

"Yes," Jill answered almost shyly. "I fought the urge as long as I could, but I wanted him as much as he wanted me, probably even more."

Bebe sat smiling at her in wide-eyed wonder. Given Jill's determination not to fall in love with Kyle at this point in her career, their making love was the one thing she didn't think would occur. Well, she thought, at least not today.

Though she wanted to hear every juicy detail, she didn't want to make Jill feel pressured by more questions. She knew Jill would tell her more in her own time. Bebe said, "I am so happy for you and I think you and Kyle will make the right decision." Then she changed the subject and added, "Now for some shoptalk: I called Don and told him we would be at the station at two P.M., and he said that would be fine."

"Good. Thanks, Bebe. I guess we should get started over there."

"Sounds good to me," Bebe said. She stood up and grabbed her purse.

"I'll meet you at the Jeep. I have to run back to my room and get my purse too."

"You might want these," Bebe said. She handed Jill the sunglasses that she had left in the Ranch House.

"Yes, thanks for bringing them with you. I'll only be a moment," Jill said.

They left the office, Bebe walking toward the parking lot, Jill going to her room. She couldn't help wondering what Bebe was trying to tell her about Kyle. At least it was something good. Jill was glad Bebe was letting things progress between herself and Kyle with time, and not trying to push things along. Jill certainly didn't want things to turn out between Bebe and herself as they had between Grace and Sharon.

Jill retrieved her purse and checked her hair in the bathroom mirror. She saw her windblown reflection and quickly grabbed a comb to fix her hair. She applied a little more makeup and then hurried out the door.

As she walked to the parking lot, she thought of what Bebe had said about Kyle. She had told Jill that there was more to Kyle than met the eye. Everything she had learned about him so far made her fall for the guy. He was fascinating, Jill thought. How could there be anything else that would make him more of a dream come true? She decided not to try to overthink the issue. Bebe had said that Kyle's past was good, so she wouldn't allow herself to worry. Still, she couldn't help feeling that there was something major about him that she was missing.

When Jill reached the parking lot, Bebe had the engine running and was waiting for her. Jill got in and they headed toward the television station.

"When we get back, let's get started on the invitations," Jill said.

"All right," Bebe agreed. "Did you have lunch already?"

"No, I didn't. We had some iced tea, and then Kyle showed me his log cabin. I have never seen anything so beautiful."

"Did he tell you that he built it himself?"

"Yes, and I find that amazing too."

"Actually, he and his brothers built it."

"I know. I can't believe that they are all so talented. Do Eric and Sharon have a log cabin too?"

"As a matter of fact, they do. And they built that one also," Bebe said. She turned on the radio, hoping to hear her radio spot. Jill smiled at her friend and silently prayed that the commercial would air soon too. Though they had heard it at the radio station, she still wanted to hear Bebe's voice over the air.

"Bebe, let's stop in town for a bite to eat after we leave the station."

"Why? If we go to the Ranch House, we can get started on the invitations right after we eat."

"I know, but if I run into Kyle I'm afraid I won't get as much work done as I should," Jill said. She looked out the window and tried not to show much emotion.

"Jill, if you want to spend time with Kyle, that's fine. I can get started on the invitations. You just have to look over those contracts and send them out," Bebe said. She hoped Jill would take her up on her offer. She really didn't mind if Jill spent more time with Kyle; in fact, she encouraged it.

"No, Bebe. I came out here to do a job, and that should be my first priority," Jill said with conviction.

Bebe turned and smiled at her friend. "No matter how hard you try, you can't change fate."

Jill sighed. "I know."

"Oh, Jill, turn up the radio, the commercial is on!" Bebe said. Her eyes widened and she drove with one hand and excitedly put the other hand over her mouth.

"Are you trying not to scream?" Jill laughed.

They listened intently to Bebe's commercial. She came across just as Jill had predicted, like she was knowledgeable about the resort and had a passion for it. Bebe smiled, feeling very pleased with the work she and Jill had done.

"Jill, I have never had as much fun as I have had working with you. I wish we could work together all the time," Bebe said when the commercial ended.

"Bebe, you truly did a wonderful job on the commercial. You've done a great job on the whole project. I think you would make a great public relations executive, but it's not as glamorous as people think."

"What do you mean?"

"I mean that you have to be available to your clients twenty-four hours a day, seven days a week, when you are on an assignment. Sometimes you have to leave your family and friends for weeks at a time. And all firms aren't as wonderful to work for as Iguana. The people at Iguana are like family to me."

"But you found a group of people that you work and play well with, right?"

"Yes, I did."

"Isn't that what you've found here too?" Bebe asked simply.

"I guess I have. But I just can't move out here."

"Maybe one day you will," Bebe said. She pulled into the Channel 4 parking lot and found a space right away.

Bebe parked the Jeep, and the two women exited and went inside the station.

Once inside, they waited only a few minutes before Don came out and greeted them.

"I think you will be quite pleased with what we've got," Don told Jill. He led the women back into the production room and asked them to have a seat. Then he signaled to another man in the projection room to roll the tape. Don took a seat next to Jill and Bebe as the commercial began to play.

The tape was crisp and clear, and Don hadn't forgotten to showcase the special features of the ranch such as the spa, pools, riding trails, and restaurants. Jill loved the commercial and was pleased with his work.

When the commercial ended, Don turned around to see the satisfied looks on their faces. "Do you like what we've done so far?" he asked knowingly.

"Don, you've done a superb job," Jill said.

"I thought you would be pleased. Bebe, are you ready to do your part?" he asked.

"Yes, I am, Don," Bebe answered. Don and Bebe stood and he led her away into the sound room, where her voice would be added to the commercial.

Jill could not hear anything, but she could see them talking through the window. Bebe sat in a chair in front of a microphone, and Jill could see her watching the commercial as Bebe recorded what she wanted to say about the resort. A half hour later, Jill saw Bebe shaking Don's hand, and imagined that Bebe had done a good job and was finished recording.

"Jill, I think we have something close to perfection," Don said. He signaled for the projectionist to roll the tape again.

Jill smiled as she watched the finished production. She was pleased with what Don and Bebe had done.

When it ended, she turned to Bebe and said, "I think you're a natural, Bebe. You did an excellent job."

"I'm glad you like it," Bebe replied.

They thanked Don again for all his help and assured him that he would receive an invitation in the mail. Then they left the station feeling like they had accomplished all the major elements concerning the grand opening.

Jill and Bebe returned to the Jeep, still flying high from the masterpiece they had completed.

As Bebe drove toward the restaurant, Jill said, "Bebe, you did such a nice job. You were able to cover all the highlights of the resort and still mention the grand opening."

"Did I sound like I was rushing?"

"Absolutely not. You came across as being very professional. I loved it."

"Do you still want to eat in town?"

"Sure, but I don't want to lose momentum. I'm anxious to get back to your office and start on the invitations and send out the contracts," Jill said. "Can we grab something quick?"

"I know just the place, and it's just around the corner," Bebe said, reading Jill's mood.

Jill turned on her laptop and quickly e-mailed Lois to let her know how nicely the project was progressing before she began composing the contracts and payments for the vendors. Bebe was busy making address labels for the invitations. It took her some time to input each name, but once she had the information in her computer, they printed out quickly.

Jill kept a running log of the invitations she labeled. She kept referring to her list of guests, and was meticulous as to making sure no one was forgotten. When she affixed the last address label to the final invitation, she stood and stretched. Her shoulders were tight and her back ached, but she was very pleased having accomplished their goal. Tomorrow she could enjoy herself and not worry about all the work she should be doing. Now her only concern would be to finish up a few odds and ends, and to take care of whatever problems would arise. Though she could foresee none, it was nice to have the time to take care of a problem if one did arise.

Bebe rubbed her temples and stood up too. "I have a headache."

"Do you think it's because you're hungry?" Jill asked.

"Maybe, we've been at this for hours."

Jill quickly looked at her clock and saw that Bebe was right. "I can't believe how long we've been working."

"Me either, but it does feel good to have everything done."

"Yes, it does. Hey, why don't we go get something else to eat, and then hit the hot spring?" Jill suggested.

"That sounds great," Bebe said.

She and Jill shut down their computers and stacked the invitations, payments, and contracts in a box to take to the post office. They shut off the lights in the office and left. They cut through the main lobby to the side of the building. Walking along the path on the side of the main building that led to the pool, they could hear the music pounding loudly from the Ranch House.

"I don't know how good all that noise will be for my headache," Bebe said.

"Do you want to go somewhere else?"

"No, I have some aspirin in my purse. As soon as I get some food in my stomach I'll take them."

The sun hung low in the sky and was streaked with hues of magenta and pale blue. Soon the stars that Jill loved would be putting on her favorite show.

"Hey, Bebe, I haven't seen you all day," Tony said. He and Kyle were coming from the corral and were headed for the Ranch House too.

"I know. We had a lot of work to get done today," Bebe answered.

Jill smiled as she saw Kyle, and his face lit up too.

"So you got a lot of work done?" Kyle asked. He took her hand and kissed the back of it.

Jill continued to smile and answered, "Yes, we did, but now my back aches and Bebe has a headache."

"Are you sure that you want to go into the Ranch House? Your head will only throb more if you go in there," Tony said.

"Not really, but we haven't eaten yet and I'm starving. My headache will probably go away after I've had dinner."

"Why don't we all go back to my cabin? It's quieter there and I can make us all something to eat," Kyle suggested.

"Aren't you too tired to cook for all of us?" Jill asked.

"It won't be any trouble at all; besides, I love to cook," Kyle said. He was still holding her hand and brought it up to his lips to kiss again.

"Hey, big brother, that sounds like a great idea," Tony agreed.

"How are we going to get there now? The sun is setting and soon it will be too dark to ride a horse back to your cabin," Jill said.

"Why don't you two go and get what you need for the night? I'll ride Patches home and drive back for you."

"That works for me, what about you, Bebe?"

"I'm up for it," Bebe said. "I can wait to eat."

"Great, I'll meet you all back here in about an hour," Kyle said.

He and Tony turned and were just about to leave when they ran into Eric.

"Hey, what are you all up to?" Eric asked.

"We're going back to Kyle's place for the night. He's going to cook dinner and then we're just going to sleep over, since we're going to start out early tomorrow to go rafting," Tony told him.

"Would you and Sharon like to join us?" Kyle asked.

"Spending the night sounds like a good idea. That way, I don't have to get up any earlier than I have to. Let me run it by Sharon and see what she says."

"See you later, bro," Tony said as Eric walked off. His brother was anxious to find his wife, and hoped she would be up for a night at Kyle's also.

"All right, ladies, I guess we'll see you back here in a little while," Kyle said. With his gazed fixed on Jill, he slowly backed away, before he finally turned to leave.

Jill stood quietly watching him walk away. She exhaled slowly, only to draw in another deep breath. Bebe waved her hand in front of Jill's eyes, and Jill let out a girlish giggle.

"Come on, let's grab everything we'll need for tomorrow," Bebe said. She wrapped her arm around her friend, and they began walking back toward their room.

"Bebe, I must admit, I'm having a ton of fun out here."

"I'm glad. I think you more than deserve it. Aren't you glad we got everything done?"

"Yes, I am. Oh, Bebe!" Jill said. She stopped walking and put her hands on her head.

"What's wrong, Jill?"

"The invitations! We have to get them in the mail tomorrow. I know it's Saturday, but Monday makes us run a little short on time," Jill said, obviously frustrated.

"Well, we'll just have to ask Kyle to run us to the post office before we go rafting," Bebe suggested.

"Do you think he will?"

"I know he will. You, my dear, have Kyle Roberts wrapped around your little finger," Bebe said. They began walking again, and Jill smiled to herself. "In fact," Bebe continued, "if you told that man you had to make a pitstop on the moon, he would find a way to get you there."

Bebe and Jill went to their rooms and packed an extra set of clothes, towels, and toiletries. Then they went to Bebe's office and picked up the invitations before they headed back to the parking lot to wait for Kyle and Tony.

They sat on a bench enjoying the warm evening air. Jill couldn't help thinking about Kyle. She let her mind replay their lovemaking session, and a faint smile played upon her lips.

Bebe noticed the look of sheer pleasure on her friend's face and asked, "What are you thinking about?" Jill said nothing, but quickly glanced at Bebe before lowering her eyes to the ground. "You sure seem to be looking forward to spending the night with Kyle. Ooops, I'm sorry. I meant to say at Kyle's," she teased.

Jill was surprised at how well Bebe could read her facial expression. Still, she answered her honestly. "I'm looking forward to being with him. I can't help it, Bebe, Kyle makes me feel like making love to him every time I'm near him," Jill said, and again her face showed all the desire and passion she had been letting her mind reminisce about.

In the distance, they could see Kyle approaching. They gathered their things from the bench.

Kyle pulled up in front of them and quickly got out to assist them with their bags. Tony got out too and opened the doors for them. Once everyone was inside, Kyle pulled off and headed in the direction of his cabin. He glanced over and smiled at Jill, who was lost in her own thoughts.

She wondered about the vehicle she was riding in. How could a ranch hand afford such an expensive automobile? He wasn't married, so his money was all his own. She imagined ranch hands made a good living in Durango, and would have to leave it at that. She wouldn't dare ask him about his income, embarrassing herself and him.

Kyle reached over and caressed her cheek, and Jill turned to look at him. She smiled at the man whom, until just a couple of weeks ago, she didn't know. She wanted to know more about Kyle Roberts, and hoped that tonight would give her another glimpse into his life.

"We're almost there, Bebe," Kyle said. "As soon as we get in, I'll get started in the kitchen."

"I hope so, because I'm still starving, but my headache is ebbing," she replied.

Jill turned around in her seat to look at her friend. Bebe sat closely to Tony, and his arm was around her shoulder. Bebe sat relaxed, her eyes closed. Jill turned around and continued to look out the window.

Kyle pulled into his two-car garage and parked next to his fishing boat. Jill reached for her overnight bag, but Kyle got it first.

"I'll carry that for you," he said. He opened the door and got out, then walked around to Jill's door and helped her out. Tony and Bebe walked behind them.

Kyle unlocked his cabin door and everyone went inside. The phone was ringing when they entered, and Kyle went to answer it.

"Hello," he said. "Oh, that's great, man. I'll see you in a bit," Kyle finished and hung up the phone. "That was Eric. He says that he and Sharon will be here in about an hour."

"Kyle, I have a little problem," Jill said.

"What's that?"

"I have to get the invitations in the mail tomorrow morning. I know I should have told you earlier, but it slipped my mind."

"That's no problem. I can take you to the post office first thing in the morning. Is that what's in the box that Bebe had?"

"Yes," Jill answered.

"No problem. We'll take care of that before we go rafting," he said, and then headed into the kitchen. Jill turned and looked at Bebe, who was sitting on the sofa, giving her friend a knowing smile. Jill smiled too. She looked down at the floor and then followed Kyle into the kitchen. She saw that Kyle was already getting started with dinner. He had a major chore in front of him cooking for six so late in the evening. It was an impromptu gathering, but Kyle seemed to have everything under control.

"Is there anything I can do to help?" she asked. Jill stood on the other side of the island and saw that Kyle was preparing barbecued chicken, coleslaw, baked beans, and corn on the cob.

"You can keep me company," he said. He glanced up quickly from what he was doing and winked at her.

Jill pulled out a stool from under the island and began to shuck the corn. Kyle smiled, but said nothing to stop her.

"Tell me about yourself," she said softly.

"What do you want to know?"

"I want to know everything."

"Do you mean from birth? Because if you do, we

could be here all night," he said playfully, and Jill smiled.

"No, I don't mean from birth. I can't help getting the feeling that there is more to you than meets the eye."

Avoiding eye contact, Kyle answered, "Well, I'm almost thirty-one, I've never been married, no kids—oh, and I love to travel," he said.

"I love to travel, too," Jill said, still smiling.

"I graduated from the University of Colorado with a degree in architecture."

"Aha, so that's why this place is designed so beautifully," Jill said. She was happy to get a better picture of what Kyle was all about, but didn't understand why such an educated man wanted to work on someone else's property as a ranch hand.

"Yes, that's just why this place is so beautifully designed," he agreed.

Just then, Sharon and Eric entered the cabin. Tony had put on some music and Jill had a feeling that Bebe's headache had disappeared. Jill could hear them laughing and talking in the living room.

Kyle turned on the stove. "I guess we should go in and say hello, babe," Kyle said. He was almost at the kitchen door, when Jill caught him by the arm.

"What did you just call me?" she asked, looking him straight in the eye.

Kyle thought for a second, and then his own smile softened. "I called you babe," he said quietly.

"Why?"

"I guess it's like I told you before, I feel as though you're already mine. I'm just waiting for you to realize it," he whispered. Kyle kissed her softy on the lips and then took her hand and walked into the living room.

Kyle walked over to Eric and gave his younger

brother a bear hug. Then he turned to his sister-in-law and gave her a kiss on the cheek.

This was a side of him Jill hadn't seen. She had seen him interact with his brothers before, but she had never seen him hug them. They were a close-knit clan, and Jill admired Kyle's leadership and sense of family.

"I'm glad you guys were able to come up," Kyle said.

"I am too," Eric said. "Listen up, everyone, Sharon has something she wants to tell you."

Jill had never seen this side of Eric either. The usually quiet man didn't seem to mind being the center of attention. This had to be big for Eric to be making an announcement. Jill sat down and fixed her eyes on Sharon.

"Well, we're all family here, so I wanted you to be the first to know that Eric and I are going to have a baby!" she said. With one hand around her husband's waist, and the other resting on her belly, she looked around the room glowing with happiness.

Bebe was the first one to congratulate the couple, followed by Tony. Jill felt a dull ache in the pit of her stomach. She instantly thought of Darlene and Mike, and their baby, Helena. She remembered how she had felt the first time she held the little girl in her arms.

Her thoughts drifted to her sister, Barbie, and how she enjoyed being a mother. Jill could also hear her mother's voice, telling her to find a man. She desperately wanted to see Jill married with children of her own.

Jill forced the thoughts away. Now wasn't the time for her past to haunt her. She made herself look at Eric and Sharon. Kyle was hugging Sharon, and Jill willed herself to stand. She forced a smile on her face and put her best foot forward.

"Sharon, I am so excited for you. When is your baby due?" she managed to ask.

"I think April, but I'm not sure," she said, rubbing her flat stomach. "I'll have to wait and see what my obstetrician says," she said, beaming. Jill gave Sharon a hug and congratulated her and Eric again before she went into the kitchen to check on the food.

She wanted to cry, but wouldn't allow herself to. She lifted the lid on the pot and saw that the corn was boiling. Jill stood there and fidgeted for a second and then went into the bathroom. Unable to hold back any longer, she began to cry.

She threw cold water on her face, then patted it dry. She didn't want to do this, not right now. Jill sat down on the toilet and blew her nose. "Why am I crying?" she said softly to herself. "My life is going just the way I planned it. Why can't I be happy with what I've got?"

Someone would come looking for her soon. She had to pull herself together. She threw cold water on her face again and patted it dry. She sat for a minute more and then left the bathroom.

When she walked out, Bebe was leaning against the kitchen's island waiting for her friend. She walked over to Jill and whispered in her ear, "What's wrong?"

"Nothing, Bebe, I'm fine. I just had to go to the bathroom."

"Well, you forgot to flush the toilet."

Realizing that Bebe knew she was lying, Jill said, "Bebe, we'll talk about it later, now is not the time."

"What do you two want to drink?" Kyle said. He entered the kitchen and checked on the meal he was preparing and then walked over to the refrigerator.

"Do you have any more iced tea?" Jill asked.

"I sure do."

"I'll have a glass please."

"I'll have the same, Kyle," Bebe said.

"The food should be ready in a minute, Bebe. You

guys missed it; Tony was doing some impersonations again. He really had us laughing," Kyle told them, chuckling as he recalled his baby brother's antics. He handed Jill and Bebe their iced tea, and put beers and lemonade on a tray to carry into the living room. "Come back into the living room," he said to Jill. "I want to dance with you."

Jill smiled and followed him, with Bebe close behind.

Once in the living room, Tony grabbed Bebe's hand and the two started to dance. After Kyle gave everyone their drinks, he and Jill started dancing, too. Sharon sat contently on the sofa with Eric and sipped her lemonade.

When the song ended, Kyle went back into the kitchen and prepared platters of food. He placed them on the table. Jill came in shortly and offered her assistance.

"Can I set the table for you?" she asked.

"You sure can, the dishes are in that cabinet over there, and the silverware is in that drawer," he pointed out.

Jill set the table, and Kyle put the food and serving utensils in the middle. He stood back and proudly observed his quick culinary masterpiece before calling everyone in to eat.

Everyone came into the kitchen and sat at the table. The scent of Kyle's barbecued chicken filled the air, making the hungry clan's mouths water.

"Kyle, no one can throw it together like you can," Tony said. He rubbed his hands together as he looked over the feast his brother had prepared.

"Everything smells wonderful, Kyle. Thank you," Bebe said.

"You're in for a treat, Bebe. I used my specially prepared barbecue sauce on this chicken."

"Are you ready to do this, big brother?" Tony asked.

"I sure am," Kyle replied.

The group held hands and bowed their heads as Kyle led them in a quick blessing before they ate. Jill added a secret prayer of her own as he ended. She looked at Kyle as he finished, and he winked at her. She knew he was something special.

The lively conversation around the table began. Jill felt contentment in her heart once again. "Enjoy yourself, and enjoy the man," Barbie had told her. If only her sister knew just how deeply she had taken her advice.

"Bebe and Jill, are you pretty caught up with your work?" Sharon asked.

"Yes, we are. Finally we can relax a little and enjoy ourselves before Jill has to return to New York," Bebe said, smiling.

"Great, I was hoping that we girls could get together one day before Jill has to leave. I haven't had a chance to spend any time with you," Sharon said.

"I'd like that very much. Maybe we could go out to dinner or shopping," Jill suggested.

"Yeah, well, what are we supposed to do while you ladies are all out having fun?" Tony asked.

"You always have so much to do around the ranch, I didn't think you'd have time to go shopping," Bebe teased.

"I'll make time for you," Eric said to Sharon. She smiled at her husband, who was now kissing her cheek.

"Hey, hey, keep all that mush at home. You're making me and Tony look bad," Kyle said. He threw a napkin at his brother, which Eric caught. Smiling, he gently caressed his wife's cheek with it.

"Aww," Jill cooed.

Kyle and Eric only shook their heads and laughed, but each wished one day soon to be like their brother.

Tony picked up a piece of chicken and bit into it. "Brother, you outdid yourself this time."

"Thanks, man, but flattery will get you nowhere. You and Eric are still on cleanup duty," Kyle said jokingly.

The rest of the meal continued magically. Jill laughed and joked with her newfound close circle of friends and found that Eric was almost as funny as Tony when he wasn't under his wife's spell. Jill imagined that Eric's losing his quietness was because he was getting used to her being around. She felt at home and as if she had known everyone around her for more than two weeks. They had shared so much of themselves with her, and she with them. Even now, at Kyle's kitchen table, she could sense a bond forming among them.

At the end of the meal, Tony and Eric started cleaning the kitchen and Kyle asked Jill, Bebe, and Sharon to follow him into the living room. Bebe and Sharon sat on the sofa and Bebe grabbed the remote and turned on the television.

"You two already know the sleeping arrangements," he said. "When I get back, you have to be off my bed."

"We'll be gone, Kyle, don't worry," Sharon told him.

Kyle picked up Jill's overnight bag and said to her, "Come upstairs, and I'll show you to your room." He took her hand and led her up the stairs and into his bedroom. He turned on the lights, after Jill preceded him into the room, and then closed the door behind them. He excused himself and went into the bathroom, shutting the door.

She sat on the edge of the bed and thought about Kyle. She wanted him to stay with her tonight, but felt uncomfortable having everyone staying the night with them. They all held her in high regard, and she didn't want to appear too anxious to all of them. Tonight she would have to sleep alone. Though she wanted to make love to him again, tonight was just not a good time.

Kyle emerged from the bathroom fully dressed. "I'm sorry I took so long. I wanted to brush my teeth and clean up for you." He walked over to Jill and kissed her on the cheek. His arms found their way around Jill's waist and he held her close as he began planting soft moist kissed from her lips to her neck.

She could feel his mounting need for her, and said, "I want to be with you tonight too, baby, but I feel a little uncomfortable sleeping with you with your house full of people." She caressed his strong chest.

"Okay, give me a minute and I'll get rid of them." He pulled away as if he were leaving and Jill started laughing and grabbed his arm.

"No, Kyle," she said. He returned his arms to her waist and she continued to laugh. "We'll just have to wait. I am worth the wait, aren't I?"

Before answering, Kyle's tongue found its way into the warmth of her mouth. He wanted her more than she realized, but tonight he would honor her wishes. His hands fell gently to her backside, and he pressed her to him before ending his kiss.

"Jill, you're more than worth the wait." Reluctantly, he released her and started walking toward the door. "Feel free to use anything in the bathroom, all right? Sleep well; we have to get up early tomorrow," he said. He turned out the ceiling light and left the room.

Jill reached for her overnight bag and went into the bathroom. It had been a busy day, and she was desperately in need of a shower. When she was finished, she slipped into her white nightgown, brushed her teeth, and applied a moisturizer to her face. Finally climbing into the massive bed, she found Kyle's pillows were big and soft and held a faint sent of him. She reached over and turned out the light on the nightstand. Caressing the pillow, she nuzzled her nose in its softness. Jill inhaled deeply, taking in the scent of his cologne. With a smile on her face, she fell asleep.

Chapter 17

A gentle knock on the door woke Jill. As she stretched and then pulled the sheet up over her chest, she said, "Come in," trying to stifle a yawn.

The door opened, and Kyle stuck in his head. "Is it all right to come in?" he asked.

Jill smiled. "Yes," she said, propping herself up on a pillow. "What time is it?"

"It's seven o'clock. I didn't want to wake you, but if you sleep any longer you'll miss breakfast. You know Tony, all is fair in love and food with him," Kyle said, taking a seat on the edge of the bed.

"Did he save me anything to eat?"

"Yes, he did," Kyle answered, unable to take his eyes off the beautiful woman who lay in his bed. With her long, dark brown hair framing her face, she looked at him through thick lashes, and her almond-shaped eyes never left his. He wanted to reach out and touch her silky cocoa skin, but didn't trust himself to stop with just one touch. "If he hadn't I just would have made you some more," he said. He looked at Jill with eyes that pierced her soul, and Jill could sense his desire.

The sheet had slid down to her waist, revealing more of the sexy white nightgown she wore.

"Do you need your room back?" she asked softly.

"No, you take all the time you need."

"I thought you said we had to start out early today."

"I would stop the earth from spinning for you," Kyle said in a sensuously deep, sincere voice. Kyle knew he couldn't compose himself much longer. Turning away from Jill, he started to leave, when she reached for his hand.

"How about a kiss good morning?" Jill asked. She spoke soft and low, and knew that he probably could detect the tone of desire that laced her voice.

He didn't say anything, but quickly took Jill in his arms and began to kiss her with as much passion as he dared to express. He pressed her delicate body against his as he kissed her fully on the lips. With one hand pressing against the small of her back, and the other on the curve of her hip, Kyle's touch melted everything away. She gently held his face to hers and with halted passion returned his kiss. Each of her worries and concerns disappeared when she was in his arms.

Kyle moved back from Jill and held her body away from him. His eyes bored through her and he held his jaw taut. "Do you have any idea what you do to me?" he asked in a voice that pleaded with heaven for help. "You are the most beautiful and fascinating woman I've ever known. You have me jumping through hoops just to be near you."

"I want you to be happy, Kyle."

"I am happy when I'm with you."

Jill ran her fingers gently across his brow and tried to ease the furrows she found there. Giggling lightly she said, "Kyle, we've been making love like we've just discovered sex. Not being together last night didn't kill us."

"Speak for yourself. I felt like I was dying knowing you were in my bed, but not being able to be with you. But I understand, you have appearances you have to keep up," he said reluctantly. "You look ravishing and I only have so much willpower," Kyle said, making himself and Jill laugh. He leaned forward and kissed her again. "I'll wait for you downstairs." Kyle stood, composing himself, and left the room.

Jill thought about what Kyle had said. He wasn't just happy to make love to her, he wanted her to be completely his. It still was all so soon. She was sure she felt something for him too, but was it really love? How could it be love? She had only known him for a couple of weeks. When she returned to New York, she would be able to clear her head.

Jill rolled her eyes at the thought. She wanted to get away from New York and Pittsburgh to straighten out her life, and now she wanted to get away from Durango so she could think clearly again. "I can't keep running," she said aloud.

She got out of bed and dressed, before she went into the bathroom and pulled back her hair. Jill washed her face, brushed her teeth, and then applied her makeup. When she was finished, she made Kyle's bed and put her things back into her bag. She headed downstairs where everyone was still gathered around the table eating breakfast and talking.

"Hey, sleepyhead," Bebe said.

"Good morning, everyone, I hope you all weren't waiting on me," Jill said. She took a seat at the table next to Kyle.

"I only came downstairs a few minutes before you did Jill," Sharon said.

"What would you like to eat, babe?" Kyle asked as he got up to get Jill's coffee.

"I can get it, Kyle. You don't have to wait on me."

"I don't mind. I have orange juice too, would you rather have that?"

"Yes, thank you."

"What time are we going to start out?" Tony asked.

"Jill and I have to make a quick stop at the post office before we leave," Bebe said.

"I have to take a shower before I do anything," Kyle said.

"Kyle, I feel so bad. Thank you for letting me have your room last night, but I feel like I put you out. You should have at least taken a shower before you gave me your room."

"I didn't mind."

"Why don't you ever offer me your room? I've stayed here many nights, and you never offer me the presidential suite," Tony said, smiling and chewing on a piece of bacon.

"The presidential suite is reserved only for Jill," Kyle said. Jill smiled, loving being considered a special guest. She also loved it when Kyle called her "babe." It made her feel as though they were more than friends, though they still weren't officially anything more.

Jill filled a plate with bacon and pancakes. She still couldn't believe that Kyle loved cooking. He was just like her father, who loved to be in the kitchen too.

"Kyle, these pancakes are wonderful," Jill said as she took another bite.

"Thanks, I made them from scratch," he said proudly. "Now, if you all will excuse me, I'm going to take a shower and get dressed."

"Kyle, would you mind if Jill and I drove to the post office? We could go and be back by the time you're done showering," Bebe said.

"Fine by me. My keys are on the coffee table," he said and headed upstairs.

Jill had finished the last of her pancakes and was ready to leave with Bebe. She rinsed her dishes off and put them in the dishwasher.

"Bebe, I'll see you in a bit," Tony said as he followed them to the living room. He gently took Bebe's arm and turned her around. Then he gave her more than a friendly smooch on the lips. He kissed her as if it were an old habit, but Bebe didn't look as casual about it.

"See you later, Tony," she replied. Bebe took Kyle's keys off the table, and she and Jill left the cabin. They walked in silence to the garage. Jill didn't know what was bothering her friend, but it seemed that Bebe's mood had changed when Tony kissed her.

They got into Kyle's Navigator, and Jill started the engine. She backed out of the garage and drove toward the main road. Jill looked over at Bebe and saw a sad expression on her face, and she rubbed her forehead as if trying to relieve stress. "Bebe, you'll have to tell me the way to the post office," Jill said in a hushed voice.

"I'm sorry, Jill. I'm just not myself today. When you get to the main road, make a left and keep straight. It's about two miles away on the right-hand side," Bebe said as she continued to rub her forehead.

As Jill drove she glanced over to see tears falling on Bebe's cheeks. She reached over and laid her hand on Bebe's arm. "What's wrong?" she asked.

"Jill, I don't want to ruin your day. We can talk about it later."

"If we don't talk about it now you will ruin my day."

"You didn't want to talk last night, remember?"

Jill smiled and said, "All right, I'll tell you what was bothering me last night, if you tell me what is bothering you now, deal?"

"Deal," Bebe agreed reluctantly.

Jill took a deep breath and then began, "Before I left New York, I went to visit my next-door neighbors. They just had a beautiful baby girl. Bebe, it's not that I don't want a husband, kids, and the white picket fence, it's just that I want the career too. I've come too far to give it all up now. But every time I see someone with a baby, or expecting a baby, I get a little insecure with my own life. I'm happy. At least that's what I tell myself."

"I can understand that. I kind of figured Sharon's pregnancy hit an emotional nerve."

"Now, what's going on with you?" Jill asked.

"Tony asked me to marry him last night."

"Oh, Bebe, that's wonderful!"

"Jill, I'm afraid of losing what we already have, and he doesn't understand that."

"It seems to me that we both have fears to face. The men in our lives seem to want more than we're ready to give. Kyle and I aren't where you and Tony are, but he wants to be and soon. I also see that you haven't been taking your own advice. Bebe, has there ever been another man you felt more passion for than Tony?"

"No. Like I said, I've know Tony since I was little. Tony, Eric, and Kyle are like brothers to me. I don't want to ruin the family."

"Maybe you would improve the family, not ruin it. Last night at dinner, everyone was so close and happy. I get the feeling it's like that around here all the time."

"You're absolutely right, so why would I want to change anything?"

"Because Tony loves you enough to want to make you his wife. Bebe, he's wonderful and you deserve him. Let yourself be happy with his love," Jill said.

"Only if you promise to do the same," Bebe said as Jill pulled into the parking lot of the post office.

"I'll try, Bebe."

Bebe grabbed the box of invitations from the backseat, and Jill took the contracts and payment invoices that she needed to mail. They quickly had everything weighed, and after paying, the two hurried back to Kyle's cabin.

When they arrived, everyone was waiting for them on the porch. Jill put the vehicle in park, hopped out, and walked around to the passenger's side. Tony opened the back door for Sharon, Eric, and Bebe to get in. Before she got in, Bebe reached and took Tony's face gently in her hands. "I love you, Tony Roberts," she whispered. She pulled his face slowly toward hers and kissed him long and passionately on the lips.

Eric looked over at Kyle and let out a shocked "Whoa!"

No one else said a word, but looked on in amazement. When Bebe finally let Tony come up for air, he had a big grin on his face. Sharon and Eric jumped into the vehicle, and Bebe entered as well. Tony, still smiling, took his hat off and followed behind Bebe.

Jill looked at Kyle and shrugged her shoulders. "What did you say to her?" he asked quizzically.

"Obviously the right thing," Jill whispered. She climbed inside and looked back at her friend, who was busy kissing the man she had known since childhood, and had loved just as long. Jill turned around in her seat and Kyle pulled off.

They had a long drive ahead of them, and the group of friends and family began talking. Kyle reached over and held Jill's hand as he drove.

"About how long do you think it will take us to get there?" Jill asked.

"Almost two hours," Kyle answered. We're going rafting down the Animas River."

"Have you gone rafting down it before?"

"I've been down the Animas several times. The current is swift, so it's good to have an experienced person with you," Kyle said. "Don't worry, you have a car loaded with experienced people."

"That's reassuring. I haven't been rafting in years, and I don't know if I remember what to do."

"Well, the two most important things are wearing a life vest and remembering to sit next to me," he said.

"I think I can manage to do that," she replied.

Kyle was attentive and loving, and Jill couldn't remember the last time she felt so well taken care of by a man. She gently squeezed his hand and he glanced over at her to see a smile of contentment on her face.

"I reserved the half-day package, which includes lunch. I figured that by the time we finished rafting we would be starving," Kyle said.

"I knew we were in good hands with you organizing this trip, big brother," Tony said.

"Do you think that you should be rafting in your condition, baby?" Eric asked his wife.

"Eric, don't worry. We just found out I'm expecting," Sharon said. The car grew silent, as they listened with concern. "Besides, we'll let the doctor decide what I can and can't do."

"I just don't want anything to happen to you or our little one," he assured her and then kissed her cheek.

Jill had the same concern, but didn't dare say anything. She could see that Sharon usually got her way, and that Eric was happy to give it to her.

After almost two hours of driving, Kyle pulled up into the parking lot of Durango White Waters and Outfitters. He parked and everyone exited the truck and went inside. There was a long line of guests, but it was moving quickly. When Kyle reached the clerk, he gave her his name and reservation number. She gave Kyle a quick once-over and smiled enticingly, before she realized he was holding Jill's hand. Though her actions were noticed by Jill, Kyle was completely oblivious.

"All right, Mr. Roberts, I have you down for a half-day package with lunch for six adults," she said.

"That's correct," he said, taking out his wallet to pay for the rafting expedition.

"Hold on to this ticket. Half is for your rafting trip, and the other half is for your meals at our restaurant across the street," the clerk explained, batting her lashes seductively at Kyle.

"Got it," Kyle said.

"Right now, you need to go outside and around to the back of the building. George is out there, and he'll get you started on your rafting excursion." She placed the tickets in his palm, letting their hands connect a little longer than necessary.

"Thank you," Kyle said.

"Yes, thank you," Jill said abruptly. She grabbed Kyle's hand and led him back outside. For an instant, Jill felt as territorial as Sharon.

The group made their way to the back of the building, where they found George.

"Hello," the gray-haired man said. "Welcome to Durango White Waters and Outfitters. I'll be getting you outfitted and on your way."

George disappeared into a shed and came back with six life vests. He gave one to each person and then led them to a raft big enough to carry their group.

"Do we have any experienced rafters here?" George asked.

"We've all been rafting before," Kyle told him.

"Good, then I don't have to give you Rafting 101," he said, laughing, then checked to make sure everyone had fastened their life vests correctly.

The small group boarded the raft and tried to distrib-

ute the weight evenly. Once everyone was seated and
had an oar, they paddled into the river. At first the water
was calm, and Jill enjoyed the sound as it splashed
against the raft. The sun's rays felt warm on her skin,
and she looked up to see that there were no clouds in the
sky.

They paddled toward the bend in the river, and Jill noticed the current picking up. The tiny craft moved faster
through the waters, and Jill felt her hair standing on end.
Before she knew it, the once tranquil waters were now
raging and she could see giant rocks on either side of
them. She smiled as they navigated past jutting rocks,
and was delighted as the raft flew up in the air, only to
land, splashing water over them.

The raft slowed down briefly and she looked over at
Bebe, who had a smile filled with exhilaration on her
face. Bebe's hair was drenched, but she looked like she
was having the time of her life.

Tony sat across from her and seemed to be having fun
as well. The two of them were perfect for each other,
and Jill was happy that Bebe was finally beginning to
see that. Eric and Sharon were in the very back. From
where she sat, Jill could only see Sharon, who looked
very pale like she was going to be sick.

"Are you having fun?" Kyle yelled. He smiled, and
his deep dimples formed in his cheek. He was wet, too,
and Jill could see his fantastic muscles bulging in his
arms as he paddled. Though she tried to stay focused,
her thoughts went instantly to earlier that morning,
when he had kissed her in bed. "Jill, are you all right?"

"Oh, yes, Kyle, I'm fine," she replied, bringing herself back to the present.

"Are you enjoying yourself?"

"This is fantastic. I can't remember ever having this
much fun," she said, smiling. Kyle's own face lit up,

knowing he had accomplished his goal, to make Jill happy. He knew in his heart that there wasn't too much he wouldn't do for her.

"I'm glad because things are about to speed up," he said.

Kyle nodded his head in the direction they were going, and Jill saw that their ride was about to take an even wilder turn. The waters became rougher, and Jill was thrilled by the current's unrelenting rage. With rocks dangerously close to them on either side, Kyle made a split-second decision to veer to the left. He navigated with expert timing and precision, and Jill added this to the list of his many talents. Kyle gained more points with her every day, making it hard for her to keep her resolve not to fall harder for him.

The waters calmed, and they passed a sign that told them where to stop. They would come to a Durango White Waters post in two miles, and Kyle directed the raft toward the right riverbank. They paddled as close to the rocks as they could safely, and Kyle jumped out into the knee-deep water and pulled the raft toward the bank.

Jill jumped out of the raft and helped him, and Bebe and Tony were next. When Jill looked back, she could see that Sharon wasn't doing well. With the raft close enough to rocks, Eric picked Sharon up and carried her to the river's edge.

As soon as she touched the ground, Sharon had her first bout of morning sickness. Bebe held her hand as Jill patted her back. Eric stood by helplessly as his brothers tried their best not to watch. Though Kyle felt compassion for her, he silently hoped his sister-in-law's sickness would be over before she got back into his vehicle.

"Is the little lady all right?" asked an employee from Durango White Waters.

"She'll be fine, she's just experiencing a little morning sickness," Tony said.

"Oh! If she's expecting, I don't think rafting is the best thing for her," he said in a fatherly tone. He handed each of them a towel as he collected all of their life vests.

"I'm fine, morning sickness is a perfectly normal part of pregnancy," Sharon said defiantly.

Jill held her tongue, fighting the urge to speak her mind. Sharon was spoiled and headstrong. She hadn't listened to her husband, and she probably wouldn't have taken Jill's advice either.

"The shuttle will be back to pick you folks up in a minute or two. In the meantime, you can have a seat over at the pavilion," the employee offered.

"Thanks," Kyle said.

Just as they were making their way to sit, the shuttle arrived. They boarded with the other rafters who were waiting. The ride back was much longer than the swift ride they had just taken on the raft. When they arrived at the main post, everyone was ready to eat, except Sharon.

They filed out of the shuttle and walked to the restaurant. It was a busy little place on the side of the road. Jill imagined that the food was good, because of the number of customers they had inside. She was sure that most of the patrons were from White Waters, but not all, because of the way they were dressed.

A hostess came to seat them. "How many in your party?"

"Six," Kyle answered. "Can we sit in the no-smoking section?"

"Sure, follow me," she replied.

The hostess gave them a large booth next to the window. Jill looked outside. Across the busy highway, she could see the beautiful mountains on the other side of the river. They were mostly covered by trees, and Jill loved the natural wonder of them. She thought of New York and wished she didn't have to travel so far to see such natural splendor.

A waitress came and handed each of them a menu, before she took their drink orders and left. A moment later she returned with their beverages and took their food order.

"So what do you have planned for tomorrow?" Kyle asked Jill when the waitress left.

"Nothing. Bebe and I have everything pretty much wrapped up, so I'm free."

"How would you like to go to the Mesa Verde National Park, just you and me?" he whispered.

Jill's eyes sparkled at the thought of spending another day with Kyle. "I'd love to," she whispered back.

"Hey, what are you two whispering about?" Tony said.

"The trip, little brother," Kyle said without lying.

"Man, I haven't had that much fun in a long time. We have to do it again real soon," Tony said.

The waitress returned with their food. They had ordered enough to feed an army and they ate as if they were one too.

"Bebe, you really enjoyed yourself out there, didn't you?" Jill asked.

"Yes, I did. I can't wait to do it again."

Sharon rested her head on the table and tried to wait patiently for them to finish eating. "Sharon, are you all right?" Jill asked.

"No, I still feel a little sick. I just want to go home and rest," she replied tiredly.

"You'll be home before you know it, baby," Eric said.

He finished the last of his food and lovingly helped his wife from the table.

The waitress returned, and Kyle gave her the other end of the ticket to pay for their meal. He opened his wallet and handed her a hundred-dollar bill as a tip.

"Thank you, sir," she said gratefully. "Come back and see us again soon."

"Thank you," Kyle said.

The rest of the group followed Sharon and Eric back to Kyle's truck.

"Don't anyone get in yet, I want to take some pictures of all of us first," Kyle said, opening the passenger door and reaching into the glove compartment for the camera. Kyle ran over to one of the White Water employees and asked him to do the honors.

The guide took several pictures of the group and then Kyle had Tony take a few pictures of himself and Jill. Jill stood in front of him, and Kyle wrapped his arms around her. They both smiled brightly and looked as natural as if they had known each other for years. Tony also took one of Kyle sitting on a bench with Jill sitting in his lap.

The group wasn't as lively on the return trip home. Jill glanced back to see Bebe in Tony's arms, and both were asleep. Seated in back of them, she could see that Eric was still awake, but his exhausted, pregnant wife was asleep in his arms as well.

Jill turned around and smiled. It had been a wonderful day, and she could hardly wait to spend tomorrow with Kyle. When she got home, she would need to get lots of rest, because Kyle wanted to get an early start.

Kyle was tired, but concentrated on the drive home.

Jill laid her head back and watched him. He looked over and saw her watching him.

"Are you tired?" he asked.

"I'm exhausted. Thank you for today."

"You're welcome," he said, once again finding gratification in the fact that he had made Jill happy. "If you're too tired to go to the park tomorrow, I'll understand."

"No, I won't be too tired. Besides, if it's anything like today, I wouldn't miss it for the world," she told him. She gave him the smile that always melted his heart.

Kyle smiled back. "Why don't you get some rest? You might as well get in all you can for tomorrow." He reached over, took her hand, and kissed her palm.

"No, I'd rather just sit here and watch you."

"I have a better idea; why don't you drive, so I can just lie back and watch you? You're a much more beautiful subject to look at than I am," he said.

"As handsome and intelligent as you are, I'm surprised that some woman hasn't snatched you off the market by now."

"No one has snatched me because I have never found the right one. I could say the same for you. You're beautiful, intelligent, funny, and incredibly sexy. Your father must stay worried," he said, laughing.

Jill laughed too. "My father wishes I were married, but not as much as my mother does," she said, shaking her head. "My mother has been going to extreme lengths to get me a husband. I've tried to explain to her what I want out of life, but she won't listen to me." She looked at Kyle, and then out the window, realizing that she had touched on their controversial topic.

"Do you have any brothers or sisters?" he asked.

"I only have a sister. Barbie is two years older than I

am and about a thousand years smarter. She's married, with three kids."

"She must be very busy," Kyle said.

"She is, but she's also going back to law school. Barbie is the type of woman who can juggle being a wife, mother, sister, and student and never make anyone feel as though she doesn't have time for them."

"Wow," Kyle said, impressed.

"My sentiments exactly. It would be hard to imitate that kind of woman," Jill said. Afraid that he might see the sadness in her eyes, Jill looked out the window again.

"Who says that you have to imitate any woman? Jill, you could hold your own in any arena."

She turned and looked at him and saw the honesty in his eyes. His belief that she was a powerful force in her own right made her feel as though a weight had been lifted from her shoulders.

Kyle pulled up into his garage and parked. He turned and looked at Jill, who was still looking at him, this time with admiration in her eyes. "Thank you," she said.

"For what?"

"Just suffice it to say you made me feel really good just now," was all she offered. In her heart, she knew she was thanking him for making her feel complete and for accepting her as she was. Though she knew he wanted a lasting relationship with her, she was happy that he at least offered the words that made her feel good about herself.

He reached over and touched a soft curl of hair that framed her face. "And you just made my day," he said. Kyle slid his hand to the back of her head and pulled her gently toward him. He kissed her on the lips, then whispered, "I want to be the only one who always makes you feel good."

"We better wake everyone up," Jill said nervously.

"You're right." In a louder voice, he said, "All right, everyone, this is the last stop. You don't have to go home, but you can't stay here." He opened his door and walked around the vehicle to assist Jill.

"I can't believe we're already home," Tony said, yawning and stretching.

"Of course you can't, you slept all the way back," Bebe said sleepily.

"I can't believe I got any sleep. I didn't know that you snored so loudly, Bebe," Tony joked.

"Oh, stop, you know that I don't snore."

Tony put on his hat. "Oh yeah, like a chain saw."

Bebe playfully hit his arm as he helped her out.

"Wake up, baby, we're back," Eric said. Sharon had slept all the way back home too and looked as if she had been through the proverbial ringer.

Tony held his sister-in-law's hand, assisting her in getting out of the vehicle. Eric was the last person out of the truck, and he closed the door behind him. He wrapped his arm around his wife's shoulder and said, "I had a great time, big brother."

"Don't mention it. It was my pleasure."

"Sharon and I are going to leave. I think my baby needs to get some rest."

"I have to go too," Tony said. "Eric, can you give me a lift back to my place?"

"Sure."

"Eric, can you give Jill and me a ride back to the ranch?" Bebe asked.

"No problem. Are you both ready to go?"

"We just have to get our bags," Bebe said.

"Actually, Bebe, I'm going to stay for a while longer," Jill said hesitantly. She hoped no one would make a big deal of her staying behind. She was thankful when she realized that they were all too tired to joke.

Bebe left and quickly returned with her bag. "I'm all set," she said in an exhausted voice. She was tired and anxious to get back to the resort and to bed.

Eric bumped fists with his brother. "I'll see you later, man."

"See you later, Kyle," Tony said. He followed Eric, Sharon, and Bebe to Eric's car.

"Later, fellas," Kyle said. He waved good-bye to his family, before he and Jill went to the cabin.

Chapter 18

Once inside the cabin, Jill flopped down on the sofa and said, "I am so tired."

"Can I get you something to eat or drink?" Kyle asked.

"Kyle, I really would love a beer."

"One beer, coming right up," he said, heading toward the kitchen.

He returned with two beers in his hand and sat next to Jill. He was happy to finally have her all to himself, and couldn't believe she had consented to stay with him. He handed her a beer and sat back on the sofa.

She took a long sip of the dark brew and let out a satisfied sigh. "That hit the spot. I rarely drink beer, but I just felt like having one tonight," she said. "Heineken, right?"

"Yes, I see you know your beers."

"Not really, when I want a beer this is the only brand I drink."

"It's my favorite, too," he said. He noticed that he and Jill had a lot in common and hoped she noticed, too. "I think tomorrow will be great. You'll love the park. It's one of my favorite places to visit."

"I'm sure I will love it since you haven't steered me wrong so far. I must admit, though, rafting really took a lot out of me. But I can't remember ever having that much fun," Jill said, smiling. "You always seem to be prepared for everything."

"That's because I was a Boy Scout."

"Were you really?"

"Yep, Eric and Tony were too," he said. He took a drink of his beer. "My father made all of us join. At first we hated it, because we'd rather have been riding our horses, but then we started enjoying ourselves and didn't want to miss a meeting."

"That's why you're ready for anything."

"I guess so," he said. "Would you like to watch a movie, Jill?" He put his empty glass on the table and picked up the remote to the flat-screen television.

"That would be nice." She put her beer on the table and Kyle noticed that the bottle was more than half full. Jill sat back and moved closer to him.

He turned on the television and flipped through the channels. He didn't know if Jill was into suspense or romance, but he hoped she would give him a clue. He had over a hundred cable stations and knew he would eventually find something Jill would enjoy.

"Oh, Kyle, go back a few channels," she said suddenly.

Jill wanted to watch a murder mystery. Kyle returned the remote to the table and snuggled next to Jill. He put his arm around her shoulder and she laid her head on his. As Jill watched the movie, she felt Kyle's eyes resting on her. She turned to see a content expression on his face.

"What are you thinking about, Mr. Roberts?" she said, taking his hand in hers.

"I'm just thinking how blessed I am to have you in my life," he replied as he slid his hand away from hers and placed it under her chin. He lifted her face and kissed her softly on the lips before letting his hand slide down to caress her breast.

What was it about him that made her weak in the knees? she thought. He needed only to express his need for her and she was ready and willing to accommodate him. She wanted to show him all the love a woman could hold in her heart for a man, too.

Kyle seemed never to get enough of her and Jill loved the fact that every time they had made love it was something new, exciting, and more passionate than the time before.

Kyle had her shirt off and was concentrating on getting her out of her shorts. Jill was just as anxious and began working to take off his clothes. When they were both naked, Kyle sat down on the sofa and Jill sat in his lap, straddling him.

She closed her eyes as he took her breast into his mouth and lovingly stroked her back. When he finished with that breast, he moved to the other, nibbling and sucking until she let out a little moan.

Having made love to Jill two times before, he was very in-tune to her needs. He knew she was just getting started and he would need to lovingly coax her to a higher plateau.

In one effortless movement, Kyle stood up holding Jill in his arms. He walked over to the bearskin rug and laid her down. Then he took a bottle of body oil from the table and poured some in his hand. He began massaging the front of her body from head to toe, then he had her roll over onto her belly. Kyle massaged her back, shoulders, and thighs. Jill could feel herself getting very sleepy, but before she fell into a blissful slumber, Kyle pressed his strong body against her back. Jill's eyes closed softly as a smile formed on her lips.

Then she turned her head, Kyle's tongue slid into her mouth.

They continued kissing until he turned her over. The couple stood and Kyle guided Jill back to the sofa. He sat down and Jill could see the full extent of him. Kyle worked the condom down his length and Jill saw that he was more than ready for her. Jill climbed into his lap and slid herself over him, taking in every inch he had to offer.

Though he had taken time to ready her for their love-making, it always took Jill a few moments to adjust to him. Kyle placed a hand on either side of her waist and gently moved her body up and down. After her body had managed to accommodate his immense size, she too began moving in harmony with him.

He took up every inch she had to offer and left her body craving more. In the dimly lit room, Kyle still could see Jill's perfect form. He watched her breasts bounce enticingly as she rode him. Kyle rested his head on the back of the sofa as he held her body tightly. Consumed with more excitement than his body could contain, he held her hips as he thrust himself into her. Jill cried out loudly with passion as both their bodies reached a climax at the same time.

Jill fell limp in Kyle's arms. He continued to hold her body close as their breathing began to slow. She wanted to stand, but her legs wouldn't let her. Kyle sensed what she wanted and once again lifted his queen and laid her on the bearskin rug.

He retrieved a blanket and pillows from the hallway closet. Tucking a pillow under her head, he cuddled next to her and covered them both.

Jill turned and smiled at him. "I wish I had a crystal ball," she whispered.

"Why?" he asked as he rubbed her belly.

"I just feel so good with you. When I'm with you everything fits, everything's perfect. I don't know if what I'm feeling is real or if it is just my imagination. If I had a crystal ball, I could look and see if you are always going to be in my life."

"I am. I want to be, Jill." Kyle caressed her cheek and added, "Baby, I'll never hurt you."

"I want to believe that but—"

"But time will tell," Kyle said. "I'm not going anywhere, and I won't let you either. I love you." He kissed her again. Jill felt herself giving way to sleep. She rested her head on Kyle's chest and fell asleep.

The morning sun filtered through Kyle's living room window. Jill began to stir. She slowly opened her eyes and looked up at Kyle. Seeing his handsome face so close to hers, she smiled. "Well, good morning, handsome." Jill uncurled her legs from under her and sat up, leaning forward to kiss him.

"Good morning, beautiful," he replied. Kyle sat upright and stretched. "Aahhh, my back is killing me."

"I'm sorry. It probably hurts because I was lying on you."

"Don't worry about it. It will feel better after I take a hot shower," he said. Kyle stood and took the two beer bottles he and Jill had left on the coffee table into the kitchen. Then he came back into the living room. "Do you want to take a shower first, or do you want me to?"

"I'll go first. If I don't, I'm afraid that you won't leave me any hot water."

"You're right about that. While you take a shower, I'll make you some breakfast. What would you like to eat?" he asked as he slid on a pair of boxers.

Jill walked over to where he stood and wrapped her

arms around his waist. "Why don't you surprise me?" she said. Jill tilted her head back and slightly parted her lips in anticipation of Kyle's kiss.

He held her face gently and kissed her tenderly on the lips and then her neck. Jill pulled away slowly and looked up at the rugged, handsome cowboy who had stolen her heart. "I'm going to go take my shower now," she said. Jill turned around slowly and walked up the stairs.

Watching Jill from behind was one of his favorite things to do. She was definitely not a hippy woman, but she had the walk of a runway model, and Kyle enjoyed every step she took. He watched until she was out of sight and then went into the kitchen to make her breakfast.

Jill went into Kyle's room to get an extra outfit from her overnight bag. Undressed, she went into Kyle's linen closet to get a bath towel. In the closet, she saw the white nightgown she had worn the night before. Jill stood still for a second wondering how it had gotten into the closet, when she distinctly remembered putting it into her overnight bag. She smiled as she remembered Kyle kissing her in his bed yesterday morning and knew that he had taken it as a keepsake.

Putting the gown back, she went to take her shower. The water felt wonderful on her skin. As she bathed, she thought about how her relationship with Kyle was growing. Jill had slept in his bed and in his arms. She had been out with him and enjoyed meals with him and his family. She felt warm inside and had a sense of belonging when he was around. She couldn't remember when she had felt so at peace with her life.

After her shower, Jill slathered on lotion and then applied a light moisturizer to her face. She dressed in a pair of cute denim shorts and a pale blue tank top. She remembered Kyle had been playing in her hair as she woke up, and decided to leave it down. She brushed her hair behind her ears and left the soft curls flowing over her shoulders. Then, she sprayed Chloe Narcisse behind her ears and in her cleavage.

"The shower is all yours," she said as she entered the kitchen.

"Breakfast is ready," he said in a halting manner. He stopped what he was doing long enough for his eyes to take in an appreciative look at her. "Wow, how does the most beautiful woman in the world stay so gorgeous?"

"Flattery will get you everywhere, Mr. Roberts," she said, smiling.

"I made you a western omelet, some toast, and orange juice," he said. Kyle looked at Jill's long beautiful legs and noticed that they were incredibly shapely with no marks or blemishes. Her arms were firm, but not muscular. He looked away, realizing that he was blatantly staring at her.

"I left you some hot water," Jill said as she sat down.

"I have to admit, that's more than I would have done for you."

Jill laughed. "Kyle, breakfast looks wonderful. You have to stop spoiling me. I'm going to start expecting you to cook for me all the time." She opened the linen napkin and placed it on her lap.

Kyle bent over and whispered in her ear, "You have no idea just how much I want to spoil you, Jill Alexander. He kissed her cheek, then added, "I'm going to go take a shower now." He went upstairs, hoping that the beautiful dream he had just left would not fade away.

Jill sat in the kitchen enjoying the meal Kyle had prepared. He was a fantastic cook and obviously liked being in charge of the kitchen. As she ate, she thought about the many things she had learned about him over the past few days.

He was very romantic, she thought, never missing an opportunity to hold her hand or kiss her. He was a great conversationalist and didn't mind being the center of comical attention from time to time. As she took another bite of the omelet, she couldn't help wondering why such a smart and educated man was content being a ranch hand. She had thought on the subject more than once, but still wouldn't dare ask him why he chose the profession.

She sat back in her chair and sipped her orange juice, continuing to think about the handsome cowboy who was creeping into her heart. She did enjoy being with him, and knew in her heart that she wanted to be more than friends, although she was uncertain of how things would develop between them.

As Jill rinsed her dishes in the sink, Kyle came down the stairs wearing a tight-fitting black T-shirt that showed off his well-defined pectoral muscles. The shirt was tucked into a pair of nice-fitting jeans, giving Jill a better view of his six-pack abdomen. His neat, tapered hair was brushed and wavy. Kyle stopped and picked up a pair of Ray Ban sunglasses from the counter and put them on.

"I'm all set. Let's go, babe."

Jill could smell his cologne. He was wearing her favorite, Fahrenheit, and she inhaled deeply. He had called her "babe" again, making her heart skip a beat. Jill could only hope she hadn't been staring, but she was completely aware that her jaw had dropped slightly when she laid eyes on him. "I'm ready too. I mean, I'm ready to go too," she said, trying to focus on something other than his muscles.

Kyle walked to the front door and held it open for her.

"After you," he said. He picked up her overnight bag and took it with him.

"Thank you," Jill said. She walked out into the brilliant sunlight and knew that the day was full of promise.

Kyle closed the door behind them, and he and Jill walked hand in hand to the garage. He opened the door to the truck and waited for her to climb inside.

"I guess we have a long drive ahead of us to the park, don't we?" she asked, when Kyle was inside.

"Not really. We have about an hour's drive. We're going to ride U.S. 160 West, and then we'll come to the park's entrance. We'll be there before you know it. Are you a little anxious to get there?" he asked. He reached over, deciding to hold her hand as he drove.

"I guess I am a little excited, but I don't mind the drive. It will give me a chance to enjoy your company."

Kyle looked over at her and smiled. His deep dimples caught her eye, and she couldn't resist smiling back. She rubbed the top of his hand with her thumb and relished the warmth and strength she found there. She enjoyed his touch and hoped he wouldn't let go.

"How long have you lived in New York?" he asked.

"I have been there for almost seven years. I moved there right after college and landed the job at Iguana."

"I guess you really enjoy working for them."

"I do, and it's not a long plane ride home."

"Where is that?"

"Pittsburgh."

"Do you go home very often?"

"Not as often as I should," Jill answered. She looked sadly out her window, thinking of her parents, and how sad they were to see her leave, and of Ricky, and how much he enjoyed being around her. She missed her sister too, and couldn't wait to see her at the end of the week. "I plan to take care of that though. My family misses me a lot and I miss them. I promised them I would visit more often."

"Why haven't you been able to? Is working for Iguana very demanding?"

"No, it's not. Iguana gives me pretty much everything I ask for. To be honest, I want to open my own public relations firm one day. I guess I have been so driven by the desire to succeed, and trying to make a name for myself, that I've left little time for myself or my family. But that will all change once I get my business under way. For right now, though, I am going to make visiting my family a priority," she finished with conviction.

"Along the way, don't forget to stop and smell the roses. You might return too late and find that they have all died."

Jill looked at him and smiled, enjoying his gentle analogy of her life. "I'll try not to forget," she said.

"Where are your parents?" Jill asked.

Kyle shifted in his seat and, like Jill, avoided eye contact. "Well, my mom and dad are in Chicago right now."

"Chicago, is that where they live?"

"No, my dad is on a business trip, and my mother always travels with him.

They live here in Durango, but it's hard to catch them here."

"Why?"

"Oh, because my dad travels quite a bit."

"He must be a very successful businessman. What does he do?"

"He's into real estate," was all Kyle offered. He hoped for now that what he told her would suffice, and tried to change the subject. "Are you thirsty? There's a gas station up here on the left."

"Yes, could I have lemonade please?"

"No problem," he said. Kyle pulled into the station and up to the pump. "I'll be right back," he said.

Kyle got out of the vehicle and walked back toward the store. From her rearview mirror, Jill watched him walk away. She laid her head back against the headrest and let her mind have its way with Kyle's body. All six feet three inches of him reeked of fine, and she watched him until he disappeared into the store. She smiled to herself and closed her eyes. She felt giddy inside, and wanted to shout to the world just how happy he made her.

"Here you go, babe," Kyle said. He stood at her door and handed her a bottle of lemonade.

"Thanks," she said. Though she loved it when Kyle called her "babe," she didn't feel the need to return the term of endearment just yet.

"Give me a second, and we'll be on our way."

As he pumped the gas, a white BMW pulled up on the other side of the pumps. A woman wearing a sexy, coral-colored chiffon sundress got out and walked over to Kyle. Jill sat up in her seat and looked at the brown-skinned woman as she approached Kyle.

"Excuse me, could you tell me how I would get to Mancos?" she asked him.

Kyle began giving the beautiful woman directions, and Jill angled his rearview mirror so that she could see the woman better. Her hair blew in her face, and she tucked it behind her ears. The woman took off her sunglasses, and Jill could see that she had a flawless complexion. Though she wore a pair of elegant three-inch sandals, Jill estimated that she and the woman were about the same height.

Kyle had obviously said something funny because Jill heard the woman laughing. She pushed the mirror farther out so that she could get a better look at what they were doing. She saw the woman rest her hand on Kyle's arm and hold it there as he gave her directions.

"Oh, no, she's not," Jill said under her breath. She leaned over and purposely blew the horn. The woman jumped and turned in Jill's direction. "Ooops! Sorry, that was an accident," she yelled out to them.

She sat back in her seat, but continued to watch the woman, who had turned around to finish getting directions from Kyle. A moment later she thanked him and returned to her own car. She gave Jill an irritated look, put her sunglasses on, and sped off.

"Jill, do you need anything else while we're here?" Kyle asked her.

"No, I'm fine."

Kyle pulled off and headed back to the highway. He glanced into his rearview mirror and noticed that it was askew. He shook his head and smiled. Taking Jill's hand, he kissed the back of it and continued to hold it as he drove.

"I bet you get that all the time."

"What?"

"Beautiful women throwing themselves at you."

Kyle chuckled. "She wasn't throwing herself at me."

"Yes, she was. Why is it that men can never see these things? She had no reason to hold your arm while you gave her directions."

"First of all, babe, I didn't feel as though she was throwing herself at me. Secondly, if she was, I totally missed the pitch. The only thing on my mind was Jill Alexander, and how fast I could get back to her. As far as beauty is concerned, she couldn't hold a candle to you."

"I like your comeback."

"I must admit, though, it was kind of enthralling to see you get a little jealous." He snickered.

"Jealous, I wasn't jealous. I just didn't see any reason for her to be all over you," Jill said, trying to suppress her own laughter.

"Uh-uh, it was jealousy. I'm just happy that she didn't give me a hug; then I really would have seen the green-eyed monster come out," he said in uncontrolled laughter.

Jill was laughing too, and playfully hit his arm. "Kyle, stop. I'm not like that at all."

"Whatever you say, babe. As long as you know that I only have eyes for you." He continued holding her hand and hoped she knew that what he said was true.

"We're here," Kyle said.

After the exit, the entrance gate was a mile away.

Jill looked out her window. "Oh, Kyle, this place looks amazing."

Kyle drove to the visitors' center, fifteen miles farther into the park. There, he purchased tickets for the ranger-guided tour of the Palace Cliff. Jill made sure she picked up a map of the park, wanting to know as much about the ancient grounds as she could.

The visitors' center had many Native American artifacts decorating the room. It also had souvenirs and books for sale.

As she walked toward Kyle, at the register, she saw books about the park and the Pueblo people who once lived in the area. She couldn't resist and picked one up to purchase. Kyle watched in amazement at her enthusiasm for knowledge.

"I have to get this book. Doesn't it look interesting?" she said as she handed it to him.

"Yes, it does," he replied, flipping through the pages.

She reached in her back pocket and pulled out some

money. "Would you pay for this for me?" She tried to hand Kyle the cash, but he refused it.

"Let me buy it for you."

"Why? I have money on me."

"Consider it a gift to celebrate our first date. Well, our first date alone."

She reached up and put her hand behind his head and then she gently pulled his head down toward hers. Jill kissed him on the lips and whispered, "Thank you," in his ear.

"It's my pleasure," he whispered back, in a sensuously deep voice.

Kyle paid for their items and then the couple left the center. It was a hot and sunny day, and they both were glad they had brought their sunglasses. They were going on a guided tour, and Jill was instantly thankful she had worn shorts.

"I hope you don't bake in those jeans," she said, looking at Kyle.

"I was just hoping you didn't scrape your legs," he replied as he got back in his vehicle.

Jill stopped momentarily and looked down at her legs. She didn't have a scratch on them, but now feared she would acquire some.

"Why didn't you tell me?" she asked with a slight whine in her voice.

Kyle laughed at her and said, "I'm just teasing you; you should be fine. Besides, I would never put those legs in jeopardy."

"I'm going to hold you to that. Are we on our way to the Palace Cliff?"

"Yep, it's located in the Chapin Mesa, but we have to go to the rangers' post for the tour."

Kyle pulled off and headed to the post. When he and Jill arrived, there was a nice-sized group waiting to take the tour. He parked, grabbed his camera from the back-seat, and then they both joined the onlookers.

A woman was walking around collecting the tickets. Jill was surprised to learn that she was the ranger; Jill had been expecting a man to fill the position. After she had collected all the tickets, she announced that they would begin their expedition in just a few minutes.

Kyle held Jill's hand as they waited patiently. Jill looked and saw that there were quite a few families taking the tour, and saw that one woman had decided to come alone. Jill felt sorry for her and imagined that the woman was lonely and wished she had someone to enjoy the experience with.

She wondered if that was how people perceived her when she was on an outing alone, then guessed that it was. She remembered how she felt the last time she had gone to the Olive Garden and had sat alone in the restaurant. She remembered how she felt as families conversed, and loving couples stroked each other's hands and whispered sweet nothings in each other's ears. Unable to take it anymore, she had asked her waiter to make her order to go.

Instinctively, she squeezed Kyle's hand, and she found comfort in having him by her side. Kyle looked at her and saw a distant look in her eyes. "Are you okay?" he asked in concern.

"I am right now," she replied.

Kyle let go of her hand and put his arm around her waist. He pulled her close to him and kissed her temple. Jill felt a strong sense of contentment, as if all that mattered in the universe was being with him.

"Good morning, everyone. I'm Ranger Sansone, and I'll be your tour guide today," she said. The ranger was a very pleasant woman and obviously had a zeal for the work she did. "Welcome to Mesa Verde National Park.

Mesa Verde is Spanish for green table. My job today is to give you a glimpse into the unique civilization that once lived here. The ruins we're about to tour were inhabited by Pueblo Indians about fourteen centuries ago. Please feel free to take as many pictures and ask as many questions as you would like. I love to be in pictures and I love answering questions," she announced, and the group chuckled at her humor.

Ranger Sansone led the group on its tour. They walked past giant spruce trees, colorful wildflowers and shrubs. When the ranger led them to the edge of a cliff, Jill saw an awesome view of Cliff Palace. Kyle lifted his camera and took several pictures of Jill with Cliff Palace in the background.

"Kyle, this is the most spectacular place I've ever seen," Jill said. Her eyes were wide, and her voice was filled with awe.

"Wait, it gets better."

Ranger Sansone led them down the side of the cliff. The hike descended down a steep trail, and Jill wondered if she would make it to the bottom without falling.

"This looks a little rigorous," Jill said.

"Look over there. We have to use stairs, ladders, and rock outcroppings just to get down there," Kyle told her.

An intrigued smile appeared on Jill's face. She was anxious to take on the challenge. For a chance to explore the ancient ruins, she would gladly risk a skinned knee or two. "Let's do it!"

It took them a while, but everyone made it down the side of the cliff without incident. The ranger waited until everyone gathered around her before she gave a brief summary about the site they were all getting ready to explore.

Jill listened intently as the ranger described the Cliff Palace ruins as the largest and most spectacular dwelling in the park. Some fourteen centuries ago, the Anasazi Indians had made this area home also. Cliff Palace had 217 rooms and was a massive construction project for the Anasazi tribe, who lived there for nearly one hundred years.

Jill looked in awe and admiration of an ancient civilization's incredible edifice. They had chiseled out living spaces from sand stone and rock. The Native American architecture reminded her of Kyle. She was still quite impressed by the fact that he had built his own home.

Ranger Sansone made sure everyone in her group was accounted for before she led the small gathering toward one of the many ladders they would use to climb back to the top of the cliff's edge.

Kyle turned around and took another picture of Jill as she climbed.

"Kyle, how many pictures of me do you plan to take?"

"I'll just keep taking them until I run out of film. You seem to be enjoying yourself."

"I am, but are we leaving after this?" she asked reluctantly.

"No, I thought you and I would make the rest of our stay in the park a self-guided tour. After we're finished taking our personal tour, you should be good and hungry. We can stop and get something to eat before we head back to Durango."

"That's sounds great," Jill said. It felt good having a man take care of her. Kyle was loving and thoughtful, without being overbearing. He hadn't ceased to amaze her with his quick wit and intelligence, and Jill knew that all she had learned so far about the amazing man only scratched the surface.

"It's hot out here. I wish I had bought a bottle of water while we were back at the visitors' center," Jill said.

"That's no problem, we have to go back that way to get to the parking lot. We can stop and get a couple of bottles of water," Kyle said.

When they arrived back at the visitors' center, Kyle said, "Why don't you just stay here and relax, since we have quite a hike ahead of us still? I'll go inside and get the water."

"You're really planning on wearing me out, aren't you?"

"That's not my intention, but I do have a feeling that you'll be worn out by the end of the day," Kyle told her. He brushed her cheek gently with his hand and went to the center.

Jill laid her head back and relaxed. Closing her eyes, she thought of the site she had just visited. She was enjoying herself immensely and was anxious to see more of the park. Jill opened her eyes when she felt the vehicle move.

"Here you go," he said, handing her a bottle of water. "This is nice and cold."

Jill opened the bottle and took a long drink. She hadn't realized that she was so thirsty and wished Kyle had bought two.

She wiped her mouth on the back of her hand. "Aahhh, that felt good going down. Thank you."

"You were pretty thirsty," Kyle said. He started the engine and drove toward the Morefield Amphitheater.

"Yes, I was. When we stop for lunch, I'll make sure I drink some more. I don't want to get dehydrated." She took another drink, before she put the cap back on the bottle.

As Kyle drove, Jill looked out her window and could see visitors walking along and enjoying their own self-guided tours. Just about everyone had a camera and was taking pictures of the huge beautiful mountains, trees, and cliff dwellings. On their way to the amphitheater, they passed Ranger Sansone and her group of visitors. The ranger still looked like she had a lot of energy left in her and was walking and talking enthusiastically. When they arrived at the amphitheater Kyle parked and grabbed his camera.

They got out and Kyle walked over to Jill, taking her hand in his. "We'll start from over there." He pointed at the far side of the parking lot. "Are you ready for this?"

"I'm ready, willing, and able."

"Great. Let's go then."

The two began walking up the ridge to Point Lookout. Kyle expected Jill to tire easily. Halfway through the trek he asked her, "Do you want to stop for a rest?"

"No, I don't need one," she said as she continued to take long strides. "But we can stop if you need one."

Kyle's brows furrowed. "No, I'm fine. Let's just keep going," he said with a note of determination in his voice.

Jill smiled to herself knowing Kyle expected her to whine about the steep hike. But for her, this was nothing more than a good workout on the Stair Master in her apartment's fitness center.

"Here we are," Kyle said. The two had made it to the top of the five-hundred-foot rise.

"Wow," Jill said. She looked around in astonishment at God's work. Never had she seen so much splendor in one place.

Kyle took her hand again as the two continued on the trail, which followed closely along the edge of the escarpment. Though there were quite a few people on the trail with them, Jill felt as if she were there with no one else except Kyle. Only a few clouds danced across the clear sky, and sunlight glistened off the surrounding mountains. Of all the places she could be right now, she knew she was where she was supposed to be.

Kyle stopped walking and pointed down. "That's Mancos Canyon."

"It's breathtaking." Jill looked all around at the canyon's sun-streaked beauty. Giant rocks jutted out from all sides. She could see a stream flowing through the valley too.

"And those are the La Plata Mountains," Kyle said. Then he pointed toward the southern end of the mountain facing them. "That's Mount Hesperus. The Navajo consider it their sacred mountain of the north," he finished and turned to look at Jill, only to find her eyes gazing at him in wonder. "What's wrong?"

"Nothing, it's just that I have never met anyone like you. All the men I've ever dated only wanted a one-night stand, or they were like talking to a doorknob. But you don't fall into either category. You don't try to push me into something I'm not ready for. You're patient and loving . . . I-I shouldn't have said that. I'm talking too much," Jill said. She turned and looked at the mountains again.

Kyle turned her back around and took both her hands in his. "Anything worth having is definitely worth waiting for. Jill, I know that you feel the same way that I do, but you're just afraid to give it a name. I love you and I want you to be mine. I can't let you go back to New York without letting you know that someone out here is crazy in love with you."

"It sounds so insane, but I love you too," she said softly.

"Stranger things have been said between two people. What's wrong with our admitting we love each other?"

"Kyle, we've only know each other for a couple of weeks. How could either of us be sure of what we're feeling?"

"I'm not saying that we have to book the church today, but if you wanted to, I'd be there. Jill, what I am saying is that the moment you fell into my arms, you had me. Since that night, I've thought of you every waking moment, and you even fill my dreams when I'm asleep. I've never felt like that about anyone before. I know you're something special, and I know what we feel between us is something special too."

Jill pulled her hands from his and wrapped them softly behind his neck. She pulled him toward her until their lips met. Kyle held her close and kissed her passionately on the mouth. They gave no care to the world around them. Jill knew in her heart that this was what she wanted, and that Kyle was whom she wanted to be with.

"Let's go, baby," she said. Pulling away from him, she surprised Kyle with her words of affection.

"Don't you want to see more of the park?"

"No, I just want to spend time with you."

"Fine by me, but let me get a picture of you up here first."

Jill laughed and obliged him.

Kyle stepped back and took a couple of pictures of Jill using the beautiful mountains as a backdrop. He asked another visitor to take a couple of them together. Kyle placed Jill in front of him, and the couple smiled brightly, basking in the love they had just found in each other.

The walk down was much easier and faster than their climb up. When they reached the bottom, Kyle put his arm around Jill's waist and they walked slowly back to his SUV.

"Kyle, I had a wonderful time today. I wish it didn't have to end."

"Do you mean stay in the park forever?"

"No." She laughed. "I mean I wish every day could be like today. I never have to worry about anything when I'm with you. I love the way you take care of things and the way you make me feel."

When they had reached Kyle's truck, he leaned against it. She rested her hands on his chest as he pulled her close to him. "I'm glad you feel that way when you're with me. I'm not going to lie, I want to take care of you forever. I want to be the last thing you see at night and the first thing you see in the morning."

"And I want to be the only person you hold like this," Jill said coyly.

"I hear you. I'm so into you, Jill Alexander," Kyle said thickly. He was filled with desire for her, and was happy he was wise enough to realize the kind of woman Jill was, and how to approach her.

He kissed her neck softly in an upward motion, until he reached her ear. Kyle nibbled it gently with his lips, and Jill closed her eyes and felt herself go limp in his arms. She tried hard to remember the last time a man had made her feel this way, then quickly decided that now was neither the time nor the place for such thoughts. Right now, everything was perfect, and she didn't want to tamper with perfection.

Kyle lifted his head and looked into Jill's face. Her eyes were still closed, and he smiled knowing he was the reason for giving her a sense of contentment. He didn't want to lose her and would do whatever it took, to keep her for himself.

Jill opened her eyes to see a peaceful smile on Kyle's

face. He reached up and softly stroked her hair and then pulled her to his own lips. He kissed her again, then said, "Let's get something to eat, babe."

Kyle opened the door for Jill, and when she was seated inside he closed it behind his treasure. He walked around to his door and got in. Neither one said a thing, preferring not to spoil the moment with talk.

Chapter 19

Jill looked out her window, trying to come to terms with everything that had transpired in the last hour. She had told Kyle that she loved him, and he had said the same. She tried to recount the events of the last two weeks, trying to figure out when she fell in love. If she had to pin the incident to a time, she would have to say it was the first night she laid eyes on him. She, of all people, didn't believe in love at first sight, but it had happened to her.

Kyle looked over and saw a blank stare on Jill's face. "Jill, are you all right?" he asked.

"Oh yeah, I'm fine. I'm just a little hungry though."

"I'm going to take you to the Spruce Tree Terrace for lunch. It's located in the museum area, not too far from here."

"That's good because I think all the hiking made me build up an appetite."

"I've seen how you eat; I hope there's enough room on my credit card to cover that appetite," he said, laughing.

Jill playfully hit his arm and said, "Kyle, I don't eat a lot."

"Yes, you do. I've been wondering how you stay so small the way you go at it."

"Kyle, stop," Jill said. They were both laughing when Kyle pulled into the parking lot.

They walked to the outdoor terrace and found a little table for two. The area was surrounded by big lush trees, which gave their own music as a breeze blew through their leaves.

"I like this place; it's a little romantic," Jill said.

"What do you mean? There're families with kids all around us," Kyle said. He looked up from his menu to see what Jill was talking about.

Jill playfully rolled her eyes and said, "No, that's not what I mean. I'm talking about the design of the place itself. I love the trees, the breeze, and this little table we're sitting at." The wind blew again and she brushed her hair from her face.

After a waitress took their drink and food orders, Kyle said to Jill, "You know, I was only teasing about how much you eat. You didn't have to order a salad."

"Oh no, buddy, soon you'll tell me that I've put on weight."

"Jill, I'm sorry. Really, I was only teasing."

"I know you were just joking. I really do want a salad though."

They finished their food and Kyle paid the bill. Both were tired and ready to head home.

"I know you're tired. I'll have us home in no time," Kyle said as he pulled out of the parking lot and drove in the direction of the exit.

Jill turned her head toward Kyle and rested it against the headrest. "Kyle, I want to say something, and I hope I don't offend you."

Kyle glanced over at her with a serious look on his face. He couldn't imagine what she could say that would offend him, but asked cautiously, "What's on your mind?"

"Well, you've been paying for everything, and I know it can't be easy. I mean, I don't know how much a ranch hand makes, but I hope paying for all the activities these past few days didn't put a hole in your pocket."

"Oh, Jill, don't worry about it," he said. He looked out his window nervously and shifted in his seat.

"See? I did make you uncomfortable. I'm sorry. I just wanted to let you know that I can help pay."

"No, I can't let you do that. I have everything under control." Kyle looked straight ahead, refusing to make eye contact with Jill. He had wanted to tell her that his father, Samuel Roberts, was one of the wealthy investors that had hired Iguana Public Relations to promote the ranch. And that he was no mere ranch hand, but actually the grandson of Decatur Roberts, the original owner of the five thousand acres that A Special Place sat on.

He preferred to charm her with his personality, rather than his wealth. When he realized that Jill was all class, he didn't know how to bring it up without chasing her away. Their first few meetings had been so rocky that he didn't want to risk laying too much on her at one time. If he told her now, it would be as if his intention all along was to deceive her.

They rode in silence for quite a ways. Jill felt as though she had offended Kyle and wished she could rewind the tape and take back what she had said.

Kyle drove in silence, trying to figure out when the right time would be to tell Jill who he was. He knew it had to be soon. The longer he waited, the more it would seem as if he was being dishonest with her.

They were almost back to the resort when Jill reached over and rubbed Kyle's neck. "Kyle, I'm sorry. I don't want you to be mad at me for what I said," she said sadly.

"Babe, please, I'm okay with it," Kyle said. He pulled onto the road that would take them back to the resort.

"I just want you to know I didn't mean to offend you."

Kyle pulled in front of the main building and into the rotunda. "You weren't out of line." He bent over and kissed her lips. "I have something I want to talk to you about, too," he said, unable to keep his secret anymore.

"What's that?" she asked, sitting back in her seat.

"Not right now; I know you're tired, and so am I. We can talk about it later."

"Are you sure?" she asked. Jill looked deep into his eyes trying to find any sign of frustration, but there was none.

"I'm sure. Will I see you later?" He reached into the backseat and handed Jill her bag.

"You can count on it, cowboy." She leaned over and gave him another kiss before she got out.

Jill waved good-bye and walked to her room. Once inside, she took off her shoes and clothes and got into the shower. She felt as though she were drenched in sweat and the water felt warm and cleansing as it sprayed over her body.

When she finished, she put on a short, pink floral pajama set, then opened the sliding glass door that led out to her patio before she lay across her bed.

She had several calls to make and decided to call Lois and Diane first, since they would be getting off work soon. Afterward, she would call Barbie and let her know just how well things had gone since she had taken her advice. She picked up the phone and dialed Iguana. The phone rang a few times and Jill hoped her friends hadn't left work for the day.

"Iguana Public Relations Group," Lois said in an extremely tired voice.

"Hi, Lois, it's Jill."

"Jill, we've been wondering when you were going to call. How are you?" Lois said, happy to hear her friend's voice.

"I'm fine, Lois. I'm sorry I haven't called lately, but I've been kind of busy."

"I got your e-mail. I'm glad that the opening is coming along well."

"It's coming along great. Did you get a chance to make my travel arrangements for Thursday?"

"Yes, I did, you're all set to return to Pittsburgh on Thursday morning, and then back to New York on Sunday afternoon. I can't wait to see you. Our Friday night celebrations haven't been the same without you."

"I've missed you and Di too. How is she?"

"Di is fine. She wants to talk to you, probably about her new man. They seem to be really into each other.

Jill thought immediately of the new someone special in her life. She wanted to wait until she returned to New York and tell her friends in person about Kyle, but felt she would burst from excitement if she didn't tell them now. "Lo, I'm seeing someone too," she began excitedly. "His name is Kyle Roberts, and he is a ranch hand out here."

Lois said nothing, surprised that Jill was seeing anyone at all, especially Kyle Roberts. "Lois, did you hear what I said? I guess you're just as stunned as I am."

"I'm stunned that you're seeing Kyle Roberts!"

"You-you know him?"

"Well, I don't know him personally, but I do know that he is Samuel Roberts's son."

"Who's Samuel Roberts?" Jill asked. She felt her mouth going dry at the possibility of finding out something bad about Kyle.

"Jill, Samuel Roberts is from the investment group

Davis, Sterling, and Roberts. You know, he's one of the wealthy investors that hired us to do the opening."

"Lois, you must be mistaken. It can't be the same Kyle Roberts. My Kyle Roberts is a simple ranch hand," Jill said in a puzzled voice.

"I think we're talking about the same person. Phil Harmon went out to dinner with the group to discuss the deal, and I made all the dinner and hotel arrangements for their meeting. When I saw Phil the next day, he told me all about the meeting and how they had heard about you and wanted you for the job. He also joked about Roberts having three sons, and wished he could snag one of them for you." Lois said sadly. From Jill's silence, she could tell that her friend was hurt, and hated to be the one to break the news. "Jill, he didn't tell you who he was?"

"No, Lois, he didn't. I really feel like a fool. All this time he kept telling me he wanted us to be honest with each other and honest with our feelings."

"I'm sorry, Jill," Lois muttered. "I knew they wanted you for the project, I had no idea that you would go out to Durango, or even meet Kyle.

"Today, as we were driving back from the park, I told him that I didn't want him to go broke paying for everything, and now I find out he's loaded. I feel like such a fool."

"Don't feel that way, he wasn't honest with you, and you based your feeling on the information you had. But if he's really a nice guy, you might want to discuss his being more open and honest with you in the future."

"No, Lois. Honesty is the cornerstone of any relationship, and without it, the relationship will eventually crumble. I feel so stupid. Here this guy is, living in a beautiful cabin, driving a brand-new Lincoln Navigator, and paying for all his friends' and families' outings, and

I'm thinking he's covering all this on a ranch hand's salary."

"Jill, don't be so hard on yourself," Lois pleaded.

"Lois, I have to go."

"Do you want to say hello to Diane first?"

"Not right now. Please tell her I love her and I'll see her in a few days," Jill said hurriedly.

"Take care, Jill."

"You too, Lois," she said and hung up the phone.

Jill rolled over on the bed and a tear ran down her cheek. Kyle had said he loved her. Why didn't he love her enough to trust her with the truth? He had asked so much of her and was obviously not willing to give the same.

Jill picked up the phone book and found the number to the air line. She called and made arrangements to fly out first thing tomorrow morning. She wanted to leave tonight, but there were no seats available.

After she finished booking her seat on a flight to Pittsburgh for the morning, Jill dialed her sister's phone number. She was feeling very sad and confused, and wanted nothing more than to hear her wise and loving words.

"Hello," Barbie said.

"Hi, sis, it's me," Jill said. She tried to conceal her despair, but it was a futile attempt.

"Jill, is everything all right?" Barbie said. Her voice was laced with concern as she detected the sadness in her sister's voice.

"Not really, Barbie. I was hoping to tell you that I had found that someone special, but instead I'm calling to tell you that I've been careless with my heart."

"You fell for him, didn't you?"

"Yeah, I did," Jill replied, wiping away her tears. "But

I shouldn't have. I should have done just what you told me to and just have fun with it and enjoy myself."

"Jill, we can't always control our hearts or our feelings. Though I must admit, you fell for this guy kind of quickly."

"Barbie, I'm so confused, I don't know what I'm feeling. The only thing I know is that I want to come home."

"When?"

"Tomorrow. Can you or Dad pick me up from the airport? My flight gets in at noon."

"I'll let Mom and Dad know you're coming, but I want to pick you up," Barbie said softly.

"Thanks, Barbie. Please don't tell them anything."

"I won't. I'll see you tomorrow afternoon."

"Bye, sis," Jill said and replaced the phone back on the receiver.

Jill lay on her belly and pulled her pillow under her face. She cried softly into it, partly because she felt she had been made a fool of, and partly because she felt she was losing someone she loved. In her anguish, she cried herself to sleep.

When she awoke, it was late evening. She was a little hungry, but she wouldn't leave her room for fear of running into Kyle. Jill had nothing to say to him except good-bye. She picked up the remote, turned on the television for company, began to pack. She laid out her clothes that she would wear to the airport in the morning and arranged her suitcases by the door. Next, she called a taxi service and made arrangements to be picked up by five A.M.

Jill felt terrible about not saying good-bye to Bebe, but felt it couldn't be helped. She wrote Bebe a note and left it on the desk, where she hoped it would be found. She set the alarm clock for four and lay back down.

* * *

Kyle walked into the Ranch House and over to where Bebe was sitting and joined her. "Good morning, Bebe," he said.

She sipped her coffee and then said, "Hey, good morning, Kyle."

"Where's Jill?"

"I thought she was with you."

"She was, but I haven't seen her since yesterday afternoon. I took her to the Mesa Verde National Park, and she loved it," Kyle said.

"I bet she did. You must have worn her out, because she's usually up by now." Bebe glanced at her watch; seeing how late it was, she wondered where Jill was. "Maybe I should go and see if she's all right."

"That's a good idea. Will you come back and let me know how she's doing?"

"I sure will," Bebe said. She left the table and went to see what was keeping Jill.

When Bebe knocked on Jill's door, it pushed open. "Jill, are you up sleepyhead?" she yelled out as she stepped through the entrance. She looked around and saw that there was no sign of Jill. Bebe walked farther into the room and saw that all of Jill's things were gone, but a note addressed to her was on the desk. It read:

Dear Bebe,

I'm so sorry that I didn't say good-bye to you, but I had to get away. I love you and will miss you very much. Kyle wasn't honest with me. I found out from my office who he is, and just feel like he treated me like a fool. It hurts me deeply because he wanted me to trust him and I did, but he wasn't honest with me. I thought I loved him

Bebe, but now I don't know what I feel. I'll be
back in time for the grand opening.

                                    Love always,
                                    Jill

Kyle was still there when Bebe returned to the Ranch
House. She sat down slowly across from him and
handed him Jill's note. He looked in Bebe's eyes and
saw only sadness there. He said nothing, but lowered his
eyes and read the note.

When he finished, he looked up and said, "I should
have told her from the beginning."

"Why didn't you, Kyle? What was the big secret?"

"She was so unsure of me, I didn't know how to bring
it up without scaring her off," he said. He rubbed his
hands roughly across his head, knowing that he had
messed up.

"It looks like the very thing you were trying to avoid
landed right in your lap."

"I know," Kyle said. He grabbed his hat from the
hook and left the restaurant.

Chapter 20

After collecting her suitcases from baggage claim, Jill packed them on a cart and headed toward the entrance of the airport. Before she got out the door, she could see Barbie standing in the doorway waving to her. Her pace quickened as she hurried to meet her sister outside.

Barbie gave her sister a warm embrace and Jill instantly felt some stress leave her body. After a moment she pulled away and said, "It is so good to see you, sis. Where did you park?" Jill asked hoping that her sister's van wasn't too far away.

"I'm right here," Barbie announced proudly, pointing to her car.

"I'm surprised it didn't get towed away."

"Don't be. My friend's son works out here. He let me park here, and I promised I wouldn't be long."

"Well, it must be nice to have friends in high places."

"It helps," Barbie said. They loaded the van with Jill's suitcases and then pulled off. Barbie waved at a gangly young man, and Jill guessed that was the friend's son she had referred to.

"Barbie, can we go some place and talk before you take me to Mom and Dad's house?"

"I thought you might want to. Ricky is over at a friend's house, and Lacy and James are at the sitter's. We could go back to my house if you want."

"That sounds great. I'm just not ready to deal with Mom right now."

Barbie drove in the direction of her house. There was so much she wanted to say to her sister, but knew she had to let Jill open up in her own time. Jill sat next to her quietly and considered her own thoughts.

But seeing the sadness in her sister's eyes, Barbie finally said, "Jill, Mom just wants to make sure that you're all right."

"I know, but it has to be in my own time and on my own terms."

Barbie nodded in agreement as she pulled up into her driveway. The two got out of the van and went into the house. Barbie's home seemed empty without her children running around. Jill would have wanted to see them right away, if she didn't have so much on her mind.

"Go have a seat, sis, and I'll get us something to drink," Barbie said, moving toward the kitchen.

As she took off her shoes and walked over to the sofa, Jill sat down and laid her head back, finally taking notice of how tired she was. Moments later, Barbie returned with two cups of hot green tea. She handed Jill a cup as she sat down beside her.

"You look so sad," Barbie said. She wanted to approach the situation cautiously, not wanting to press her sister for information that she wasn't ready to give, but her concern got the best of her. She asked in a loving tone, "What's happened?"

Jill took a deep breath and looked up at the ceiling. She tried to keep her tears at bay, but couldn't. "Barbie, what's wrong with me? Why is it that every time I let my guard down, I get slapped in the face?"

"What did Kyle do?"

"It's not so much Kyle as it is me. I had a goal, I had

a game plan, and I was willing to put it on the back burner for a man."

"That happened quickly."

"I know," Jill replied as she wiped away her tears. Barbie reached over and got a box of tissue and handed it to Jill. "Thanks," she said, and wiped her tears away. "What hurts the most, Barbie, is that he went on and on about how I need to be honest with my feelings. He asked me to open up to him and to trust him. Stupid me, I did."

"Well, Jill, I don't see where what he asked was so wrong."

"We had gone out together several times, but the first time we went out alone he took me to this beautiful national park and we had a wonderful time. Everything was so perfect and wonderful, and I truly felt like I was where I was supposed to be. He held me and told me just how much he loved me, and I told him that I loved him, too. Barbie, he was saying everything I wanted to hear. I know that it all happened fast, but I had never been so sure of anything in my life."

"I see you took my advice and enjoyed yourself."

Jill smiled and said, "Yes, I took your advice, but I hadn't planned on falling in love."

"And that's what's got you running scared?"

"Yes, but it's more than that. Kyle deceived me. All this time I thought he was a poor ranch hand. He lives in a beautiful cabin that he built himself, and he furnished it with all the bells and whistles. He drives a Navigator and is always spending money on his friends and family."

"Wow, all that on a ranch hand's salary?"

"Yeah, that's what I thought, too. But one night we were talking, and he told me that he had a degree in architecture, so I figured he might have made some good money from building things. I talked to Lois yesterday, and she told me that Kyle is the son of one of the investors that hired our firm. He's loaded. Barbie, he had plenty of time to tell me he wasn't just some ranch hand. I don't know if he thought I was a gold digger or what, but he wasn't honest with me. He went on and on about giving us a chance and honesty, and all along he wasn't."

"Jill, maybe you're being too hard on the guy, maybe he had a valid reason for not wanting to tell you who he was. Maybe he felt that indirectly being your employer might make you feel funny."

"You're right, it made me feel funny; it made me feel like a fool. I was ready to give up my dreams I've fought so long and hard for, for someone whom I had just met," Jill said. She grabbed another tissue and wiped away the fresh tears that streamed down her face. "Barbie, I should have kept the relationship fun and stayed friends. I let it go too far."

"Sis, it's obvious that you feel something for this guy."

"I'd be lying if I said I didn't still love him; I just can't have him in my life."

"I wish there was something I could do."

"Just tell me what you would do if you were in my shoes."

"I can't, because my shoes never did fit you. I'm the one that always lets love have its way with me, remember? Judging by what you're saying to me right now, I have a feeling that love will have its way with you, too."

"Oh no, not me, not again. I'm going back to New York and start preparing to open my own agency like I've always wanted to do."

Barbie wanted to say more, but she thought she had best leave the situation alone. She knew that if Jill was hurt, she would hide behind her career, even though she knew her sister wanted more.

"How long do you plan on staying in town?"

"I'm leaving Tuesday morning. I probably have a ton of things I need to catch up on at work," Jill told her, making an excuse. "I guess I better go over to Mom and Dad's house. I know they're anxious to see me."

"Do you feel up to it?"

"I am. I missed them too. I just wanted a chance to get my head on straight before I saw them. I know Mom will want to know if I met anyone while I was out there."

"What will you tell her?" Barbie asked. She stood up and started walking toward the door.

Jill put on her shoes and pondered her sister's question for a moment. She stood and walked over to the door where her sister was standing. "I'll tell her the truth, that I met someone, but it wasn't meant to be," Jill said honestly. "Barbie, thank you so much for being here for me."

"Where else would I be?" Barbie said, hugging her sister. "I'll always be here for you no matter what."

Barbie opened the door and led the way back to her van. They got inside and headed for their parents' home. A few minutes into the ride, Jill said, "Barbie, do you think I'm a little confused about my priorities?"

"No, to tell the truth, I don't. I think you know exactly what you want out of life, and know how to get it. You're at an age when a woman's biological clock starts ticking so loud that she can't ignore it. That, accompanied by family and friends telling you to hurry up and get married, is enough to make anyone confused."

"But I do want to get married one day. I just want to do it at the right time and with the right person."

"I know, and it will happen for you. You'll sit back

and wonder how love found you, when you weren't even looking for it." Barbie looked over and saw Jill smiling at her.

"I knew you would make me believe that everything will be all right."

Barbie pulled up into their parents' driveway, and they were quickly greeted by them. As soon as Jill stepped out of her sister's van, her father gave her a big hug.

"Oh, baby girl, it sure feels good to see you twice in one month."

Jill gave her father a warm hug back. "It feels good to see you again too." Jill smiled and her father stepped back to let her mother greet her.

"Hi, Mom,"

"Jill, I'm so happy that you kept your promise," Maddie began. "I was afraid you would skip coming back here," she continued as she hugged her daughter.

"Why would I do that when I said I was coming back?" Jill's smile faded a little, as she was confused by her mother's comment.

Maddie took a step back and said, "Well, we all know how important your job is to you. I just thought you would be anxious to get back to New York and work."

"I am, Mom, but my family is just as important to me as my job is," Jill explained. With everything else that was going on in her head, she could see that she was getting ready to lose her temper. She shook her head and bowed it in exasperation.

"Maddie, the girl just got home. She obviously wanted to see us since she made time in the middle of a project to get here," Rob said.

"I'm sure Jill is tired. Why don't we all go inside?" Barbie suggested.

Rob took his daughter's luggage out of the van with Barbie, while Maddie walked into the house with Jill.

Jill sat down on the sofa and set her purse beside her on the floor. Maddie went into the kitchen and returned a few minutes later with drinks on a tray.

"I'm sure you're a little thirsty after the long plane ride home," Maddie said.

"I had some tea over at Barbie's, but I'm still thirsty," Jill said. Her father and sister had just walked through the front door as she told her mother where she had been.

Maddie's eyes darted from one daughter to the other. Not wanting to be in the middle of what was between her mother and sister, Barbie listened but didn't make a comment.

"Why didn't you come home first?" Maddie said. Her brows lifted, and she spoke in a tone that challenged the family's importance in her daughter's life.

"Barbie hardly has any free time on her hands. It's hard to spend time alone with her between the kids, a household, and a husband. We just took advantage of the little bit of time she had available," Jill said.

"I'm glad you two had a chance to spend some time together before you head back to New York," her father said. "I'll be back; I'm going to take the suitcases up to your room, Jill."

"Thanks, Dad. Do you want me to help you?" Jill asked.

"Oh no, you just sit down. It will only take me a minute." He started up the stairs, leaving the women to talk.

Barbie took a seat across from Jill. Maddie set a tray of drinks down and then handed one to each of her daughters, before taking one herself. Then she sat down next to Jill.

"So, did you enjoy your stay in Durango?" Maddie asked.

"Yes, I did. Durango is a beautiful city."

"I guess you were quite busy with work."

"Yes, I was, but I met a wonderful woman named Bebe Simmons. She and I worked together on the project and became friends. We did manage to get everything done before I left."

"Were there any nice, charming cowboys who wanted to take you out?" Maddie asked.

Jill thought of Kyle. She had thought he was a cowboy, but it was only a pastime for him. "No, Mom, there weren't," she said, convinced that she had told her mother the truth.

"Jill, you probably didn't make yourself available for anyone to ask you out. You were more than likely caught up in the project."

"You know what, Mom, I was caught up in the project. After all, that's what I was there for," Jill said in a haughty voice. She set her drink back on the tray and stood up. "I wouldn't give a man time to talk to me, and if I did I wouldn't care a thing about what he was saying."

Rob had just reached the bottom of the stairs, when Jill brushed past him. She ran up the stairs and into her room, closing the door behind her.

Rob looked at his wife in dismay. Maddie looked from her husband to her oldest daughter. She pursed her lips together and then said, "What did I say?"

"That's just it, Maddie, you say too much."

"Rob, I just want our daughter to be happy."

"Mom, have you ever stopped to think that Jill is happy? That right now, all she really wants is your support? I can imagine that when she does find that special someone, you won't be the first to know. You've got to remember that this is her life, and she's got her own agenda for it. If you keep pushing her, you're going to push her away, and I know that you don't want that," Barbie said softly.

Maddie thought on what her daughter had just said. "Maybe I should go up there and talk to her."

"No, Maddie, give her some time to calm down. I think you really hurt her. Let her get her feelings together; and in the meantime, you think about your relationship with your daughter and if you are prepared to lose it," Rob said. He sat down in his recliner and turned on the television.

"I have to go, Mom," Barbie said. She set her glass on the tray and stood up. She bent over and gave her mother a kiss on the cheek, and then walked over and said good-bye to her father. She left the house, feeling sorry for her sister.

In her room, Jill had finished unpacking. She changed into a short pajama set and lay across her bed. She was tired of traveling and wanted to get back to her own apartment. Living out of suitcases and hotel rooms had taken its toll on her, and she desperately wanted to be surrounded by the familiarity of her own things.

She rolled over and thought of what her mother had just said to her. She had made her feel bad about herself. More importantly, Jill felt bad about the way she had spoken to her mother. Later, she would apologize.

Though it was early and sunlight still filled her room, Jill was tired and wanted to take a nap. She cuddled her pillow and began to blink slowly. She fell asleep, dreaming of the beautiful room she had called home for the past few weeks.

In her dream, she sat on the patio and looked out at the beautiful sun-drenched mountains. A familiar clear blue sky was graced with a few giant puffy clouds dancing in a distance. The wind blew gently, and she could feel her long white nightgown caress her skin. Then she saw someone waving at her. It was Kyle. He sat tall in his saddle as he rode Patches up toward her. He reached down and assisted her onto the horse's back. She rode sidesaddle away from the resort, and she didn't care where he was taking her.

With her eyes still closed, Jill grinned and ran her fingers through her hair. She opened her eyes to a darkened room. She sat up, realizing that she was no longer in Durango and no longer with Kyle.

She turned on the lights and pulled a robe from the closet. When she got downstairs, she saw that her father was asleep in his recliner. She walked quietly past him and into the kitchen. Her mother was eating dinner. She stopped when she saw her daughter standing in the doorway.

"Well, hello, sweetheart. I was wondering when you were going to come back downstairs. I made pork chops, green beans, and rice, but I'm afraid that it's not nearly as good as your father's. I'll make you a plate," Maddie said. She began to stand and Jill stopped her.

"Not just yet, Mom. I'm sure your meal turned out wonderful, but I want to talk to you for a minute first."

"I wanted to talk to you, too," Maddie said. Jill sat down at the table across from her mother and Maddie continued. "Jill, I am so sorry that I made you upset this afternoon. I know I stepped way over the line and I deeply regret doing that. I love you, Jillian, and I just want you to have everything. I see you alone, and it makes me just want someone in your life to fill the void. I never take time to even look and see if you're happy with your life just the way it is."

Jill was caught off guard by her mother's apology and sensitivity. For the first time in a long while, Jill felt as though her mother truly understood how she felt about her life.

"Mom, I know that you love me, and I love you, too. I'm sorry for losing my temper earlier. It just hurt thinking that you didn't feel as though you, and the rest of the family, were important in my life."

"Please forgive me, Jill. I know that you love each and every one of us. You live so far away, I guess that was just my crazy ploy to get more of your time and attention. I am so proud of you, sweetheart. I promise that I will leave your love life alone."

Jill arched a brow, not totally believing that her mother could deliver what she was promising. Maddie laughed and added, "It will take some practice, but I'm going to work on it."

"Thanks, Mom. That means a lot to me."

"Me too," Maddie said. She stood up and gave her daughter a hug and then went to make her a plate. "When are you going back to New York?"

"I'm leaving tomorrow morning."

"That doesn't leave us much time together," Maddie said.

Jill tilted her head and wondered if her mother had already forgotten her apology.

"What I mean is that I was hoping that we could go shopping, just you and I," Maddie said. She placed a plate of food and a glass of iced tea in front of Jill and then sat back down. She looked intently at Jill's face, half expecting to see an uncomfortable expression there. She was pleasantly surprised when there wasn't one.

Jill entered the kitchen and was quickly reminded of the last time she had seen her parents there. Her father was busy preparing a huge breakfast, and her mother looked as radiant as ever. Her skin had always been smooth and flawless and never needed much makeup.

She sat at the table reading the morning paper and wore another of her gorgeous peignoir sets, its soft yellow color richly complementing her café au lait skin tone. Jill could only hope that she would age as beautifully and gracefully as her mother.

She silently watched them. They had been married a long time and were still completely in love with each other. Their personalities were vastly different, but that worked for them because they complemented each other. Jill wondered if Kyle had been honest with her, would they have complemented each other like her parents.

Rob saw his daughter standing in the doorway and said, "Good morning, baby girl. I'll have your breakfast ready for you in just a minute." He stopped what he was doing and walked over to give his daughter a kiss.

"Good morning, Daddy," she replied.

Maddie lowered her newspaper and saw her daughter. Her face lit up seeing Jill. "Good morning, sweetheart."

Jill kissed her mother. "Good morning, Mom. I see you got your beauty sleep. You look stunning."

Rob peeked over his shoulder to see his daughter. She was obviously being very sincere and he wondered if Maddie had taken his advice. He imagined she had, given Jill's cheerful disposition. He turned around and continued to cook.

"What time did you want to leave, Mom?"

"After I eat, I'll take a bath and get dressed, and then we can leave."

Rob placed his wife's breakfast in front of her. "Where are you ladies off to today?"

"Jill and I are going to the mall and out to lunch." Maddie winked at her daughter, hoping that Jill was as excited as she was.

Rob returned with another plate filled with pancakes,

bacon, and eggs and placed it before Jill. He gave his daughter a tall glass of orange juice and made a plate for himself.

"I haven't been out to Century Three in years. I hope all my favorite stores are still there," Jill said.

Rob sat down with his own plate and said, "I'm sure they are. If not, I know that you won't come back home empty-handed," he teased.

"She gets that shopping gene from me," Maddie said. She stood and put her empty plate in the sink. Maddie kissed her husband and said, "Thank you, honey, breakfast was wonderful. Jill, I won't be long." Maddie left the kitchen and went to get ready for their outing.

"I'm glad things are okay between you and your mother," her father said.

"Me too. I didn't mean to be disrespectful. I apologized to Mom last night."

"You're a good daughter, Jill. Your mother worries about you."

"I know she worries, but she admitted to being intrusive where my love life is concerned and promised to give me some space in that area."

"As long as you two patched things up, I'm happy."

"Have you heard from Barbie today?"

"As a matter fact I did. She said to tell you that she will be over later this evening with the kids. Do you think you and your mother will be back before dinner?"

"I imagine we will be," Jill said. She stood up and started cleaning the kitchen.

"When do you have to be back in New York?"

"I'm leaving tomorrow morning. I want to get a few things taken care of before I go back to the office."

"What time is your flight? I want to take you to the airport. I see no reason for your sister to have all the fun."

Jill laughed and said, "My flight is at nine in the morning. Are you sure you want to get up that early?"

"If it's for my baby girl, I'm sure."

The doorbell rang, and Maddie yelled out, "I'll get it."

She walked to the door and opened it. It was a deliveryman from Swissvale Florist. "I have a delivery for Jill Alexander," he said.

"I'll sign for it; I'm her mother," Maddie told the man. She signed and took the box from him, then closed the door and walked into the kitchen. "Jill, this was just delivered; it's for you," Maddie said.

She set the long box in front of her daughter. Stepping back, she waited for her to open the box. Jill looked nervously at it, wondering who could have possibly sent her flowers.

"I didn't even peek inside," Maddie said in a proud voice. "Come on, sweetheart, I can't wait to see if they're from L," she added anxiously.

"From who?" Jill asked, puzzled. Then it dawned on her who her mother was referring to. Jill still hadn't told her mother that Lois had sent her the flowers. "Oh yes, L. Maybe they are from L," Jill said as she lifted the lid.

Rob and Maddie exchanged curious glances at each other, both having a feeling that much more was going on with their daughter than she let on. They said nothing, but watched intently.

Jill opened the box, and inside were one dozen long-stemmed, red roses. In the middle was a single white rose. Jill took the card out and read it.

Dear Jill,
    As you know, the red roses are for love, but the white one represents honesty.

I'm sorry.
K

Stunned, Jill lowered the card down to her lap. She sat staring blankly at the roses. She wondered how he had gotten her parents' address, and imagined that, since she was actually one of his employees, he had no problem tracking her down at Iguana.

Rob stopped eating. "Is everything all right, baby girl?"

Jill said nothing, but continued to look at the roses. Of course her parents would want to know what was going on, and she wanted to tell them. She just didn't know how to explain everything.

Maddie took the card out of her daughter's hands, read it, and said, "Does K know about L?"

Jill stood abruptly and said, "Mom, let's go." She walked out of the room and waited at the front door for her mother.

Maddie turned to follow her daughter and was stopped when her husband took her hand. "Now, Maddie, don't be too pushy. The girl obviously needs her space, and—"

"And I know what to do. Don't worry, honey, I won't blow it," Maddie said and kissed her husband good-bye.

The two walked out the door and got into Maddie's car. She was just about to back out of the driveway when Jill said, "Mom, do you mind if we don't go shopping today? I want to go to Highland Park, find a bench under a nice shady tree, and just talk."

"That sounds wonderful to me, Jill," Maddie said.

They drove to the park in silence, each wrapped up in her own thoughts. Maddie wondered what Jill wanted to talk about. She silently hoped that her daughter would open up to her. That she would trust her enough to know she would only give her the best advice she could.

Jill sat quietly and thought of Kyle. She felt that he had clouded her judgment. All along, she knew what she wanted out of life, and had a plan as to how to carry out her goals. She had even considered taking a slight detour from her endeavors in order to be with him. But if he was dishonest with who he was, she thought, how much more so would he be with other issues?

Maddie entered the park and found a parking space near a bench. She parked and they got out of the car and walked slowly over to the bench and sat down. Jill looked around at the couples walking by and holding hands. She let out a sigh and started to cry.

"Jill, what's wrong?" Maddie asked tenderly. She moved closer to her daughter and hugged her. "I know that I don't have the greatest track record for being patient or understanding, but I want to try. Please let me try."

With that, Jill gently pulled loose from her mother's arms and said, "Mom, I lied to you. The roses I got the last time I was here were from me. I had Lois have them delivered."

"Oh, so that's who L is. Who is K?"

"K is Kyle, a man I met in Durango," Jill said, holding back tears.

"Judging from the card and your reaction to it, I get the feeling that you and this Kyle have feelings for each other."

Jill nodded slowly and said, "Mom, do you believe in love at first sight?"

"I believe it can happen."

"Well, that's what it was for me; at least I thought that's what it was."

"What do you mean?"

"Mom, Kyle and I have so much in common. He's an architect and built his own home. He cooks like you wouldn't believe; he reminds me of Dad," Jill said. Her eyes sparkled as she spoke of Kyle. "He took me rafting and we had a blast. We can talk forever, and sometimes about nothing at all. He has the most beautiful horses, and he's a cowboy. At least, that's how I knew him."

"How you knew him? What happened to him?"

"In a way he disappeared. I found out he was not some ranch hand, but the son of one of the wealthy investors that hired me to do the opening. Mom, I was ready to put my dreams of opening my own firm on hold for a man I just met."

"You're in love, dear. People have been known to do stranger things in the name of love."

"That might be true, but I can't give up my life to someone who won't be honest with me."

"That may be true, darling, but only time will tell," Maddie said. She held Jill's hand and then added, "I've never seen you like this over a man before, Jill. It seems like I waited forever for this to happen, and now that it has I want you to take your time and make the right decision for yourself."

"Thanks, Mom," Jill said.

"I hope you know, Jill, that I truly only had your best interests at heart."

"I've always known that. It was just a little hard to take sometimes."

Maddie smiled at her daughter and said, "Do you still want to go to the mall?"

"Not really, I want to go back home and spend the day with my family."

Jill stood up and walked arm in arm with her mother. She felt good being able to talk to her mother without being pushed into something she wasn't ready for.

They got back into Maddie's car and headed home. Jill thought about the events that had occurred over the past seventy-two hours. She had found a love, and lost a love, and in the end, begun to enjoy a closer relationship with her mother.

"So tell me, Jill, what does Kyle look like? Is he hot?" Maddie asked. She glanced at her daughter, who looked at her mother in stunned silence. "What? I was young once, too."

Jill rolled her eyes and said, laughing, "Yeah, Mom, he's hot."

"Is he tall or short? Does he have one eye and a pointy head? Tell me more about him?" Maddie said with great interest.

Jill sat back and thought about the man she had left in Durango. "Mom, he's the most beautiful specimen of a man I've ever seen," Jill said in a distant voice. "He's tall and very muscular. Every time I see him in his tight jeans and his cowboy hat on, I feel my heart race." Jill looked at her mother and saw a knowing smile on her face.

"What are you thinking?"

"I'm thinking that you got it bad for this young man." In keeping with her promise, Maddie said nothing else.

Maddie pulled into the driveway and parked. Jill saw Barbie's van and hoped she had brought the kids with her. Jill rushed into the house and was greeted by Ricky.

"Aunt Jill!" Ricky ran up to his aunt and gave her a big hug. "I'm so glad you're here."

"I'm so glad I'm here too, Ricky," Jill said. She hugged her nephew warmly and smiled at her sister.

"Mom, I have a surprise for you. Dad said it would be all right if we spent the night tonight," Barbie said. She waited for her mother to complain and watched her face to see if a dismal expression appeared.

"Oh, that's good, Barbie. I want the kids to spend

some time with Jill before she leaves in the morning," Maddie said. She kissed her eldest daughter and then went to greet her grandkids.

Barbie looked at her mother, stunned, and then whispered to Jill, "Okay, who's that woman, and what have you done with our mother?"

"Let's just say that the last twenty-four hours has been a mellowing experience for both of us. I apologized for my actions yesterday, and she promised to leave my love life alone."

"She did?"

"Yeah, and today I totally lost my head and told her about Kyle."

"You did lose your head," Barbie said.

"Mom, Aunt Jill, come on, Granddad is starting the movie and I've got the popcorn," Ricky said.

For the rest of the evening, Jill enjoyed her family and the movie, and tried to keep thoughts of Kyle out of her head.

Chapter 21

Jill kicked off her shoes and looked around her empty apartment. There was a pile of mail on the table that Marie had left for her. Jill thumbed through it quickly and decided that all of it could wait.

She took one suitcase at a time into her bedroom and neatly put them in her walk-in closet.

Next, Jill checked her phone messages. There was one from Barbie, telling her that she loved her and would call her soon. Another message was from Bebe; she said that she felt bad about what had happened and would see her soon.

Her place felt so quiet and empty. Her senses had become accustomed to fresh air and good people. Now there was no one but herself.

Feeling restless, Jill didn't know what to do. She quickly decided to go to Iguana and visit her friends. She went back down to the garage and got into her silver-gray Mercedes.

Jill had missed Lois and Diane, and couldn't wait to see them. Even though it wasn't Friday night, she hoped she could persuade them to come to her place after work.

Jill pulled into the parking garage and walked toward her building.

As the elevator door opened on Iquana's floor, she could see Lois working at her desk.

Jill walked up quietly to her and said, "Boo!"

Lois jumped as she looked up. "Jill! I wasn't expecting you until Thursday." Lois walked around her desk to greet her friend with a big hug. "What are you doing home so early?"

"Let's just say I missed you guys," Jill said, laughing.

"We missed you, too," Lois said. She picked up the phone and buzzed Diane. "Di, you'll never believe who's here. No, I won't tell you. Come see."

"Is everything going all right with the project?" Lois asked cautiously.

"Everything is fine. We're all set for the grand opening."

"Oh my goodness, Jill, is that you?" Diane said.

Jill turned around to see her friend rushing toward her. "Hey, Diane, it's me."

She gave Jill a warm welcome-home hug too, and then said, "Girl, did we ever miss you! But I thought you weren't coming home until later this week."

"Yeah, well, there was a little change in plans. Have you guys had lunch already?"

"As a matter of fact, we haven't. It's been so crazy around here, we haven't had time to squeeze in time for lunch," Lois told her.

"But we will now that you're here," Diane said.

"I know you're busy, so why don't we just go down to the café and grab a quick bite to eat? I want to hear about everything that has been going on, and I have a lot to tell you," Jill said.

"I'm ready," Lois said anxiously

"Give me a second to grab my purse," Diane said, almost running back down the hall.

"We'll wait for you by the elevator," Lois yelled out to her.

"You know I leave for Hawaii in three weeks?"

"Yeah, I have to be back in Durango by that time. I really wanted to be here to see you off."

"Don't worry, it's my turn to send you a postcard," Lois teased. "Besides, Matt wants the entire office staff in Durango, so Curtis and I will probably be leaving for Hawaii from there. We've never done this much traveling," Lois finished excitedly.

"That will be great, Lois," Jill said.

"Okay, I'm ready," Diane said, walking toward them.

The three friends got on the elevator and rode down to the building's café. Jill could smell the food from inside, and then realized that she had missed breakfast and had almost missed lunch.

"I'll have dragon breath later," Diane said, joking about her lunch order.

The lunch crowd was pretty much gone, so they had no trouble finding seats near the window after they'd bought their food. When they were seated, Diane began telling Jill about the excitement that was going on in her life.

Diane reached into her purse, pulled out a picture, and handed it to Jill. "This is Brian, the new and permanent man in my life," she said, beaming.

"Oh, Di, he's handsome," Jill said.

"A little too good to her if you ask me. They have only known each other since the day after you left, and he has already asked her to fly to the Florida Keys for a long weekend, and she deserves it," Lois said, smiling at her friend.

Jill squinted her eyes slightly and said, "Really, Di?"

"Yes, really. Jill, I can't wait for you to meet him. He's funny and smart, and such a gentleman," she said as she put down her burger. She took the picture carefully back from Jill and returned it to her purse. "What about you, Jill? Did any of those handsome cowboys catch your eye?" Diane asked.

Though she had a forkful of salad in her mouth, she stammered as she tried to talk. "I-I did meet someone," she said.

"I knew it, I knew it, stop wasting time and tell us all about him," Diane said.

"I can see it in your eyes that he was more than just a friend," Lois said excitedly. Though she knew who it was, she wanted Jill to tell her story.

Jill looked at Lois curiously and then said, "Lo, did you tell Kyle how to find me in Pittsburgh?"

"Who's Kyle?" Diane said.

"Yes, I did, Jill, but before you get mad at me, let me explain," Lois said and swallowed hard. "He called Iguana and said that he had an urgent matter to discuss with you. I knew you weren't in New York so I told him to try you at your parents' house. But I didn't know that you were coming to New York today," she said, trying to redeem herself.

"Who's Kyle?" Diane said again.

"It's all right, Lois. If you hadn't told him he would have gotten the information from someone else. He has the connections and the resources to get anything he wants."

"For the last time, will someone please tell me who Kyle is?" Diane said in frustration.

"Kyle Roberts is the man I met in Durango. I thought he was just a ranch hand, and I fell in love with him. He is the most magnificent and intelligent brother I have ever met. He enjoys things that are out of the ordinary," Jill said, smiling as she recalled Kyle's attributes.

"But is he a good kisser?" Diane asked.

Jill blushed and dropped her head. She said nothing but smiled and gently rubbed her forehead, not knowing what to say.

"Ahhh, so the brother knows how to touch the intellectual Jill, as well as the physical Jill," Lois said knowingly.

"Yes, he did," Jill said, losing her smile.

"Did, what do you mean by did?" Diane asked.

"Jill found out that Kyle wasn't being completely honest with her. It turns out that Kyle is the son of one of the investors that hired our firm. He conveniently forgot to tell Jill who he was. She only found out a couple of days ago. I was the bearer of bad news," Lois told Diane.

"So, he didn't mention that he's loaded; I don't see where that puts a wrench in the works. In my opinion, that only sweetens the pot. Uh, try living without money," Diane said and took another bite of her burger.

"Honesty is very important to me, especially if a relationship is going to have any longevity. I was going to give up my dreams just to be with him. What a fool I was. I shouldn't have been doing ninety when the speed limit is fifty-five."

"Jill, don't be so hard on yourself," Lois said, caressing Jill's arm. "I'm glad you're home. We can all get together and talk about this some more. Right now, we have to get back to work."

"Why don't you guys come over my place tonight? I sure could use the company," Jill told them.

"Oh, Jill, I can't. Brian has dinner reservations for us tonight," Diane said.

"I can't either, Jill. My in-laws are coming over tonight. If there was any way I could get out of it, I would," Lois told her.

"Well, by the off chance either of you can show up,

I'll leave word with the doorman to just send you up," Jill said.

They all stood up and began to leave. Jill felt empty inside, but didn't want to ruin her friends' plans. She was sure that in a few days she would be back to her old self, so she put on a happy face and walked them to the elevator.

"Jill, I'm so glad that you're back. I hope we're on for Friday?" Lois said. She could tell that Jill wasn't herself and deeply regretted not being able to visit her tonight.

"We're definitely on for Friday," she said with a forced smile.

"Okay, sweetheart," Diane said and gave Jill a hug good-bye. "You take good care of yourself, and I'll see you soon." The elevator arrived and they stepped inside. Jill waved good-bye to her friends and turned to leave.

Jill walked back to the parking garage to get her car. As she started her engine, but before she pulled off, she wiped the tears from her eyes. She put her sunglasses on and drove away.

When she arrived at her apartment building, she parked her car, and went directly to her apartment and closed the door behind her. She went into her bathroom and ran a hot bath, then went back to her bedroom and found a comfortable pair of pants with a matching top and laid them across her bed.

She returned to the bathroom and poured a jasmine-scented oil into her bath and then undressed. Jill stepped in and submerged her body under the water. She lay there hoping that its silky warmth would ease away all the tension she had inside.

After her bath, Jill dressed in the pale blue, two-piece lounge outfit she'd put out. Just in case Lois and Diane were able to come over, she didn't want to have on her nightgown. She pulled her long hair into a high ponytail and went into her kitchen to make herself a cup of chamomile tea, and grabbed a bag of unsalted pretzels.

She sat quietly in the living room, sipping the warm liquid. She watched mindlessly as the television played, oblivious to the program. Her mind was a million miles away. She thought of the endless Colorado sky with only its gorgeous mountains giving evidence to a divide between earth and heaven. Jill thought of all the friends she had left behind and the good times they had shared.

Why did things turn out the way they had? she wondered. Why couldn't Kyle have just been honest with her, instead of playing the part of a lowly ranch hand? He obviously didn't know her well if he thought he had to hide who he was. He thought of her as a golddigger, and she couldn't bear the thought.

Jill wiped the tears from her eyes and promised herself that she wouldn't cry anymore tonight. She got up and went back into the kitchen and got herself another cup of tea. On her way back to the living room, there was a knock at the door.

Jill hurried back to the living room and set her tea on a coaster. She was happy that Lois or Diane had made it over.

"I knew you guys would come," she said as she swung open her door. To her surprise Kyle stood there and he took Jill's breath away. His six-foot-three frame was draped in a navy blue Armani suit. His thick, muscular chest was covered by a light blue dress shirt and a navy blue tie. Kyle was clean shaven, and Jill could smell the sensuous cologne he wore. He sported a Rolex on his left wrist and his class ring from the University of Colorado on his finger.

"Can I come in?" he asked in a hushed voice.

In reply, Jill stepped back so that he could enter. She turned around and picked up her cup of tea, and walked over to the window and looked outside. She had so much to say to him, and then again, she had nothing to say at all.

Kyle walked up behind her and laid his hand on her shoulder. Jill turned away and walked back over to the sofa.

"Jill, I'm sorry."

"Not half as sorry as I am. You hurt me."

"I never meant to hurt you. That was never my plan."

"You know, I thought I had met the man I would spend the rest of my life with. I trusted you and I thought you trusted me. You played me for a fool, Kyle!"

"No, Jill, I never played you for a fool."

"Well then, you must have thought I was some gold digger, just out to get my hands on your money," she said angrily. "Why didn't you tell me who you were? I gave you plenty of chances to tell me."

"Because you were so unsure of me, I wanted to give you time to get to know me," Kyle said honestly.

"But I didn't get to know you, did I?" Jill said hotly.

"Yes, you did. I'm sorry I didn't tell you who I was right off the bat, but I didn't want to scare you off. I'm still the same person," he said as he walked closer to her. "I am the man who loves you, and the man you fell in love with. You already know the real Kyle."

Kyle reached into his suit pocket and pulled out a red velvet Cartier ring box. He took Jill's hand and placed it in her palm. Jill's mouth dropped open as she realized what he had place in her hand. She didn't open it, but stood in stunned silence looking at the box.

"I am flying back to Durango tonight. Just know that there's a man out there that loves you with all his heart. I'm not playing games, I'm playing for keeps," he said, and kissed her gently on the lips. "And all you have to do is say yes," he whispered.

Kyle turned and walked away, and as he did, he left another package on the coffee table for her. He left Jill's apartment and closed the door behind him.

Once Kyle left, Jill sat down on her sofa. She slowly opened the box he had given her and saw a four-carat, emerald-cut diamond engagement ring set in platinum. Jill pulled the beautiful ring from its case and placed it on her finger. She held her hand out and admired the exquisite piece. It sparkled and shined with every turn of her hand. She took it off and placed it back in its box.

Jill got up and put Tomahawk's CD on. As the music played, she remembered how she felt the first time she heard the song "Pounding Heart." She returned to the sofa and sat down. Jill opened the other package Kyle had left for her, and was surprised to see all the pictures he had taken of the two of them. He had included pictures of their rafting trip, as well as pictures in the Mesa Verde National Park. In every picture she smiled brightly and remembered how Kyle made her feel every time she was with him.

She sat staring at the picture of them with her sitting on his lap after they had come from rafting. She couldn't remember ever having been so happy. Jill listened to the music. She closed her eyes and, for an instant, felt as though she was back in Colorado wrapped securely in Kyle's embrace. The music ended, and she opened her eyes. A tear rolled down her cheek as Jill got up and turned out the lights.

She went back into her room and lay across her bed. She picked up the phone and called her sister.

"Hello," Barbie said.

"Hi, Barbie, it's Jill."

"Hey, sis, are you home and all settled in?"

"Yes. Barbie, I just had a visit from Kyle."

"Wow, he's a persistent little bugger, isn't he?"

"I would have to say so. He said that he didn't mean to deceive me. He told me that he loved me."

"Well, he's definitely winning points with me."

"Barbie, he gave me an engagement ring."

"What? Jill, are you kidding?" Barbie asked.

"No, I'm not."

"Well, what did you say?" Barbie asked anxiously.

"He didn't wait for an answer. He only said for me to know that he loved me with all his heart, then he kissed me and left."

"I guess he wants you to come to terms with the situation in your own time. Jill, if you love him, try to find a way to pursue your dreams and include him in them. If you're happy, then go for it."

"I don't know; I have to clear my head. I have so many thoughts going through it right now. I just don't want to make a mistake."

"Whatever you decide, you know I'm in your corner."

"Thanks, sis. I have to call Mom and Dad now."

"They're not home right now. Dad took Mom to the movies. If I talk to them later, I'll let them know that you got home all right."

"Please don't tell them about the ring. I have no idea what I'm going to do, and I don't want to get them all excited, only to let them down."

"I won't. That, my dear, is for you to announce. Good night, sis."

"Good night," Jill said and hung up the phone.

She opened the velvet box again and looked at the ring. She closed the box again, and placed it on her nightstand. Turning out the light, she lay down.

Her bed felt awkward and huge. She tossed and turned, trying to get comfortable. Jill squeezed her pillow and nuzzled her nose into its softness. She half expected to inhale the scent of him, but it wasn't there.

Jill opened her eyes and sat up. She turned on the lights, got out of bed, and went back into the kitchen.

Jill sat at her kitchen table and pulled her knees to her chest. She felt painfully alone. She had hoped that Lois and Diane would have been able to come over, but she realized that they had their own lives and couldn't just drop everything because she had a problem. The apartment was void of sound except for the low hum of a few appliances. She got a bottle of wine from the refrigerator, poured a glass, and went into her living room.

Sitting on the sofa, she picked up the book she had been trying to read for over a month, and finished the love story in just a couple of hours.

Tucking herself into bed, Jill had hoped for a peaceful sleep. Instead, her mind was filled with vivid dreams of Kyle. He was there, laughing with her and kissing her. He took care of all of her needs and made sure she wanted for nothing. She could feel his warm hands on her skin and the gentle touch of his lips on hers. In her dream, she saw someone else, too. He was much smaller than Kyle, but looked just like him. It was a child, and he was their son.

Chapter 22

The morning sun was shining through her window. Jill sat up quickly in bed. She looked around and saw that she was home and had only been dreaming. Jill glanced over to see that the red velvet box was not part of her dream. She opened the box and took the ring from its satin lining. Jill placed the ring on her finger and smiled, finally knowing what she wanted to do.

It was only seven A.M., a little too early to call Lois and let her know she was going back to Durango, so she decided to call her parents.

"Hi, Mom, did I wake you?"

"No, sweetheart, we were up. How are you doing today?"

"Mom, I'm fantastic. I'm engaged!" Jill yelled excitedly.

Maddie almost dropped the phone from shock. "What did you say, baby?"

Jill giggled and then repeated herself. "I said I'm engaged."

"Jill, this is so sudden, you just got home. Who asked you?"

"Kyle, he came to New York and gave me a ring," Jill said in a tickled voice.

"Where is he now?"

"He's in Durango, he left last night."

"I don't understand, Jill, why did he leave?" Maddie asked, confused.

"Because we hadn't settled our differences. He apologized for not being honest and telling me who he was from the beginning. He said that he never meant to deceive me."

"What did he mean to do?"

"He meant to take it slow, so I wouldn't run away from the relationship."

"Well, I can understand that; I like him already. Jill, your father wants to talk to you, do you have time?"

"I sure do, Mom."

Maddie handed the phone to her husband. "Hello, baby girl."

"Hi, Daddy, I have some exciting news for you," Jill said, smiling.

"The way your mother is running around the house I would have to say that you do. What's going on?"

"Daddy, I'm engaged!"

"Oh, let me guess, to the flower guy?"

"Yes, Daddy, to the flower guy. I can't wait until you meet him. You two have so much in common."

"Is he there now?"

"No, he flew back to Durango last night. I haven't told him yes yet."

"Jill, do you love him?" Rob asked pointedly.

"With all my heart, Daddy."

"Then get yourself out to Durango, and get me another son-in-law!" he said lovingly.

"I'm packing right now, Daddy."

"I love you, sweetheart."

"I love you too, Daddy," Jill said and hung up the phone.

She packed quickly, throwing only what she needed in one suitcase, which included Tomahawk's CD and the pictures Kyle had given her. She wanted nothing slowing her down and called the airline as she packed. Jill wanted the next flight out to Durango. She was in luck. The reservation agent told her that there was a flight leaving for Colorado at noon. She would have to hurry if she wanted to stop and say hello to Dar and still make her flight.

Jill threw her cosmetics case into her carry-on bag. Except for her gold hoop earrings, Kyle's ring was the only other piece of jewelry she wore. She put the rest of her jewelry in a case and placed it in the inner side pocket of her carry-on bag. Jill walked to her door with the two pieces of luggage in one hand and dialed Lois with the other.

"Iguana Public Relations Group," Lois said in her usual business voice.

"Hey, Lo, it's me," Jill said in an upbeat voice.

"Hi, Jill, you sound like your mood has changed for the better. I'm sorry that I didn't make it over last night. Was Diane able to come by?"

"No, she wasn't, but that's all right. I know you two had other things going on. I just wanted to let you know that I'm leaving for Durango this afternoon."

"Why? I thought you would be in town until the grand opening."

"I thought so, too. I had a visit from Kyle last night. He loves me, and heaven help me, Lois, but I'm deeply in love with him, too."

Lois smiled as she realized that her friend had found what she was looking for all along. "Jill, I'm so happy for you."

"He gave me a beautiful ring," Jill said. She stopped what she was doing to admire it again.

"An engagement ring?" Lois asked with a mixture of surprise and excitement in her voice. She couldn't believe all this had happened since she had seen Jill last. She secretly wished she had ditched her in-laws to be with her friend.

Jill laughed and said, "Yes, an engagement ring."

"Congratulations, I can tell by the joy in your voice that you already told him yes."

"No, I didn't, but I'm going to," Jill said assuredly.

"Don't just stand there. Get going!"

"I'm on my way. Oh, and, Lois, thanks for everything."

"Don't mention it. Bye, Jill," she said and hung up the phone.

Jill quickly dressed in comfortable clothes for her long flight back to Durango. She grabbed her purse and her luggage and left her apartment. She placed her suitcase next to the elevator and then walked toward Darlene and Mike's apartment. Jill knocked on the door. A moment later, Darlene opened the door holding her infant daughter.

"Jill, hello. I've been waiting to hear from you," Darlene said. She held Helena in one arm and hugged Jill with the other.

"Hi, Dar, I'm so sorry that I haven't been in touch, but I had a ton of work to accomplish, and a lot on my mind." Jill looked at little Helena. She was awake and sucking on her fist. "Dar, she's more beautiful than I remember."

"Thanks, Jill, but I can't take credit for that. I think she looks more like my sister. Now, *she's* a beauty. Do you have time to come in for a visit?"

"Actually, I don't. I'm on my way to the airport. I just wanted to stop by before I left town again."

"Jill, I'm so sorry for the way things turned out with Dre. He is my brother-in-law, but he's kind of a jerk." Jill nodded her head in agreement as Darlene lifted

Jill's left hand. "Is this what I think it is?" she said in surprise.

"Yes, it is," Jill said, blushing.

"Oh, Jill, I'm so happy for you," Darlene said sincerely.

"Thanks, Dar. Listen, I have to go, but I'll be in touch," Jill said as she gave Darlene another hug and bent down to kiss Helena's cheek. "Bye, Dar."

Jill pushed the elevator button and picked up her luggage. She rode down to the first floor and walked onto the busy New York sidewalk. Jill inhaled deeply as she realized that she was taking a major step in her life—a step that would take her somewhere she had never been before. She wasn't afraid of the unknown, but rather embraced it, positive that what was on the other side was something special and meant just for her. Jill stepped to the edge of the sidewalk and hailed a taxi.

It was early evening when Jill arrived in Durango. And she caught another taxi to the resort. After paying the driver, Jill walked into the dimly lit main building and set her luggage down behind the counter. It felt good to be back, and instantly she had a sense of belonging.

Jill walked toward the Ranch House. She could hear loud voices and music long before she even got to the building. She remembered all the good times she had had there and was happy to be back.

Inside, just about everyone was dancing and she could see Bebe and Tony on the floor. Many people were standing at the bar laughing and talking, but she spotted Sharon and Eric sitting snuggled together in a booth. Jill looked around, but she didn't see Kyle.

Jill walked over to the booth Eric and Sharon shared and said, "I thought I'd find you all here."

"Jill!" Eric said, smiling. "When did you get back?"

"Just now," Jill said. She sat down with them and could tell they were happy to see her.

"I'm so glad that you're back. I was really looking forward to spending time with you," Sharon said.

"I was only gone a few days, but I really missed you guys, too. Sharon, you look great. Has the morning sickness subsided?"

"A little bit. I am feeling better," Sharon answered proudly, rubbing her flat abdomen.

"Have you seen Kyle?" Jill asked them.

Eric tipped his head in the direction of his brother. Jill's eyes followed, and she saw Kyle standing in the back of the room playing darts alone. She mouthed a silent thank-you to Eric, then stood and walked over to Kyle.

He threw effortlessly at the board, but didn't land a single dart near the bull's-eye. "If you raise your hand to eye level and keep your sight on the center of the board, you just might hit the middle," she said in a low soft voice.

Kyle lowered his hand and turned around. He smiled brightly at the sight of her and put the darts down. "Do you know who I am?" he asked.

She wrapped her arms around his neck and let her body lean into his. "Yes, I do," she replied before she kissed him. "You're the man I love."

Kyle hugged her back and planted a kiss lovingly on her lips. He stopped and picked up her left hand and saw that she wore his ring. His smile broadened until those irresistible dimples Jill loved appeared. "I love you, Jill. Will you marry me?"

"I will," Jill said, smiling and kissing him again. "But you still have to clear it with my father." She laughed.

"I can do that."

"Good, I think in about a year's time I can put a wedding together."

"Take all the time you need; I'm not going anywhere," he said. Kyle kissed her one last time before letting her go. He grabbed a stool and stood on it. With a loud piercing whistle, he got everyone's attention. "Hey, everybody, I have an announcement to make. I just asked Jill to marry me!" he said, still smiling.

"What did she say?" Tony yelled back at him.

"What do you think she said, smart aleck? She said yes!" Kyle finished and jumped down off the stool. The noise in the Ranch House exploded as friends and family congratulated the newly engaged couple. Rounds of beer were served on the house and Jill was the happiest she had ever been. She knew she had found a new home.

"Jill, I'm so happy for you. I must admit, this is what I was praying for," Bebe said as she hugged Jill.

"Thanks, Bebe, I guess I just needed some time to see that what I really wanted was right in front of my face. I'm going to quit my job in New York, but I still wish I could open up my own firm."

"Who says you can't? What about the dynamic team of Alexander and Simmons?" Bebe reminded her. "Jill, your life doesn't have to be this or that, you can have both."

Jill's eyes sparkled as she understood what Bebe was getting at. "Are you saying that we should go into business together?" Jill asked excitedly.

"That's exactly what I'm saying; and I already have a name picked out for our company, Desert Star, what do you think?"

"I think I like it!" Jill said.

The two friends shook on their newly formed partnership. Jill was still in a state of disbelief over how her life had become so perfect. Barbie was right. It felt like a dream, but she was awake and decided to enjoy all the pleasure she was experiencing.

"Bebe, do you mind if I steal my fiancée away for a moment? I have to show her something."

"No problem, I'll see you later, Jill," Bebe said.

Kyle took Jill by the hand and led her out the door of the Ranch House. The two walked up the lighted path toward the main building.

"What do you have to show me that's so important?" Jill asked.

"You'll see," Kyle said. He opened the front door to the main building and guided her inside.

They walked in the direction of the formal dining room, and just as they got to it, Kyle made Jill close her eyes. She did, and he walked away from her.

"Now, no peeking," he said.

"I'm not," Jill said, laughing.

"Okay, open your eyes," he said and stepped back behind her.

When Jill opened her eyes she saw her name in lavender neon lights. Just behind the letter J in her name was a white dune evening primrose. Kyle had named the formal dining room Jillian's.

"Oh, Kyle, it's beautiful," she whispered. "You must have been awfully sure of yourself to do this before I said yes," she teased.

He turned her around and held her close, saying, "The only thing I was sure of was my love for you." He kissed her again and made a solemn promise to himself to love her for the rest of his life.

It was the end of a very busy and tiring day. Kyle es-

corted Jill to her room with her suitcases, and with a last
kiss good night, he left for his cabin.

Jill basked in the familiarity of her old room. She
opened the sliding glass door and stepped out on the
patio. Jill looked up at the star-studded sky and touched
her ring. She was happy to be home.

The Grand Opening

Everything Jill and Bebe had worked for had led up to this moment. Jill was as nervous as she could be and felt as though more than her reputation was on the line. She checked her appearance in the mirror and smiled back at herself, loving how the sleeveless black dress fit her. Her long hair was pulled back into a sleek French knot, with just a few tendrils framing her face. Jill put on a pair of pear-shaped diamond earrings, did her makeup, and put on her Chloe perfume. She glanced at her reflection one last time before she left.

Jill headed for the main dining room and hoped she would find Bebe there. A Special Place was in full swing, with its entire staff in place. The registration and spa staff was in uniform and ready to greet the press and give tours of their areas. Jill looked outside and saw the television and radio station vans in the parking lot and imagined that Charmaine Perry and Don Ashton were somewhere around. Though they were working the event, she had sent them invitations and told them to feel free to bring a guest.

Jill smiled and walked outside as she saw the car with Matt Singletary and his wife, Joan, approaching. Behind them she could see Phil Harmond and his wife, along with Lois and Curtis and Diane and Brian.

"I'm so glad you all are here," Jill said. She shook

Matt's and Phil's hands, said hello to Joan, and then gave Lois and Diane a warm hug.

Curtis greeted Jill excitedly, enjoying the first part of his trip. Diane introduced Brian to Jill, and Jill shook his hand, too.

"I can see why you fell in love with this place," Lois said.

"It's breathtaking," Joan added.

"Yeah," Matt Singletary chimed in. "It cost me my best executive." He smiled and then said, "Congratulations, Jill, I couldn't be happier for you."

"Thanks, Matt," she said. "Let's go inside. I'm sure you'll see some people you already know."

Jill began to follow them and saw two taxis approaching. She looked closer and could see her family inside. The taxis pulled up and her mother and father got out of the first car. Barbie and her family were in the second one. Jill smiled with delight and hurried to meet them. A bellhop came and took their luggage as Jill greeted her family, hugging each one of them.

"We wouldn't miss it for the world, baby girl," her father said.

"Ricky, you look so handsome!" Jill said, bending to embrace her nephew.

"Thanks, Aunt Jill," he replied proudly.

Jill led them into the main dining room, and her father saw his daughter's name in neon lights. "He must really love you," he whispered in Jill's ear.

"He does, Daddy," she whispered back.

"This is just gorgeous," Maddie said, looking around the impressive restaurant. Gentlemen of the Four Corners played inside Jillian's and gave the restaurant a serene atmosphere.

"I'm glad you like it, Mom. If you want, you can sit

outside near the pool. Food and drinks are being served out there as well."

"That sounds nice," Maddie said, impressed.

Jill led her family out to the pool and could see the festive atmosphere was growing with excitement. She saw Bebe and signaled for her to come over. Bebe walked over to her friend. "Bebe, I want you to meet my family."

Bebe extended her hand to each of them, saying, "It's so nice to finally meet you all. Jill has told me so much about you that I feel like I already know you."

"Good, because I could use another sister," Barbie said.

Bebe smiled at Barbie's comment and continued talking with Jill's family. Out of the corner of her eye, Jill saw someone waving. She looked and saw that it was Kyle. He was signaling for Jill to come to him.

"I'll be right back," Jill said, excusing herself.

"Hey, babe, I was wondering when you'd put in an appearance," she said, taking Kyle's hand as she kissed him lovingly on the lips.

Standing next to him was an elegant-looking older woman. She was very beautiful, Jill thought, with her hair swept up in a chic twist. She had flawless skin like Jill's mother, with just a touch of silver gray at her temples. The man with her looked very distinguished and kept his eye on Jill. Kyle looked up sheepishly at the older couple standing next to them. "Jill, I want you to meet my mom and dad."

Though his parents stood looking at Jill with approving smiles on their faces, she immediately dropped Kyle's hand and tried to display a more businesslike demeanor.

"Mom and Dad, this is my fiancée, Jill Alexander," he

said proudly. Then he added, "Jill, these are my parents, Samuel and Regina Roberts."

Jill stuck out her hand. "It's so nice to meet you."

Regina looked at Jill's hand and said, "My darling, you're soon to be my daughter-in-law. I think a hug is in order." She quickly stepped forward and welcomed Jill into her family.

"Wow, son, you sure know how to pick them, she's beautiful!" Samuel said. "Welcome to the family, Jill," he said as he gave her a hug too.

Jill was overwhelmed by their acceptance of her and their obvious approval of Kyle's choice for a mate.

"Thank you, I am so happy to meet you both, too," she said. When the shock of meeting her future in-laws finally faded, it was replaced with a blush. Everything that was happening to her was exciting, new, and wonderful, and she hoped things would forever stay this way. "Would you mind following me out to the pool? I'd like for you to meet my family, too," she said.

"Sure, darling," Kyle's mother said.

They made their way through the crowd of people. Jill took note and saw that everyone was enjoying themselves. Tomahawk's music was playing, and Paulina's staff was busy making sure that everyone was eating. She was right, Jill was completely pleased with her catering service.

As they walked, Kyle whispered nervously into Jill's ear, "When you say family, do you mean that your mom and dad are here?"

"Of course I do," she answered with a teasing smile.

"I'm a little nervous."

"At least I gave you some warning. You let me walk up and start kissing on you in front of your parents."

"Believe it or not, that sealed the deal with my mom. You're her favorite now."

Jill's family was sitting by the pool still talking to Bebe. They were all sampling Paulina's fabulous food and enjoying the music. As Jill approached them, she could see Lois and Diane had found her parents.

Still holding Kyle's hand, she walked up to them and said, beaming, "Everyone, I'd like for you to meet Kyle Roberts. And these are his parents, Samuel and Regina Roberts. Kyle, these are my parents, Robert and Madeline Alexander."

"Hello, sir, it's nice to meet you," he said nervously to her father. His usually firm handshake seemed weak even to himself, and he felt his throat go dry.

"What's this 'sir' stuff? You're about to become family."

"Yes, sir, I am. I want to ask you for your daughter's hand in marriage." He strained to control his voice, but his nerves wouldn't let him.

Rob looked at the young man from head to toe. He saw a strong man, with the brains and ability to make his daughter very happy. An approving smile curled on his lips. "Yes, you may have my daughter's hand in marriage, but only if you find another name for me besides sir."

"I can do that," Kyle said, smiling nervously.

Jill looked on happily and then continued introducing everyone. It felt good having everyone meet each other. Somehow it gave their engagement a definitive feel. Tony, Eric, and Sharon came over to their table, and Jill introduced them to her family.

"You all will have to excuse me," Samuel Roberts said. "I'm being summoned to the bandstand."

Tomahawk had stopped playing and the guests grew quiet. The television crew focused their cameras on the bandstand, and the radio stations moved closer with their microphones.

"Ladies and gentlemen, may I have your attention please? I'm glad to see all of you out here tonight, and I thank you for coming. My name is Samuel Roberts. I'm one of the owners of this fabulous resort. Please let me introduce two of my partners in crime. This is William Davis," Kyle's father said as he shook Davis's hand. He stepped over and said, "And this is Malcolm Sterling."

The guests applauded the investors, and Samuel waited for their enthusiasm to die down before he began again.

"This is quite a grand opening," he began again. "None of this would have been possible if it weren't for the efforts of two extraordinary women. Thank you, Bebe Simmons and Jill Alexander, for making this grand opening spectacular."

The cameras turned around to face Jill and Bebe. Jill waved to the guests in acceptance of their adulation, smiling easily as she looked at the camera. Bebe wasn't quite as comfortable being the center of attention, but she took a cue from Jill and did the same.

Samuel waited a third time for the joyous noise to die down. When it did, he said, "I have one more thing to say before I let you all return to having fun. I just want to announce the engagement of my eldest son to Miss Jill Alexander. Jill, welcome to our family."

Jill smiled appreciatively and blew a kiss to her future husband as the crowd looked on.

Among the oohs and aahs, Kyle approached her and wrapped his arms around his fiancée. Tenderly, he took her in his arms and kissed her lips. "Welcome to my love," he said.

Dear Reader,

I hope you enjoyed reading this book as much as I enjoyed writing it. Jill Alexander, Bebe Simmons, and all the Roberts brothers were wonderful characters to create and develop. Though they are all products of my imagination, I couldn't help but fall in love with each and every one of them. In a way, they became part of my family, and I hope they will become part of yours.

I have started writing a sequel to *A Special Place*. All of the characters that you have welcomed into your passion-filled hearts will return, along with a few new characters.

Romance is part of all of our lives. We are either living it, watching it, listening to it, or reading about it. In its latter form, I have found a home to express my visions of love and tenderness. As a writer, it is my desire to whisk you away to a place where your dreams and fantasies are allowed to breathe if only for a few hundred pages.

Thank you for supporting me in my first endeavor as a writer. I hope you enjoy the forthcoming novels from me as well, which are all filled with love, passion, and the need we all have to follow our hearts.

I would love to hear from you. Please feel free to e-mail me at: carringtonbooks@yahoo.com.

With love and happiness,
Kim Carrington

ABOUT THE AUTHOR

Kim Carrington is a graduate of the University of North Florida School of Education. She is an employee at the DePaul School, an educational facility for children with learning disabilities. Kim is married with two children.

More Sizzling Romance From
Gwynne Forster

__Obsession   1-58314-092-1   \$5.99US/\$7.99CAN

__Fools Rush In   1-58314-435-8   \$6.99US/\$9.99CAN

__Ecstasy   1-58314-177-4   \$5.99US/\$7.99CAN

__Swept Away   1-58314-098-0   \$5.99US/\$7.99CAN

__Beyond Desire   1-58314-201-0   \$5.99US/\$7.99CAN

__Secret Desire   1-58314-124-3   \$5.99US/\$7.99CAN

__Against All Odds   1-58314-247-9   \$5.99US/\$7.99CAN

__Sealed With a Kiss   1-58314-313-0   \$5.99US/\$7.99CAN

__Scarlet Woman   1-58314-192-8   \$5.99US/\$7.99CAN

__Once in a Lifetime   1-58314-193-6   \$6.99US/\$9.99CAN

__Flying High   1-58314-427-7   \$6.99US/\$9.99CAN

Available Wherever Books Are Sold!

Visit our website at **www.BET.com**.

BOOK YOUR PLACE ON OUR WEBSITE AND MAKE THE ARABESQUE ROMANCE CONNECTION!

We've created a customized website just for our very special Arabesque readers, where you can get the inside scoop on everything that's going on with Arabesque romance novels.

When you come online, you'll have the exciting opportunity to:

- View covers of upcoming books

- Learn about our future publishing schedule (listed by publication month and author)

- Find out when your favorite authors will be visiting a city near you

- Search for and order backlist books

- Check out author bios and background information

- Send e-mail to your favorite authors

- Join us in weekly chats with authors, readers and other guests

- Get writing guidelines

- AND MUCH MORE!

Visit our website at
http://www.arabesquebooks.com